One Red Shoe

Diane Burton

Praise for

Numbers Never Lie

Numbers Never Lie, has just the right mix of romance, mystery, and humor . . . – Janet Glaser (aka J.Q. Rose, author)

The Case of the Meddling Mama

What a fun read . . . Ms. Burton had me biting my nails by the end of the book. ~ Maris Soule, author of *A Killer Past*

The Case of the Bygone Brother

"...plenty of action and sexual tension that kept me turning the pages. I loved this book and these characters. I'm glad this will be a series. I can't wait until O'Hara and Palzetti are back together again." ~ Marilyn Baron, author of *Landlocked*

". . . a wonderful modern love story made sweeter with humor, family values, and Sam Spade suspense." ~ Rolynn Anderson, author of *Fear Land*

Also by Diane Burton

Dedication

To my amazing daughters, Liz and Katy

To my terrific sons Doug and Matt

To my grandchildren who bring so much love into my
life

And especially to Bob, my best friend and hero

Acknowledgements and Thanks

Thanks to the following people for their help and support:

Chief Ed Edwardson (ret.) Wyoming (MI) Police Dept. for his assistance with weapons, for telling me when things don't work then makes suggestions for an even better story.

Matthew Carr, MD for his assistance on gunshot wounds, my go-to guy for things medical.

Mistakes are mine.

Thanks, also, to the LaSenorita critique group: Jolana, Deanna, and Dickie (RIP); to Nancy Gideon for her invaluable advice; to the Mid-Michigan RWA chapter; to Alison Henderson for the lovely cover and to Alicia Dean who did the original editing.

Last and most special, thanks to my wonderful family for all their support and encouragement, especially to Bob, my rock, who quietly takes such good care of me. I'm so glad our friends fixed us up on my first and only blind date.

CHAPTER ONE

Friday, Prairieville, Iowa

"Daria Jean, you are not going to New York City and that's final."

With a thudding heart and sweaty palms, Daria Mason zipped shut her suitcase and gritted her teeth. "Jimmy, we've been over this before."

Only about twenty times.

She lifted the suitcase off her twin bed. Since Jimmy blocked the doorway, the other boys who crowded behind him in the hall couldn't rush in—either to help or hinder. It was a sign of Jimmy's discombobulation that he didn't march in and grab the suitcase out of her hands.

She took one last look around her bedroom for anything she might have forgotten. In that fleeting moment, she realized her room looked faded and worn. With the exception of her computer desk where the doll's house her father built used to be, the room looked exactly the way it had on her thirteenth birthday. Same twin bed, same wallpaper and curtains she and her mother had chosen for that landmark birthday. No wonder the boys still treated her like she was thirteen instead of six months shy of the Big Three-Oh.

With her tote slung over her shoulder, Daria picked up the handle of her rolling suitcase and headed for the blocked doorway. "Okay, boys, I'm ready to go."

To her surprise, Jimmy stepped aside. Immediately, Billy grabbed the handle of her suitcase. "Maybe you shouldn't go," he said, following her down the hall that overlooked the living room. The others trooped after him. At the top of the stairs, she looked back along the white balustrade. *Dear Lord, I'm a drum majorette leading a parade.*

"I went on line," Andy said. "Maybe you should

1

reconsider. There are writers' conferences closer than New York City."

"It's Sodom and Gomorrah, for sure," Tommy said.

"C'mon, boys. Don't spoil my Spring Break. This conference is really important to me." Daria kept walking through the kitchen. "I left our itinerary on the board next to the phone." She pointed but didn't stop on her way out to her car.

Billy stowed her suitcase in the trunk next to the picnic cooler. "I made sandwiches for the trip," he said. That earned him a dark look from Jimmy. "And I loaded the cooler with the fruit and yogurt you bought so you and Ginnie won't need to spend too much money on food."

"Are the chips and pretzels your contribution to their nutrition?" Andy mocked. "By the way, DJ, you're all gassed up." Another dark look from Jimmy.

"I checked your car over thoroughly and it's good to go," Tommy said.

She blinked back a tear. "You boys are so sweet for going to all this trouble."

Jimmy bent down to look at the right front tire. "I don't like the looks of this."

"The tire is fine," she said.

The others ignored her and all bent down to look. While they debated whether she should get a new tire, Rover dashed up. The reddish-brown mutt of indeterminate heritage nearly knocked her over with his usual enthusiastic greeting. She gave him a quick hug and ruffled his fur.

"Billy, don't feed Rover any table scraps. Only two cups of kibble a day. Andy, you're going to put food in the barn for Archy and Mehitabel, right?" She didn't wait for his response. "And, Tommy, you'll take care of—"

Jimmy straightened. "For crissake, Daria, it's a goddamn zoo around here."

At least he wasn't trying to delay her with talk about new tires. She reached up and patted his cheek. "Don't swear."

"I mean it, Daria Jean," Jimmy said. "Don't you dare bring home some wounded stray. I don't care if it's bleeding. No more." He ran his hand through his hair. "You have no idea what you're getting yourself into. You've never even been east of Chicago."

She smiled. "I know."

"I hoped you'd get this foolishness out of your system." He blew out a breath and thrust a small item at her. "Since you're determined to go, this is a top-of-the-line cell phone. It has GPS tracking so if you have car trouble and call for help, they'll know exactly where you are."

Daria ignored the first part of his rant. She'd heard it before but was surprised at his thoughtfulness with the phone. She gave him a hug then the others. Standing back, she looked at the four of them. Tears threatened. She blinked rapidly. For goodness sake, it wasn't like she was leaving forever. A week away from home, that's all. She got into her car, eager to get started.

"Call every night," Jimmy ordered. He just had to spoil the moment. "So, we know you're okay." The others nodded. They meant well, she reminded herself.

She put the key in the ignition. *Oh, God.* This was it. She was going after her dream. A mixture of fear and excitement shot through her. She hadn't felt like this since. . . since leaving for summer camp when she was ten. How pathetic was that. When she got back, things were going to change. First, she was going on a real adventure.

New York City, here I come.

Saturday, Smolensk, Russia

Sam Jozwiak slid open the door to Korioff's inner sanctum. It had been blissfully easy. One guard, now sleeping quietly along with the rest of the compound. Locks a rookie could open. The computer password taped under the mouse pad. You'd think even a minor kingpin in the Russian Mafia would have better security.

Hold on. No modem. No cable, DSL, broadband, not even dial-up. No way to transmit data. *Well, shit.*

Okay, on to Plan B.

In the dark, with only the glow from the computer screen, Sam copied files onto a tiny memory chip. The financial records and client lists would make for fascinating reading back at headquarters. As the personal files were being copied, a name caught his attention. Why the hell did the Russian Mafia have a file on a U.S. senator? Especially, that senator. Sam opened the file. *Holy shit!*

Intel this dangerous couldn't wait for the normal fourteen-hour transport home. The hearing was next week. What he just read would send shockwaves through Washington, through the country. He had to report this to the Director now then upload that file to the agency.

An hour later, he raced up the worn wooden stairs of the shabby hotel. He'd contacted the Director who wasn't pleased about the change in plan. Sam had wasted too much time explaining why he couldn't hook up a connection instead of copying the files. The Director insisted that the *package* be hand-delivered. While that seemed odd to Sam, considering the tight time frame, the Director did have a reason. The intel was too sensitive to trust to the Internet. He ordered Sam to meet him in New York City. Again, odd. But he learned long ago not to question his superiors. All he had to do now was grab his gear and get the hell out of Dodge before Korioff discovered the little surprise in his computer.

Sam unlocked the hotel room, realizing too late that it wasn't locked.

"Hello, Samuel. Long time no see, as you Americans say." Yuri Grashenko sat in the corner of the small room, his smile as deadly as the Walther PPK in his hand. "Please return what you stole from my employer. He is most unhappy."

Jesus, how did he know? How did Grashenko get here so—

"Why you talk nice to thief?" The male voice came from behind.

Sam spun low with a move he hadn't forgotten from his college basketball days. He slammed into the newcomer as a bullet from the PPK slammed into the wall where Sam's shoulder had been seconds before. One good thing. Yuri wasn't trying to kill him. Not yet, anyway.

Sam and the newcomer rolled down the dark stairs in a tangle of arms and legs. *Jesus, the guy was big.* Elbows and knees wreaked as much havoc as the wood steps. He was going to have bruises on bruises.

His dad was right. Sam should have gone to work in the steel mill. Shoveling slag had to be easier than this.

CHAPTER TWO

Tuesday, New York City

Teller was late. And Sam Jozwiak was freezing his ass off.

One more screw-up in one hell of a long line of screw-ups. Why the hell did the Director want to meet in such a deserted area?

Sam's light jacket had been fine for April in Paris. But, spring warmth was nonexistent on the fifth floor of the old Guttschenheimer Department Store. He searched the entire floor. Teller hadn't given him an exact location. Geez, did the guy know what a rabbit warren this was? Sam wished for Ariadne's string as he negotiated the labyrinth of shelving units holding long-forgotten inventory.

Finally, he staked out a spot where he could watch the heavy fire door to the stairs. He'd already ruled out the elevator. Teller was smart enough not to use the antique contraption, especially since he would have to walk past the workers in the first floor antique mall. If Teller was anxious to keep this operation under cover, he wouldn't want to be seen. Besides, the elevator looked like Elisha Otis's original.

Sam rubbed his arms and walked in tight circles—anything to keep the circulation flowing. After running for three days across Europe, he had to keep moving, if only to stay awake.

As soon as he heard footsteps on the metal stairs, he froze. Either Teller was a heavy treader or he brought company. Sam slid behind an industrial shelving unit in the maze of units throughout the former sales floor where New York City's not-quite-finest once shopped for housewares and linens. He controlled his breathing. No sense sending up smoke signals in the event this wasn't Teller.

The air moved imperceptibly, as the fire door opened.

Sam heard the scuff of a shoe. He hoped Teller had enough sense to reconnoiter, like Sam did, and not call out like the non-operative he was. Sam had a narrow view of the door. What he saw coming through made him glad he'd stayed concealed. A hand holding a Walther PPK. As far as Sam knew, the Director didn't know one end of a revolver from the other.

Sam moved silently to get a better view. He peered between the boxes of Cannon towels—if he believed the faded printing—and Dreft. The scent of the pink powdered detergent his mother used to use overpowered that of mildew and mice. He found evidence of them earlier. Sam's nose twitched as he controlled the urge to sneeze.

The hand holding the Walther PPK was that of his old adversary, Yuri Grashenko, Korioff's primo hit man. *Damn, they found him again.*

Sam would give anything for his Sig. Or, a Magnum, a Glock, hell, even a wimpy PPK. He had to ditch his weapon at Charles de Gaulle. The airlines were finicky about people carrying guns aboard. Come to think of it, Sam was pretty finicky, too, about passengers being armed . . . unless it was him. He expected to pick up a weapon when he arrived at JFK. Heads were going to roll when he got back to headquarters. Someone from the agency should have passed him along the concourse and handed off a gun. Teller probably didn't think about that. Obviously, he hadn't told even Ryerson about this op. *Stupid. Really stupid.*

Sam moved with the stealth of long experience. He slithered between shelving units, avoiding his pursuers. He needed higher ground. Nothing would spoil his day more than turning a corner and running into Grashenko and his buddy, the Hulk. Fear of making a sound while climbing ancient shelves kept him on the move.

The scrape of a shoe and a hissed silencing whisper came from the next aisle over. With the moldering boxes jammed tight against each other, Sam could barely see through the space between the top of a box and the underside of the shelf above. Grimy windows near the ceiling on two sides of the cavernous room let in weak late afternoon light. The only other illumination came from the two exit signs kitty-corner across the huge expanse from each other. Despite the low visibility, he could just make out the backs of the two who'd had been on his tail since Smolensk. Backs were good.

"He not here yet," came a whisper now at the end of that aisle, which was promptly followed by an exasperated sigh and a hiss to search by the elevator.

While reconnoitering the area, Sam dismissed the obvious hiding places, like the restrooms or the area behind the service desk. Next to the elevator at the back of the building was a set of emergency stairs. *His* emergency exit if the situation turned nasty. Like the one in front, the back stairwell was separated from former selling floors by a heavy fire door.

A twack, a gasp, the shudder of a kicked steel unit and a "Sorry, Yuri" in Russian.

"Speak English, you fool," came a softer retort. "And watch where you're going."

Where did Yuri get such a bumbler? The Hulk was greener than grass and twice as dumb. Having a partner was out of character for Yuri. He worked best alone. And was all the more dangerous for it.

The footsteps sounded farther away now, with no attempt at stealth. Yuri was moving down an aisle over two and to the right of Sam's location. A soft curse. Yuri must have wandered into a dead end. The shelving units marched in straight rows, except when one did a ninety, ran for a bit and did another ninety. It was often a veritable maze with no rhyme or reason. Whoever designed it was either drunk or sadistic.

"I know you are here, Johnston." Yuri spoke with the cultured British accent he often affected. A trained linguist would hear the hint of the backwater Georgian town Yuri came from, along with the polish of metropolitan Moscow where he'd spent much of his adult life. Sam Jozwiak knew more about Yuri Grashenko than he did about his own boss.

Now, there was a piece of work. Teller couldn't even make it to a rendezvous *he* set up.

Yuri knew just as much about Sam. They'd been adversaries for the past twelve years. Ever since Sam's first op for the Orion Agency, their paths crossed frequently. A few times, they even collaborated. Yuri knew Sam's real name. So he had to wonder why Yuri was calling him by his *Johnston* alias.

Their cat-and-mouse game was going to end as soon as Yuri retrieved the files. He couldn't let Sam live. And since Sam wasn't fond of that scenario, he would have to kill Yuri. Killing was not a normal part of his mission. Get the intel and get out. Protect the intel, protect self—in that order. All Sam had for protection were his hands.

"Do not make things difficult for yourself, Samuel," Yuri continued from the end of the aisle. "Give me what I seek, and we shall go our separate ways—as we have before."

If Sam believed that, Santa existed, and pigs could fly.

After several moments, Yuri called, "Johnston? Why do you not—"

Two shots fired through a silencer made Sam's heart stop. He debated whether he needed CPR or a defibrillator. He didn't feel the familiar jolt of a bullet slamming into his body. And he was still conscious. He released his breath. His heart started pumping, wildly but still pumping. The shots came from the area Yuri told his partner to search.

"I got him," the trigger-happy kid shouted.

Hard-soled shoes slapped the worn asphalt tile floor. Yuri must be running toward the elevator. Sam used the commotion to scale the eight-foot high unit. He had the advantage now. He could see across the field of metal skeletons to where the big guy stood looking pleased with himself.

As Grashenko came running, he said, "Korioff, you idiot. We need him alive."

"Was big rat. Very big rat." The partner's voice was high, excited.

Sam shuddered. Rats. He felt like Indiana Jones looking down into the room full of snakes. Why did it have to be rats? Like Indy's father, Sam hated rats. He hoped Korioff got more than one.

Hold on. It couldn't be. The mouth-breather tagging along with Grashenko was the Korioff who headed an arm of a powerful crime syndicate? The Korioff whose financial records Sam stole? The Korioff who sicced Yuri on him?

Fatigue must have dulled Sam's brain. Running through Europe with those two hot on his trail for three days would have exhausted a young man. *Younger* man, Sam corrected. Thirty-four wasn't old, but no sleep and less food caught up with him quicker now than when he was twenty-two.

The guy with the itchy trigger finger had to be Korioff's son. If so, the syndicate was in big trouble. *Oh, darn.* Sam smiled for the first time since the wee hours of Saturday morning when he found Yuri in his hotel room and rolled down the stairs with the bumbling partner. Only sheer dumb luck enabled Sam to escape then. Luck wasn't with him now.

The two made no effort to conceal their locations. Yuri was searching one side of the room and Junior the other. Since they were separated, Sam could take them out one at a time. Christ, he hated hand-to-hand combat. Too close, too personal. Unlike a bullet. Though trained in self-defense, Sam was no assassin. Unlike Yuri.

Zzt-ping-ping-thud. Christ, the kid was shooting again. Bullets ricocheted off the industrial shelving and penetrated boxes. Yuri yelled at him again. From the vantage point of height in the center of the huge room, Sam watched the shadows of the men searching for him. One, big and clumsy. The other, shorter with the stealth of experience. And no Teller. Could the day get more screwed up than this?

Zzzt-ping-ping—

Fire streaked across Sam's butt. He clenched his teeth to keep from sucking air or, worse, crying out in pain. Carefully, he looked over his shoulder.

Damn. Those were his favorite jeans.

Daria Mason was in love. Or heaven. Rows and rows of books. Stack after stack, so tall she needed a ladder to reach the top. And on the floor, boxes and boxes of books. She could have wept for joy.

Two of her new writer friends mentioned the used bookstore last night at the hotel bar. Though she felt a pain of guilt, she skipped the afternoon workshops in favor of shopping. The conference was great and well worth standing up to her brothers. The best part, the most exciting part was that at ten o'clock tomorrow morning she had an appointment with an editor. A real live editor from a major publishing house. Daria grinned idiotically.

Doing her best to contain her excitement over the prospect of pitching her novel to an editor, Daria had climbed the stairwell of a former department store. The floor at street level had been converted into an antique mall while the second floor was filled with books. She hadn't seen signs for businesses on the upper floors. No matter. She'd found paradise. Unfortunately, just like the biblical Eden, this one came with a snake in the form of the proprietor. The surly, young man made it clear he couldn't wait to get rid of his dead grandfather's *trash* and turn the place into a dance club.

Hang on. Was that . . . ? All thoughts of the kid who didn't recognize the treasure he inherited went right out of Daria's head. She moved two books aside and pulled out the blue book with thick pulp pages. It was, Daria sighed. A 1930 edition of *The Secret of the Old Clock*. The very first Nancy Drew mystery.

It was dusty, like the rest of the books, but in excellent condition. Reverently, she held the book for several seconds. This was what sparked her grandmother's love of mysteries. A love Gram passed on to Daria. Now, she wrote her own mysteries featuring a kick-butt detective named Alexa Tremaine, a worthy successor to Nancy Drew.

Daria crouched on the floor, which could use a good sweeping, and pulled out books. She searched behind others. If there was one original Nancy Drew, there had to be more. She found six before it occurred to her that she might not be able to afford them. Her cash supply was limited, just what she'd budgeted for inexpensive meals and, of course, the entrance fees to the Women's Rights Museum, the Rock & Roll Hall of Fame, and the Gateway Arch—her three must-stops on the drive home.

After picking up a couple of other books at random, she put one of the blue-covers between them. She'd shopped at enough flea markets and garage sales to know that prices were negotiable. Don't appear eager or the price will be higher. She casually walked to the check-out counter where the proprietor sat on a stool moving his head in time to whatever beat pounded through his earbuds. Behind him was a large sign. How had she missed it before? Black magic marker on white poster board: "A buck a book. No checks. No CCs. Cash only." All right. She went back to the stacks. There had to be more Nancy Drews.

She was glad she'd worn her new coat. Even though it was April, the old building retained winter's chill. The antique mall on the first floor, which she'd skirted to get to the stairwell, was warm and cozy. Not so the bookstore. The new owner obviously didn't waste his inheritance on heat. She wasn't complaining, mind you.

Her search paid off. She found three more Nancy Drews and two hardcover copies of *Charlotte's Web*. Her second graders vied for the single copy on her classroom shelf. At a dollar apiece, she could splurge. She stooped to search through boxes stacked haphazardly on the floor. She didn't care if her skirt, which hung lower than the hem of her coat, trailed on the floor. Better her skirt than the new coat.

She had been thrilled when she found the cape-style coat at home. Very chic, she thought, until she got to New York City. The women she passed on the streets epitomized style. Those women exuded purpose and power. Excitement. Daria was sure they saw *country bumpkin* written across her forehead. At least, her fellow writers made her feel like she belonged. She'd even met three of her online critique partners. It was their encouragement that convinced her to attend the conference.

After her brothers' sendoff, Daria and her best friend Ginnie started out last Friday with enthusiasm and hope. Ginnie wasn't as gung-ho about writing as Daria, but she was always up for a trip, whether it was shopping in Des Moines or a trip to the Big Apple. That and wanting to get away from three pre-schoolers. Even so, Daria still felt bad Ginnie had to leave right after Sunday Mass at St. Patrick's Cathedral because of her mom's emergency surgery. Ginnie would have loved this store.

Even though her friend left, Daria stayed. No way was she heading home until Thursday, especially now that she had an editor appointment. What a fluke. One of her critique partners got The Call yesterday. Daria and the other two were celebrating the new author's first sale last night when she found out Daria didn't have an editor's appointment. Because she sold to a different publishing house, she offered Daria hers. The three of them insisted on meeting tonight so she could practice her pitch on them. She couldn't believe how lucky she was. Their support was so different from her brothers' attitude about what they called *Daria's little hobby*.

She stood and shook the dust from her skirt. She'd made it through half the store and found twelve—she couldn't believe it—*twelve* original Nancy Drew books. However, she'd ignored her bladder's call for the past ten minutes. She just didn't want to give up her quest for more books. There must be a restroom. She could take care of her needs then continue shopping.

"Excuse me?" She waved her hand in front of the young proprietor's face. At twenty-nine, Daria felt positively ancient next to him.

"Yeah?" His tone was surly. Despite her intense search for books, she'd heard him speak in the same manner to other customers, not that there had been many. He might have gotten more if he advertised. A sign at street level, one that could be seen from the sidewalk, would have helped.

She set her books on the counter and brushed the dust from the sleeves of her coat and down the front. The owner watched avidly, his eyes following her hand.

"Excuse me," she repeated, flustered at his ogling. "Where is your restroom?"

"Restrooms are on the fifth floor."

"No, I mean here," she said.

"Fifth floor."

"Surely, you don't—"

"*Public* restrooms are on the fifth floor."

"All right. I'll just leave my books here while—"

"You want those books you pay for 'em now. Somebody else wants 'em, I'll take their money. You might not come back, and I gotta get rid of all these damn books."

Daria was not leaving her treasures for someone else. She reached into the purse that she carried across her body instead of just hanging on her shoulder the way she always did at home. Jimmy, in his "how to survive in the big city" lecture, said it would foil a thief who could snag the purse strap as he ran past. Despite her exasperation with her brothers and their endless lectures, she knew they meant well, and she did listen. She paid for the books and asked for directions to the *public* restroom.

"Top floor. Way in the back, near the elevator."

"Are there other stores up there?" She hoped there would be in case she had to ask directions. Give Daria a map and she could go anywhere. Verbal directions? Forget it.

"Nope. Used to be storage for some company that went out of business. They just left their stuff up there."

Stuff. Storage. And nobody to ask for directions. "You said the restroom is near the elevator? Why don't I just take it up from here and I'll be right—"

"First," he interrupted again, which was annoying, "if I let you walk through my store, you might take more books with you. I want to get rid of the damn things, but I'm not giving them away. Second, nobody takes that elevator. Hasn't been used in years, according to the old bat who runs the antique mall. That's why all that junk is still up there. That's why you're not going to use the elevator. I'm not going to get sued when it crashes and you get killed."

Wasn't that a cheery thought. "Okay, if there's an elevator, there are emergency stairs. How about if I just go through your store and use the back stairs?"

"I *said*." His exasperated tone grated on her last nerve. "You could swipe—"

"Yes, I remember." It was her turn to cut him off. "I'll take the front stairs."

As a concession to potential customers, the bookseller had propped open the heavy steel fire door. She was pretty sure that was a violation of some fire code. But then, this whole building was probably in violation of many codes. In fact, when she opened the door to the stairs from the antique mall, she noticed there was no outside door. The stairs continued below street level into darkness. What kind of emergency exit was that?

She started running up the stairs to the fifth floor, hoping she would get to the restroom in time. As a teacher who couldn't leave second-graders alone, she'd trained herself to hold it until scheduled breaks. But, she should never have waited this long. Despite the cramping in her legs, she put on a burst of speed. As she passed the door to the fourth floor, she realized the stairs had gotten darker. She looked up to see if a light was out. On the halfway landing stood a man . . . pointing a gun at her.

She nearly wet her pants.

CHAPTER THREE

"What are you doing here?" the man demanded as he whisked his gun out of sight.

Daria froze. She clutched the rail with one hand, her bag of books with the other. She suddenly understood the line from *Romancing the Stone* because, just like Joan Wilder, Daria was paralyzed from the neck up. The rest of her wasn't moving, either.

"Where are you going?" He had a faint accent. British? His eyes flickered with impatience. Hard glacial blue eyes. His voice, cultured with a hint of menace, frightened her more.

His shoes were level with her eyes. Shiny brown Florsheims—just like the kind Andy wore. The guy's jeans were new with distinct creases from being folded. They brushed the tops of his polished dress shoes.

Brown Shoes came down three steps and halted. He reached inside his black light-weight jacket, and Daria prayed it wasn't for a gun. That made no sense. Why didn't he use the one he'd tucked behind his back? He pulled out a leather folder and flipped it open. A gold badge. He was the police. Daria sagged in relief.

With a quick motion, Brown Shoes flipped the folder closed and stuffed it back in his pocket. "What is your business?" He tapped his brown shoe impatiently.

Her throat began to close in fear from his anger.

"Did a man pass you on the stairs?" he demanded.

She shook her head. Brown Shoes was in pursuit. No wonder he was impatient. But if he were chasing someone, why had he been standing on the landing? Her mind raced a mile a minute, just like her heart. Why he did he put his ID away so quickly? From mystery books and movies, even cop shows on television, Daria knew Brown Shoes should have given her more time to examine his identification.

16

He gave her a stern look. "Do you speak Eng—"

A muffled voice came from under his jacket. He pulled out the cell phone from a holder hooked to his belt. The phone must be functioning like a walkie-talkie. Even though Brown Shoes put the small phone up to his ear, Daria could still hear.

"I find him," a male voice said in an accent different from Brown Shoes.

"Where?" he demanded into the phone.

"Third floor," came the reply.

Brown Shoes dashed down the stairs. His hard-soled shoes clattered on the gray metal steps. Daria flattened herself against the wall. He brushed past her without even an "excuse me." She guessed that manners took a backseat to apprehending a fugitive. Through the open stairs, she saw him stop at the door to the third floor. He hooked the phone on his belt loop and pulled the revolver out of his back holster. Holding the gun high, he reached for the door.

"Hurry," came the faint voice on the phone. "Before police come."

Brown Shoes reached to his side and clicked off his phone. Cautiously, he opened the door.

Daria continued up the stairs. Fear had temporarily stopped her need for the restroom. Now, she really had to go. She opened the door to the top floor as cautiously as Brown Shoes had. She held the door so it closed just as quietly.

Oh, dear Lord. Shelving units nearly reached the ceiling. Even standing on tip-toe, she couldn't see the exit sign where the stairs and the elevator should be. She tried to picture the lay-out of the bookstore. The sign for the emergency stairs should be kitty-corner from the stairs she just came up. The manner in which the shelves were jumbled, she just knew she'd get lost if she tried to cut across the floor. She turned left. Once she got to the last aisle, she could follow it until she found the elevator and, more importantly, the restroom.

Something Brown Shoes' partner said gnawed at her. Something so faint she thought she hadn't heard right. *Hurry. Before police come.* Hold on. Brown Shoes showed her a badge. He was the police. Wasn't he?

Other odd things started to register. His attire. Dress

shoes with blue jeans. Jeans so new they made noise as he hurried down the steps. When he unclipped the phone from his belt, something seemed out of place. The belt. It belonged with dress pants, not jeans. She wasn't the Fashion Police, but even so it seemed odd.

The men had accents. One, British. The other, not. She didn't have an ear for accents. The obvious ones, like British and Hispanic, of course, but not . . .

Still puzzling over the man with no fashion sense, Daria reached the last aisle. She turned the corner and began walking between the units. It was darker now. The farther she moved down the aisle, the darker it got. She expected to see the exit sign at the end. But, ahead of her were more shelves.

She puzzled over those men. They were searching for someone. The one said he'd found *him*. Unless he was being held at gunpoint, the man they were searching for would surely be alerted by the noise of the walkie-talkies. She hoped she didn't run into the hunters again or their prey. Just finding the restroom was challenge enough.

Daria looked up at the shelving units surrounding her. She'd walked into a dead end. Maybe her brothers were right. She couldn't walk and think at the same time.

As soon as he heard Yuri close the fire door, Sam Jozwiak limped toward the old customer service area. Yuri had dispatched the Korioff kid down the back stairs to search the other floors. But the wily ex-KGB man didn't leave the fifth. He'd waited in silence until footsteps on the front stairs drew him out into the stairwell. That was all Sam needed to move from his second hiding place—where he'd found a box knife a careless worker must have left behind. Not much of a weapon, but better than nothing.

The burning in his rear end was nothing compared to the fire from the swath another ricocheted bullet cut through the fleshy part of his calf. Warm blood was running down his leg. He needed to stop the bleeding before he left a trail even Korioff Junior could follow.

Sam found a door with a push plate and faded square

where a sign used to be. This had to be it. He carefully pushed open the door. No noise to attract Grashenko & Company if they came back. Good grief, the restroom was an explosion of pink. Pepto-Bismol pink with black trim. Sam didn't have time to find the men's room now. He would stop the bleeding and get out of this potential trap.

Skylights, dirty like the rest of the windows in the building, let in enough light to see. That was good. He didn't want to risk turning on a light that would shine under the door. Around a corner, hidden from the door, he found a long counter with a row of sinks and a mirror above. All the better to examine the damage done by that trigger-happy fool.

Sam unzipped his jeans and worked down his briefs to expose his hip. What a mess. Not for the first time, he cursed Grashenko for showing up in that hotel room in Smolensk. Sam's hasty departure, with Yuri and Korioff on his tail, meant leaving behind his gear. His clothes, sunglasses, and emergency medical supplies would bring top dollar on the Russian black market. He would have to make do with what he had. Carefully, he turned a faucet to wet his handkerchief. He blew out a breath in relief the plumbing still worked and was used on a regular basis. No air hissed or sputtered, which would've brought Grashenko and Korioff back in a hurry.

With much twisting to see, Sam wiped away the worst of the blood. Amazed that there were paper towels in a dispenser, he folded several and stuffed them inside his briefs. He tried to zip his jeans but the bulge in back pressed on his raw flesh. Hell, he'd zip up when he was done.

When he bent to check his calf, he nearly keeled over from dizziness. He grabbed the counter. His shoe had absorbed the blood. None on the floor, thank God. No trail. Sam patted his shirt pocket and took out his agency cell phone. He needed to find out where the hell Teller was. That idiot better have a damn good reason for doing a no-show. Didn't he realize the consequences? Didn't he realize how little time they had to—

The air moved—his only warning that the door to the restroom had opened. A whirlwind in beige blasted past him. In that split second, Sam instinctively cataloged the intruder. Female, five-ten, weight uncertain due to voluminous coat, late twenties, long dark single braid, penny loafers. And a large button clipped to her purse. *Shit*. More dangerous than a Russian Mafia hit man. A wide-eyed innocent. The kind he'd sworn to protect. And here he was bleeding like a stuck pig, so dizzy he was going to fall flat on his face.

For the second time in her life, Daria Mason came face-to-face with a man pointing a weapon at her. A pervert, with unzipped jeans, wielded a green box knife. Because she'd raced into the restroom without checking out the situation, he now stood between her and the exit.

She was at the end of the proverbial rope. After walking in circles, she finally found a restroom, and nobody was stopping her from using it. Especially not someone who was playing copycat with that guy in the movie who wore one red shoe.

"I am having a really bad day," she declared in the *don't cross me* voice she used on her brothers. As soon as her words echoed off the hideous pink and black tiled walls and floor, she lowered her voice. "You are in the wrong place, mister. Now, zip up and get out." She pointed straight-armed toward the door.

The man shook his head and set the flimsy knife on the counter. "Lady, you have more guts than sense. *You* are in the wrong place, at the wrong time." His voice was even softer as hers. He eyed her with a look so dark and intense it paralyzed her like a hawk freezes its prey. She swallowed past the fear in her throat, certain it sounded like a gulp.

"Before you embarrass both of us by peeing on the floor . . ." He jerked his head toward the stalls.

Daria's cheeks burned with embarrassment. She hesitated for a moment, certain that if this were a movie, she was the heroine too stupid to live. But, darn it, she had to go. She beat it around a corner and headed toward the end stall, as far away from him as possible. By the time she finished, Daria fervently hoped the man was gone.

She squirted hand sanitizer into her palm and rubbed her hands as she came around the corner. So much for fervent hopes. He was still there. At five-ten, she didn't often look up at a man, or at least not very far. He had to be six-two, with the lean hardness of a man who took care of himself. He had a scruffy beard, and she was sure his dark hair hadn't seen a comb in days. He'd propped his foot—the one with the red shoe—on the sink counter and was using a box cutter to slit his pantleg.

Over his shoulder, he looked at her. "Go Hawks."

"What?"

Using the box cutter, he pointed to the black and gold University of Iowa button she had clipped to the strap of her purse so long ago she'd forgotten about it.

"How do you know— Oh, my goodness, are you an alum, too?"

He gave her an exasperated look. "You might as well wear a sign: *Tourist here. Take advantage of me.*" He pulled aside the slit pantleg and began using a handkerchief to wash blood away from a ragged wound.

At that moment, several things came together. The man's ashen pallor, the white creases along his tightly-clenched mouth. Dark stains on the back of his jeans, the pocket of which was so ragged she could see his red shorts. His shoe. Oh, dear Lord, his shoe. His sock and one athletic shoe were stained with blood.

The cloying, coppery smell of blood assaulted her nose. Somehow, she missed it before. Now, the scent overpowered mildew and God only knew what else in a restroom that hadn't been cleaned since Reagan was President.

She dropped her bag of books. "Dear God, what did you do to your leg?"

"Cut myself shaving."

She tsked. "You're hurt."

"Very observant." Red Shoe raised an eyebrow and went back to washing his leg.

His caustic tone stung. What else should she say to a bleeding man? Years of patching up her brothers, assorted animals, as well as her second graders, spurred her into action. "That handkerchief is making it worse."

She set her purse on the long counter, a good distance from the man, and dug around for packets of moist towelettes. She set them closer to him before ripping one open. The astringent smell dissipated all other odors in a ten-foot radius.

"You carry hand sanitizer and wipes? Who are you? Monk's sister? Aren't you taking cleanliness too far?"

She'd heard that before from her brothers. She sniffed. Stale sweat. "And you don't take it far enough." She was instantly appalled at her rudeness. Alexa Tremaine, the heroine of her story, might smart off, but Daria didn't.

With exaggeration, he lifted his arm and sniffed his pit. "I don't smell anything."

What a clown. Just like her brothers.

"Unless you're carrying plastic gloves in that suitcase—" Red Shoe pointed to her purse, which wasn't *that* big. "—you'd better give me the wipes."

Daria gave him a smug smile, unzipped a side pocket and pulled out a pair of latex gloves. "I believe in being prepared." She ignored his derisive groan. "Make yourself useful and open the packets. One wipe won't be enough."

"Yes, ma'am."

"Can you balance with your foot on the counter or do you want to put it down?"

"I can balance."

She shoved the slit denim past his knee, to get it out of the way, and used a wipe to clean around the wound. He sucked air, wobbled, then put his hand on her back.

"That hand goes any lower," she said without stopping her ministrations, "and you'll be picking your teeth up off the floor."

Whoa. What was happening to her? That's exactly what Alexa Tremaine would say. Alexa was brave and boldly went where others . . . didn't. Daria so wished she was like her heroine instead of a wimp who got squeamish at the sight of blood.

"No need for sarcasm," Red Shoe said.

She felt the tension in his hand on her back. And a tremor. "You'd better get your foot off the counter before you fall over."

When he did, she stooped and used four more wipes. "The bleeding has slowed but it isn't stopping. You need to get to a hospital. For stitches."

"No hospitals. That's the first place they'll check."

"Who? The men who are looking for you?"

Red Shoe hauled her up by her arms. "What men?"

Daria's heart zoomed into marathon speed. His brown eyes had turned to shards, menacing. And for the third time that day, she was scared spitless. Where was Alexa's nerve now? *She* wouldn't hesitate to deck the guy. Never mind he was holding her arms. Alexa would have found a way. Daria just gaped like the guppy in her classroom fishbowl.

"B-Badge." She hated the shaky sound of her voice. "M-Man with a badge. Didn't see the other. Heard him on a w-walkie-talkie."

He tightened his hands around her upper arms. "Where did you see the one?"

Her fear escalated. She was alone in a deserted restroom on a deserted floor. Nobody knew she was up there—except the bookseller, and he wasn't likely to even pay attention whether she returned or not. Jimmy was right. No good deed goes unpunished.

"S-Stairs."

"Tell me about him." Red Shoe sounded even angrier.

Her heart banged against her ribcage. Her breaths came so fast she was going to hyperventilate. She started to pull away from him. Away from the wounded man whose name she didn't even know. And she wondered why that even seemed important.

He eased his grip. "Tell me about the man on the stairs," he said, not as harshly.

Daria struggled to control her breathing so she could talk. Alexa wouldn't let the man know he was scaring her. She would square her shoulders, jut out her chin. She'd order the man to—

Hang on. If men were chasing him, maybe Red Shoe was scared. Daria learned from her brothers that when men were frightened they acted angry.

"Middle age, my height," she said, pleased that her voice wasn't quavering.

He loosened his grip even more. "Go on."

"Brown Shoes had a slight paunch. A mus—"

"Brown Shoes?"

"He wore brown Florsheims. That was the first thing I noticed out of place. Brand new jeans and dress shoes." When Red Shoe didn't mock her, she went on, "He had a mustache. Dark, but graying like his temples. And an accent. British, I think."

"Where did he go?"

She took a breath. Her heart had slowed down . . . a little. Her lungs took longer to catch up. "Another man—one with an accent, a different accent—called him and he raced down to the third floor."

"Good." He let go of her and yanked the scarf from around her neck.

Dear Lord, he was going to use her own scarf to strangle her.

To her surprise, he bent over and began to wrap the scarf around his calf. His hands shook, and he was weaving now that he wasn't hanging onto the sink or her arms. He'd released her. She was free to leave. He could barely stand, let alone chase after her if she fled. Yet something about his trembling hands as he fumbled with the scarf stopped her. The man's vulnerability got to her. Just like Rover when she found him in the ditch in front of her house.

Daria stooped and brushed his hands aside. She rewrapped the scarf around his leg. That would stop the bleeding. Wouldn't do a whole lot of good for the scarf, though.

"The man showed me a badge," she said calmly. "I didn't see it well. He was too fast. Something was wrong. He should have let me see the badge, right? Tell me he isn't a real cop. I don't think he is. Is he?" Now, she was babbling.

The man snorted. "Probably got the badge out of a cereal box."

With startling insight, she looked up. She took in the whole man—not just the rumpled clothes and hair and the scruffy beard. Past the pain in his eyes and the clenched jaw. And she knew. "He's not a cop, but you are."

Law enforcement officers had an aura about them. The way they held themselves, the way they talked and walked— although the latter was hard to tell with this man. Knowing they were the good guys, they exuded confidence. Red Shoe had those qualities. Having lived in the same house with one for sixteen years, Daria knew she was right.

"No," he said. "But, you have good instincts."

That was all? Just *no*? No, Brown Shoes wasn't a cop? Or, no, *he* wasn't? Daria shook her head. Like she expected Red Shoe to declare he was a good guy. He was probably undercover. Disguised as a streetperson, maybe. That would explain his disreputable appearance. She knotted the scarf and tucked in the ends.

"Get up off that goddamn filthy floor."

Again, the pain in his voice overshadowed his rough words. She stood and carefully stripped off the latex gloves the way the First Aid instructor said. After tossing them in the wastebasket, she picked up her purse and bag of books. "You don't have to swear."

She'd gotten hurt more than once by a wounded animal who didn't realize she was trying to help. She still had a scar on the top of her hand from a dog she found along the side of the road who wouldn't let her treat him. Wounded animals often lashed out in defense. This man was no different. But, she'd had enough of his caustic remarks.

She did her good deed for the day. And been verbally kicked in the teeth. "You would do well to get medical help for your leg. I've done the best I could, and now I am outa here." She started for the door.

"No."

She turned around. "Excuse me?"

"I mean, no, you can't leave." He picked up the box knife from the counter.

CHAPTER FOUR

"I most certainly am leaving. And put that thing away." The woman hefted her shopping bag loaded with books. "All it would take is one good swing, and you'd be flat on your face. You can hardly stand as it is."

Sam Jozwiak found her bravado amusing. He hated to admit it, but she was right. He wasn't steady. Had he lost that much blood? Or, maybe just whacked from next to no sleep for three days. But, she was a problem. He couldn't let her leave. She'd seen him. She knew he was wounded. He couldn't let her run into Grashenko again or, worse, Korioff Junior. If the kid was like his old man, his torture techniques made Gitmo seem like kindergarten. Sam couldn't expose her to that. Then, there was Grashenko, with his supply of official badges. He could easily intimidate a fresh-faced tourist from Iowa.

Sam knew from the beginning she wasn't a shrinking violet, but his initial assessment of her wasn't too far off the mark. She was fresh off the farm. Red plaid skirt, penny loafers, Sears raincoat; long, dark brown French braid and cutesy bangs; wide-eyed emotions all there on her face. The clincher was the Iowa Hawkeye button on her purse strap. What were the odds of encountering a fellow grad in a New York City restroom? The basketball scholarship to the University of Iowa had been his ticket out of the steel mills— the career path of most of the guys in his southside Chicago neighborhood.

Yet for all her outward naïveté, she had gumption. She didn't deserve to be caught up in his problems. Yet, he knew without her he'd never make it out of the building. He blew out a breath. "Please." It galled him to ask. Finally, he said, "I need your help."

Sam hated like hell to involve a civilian, but she was already involved. She'd seen him, knew how vulnerable he was. He realized his limitations when he lost his balance. Damn. His leg hurt. And his butt. He could imagine the jeering laughter from the other field agents. *Didja hear Joz took one in the ass?*

"You probably trust me as far as you can throw a horse, but I need your help getting out of the building." God, he hated to admit that. He took a deep breath. What could he say to convince her? "It's a matter of national security."

She all but rolled her eyes. *"True Lies."*

"What?"

"It's a movie. Jamie Lee Curtis and Arnold—oh, never mind. At least, you didn't claim the Fate of the Western World hangs on my assisting you."

He let the corner of his mouth quirk—as much of a smile as he could muster. As he thought before, she had guts. Not much sense, but real guts.

"For what it's worth, you had me at 'please.' She unslung her purse and once again set it on the counter along with the books. "We'll have to go through the antique store. Those guys are probably waiting down there for you. So, we'll have to throw them off the track." As she talked, she pulled off her long coat. "Put this on."

She wore a dark red plaid dress, sleeveless with a scoop neck. He thought it was called a granny dress, although he'd never known any grannies who wore such a thing. Underneath, she wore a short sleeve, white T-shirt with a scoop neck higher than that of the dress. Hanging from a thin, gold chain, a Guardian Angel charm nestled in the hollow of her throat. Ironic. *He* was supposed to be guarding his country's security and people like her.

She shivered. "You'd better give me your jacket."

After taking his navy windbreaker, she set it on top of her purse before slinging her cape-style coat around his shoulders. Goose-bumps were popping out on her bare arms, yet she took care of him first. Sam wasn't used to such altruism.

"Okay, bend down." She pulled a blue flowered scarf out of the coat pocket.

"Just like a magician," he said. "You pull scarves out of thin air."

"Nope, just my pocket. I always keep a spare." She tied the scarf, babushka-style, around his head. "I don't like to feel my coat collar against my bare neck."

Bare neck? All kinds of inappropriate thoughts raced through his brain. Thoughts he had no business considering.

He glanced up. The mirror told him he looked like the Polish grandmothers in his old neighborhood. A really ugly grandmother, complete with a four-day stubble. He pulled the scarf lower on his forehead.

She gave him a dubious look. "Hunch over, and you might fool people."

"Only if they're blind." As a make-shift disguise, it would do. It had to. "Put on my jacket. We need to go."

As tall as she was, the sleeves of his jacket hung below her fingertips. Considering he'd worn the jacket for four days straight, it was a wonder she didn't rip the filthy thing off and fling it across the room. Instead, she shoved up the sleeves and pulled her long braid out of the collar. A crazy thought went through his brain. Could she sit on her hair when it was loose? He'd like to see that.

Crazy thought, indeed. As soon as he was done with her, he'd never see her again.

Sam slung his arm around her sturdy shoulders. As he noted before when he used her for balance, she wasn't a fragile damsel, too scared to help herself . . . or anyone else. They walked to the door. He pulled the box knife out of his pocket and thumbed out the blade. She stifled a gasp.

"It's not much, but it's protection." He let go of her, staying to the right of the door. "Slowly pull the door open. Stand behind it while I check the area."

He didn't think Grashenko would return to this floor. They were probably waiting downstairs. Yuri would watch the back stairs since that was the logical one Sam would use to escape.

When she opened the door, he motioned for her to wait. He listened. Just the creaks and groans of an old building. Even the rats were quiet. Maybe too quiet. He had to find out before letting her out from behind the door. It was solid wood. Wouldn't totally stop a bullet, but it would slow the sucker down. That was about as safe as she was likely to be

28

until they got away from this building. And he got her away from him.

On his good leg, Sam stepped through the half-opened door. The knife became an extension of his arm—just like his Sig would be. When he deemed it all clear, he crooked his fingers in the universal "come here" signal.

She came. No argument, no sass. He could live with that. As she walked out, she looked around cautiously. She seemed to have good instincts.

"Wait a sec," she whispered. "I have an idea. The elevator."

"Too noisy. Let's go. No talking and walk as quietly as possible."

"That's the point. Brown Shoes and his buddy will watch the elevator, and we can slip past them." She motioned for him to stay.

Daria was surprised he stayed. His mouth was pinched as he leaned back against a wall. If possible, his face had gotten paler than when she first saw him. He closed his eyes and shuddered. She had to hurry. He was in pain. As she rushed to the elevator, she hoped her plan worked before he collapsed.

The old-fashioned elevator had an arrow above the door that pivoted from one numeral to the next. The arrow pointed to the five. Good. If she had to call it up from a lower floor, the men who were hunting Red Shoe might race up the stairs and catch them. She hoped when she sent the elevator down it would make enough noise to draw Brown Shoes' attention. She pushed the call button.

Nothing happened.

Come on. Don't mess up my plan, she told the recalcitrant, inanimate object. She punched the button again. Not one of those lighted display buttons. This one was spring-loaded, and she got perverse delight out of punching it hard.

The door finally opened with a shriek worthy of a banshee. Straddling the opening, she reached in and hit the button for first floor.

Quickly, she stepped out. And nothing happened.

Sugar jets. No wonder Snidely Whiplash, aka the ungrateful bookstore inheritor, said no one used the elevator. Her plan wouldn't work if the elevator didn't.

This time, she stepped gingerly inside and prayed the elevator wouldn't plummet to the basement with her inside. She quickly hit every other button, including *B2*, which she presumed was the dungeon. When she hit the close door button, miraculously it did. She squeezed through the opening just before the rumbling started.

The elevator groaned, like a giant reluctantly awakened from slumber. Machinery clanked and clattered. Chains rusty from disuse went into action. Daria was sure the sounds could be heard all over the building. Halleluiah and amen. If the noise didn't bring that British guy and his buddy running, nothing would.

While the elevator moaned and groaned, she ran back to the wounded man, not bothering to keep quiet. She tucked her shoulder under his arm and muttered, "Tell me I'm not going to live to regret this."

"You'll regret it," he said softly. "But, you'll live. I'll make sure of that."

"Right. You can't even get out of this building without my help."

They did a three-legged race to the stairwell. He seemed to have an uncanny ability to choose the right aisle and avoid the deadends. With every other step, he sucked air through his teeth. His limping became more pronounced and his arm heavier. When they got to the door to the stairwell, he stopped. He bent over, bracing his left hand on his knee. He breathed so hard Daria worried he'd have a heart attack.

She reached for the heavy fire door just as the elevator stopped and shrieked. Would her ruse draw the bad guys? Oh, Lordy, she hoped so.

The wounded man seemed revived by the brief respite. "Open the door," he whispered. "And stay behind it."

Once again, he pressed himself against the opposite jamb then went through with the knife at the ready. He motioned for her to come. "Quietly," he whispered. Even that small sound seemed loud in the stairwell. She started to go ahead of him so, if he fell, she could stop him or at least slow him down. He hauled her back. "Stay behind me."

She stepped as quietly as possible with leather-soled shoes on metal stairs and wished she were wearing sneakers. Her father had been a big man but marvelously light on his feet. He expected his children to be so, too. After hearing him chew out the boys for clomping down the stairs, Daria learned to be quiet. So quiet, she could sneak up on them, which irritated her brothers to no end. More than once, she'd eavesdropped on them and learned more than they wanted her to.

The elevator started up again. Next stop, first floor. They needed to hurry. Once it reached the antique mall, the bad guys would know it was a trick.

She and Red Shoe passed the second floor. The door to the bookstore was closed. It was a good thing she hadn't left her books behind. They stopped on the landing at the first floor. The stairs continued down into darkness.

"Do you think there's an outside door down there?" Daria shuddered at the thought of descending into the bowels of the building. Rats as big as cows might be down there.

"No, I checked. Have to go past the antique mall." His whisper sounded thready.

"You don't look so good."

"You ought to see it from this side."

"Remember to scrunch down. Lean on me. Act weak."

"That'll be a stretch." Despite his sarcasm, pain swam in the muddy depths of his eyes. He quickly looked away.

"You'd better not keel over on me in there, mister. It'll cost a fortune if you break one of those old knickknacks."

"Probably cost me my life," he muttered.

His life?

She could almost hear Alexa Tremaine's derision. *What? You thought this was a game? Did you think he got that ragged wound by catching his calf on a nail or jagged rock or . . . shaving?* He'd been shot. And those guys were waiting to finish the job. Dear Lord, what had she gotten herself into? Fine time to be thinking about that, she mentally scoffed. It wasn't too late to back out, to leave this guy on his own. For all she knew he really was a bad guy, and she was abetting a fugitive.

Straightening her shoulders, she determined to see this through. She remembered her earlier assessment—he was one of the good guys. She had to believe that. Now, all she had to do was get him out of the building. Then, she could go her own way.

"Pull the scarf lower," she said. "I'll go first. Crouch down and stay behind me."

When he shook his head, she grabbed the lapels of her coat which barely covered his front. "Listen up." She talked to him the way she talked to her second-graders and her brothers. "Brown Shoes will dismiss me, and you can check out the area."

Reluctantly, he nodded. "Let's do it." He slid the knife up the sleeve of his faded blue denim shirt.

She hadn't expected him to do that, but it made sense. A knife-wielding *Granny* would draw attention. Now, he had no weapon at the ready, already more vulnerable. He depended on her to get him outside. To safety. She was all the protection he had.

Sam hated hiding behind anyone, especially a civilian and a woman, at that. Her plan was good, though. He tucked his head down into the collar of her coat, which smelled like her. Familiar scent. He couldn't figure out why.

She straightened her spine and opened the door boldly, as if she had nothing to hide. "Now, Gran, no stopping to look at the toys you played with as a kid."

She led him through the antique store crowded with booths and shoppers, including a twenty-something man in a gray sweater. He was holding a figurine that looked like the Lladro ballerina Sam and his sister had given their mother. The man had his head bowed, examining the expensive statue.

Sam and the woman made it to the large glass doors. She even had her hand on the metal bar to push it open, when a strident female voice said, "What's in the bag?"

They froze.

"Wait here, Gran." She patted his shoulder then turned to face the woman. "We bought books upstairs. My grandmother's really tired. I need to get her home."

While she held up her bag and made excuses, Sam pushed open the door. He kept his head down, scrunched up like a turtle. Out of the corner of his eye, he saw Gray Sweater. Jesus, he was thinking in clothing terms like the woman. He'd seen that sweater before. He looked more closely. At the same time, the man looked up. Recognition sparked across thirty feet of antiques.

"Go on, then," the antique store woman was saying. "That kid up there—"

There was a crash. Sam grabbed his *granddaughter's* hand and hauled ass.

Outside, he was surprised that it was evening. The streetlights and storefront lights made it almost as bright as day. Not good. All the better for Gray Sweater to see him. The klutz who dropped the Lladro had to be Junior Korioff.

Dragging the woman behind him, Sam darted down the crowded sidewalk. He caught his reflection in a storefront window. Christ, he looked like Groucho Marx in a babushka. They crossed one street. He needed more support. He let go of her wrist and wrapped his arm around her slender waist, adhering her to his side tighter than jelly on bread.

When they finally stopped so he could catch his breath, she said, "We made it."

"That's usually—" His chest heaved from exertion. "— when the bottom falls out."

Sam whipped off the scarf. While he and the woman exchanged coats, a cab pulled up to the curb at the end of the block and disgorged its passengers. Sam whistled shrilly. "Run ahead," he ordered. "Grab that cab."

No questions asked, his rescuer did. She leaned in and said something to the driver. Sam limped along as fast as he could. He heard a shout behind him. He knew that voice. He didn't look back, just put on a burst of speed. Four feet from the cab, he faltered, nearly fell and lurched against the corner of a building. He'd run out of steam.

The woman started toward him when the cabbie hollered, "You gettin' in or what?"

"In. Hang on a sec." She ran toward Sam.

He made a final effort and lurched into her arms. She faltered then steadied herself, and him.

"Get in the cab, honey." She pushed him inside. "You are too drunk to walk."

He fell across the seat and barely righted himself before she jumped in and slammed the door. When she landed against him, he nearly lit up with pain. Still, he managed to scoot across the seat on his left hip.

"Okay, folks, where to?"

Sam glanced out the back window. Korioff was racing toward them. "Just drive," Sam said, his words slurred. "Take a right at the next block."

He was losing it. He couldn't think. He used up the last of his reserves in that burst of speed down the sidewalk. Everything caught up. Exhaustion. The loss of blood. The fear that he'd failed his mission.

Daria Mason looked over at the man slumped against the side door of the cab. Now what was she supposed to do?

"You folks have a destination, or are we on a sightseeing tour?" the driver asked. "It makes me no never mind, but this isn't exactly the best part of the Big Apple."

The area they were driving through was becoming more run-down. Daria had no idea where they were, but she knew enough not to be in this neighborhood.

"When you get a chance," she said. "Go around a corner and head back the way we came but not on that street." That should buy her enough time to think.

Daria had never really known fear before. She'd been scared . . . of small things like spiders and forgetting to pay her credit card bill. Not this run-for-your-life terror.

"Somebody chasing you?" The driver smirked in the rearview mirror.

"No," she said a little too sharply. "My husband's . . . sick."

"You need a hospital?"

"No." Again, too sharp. Red Shoe said that's where they would check and find him. "I mean, not that kind of sick."

"Tied one on, hey? Don't let him throw up in my cab."

She leaped at that. She'd said something about him being drunk before getting into the cab. She'd better keep her stories straight.

"Yes," she told the driver. "I mean, I won't. I am just furious. We have tickets to see 'Wicked' tonight and he had to go and get himself drunk and I had to—"

"I don't need your life story, lady. Just tell me where you want to go." He paused. "Or, I can drive around until you make up your mind. Meter's running, either way. I just don't want you to think you got ripped off by a New York cab driver."

Daria was surprised at the driver's concern. She'd always heard New Yorkers were rude and yet, other than the bookseller and Brown Shoes, she hadn't encountered rudeness.

She looked over at the man slumped against the opposite door. His pallor was even grayer than when she first saw him. It might be the streetlights, but she didn't think so. He needed help. If she were back home, she'd know what to do, where to go, how to keep him safe. But here, in a city so big, so confusing, she wasn't sure.

He needed medical help, yet he said no hospital. Dear Lord, what should she do? What would Alexa Tremaine do? Then she thought, *forget Alexa*. This was no fictional adventure. This was real life and it was up to her, Daria Mason, to make a decision. It was up to her to keep this man alive.

There was only one place she knew where he would be safe until she could come up with a plan. It was dangerous. Her brothers would have strokes if they ever found out. But . . . she thought hard. It felt like the right thing to do.

"We'll just go back to the hotel," she told the driver. "The Harbizon."

CHAPTER FIVE

"Yuri, I lose him."

Yuri Grashenko, former KGB, now in a more lucrative line of work, blew out a long breath and tightened his grip on the mobile phone while he watched the alley.

When the elevator started in the old building, Korioff rushed toward the sound. If someone really were inside, it wouldn't be Jozwiak. He wasn't stupid. While Korioff waited impatiently for the elevator, Yuri headed for the back stairs. But there was no place to hide to surprise his prey. Unlike the front stairwell, this one had an exit to the outside.

Yuri had planted himself out in the alley along with the refuse and a smell worse than the Volga on a hot summer day. There were plenty of places to hide. He just had to watch where he stepped.

"Korioff," Yuri said not bothering to hide his anger or exasperation. "Of all the things you could tell me 'I lose him' is not what I want to hear."

"Y-Yes, Yuri. I see him. I drop . . . figur—statue thing. Store lady yell much." When he got excited, Korioff forgot what little English he knew. He needed to learn the language before he'd ever succeed outside the Motherland.

"Stop. Think. Speak slowly."

"Yes, Yuri. Oh, I learn new American saying in store. 'You break it, you buy it.' I not like that saying. I have to use credit card. Very expensive."

Yuri clutched the mobile harder, wishing it was Korioff's neck. "What about Johnston?"

Yuri knew Jozwiak's real name. He had to keep some information back from Korioff. One never revealed all one knew.

"He gone when I leave store. I run down street. See him get in taxi—"

The back door started to open. Yuri clicked off his phone

36

and flattened himself against the wall next to the dumpster. If he squinted, he could see between the wall and the brown metal receptacle. A man leaned out and looked around. Bart Teller. Was this Jozwiak's contact? Strange how these Americans operated. Jozwiak should have gone to Washington to deliver intel that would ensure the painful demise of Yuri's employer. Korioff's clients were not the forgiving kind.

When Yuri learned that New York City was Jozwiak's destination, he thought his nemesis was selling the intel—a bizarre thought, since Jozwiak was such a straight arrow. The American colloquialism seemed appropriate. Which begged the question—why did the Director of the Orion Agency want to meet Jozwiak in such an unusual place?

Maybe Teller feared his own agency had a traitor. Very interesting. A piece of luck practically falling into Yuri's lap. Capturing the director of the Orion Agency would ensure Jozwiak's cooperation.

Before Yuri could grab Teller, the woman from the antique store began yelling at him. She shouted that he couldn't use the back entrance. Couldn't he read the sign that said "No exit except in an emergency"? To Yuri's surprise, Teller didn't argue and went inside.

Disgusted, Yuri headed for his rental car. Jozwiak was gone. Teller would have been a bonus. Yuri would have to find out what else Korioff was going to say. Something about Jozwiak and a taxi.

"I do not like it when you hang up on me, Yuri," Korioff said in Russian in a surprising imitation of his father. "You will not do that again."

"I will when necessary. Now, what was that about Joz— Johnston getting into a cab?" Yuri didn't often make mistakes, but he nearly let slip the man's real name. "Check with the cab company to find out where it took him."

"Please pull around to the side entrance," Daria directed the cab driver. "I, uh, I don't want anyone to see my husband. This is *so* embarrassing."

"Honey?" She jiggled the man's shoulder. "We're at the

hotel."

"Huh?" His eyes were still closed.

Good Lord, how was she going to get him out of the cab let alone into the hotel? She paid the driver an exorbitant amount of money then got out of the cab. "We're at the hotel, *honey*." She tugged on his wrist. "C'mon, big guy."

"You should maybe get some coffee in him," the driver said. "Otherwise, he's going to have one hell of a hangover."

"Serve him right," she snapped, tugging harder.

The man cooperated this time and lurched out of the cab and into her arms. She staggered for a moment but held her ground. He nuzzled her ear, sending tiny thrills through her. "Don't lose yourself in the part, *honey*," he whispered.

Daria jerked back. She wanted to deck him. Had he been faking in the back of the cab? She was sure he'd been out. He was awake now and he could jolly well help her.

"Try not to look drunk," she said through clenched teeth.

"Would you rather I look amorous?" He leered at her. Actually, leered.

"Could we please get inside? The elevator is on the right."

They made it to the elevator without meeting any of the other writers. This hall wasn't used much, she'd noted during her stay. Neither was this elevator. It was a distance from the lobby and the main elevators. She'd noticed the housekeeping staff push their carts into it.

Red Shoe leaned in the corner, his hands braced on the walls of the elevator. He didn't speak. The bright light inside accentuated the deep groves along his mouth and the shadows under his eyes. He looked like he would fall over at any minute.

When they reached her floor, she tucked herself under his arm. Again, she wrinkled her nose. "You really do need a shower."

He leaned heavily on her. "Wanna scrub my back?"

She ignored his soft words. She'd grown up trying to stay one step ahead of four brothers. Ignoring them often took the wind out of their sails.

She got him out of the elevator, grateful her room was close. After opening the door with her key card, she reached inside to switch on a light. He moved faster than the speed of sound, muscling her into the room, his box knife out. His eyes darted everywhere. He even slammed the bathroom door against the wall and nearly ripped the shower curtain off the hooks. All the while, he kept a tight grip on her wrist. Finally, he tore her purse off her shoulder. The strap tangled in her braid. She yelped when stray hairs caught on the buckle.

"You want my purse?" she cried. "Why didn't you take it on the street? Or in the restroom?" So much for her instincts telling her she'd done the right thing bringing the wounded man up here. What a fool she was.

Red Shoe bumped into the desk chair, upsetting it on his way across Daria's hotel room. He shoved her ahead of him, making sure he stood between her and the door. No escape. Her heart now beat faster than the speed of light. Her chest heaved as her lungs tried to find oxygen. She *was* too stupid to live.

After dumping the contents of her purse on the queen bed next to the window, the first thing he grabbed was her wallet.

Oh, God. He was a thief. A common thief.

"Give me that." She'd been watching his actions in dumbfounded horror. Now that he was going to take what little cash she had left, she not only found her voice, but she charged toward him. "You are not taking my money."

He looked up and with one hand raised—like a traffic cop—he said, "Stay."

She obeyed, better than Rover ever did.

He pulled out her driver's license. "Daria Mason." He pronounced her name as if it began like *dare*. People often did.

"It's Dar, like jar," she corrected. "Daria."

"Dahria, from Prairieville, Iowa. Couldn't they have come up with something more original?" he sneered and tossed it on the bed. "How corny."

If she hadn't been so mad about rescuing him only to have him steal from her, she would have rolled her eyes at his bad pun. "Iowa is known for more than corn, you know."

Ignoring her, he examined every card in her wallet, then

tossed them one by one on the bed. "Insurance, Triple A, Voter Registration, MasterCard. Hallmark Crown?"

"Just what do you think you're doing?" she demanded. "What do you want?"

"Who do you work for?" he asked with more menace than she'd heard so far, except when he pointed the knife at her the first time.

"What?"

"What agency? Who sent you?" He fired questions at her while checking her tube of Barely There lipstick and examining her cell phone. Other than a quick glance, he didn't bother with her pocket calendar or notebook. If he started to read the latter, she would have to hurt him. She'd rip it out of his hands so fast his head would swim.

"Nobody sent me. I don't know what you mean about an agency." When he continued to stare at her, she heaved an exasperated sigh. "I work for the Prairieville Public Schools. I teach second grade at Prairieville Elementary."

"You know." He sat heavily on the end of the other bed, the one closer to the door. "I almost believe that." He was still between her and freedom.

"Lucky me. Are you through? I would like to reorganize my purse."

He gave her an appraising look. "You're a cool one, aren't you?"

Cool? She was shaking in her boots. Okay, in her penny loafers. What had she gotten herself into? She'd never done anything like this in her entire life. Back in Prairieville, her life was so predictable, so . . . boring.

It wasn't boring now. Her heart was thumping, adrenaline flowing. He could probably hear her knees knocking.

He scrubbed his hand down his face. "I need to know. Why are you helping me? My line about national security sounded lame even to me."

Daria stared hard at him. "Was it the truth?"

He nodded. "Why did you help me? And don't say it's out of the goodness of your heart."

She began to put her belongings back in their correct places. An organizer purse made things so much easier to find. *If* she remembered to put things back in the right place. "You remind me of a dog I knew," she muttered.

"A dog?" He stopped rubbing his eyes and stared at her. "I remind you of a dog?"

"Somebody dumped him in the ditch. I tried to help him, and he bit me." She held out her right hand. "Nine stitches."

"Dumb dog," he muttered.

"I couldn't save him. He wouldn't let me save him." Before the prickling behind her eyes grew worse, she shook her finger at him. "So, you'd better not die on me."

The corner of his mouth started to curve. "I'll try not to." He closed his eyes, as if he couldn't hold them open anymore. He swayed and fell back on the bed.

Daria didn't know what happened. One minute, Red Shoe was promising not to die and the next, he keeled over. She raced to his side and shook him. "Are you okay?"

No response. She placed two fingers under his jaw. He had a pulse. Then, he started to snore. No question that he was breathing.

Now, what was she supposed to do? She picked up the toppled desk chair and sat. *Think, girl.* After the way he scared her ripping her purse off her shoulder, she should just leave him there. Half on the bed.

For goodness' sake, he was going to fall off. She jumped up and tried to scoot him higher on the bed. Good Lord, he was heavy. Somehow, she got him under the covers.

She sat on the chair again. All right now. He was safe and as comfortable as she could make him. She'd done what she could. She'd gotten him out of that building, away from the bad guys. Time for her to get away from him. Time to pack up and go home. That was enough excitement to last her several years.

No, she couldn't go home. Not yet. The conference wasn't over. She had the appointment tomorrow. That opportunity was too important to miss. She had a chance to intrigue an editor into reading her manuscript. She couldn't blow this. If she went home empty-handed, so to speak, her brothers would never take her work seriously. They'd figuratively pat her on the head and either say "about time you got this out of your system" (Jimmy) or "enjoy your little hobby" (the rest of them). She couldn't bear either thought.

The man rolled onto his right hip, groaned then rolled over on his left, dragging the covers with him. Where he'd momentarily lain, there was a blood stain on the sheet. Oh, dear Lord, he had another wound.

She jumped up again. "Mister?" She shook his shoulder. "You're bleeding."

Several seconds passed. Still, she waited. No response.

She had to do something. With a gulp, she walked around the bed. She had to check his backside. She unbuckled and unzipped his jeans. Then, she raced around to the other side. No way was she looking at the front of him. Backsides, she could handle. She'd pulled splinters out Andy's backside when he slid off a plank in the barn. And quills out of Tommy's butt when he tangled with a porcupine.

Nurses saw backsides all the time. Although Daria wasn't a nurse, she'd taken a First Aid class and refresher courses. She could handle this. First, she needed another pair of latex gloves and the First Aid kit she kept in her tote.

Now, she was ready. She rolled him on his stomach and then pulled down his jeans and the waistband of his formerly white briefs. The red through the hole in his jeans that she mistook for his underwear turned out to be wadded paper towels soaked with blood. She peeled the mess away.

And nearly gagged at the sight of ragged flesh. This was much worse than the wound on his calf. It, also, went beyond the meager supplies in her small First Aid kit. He needed professional help. Until then, she'd have to come up with something else.

When she finished, she stood back. Now, both pockets bulged. His wallet was probably in his left. For a moment, she debated checking it. Then, she thought about him ransacking her purse and put aside her qualms about invading his privacy.

Ironic. Here she was worrying about violating his privacy when she'd pulled down his drawers and examined his butt.

She pulled out his wallet. She was going to find out this man's name. Not just who but what he was. She noticed something behind the wallet and pulled that out, too. A passport. Too bad he didn't carry his wallet and passport in his right pocket. They might have slowed down the bullet and prevented him from getting so badly hurt.

Sitting in the desk chair, she examined her find. His name was Sam Johnston. He lived in Arlington, Virginia. And he was thirty-two. He looked older. She rifled through credit cards—American Express and VISA—and a frequent diner's card from a Washington, DC restaurant. No emergency contact info. No Fraternal Order of Police membership card. She thought about that. If he were undercover, he couldn't very well carry that kind of identification. If he was from Washington, he could be one of the alphabet agencies—FBI, DEA, ATF, or even CIA. The more she thought about the men with foreign accents, the more she thought he must be CIA.

Holy cow! She had a spy in her bed.

When she pulled out a small wad of bills, she almost fell off the chair. There weren't many, but they all had Ben Franklin's picture on them. Whoa. It was over a thousand dollars. She never knew anyone who carried that much cash. And she'd been worried about him stealing hers. It was a wonder Sam Johnston hadn't laughed in her face.

As she stuffed the bills back into the wallet, she noted the edge of white under a flap behind the bills. The folded piece of paper was an airline ticket. He'd flown from Charles de Gaulle Airport to JFK. She looked at the date. Today. This morning, actually. *Wow*. He arrived less than two hours after leaving Paris. The wonders of traveling west across several time zones.

She turned her attention to his passport. Same information as his driver's license.

She put his identification on the nightstand. She really had no right to snoop. Especially since she wasn't sticking around. He was sleeping soundly. He would be all right now. Or as all right as a wounded man could be until he got medical help. She'd done her best. No more Good Samaritan. He was on his own. She could bunk in with one of her critique partners.

She checked her watch. She was supposed to meet them in the bar in an hour. Okay, now she had a plan. She'd clear out of this room and find somewhere else to sleep tonight. No way was she missing that appointment tomorrow.

She jumped up again, feeling like a deranged jack-in-the-box, and started packing. Leaving her precious Nancy Drew books in the bag since they were dusty, she made room for them in the suitcase. When she finished, she put on her coat then rolled her suitcase to the door. After making sure she had the key card, she slung her purse and tote over her shoulder. She looked back at the man she'd rescued. Who would've thought her little trip to a used bookstore would end with such a bang?

Poor choice of words.

"Good-by, Sam Johnston," she whispered. "Be safe."

Daria made it all the way down to the parking garage without encountering a single soul. A lot of noise came from the first-floor bar. After what she'd been through, she was getting a strong drink. The Good Lord knew she needed one. Her friends were at a different hotel. As soon as she stowed her luggage, she would settle her bill and move her car over to the other hotel.

She hefted her suitcase into the trunk of the Gray Goose. The Buick wasn't a Mom-mobile, like Ginnie's station wagon, but it didn't cry out "smoking hot babe," either. Five years ago, when she drooled over a sporty red Camaro, Jimmy steered her toward this car at Lucky's—'If you don't buy from us, you won't get Lucky'—Used Cars.

Jimmy had scoffed at the Camaro. "Muscle car. Cops can't wait to pull over a muscle car." He should know.

Alexa Tremaine would have said, "It's my money, and I'll damn well buy the car I want." But, Daria hadn't *met* her heroine yet, so she let her brother browbeat her with statistics about the safety, low mileage and dependability of the dull gray Grandpa-mobile. "Nobody'll steal this baby," Jimmy said proudly.

He was right about that. Nobody would *want* it.

Daria closed the trunk. Okay, that was that. All she had to do was check out and meet her friends. The maid would find the wounded man in the morning, if he was still there. Let the police handle this. It was their job to protect and defend.

"Leaving for good this time?"

Daria jumped at the voice behind her. The parking attendant. She'd talked to him yesterday when she brought her empty picnic cooler down to the car. When things were quiet, he'd told her, he ran laps around the cars for exercise.

"Hi," she said. "How did your test go today?"

"Great." The Columbia journalism student gave her a cocky grin. "Aced it."

"Uh, listen, could you do me a favor?" She pulled out a ten. This was going to be a costly favor, but she could skimp on meals. Besides, he could use the money. "If—If anyone comes looking for me, could you forget you saw me?"

He gave her a mocking smile. "Skipping out on your bill?"

"No. No, nothing like that. It's just . . . just that I, uh, I met this guy and . . ."

"Say no more." He took the money. "Anybody comes looking for you, and I'll steer 'em wrong."

"Great. I'll meet you at the exit booth." She got into the Buick and started the engine. She would put the parking charges on her credit card, drive up to the entrance and settle her bill. Then, she was going to get the largest margarita and maybe her hands would stop shaking. Maybe the drink would drown out her conscience that said she was abandoning a defenseless man.

CHAPTER SIX

Sam Jozwiak awoke lying on his stomach in a woman's bed. With his eyes still closed, he slowly inhaled. Definitely a woman's bed. Strawberry shampoo and *White Linen* perfume. Sally used to wear *White Linen*. He smiled, remembering.

Pressing his face into the pillow, he inhaled again. Underneath the perfume was the delicious scent of *woman*. God, he loved the smell of waking up in a woman's bed.

Wait a minute. Whose bed?

He rolled over and sat up with a jerk. Pain screamed from his right hip. He sucked air before scanning the room. An empty hotel room. Now, it came back. The woman who helped him. Daria Mason from Prairieville, Iowa. She was gone. Although he was glad to see she had some self-preservation, he felt oddly bereft.

He swung his legs over the edge of the bed. His right one hurt like a son of a bitch. He looked down at his gaping jeans. He'd been out of it, but he was pretty sure he would have remembered unzipping his pants. His left hip felt . . . different.

Goddamn it, the bitch rolled him before she left.

Served him right. He'd been stupid. Downright stupid. Her ID was as fake as his. Iowa school teacher, his ass. If he ever saw her again, he'd shake—

In the dim light from the nearly-closed bathroom door, he saw his wallet and passport on the nightstand. He checked and offered a silent apology. So, she was honest. But, what if she left to find Grashenko? Or, worse, the terrorists Yuri's boss worked for.

Korioff was the bagman for a small group of Middle Eastern extremists. They were going to shit bricks when they discovered their financial records were the victim of a computer virus. Oh, gee, darn. Korioff better hope they didn't find out before he pieced together records of their transactions. Because he sure as hell wasn't getting them back from Sam. He would destroy the memory chip before handing it over.

That would pretty much destroy any chance of Sam's getting away alive.

First, he had to get out of there. As he levered himself off the bed, dizziness swept through him. He sat down until the weakness passed before hobbling into the bathroom. In the mirror, he checked his butt wound and found her handiwork. The *bandage* looked like white cotton underpants duct-taped to his skin. Inventive. He smiled. Not much of one but a quick smile, nevertheless. He wished he'd been awake for her First Aid thing.

His reflection in the mirror reminded him of how old he felt. Where was the idealist fresh out of college? The one who would make the world a safer place? The past twelve years had not been kind to him. The harsh overhead light illuminated each line, every crease. He rubbed his hand over the black stubble on his jaw. He didn't just feel like hell, he looked like it, too.

He was getting too old for this business. The life of a field agent was short. Reflexes got slower. His edge not as sharp. He thought he was in line for a desk job when Mac retired last year. Sam knew he wasn't ready for the Director's job, but he'd hoped for Assistant Director, at least. Instead, he still skulked, eavesdropped, snooped—otherwise known as gathering intel—while The Powers That Be appointed that weeny Teller to the Director's post.

With an effort, Sam propped his foot on the lid of the toilet and checked his leg. Her scarf was matted to the dried blood around the hole in his calf. Four inches higher and his knee would have been shot to hell. He needed better bandages and a good dose of antibiotics. Otherwise, he wouldn't have to worry about his butt or leg. He didn't escape with his life from the Russian Mafia to lose it to gangrene.

What the hell happened to Teller? Why set up a meeting and then do a no-show? Another thing bothered Sam. How did Grashenko find the rendezvous? Sam thought he lost the two Russians in Paris. He needed to think. Despite his nap, fatigue still clouded his mind.

When he heard the click of the hall door, he grabbed the box knife. He waited behind the bathroom door. Stealthy footsteps crept into the room. Feminine footsteps. Sam stepped around the bathroom door.

Daria Mason gave him a quick smile. "Hi, honey. I'm home."

Sam propped his arm on the doorframe. "Forget something?"

Her mouth twisted into a wry grimace. "Yes. You."

CHAPTER SEVEN

"Tell me again how an empty parking space was a sign."
Sam stood in the bathroom doorway. Though he'd washed
his face, it hadn't done much for his appearance. He
buttoned his denim shirt and watched the woman who said
she'd come back for him.

Daria Mason had shrugged out of her beige coat. It
rested, ivory lining out, behind her in the upholstered chair.
She'd turned on the lamp in the corner next to the chair
while he washed. The tiny angel charm resting in the hollow
of her throat gleamed in the light. She certainly was *his*
Guardian Angel.

"When I came out of the parking garage, I drove around
to the front," she said. "I was going to take care of my bill."

"Why didn't you do it through the television?"

"I didn't know. Anyway, there were no parking spaces
along the street and a stretch limo blocked the drive out
front. I circled the block, and a car pulled out of a parking
space right next to the door where the cab let us off." She
looked at him, as if to make sure he knew which door. "First,
I thought I was just lucky. Then, I remembered I kept the key
card. I should've left it in the room. That was another sign,
you see."

"You put a lot of stock in *signs*?" When he unbuckled his
belt to tuck in his shirt, she quickly looked away. A faint
blush tinged her cheeks.

She propped her elbows on the arms of the chair and
interlaced her long, slender fingers. She wore a gold ring with
an opal on her right hand. Her jewelry was discreet, tasteful.
Gold studs in her ears, the thin necklace with the angel
charm, a practical Timex on her wrist. No ring, not even a tan
line, where a ring used to be, on her left hand.

As a trained professional, Sam always made note of
details. Nothing personal. He just wondered why the men in

Iowa let a good-looking woman remain single.

"Yes, I believe in *signs*." She didn't appear to notice him taking inventory. "Gut instinct, if you like. When I saw the parking space and realized I still had the key card, I knew they were signs my job wasn't done."

"What job is that?"

"Rescuing you." She gave him a cocky grin.

His leg ached from standing, rather leaning, against the doorframe. His first step into the room on his right leg about brought him to his knees.

"Are you going to faint?" She jumped to her feet.

Clutching the doorframe, he shot her a baleful look. "Men don't faint."

Easing back into the chair, she sat on the edge. "Pardon me. Are you going to pass out?"

He took several deep breaths, ignoring her. He held onto the wall and hobbled to the desk. Just that small exertion caused sweat to break out on his forehead.

He glanced at the clock/radio on the nightstand. Eleven o'clock. He'd been out for over three hours. He never slept well away from his condo. There, his sophisticated surveillance system gave him the security he needed to sleep without waking at every little noise. Yet, he'd slept so soundly he never heard her pack, never felt her bandage his butt.

Must be fatigue. After the nap, he thought he was good to go. His little trip from the bathroom convinced him he was too weak to go anywhere. He hated like hell to admit it. He was too goddamn weak.

He eased onto the chair at the desk, careful not to sit square. He patted the side of his hip. "Interesting field dressing."

Again, she wouldn't look at him. Her cheeks bloomed.

"Duct tape?" he said. "Who carries around duct tape?"

"I do." She jerked her head up and shot him a defiant look. "It has many uses. The astronauts even used duct tape to fix the space shuttle."

"O-kay." He'd better play nice. "You mentioned a car. Rental?"

She shook her head. "It's my own. I've never flown before. Besides, I couldn't afford it. Although for the price of parking," she muttered, "I probably should have tried the friendly skies."

"You drove all the way from Iowa to New York City by yourself?" Sam admired her stamina and her guts. But, then he knew she had a lot of guts considering the way she got him away from Grashenko.

"My best friend helped with the driving."

Sam went still. "Where is this friend?"

Daria sighed. "Her mom had emergency surgery Sunday. Ginnie flew down to Florida to be with her. She was really looking forward to the conference."

"Conference?"

"A writers' conference."

"You're a writer," he probed. "Are you published?"

"Not yet. I write, ergo I am a writer." She lifted her chin.

"Ergo? Who uses the word ergo?"

Ignoring that comment, she glared at him. "I'm asking the questions now, Sam Johnston. And I want answers."

She must have gotten his name from his wallet and passport. He almost told her his real name then decided against it. The less she knew, the better.

"You were shot, weren't you?" she continued.

"You don't believe I cut myself shaving?"

She shot him a look. His mother and every one of his teachers used that look on him. Must be something they learned in a teacher education class. Vile Looks 101.

Then, the corner of her mouth quirked. "I've heard of men shaving their legs. But, tell me, Mr. Johnston, why would a man shave his butt?"

She had him there.

"Why are those guys hunting you?" All trace of amusement was gone. "And why would they shoot at you?"

Sam leaned forward and dangled his hands between his knees. "The less you know, Ms. Mason, the safer you'll be."

"No. You are not going to use that line of bull hockey on me. I deserve to know what I've gotten myself into."

"Bull hockey? Don't writers from the Heartland use naughty words?"

This time, the look she gave him came from the advanced class. Vile Looks 470.

He relented. "I stole something. They want it back." When she opened her mouth—in all probability to ask what he'd stolen—he held up his hand.

She ignored it. "You're a thief. Hmph. That's what I thought when you grabbed my purse. A common thief."

"No, not a *common* thief. I'm an extraordinary thief."

"Do you think I'm going to be taken in by your little boy smile? Does your theft really have something to do with national security? Or, was that another line of bull?"

"No bull," he said. "Enough questions."

"No, one more. Which country?"

"What?"

"You said *national* security." She pursed her lips. "Which nation?"

"Have you found our boy yet?" Teller paced the living room of the small apartment he kept in New York City. Hardesty had come with his magic laptop.

"In the last three minutes, boss? No."

"Don't be a smart-ass, or this is your first and only chance to be a field agent."

"Yes, sir. I'm monitoring his cell phone, and I've rerouted calls to your office here. And before you ask again, yes, I'm still monitoring the police bands. Plus, I'm checking hospital databases since you said you found evidence of an injury at the rendezvous."

Teller continued to pace the small confines of the room. "Try his cell phone again. Why doesn't he pick up?"

"A good field agent turns off his phone so it doesn't ring at inopportune moments." Hardesty sounded as if he should know that.

Teller hadn't thought when he tapped the rookie for this op, Hardesty would give him so much grief. He did think the computer geek should be more appreciative of the opportunity.

"Keep searching," he ordered. "We have to find Joz."

"Sir, wouldn't it be more efficient to use the resources at headquarters?"

"No," Teller snapped. He forced himself to regain

composure. "We're dealing with very sensitive intel. We can't risk a leak. I'm trusting only you on this mission. I have been quite impressed with your—"

"Hang on, boss. He's using his cell. If he stays on long enough, I can get a fix on his position."

"Yes." Teller punched the air. Finally, something was going right.

"Got him." Hardesty grinned broadly.

Yuri Grashenko wondered why Jozwiak wasn't using his mobile phone. He should have called for backup right away. Yuri even tried calling him to get a fix on his position. Yuri's boss was a stingy son of a bitch regarding technology. Korioff did, however, pay very well for Yuri's services. The small computer resting on the seat of the rental car beside him was state-of-the-art, paid for out of his generous salary.

Unlike many of his former colleagues, Yuri saw the future and knew technology was its major weapon. Information was the key to success. His peers deemed themselves too old to learn new ways. Not Yuri.

He hadn't planned to spend the night in the Lincoln Towncar, but he needed space from Korioff's son. Yuri leaned his head back against the rest, pleased at the comfort of this fine American automobile. He closed his eyes. After all the running through that drafty old building, his body had begun to rebel. Aging was hell.

He shifted, trying to escape the chafing from the new denim trousers—blue jeans, he amended. He could lay their inappropriate attire on Korioff who had been in charge of their wardrobes and thought all New York detectives wore jeans.

The directive to teach young Korioff another aspect of his father's black market and money-laundering business cramped Yuri's style. Solo, he could have accomplished his mission within the first hour.

As soon as the intruder entered Korioff's study early Sunday morning, Yuri's watch had vibrated. He'd checked the monitor of the surveillance camera he cleverly disguised in Korioff's bookcase. So cleverly, that even Korioff didn't know it was there.

Recognizing the intruder immediately, Yuri watched Jozwiak hide the memory chip. Before Yuri raced across the compound to the study, Jozwiak was gone. When Yuri checked the computer to see what Jozwiak copied, to his horror, a yellow ball appeared—a profile with an eye and an open mouth.

As the figure zoomed across the screen, row by row, its mouth opened and closed, simulating that it was gobbling files. Yuri stared, powerless to stop it. Waking up his employer with the news that all his files were gone was worse.

Had Korioff's son followed instructions and captured Jozwiak in the Smolensk hotel hallway as instructed, Yuri would have confiscated the memory chip.

The beep of the computer brought him out of his ruminating. Yuri smiled. At last, he found his prey. Nothing would stop him now.

"What the hell kind of question is that?" Sam said. "What do you mean which nation? The good, old U.S. of A. What did you think?"

"How was I supposed to know? You could be working for—"

"Don't even think that," Sam snapped. "My loyalties are not for sale."

Daria blew out a breath. She didn't mean to impugn his integrity. After she used the express check-out through the television, she faced him. "We can leave now."

He stood up and sat back down quickly. He sucked in a breath. "Damn. I gotta quit doing that." His face looked as white as the Elmer's glue her students used prolifically.

She rushed to kneel in front of him. "I hate to sound like a broken record, but you do need to see a doctor."

"And you're going to take me to one."

Sam spoke to her the same way Jimmy did. Like when he ordered her to call home every night. To keep the peace, and to keep Jimmy from hounding her, she did. Even tonight while she sat in the car debating what to do, she called home.

She told Tommy about her Nancy Drew books. But when it came to what happened later . . . The less her brothers knew the better.

Sam Johnston expected her to do his bidding, just like them. If he didn't have two bullet holes in him, she'd give him an attitude adjustment for ordering her around. Alexa Tremaine wouldn't put up with that garbage and neither would Daria. Not anymore.

Before she could tell him so, he said, "Got anything for pain?"

His brown eyes clouded in pain. If he were anything like her macho brothers—and the resemblance was disgusting— he must really hurt to ask for pain medicine. She handed him a bottle of Tylenol from her purse. After he washed down the pills, she said, "Do you need help getting up?"

"I'm not a total cripple."

After that remark, she'd be darned if she offered her help again. He could just struggle. "Fine. I'll check and make sure we didn't leave anything behind."

She knelt and looked under the bed. When she got up, she realized he'd been staring at her rear. Had her dress ridden up?

He didn't seem to notice her embarrassment. "What were you doing in that building? Before you had to use the restroom?"

She'd rather he didn't remember the reason they met. "Shopping."

"Ah. What's a trip to New York without a shopping spree?"

"Uh huh." She made a last check of the dresser drawers. "At the used bookstore on the second floor."

"I'm surprised you weren't at Bloomie's or Saks."

She turned around and indicated her granny dress and loafers. "Do I look like a person who would shop at Saks?"

"Can't say you do. So, instead of shopping for clothes, you went to a bookstore?"

"And found the most wonderful treasures," she enthused. "Nancy Drew mysteries. Blue covers. Original editions."

"Aren't those a little out of date? My mom had the series

from when she was a kid and my sister read them." He paused. "I thought the covers were yellow."

"That was a later edition." She sighed. "Oh, well . . ."

"All right. What's with the sigh?"

"I was going to go back for more, but then I ran into you."

"Go back in the morning. After you take me to Doc's."

"No. Too much to do before going home. I'm attending the rest of the conference, then a trip to Ellis Island and the Statue of Liberty. I was going to tell my writer friends what I found at the bookstore at dinner tonight." She glanced at her watch. After midnight. "I mean, last night. But I didn't. Meet them, that is."

"People were waiting for you?" There he went, demanding answers again.

"I called them from the car while I was debating whether to come back here. They were concerned that I didn't show. I told them I had to rescue a tall, dark and handsome spy from the Russians."

His jaw dropped. She'd never seen anyone actually do that before.

"You're joking, right?" he said.

After his crack about shaving his leg, she figured he deserved a little payback. He stared hard at her and she finally relented. "I told them I ran into an old friend."

"Good. Good thinking."

She heard relief in his voice and began to wonder. "*Are* you a spy?"

"You think I'm handsome?"

"Yuri, I find cab driver."

"It's about time." Grashenko tucked the mobile phone between his chin and shoulder. He had almost reached the location where Jozwiak's call originated. Korioff's info came too late.

"Not my fault. I wait at depot until driver return."

"All right, all right. What did you find out?"

"I not sure right man. Driver say woman say he drunk."

"Woman?" That was a new development. "Why didn't

you tell me about a woman helping him?"

Korioff blew out an exasperated breath. "I try. You hang up."

"Tell me now."

"I see her in antique shop. When Johnston run down street—he look like old woman. I not recognize him." Korioff was starting to sound defensive.

Placate him, you fool. "You did well," Yuri said. "What else did you learn?"

"Driver say he so drunk she have to help him. I think this not right man."

"If he was wounded, he could appear drunk."

"I shoot him?"

Since Korioff was the only one firing, that would appear to be the case. "Possibly." No sense letting Korioff get cocky.

"I shoot him." The kid sounded full of himself. Wait until he found out Yuri was about to capture the American spy. Alone.

"A woman is helping him?" Yuri thought about that. "Describe her."

"Tall. Big, like peasant farm woman. Dark hair."

"In a long braid?"

"Yuri, you amazing. How you know that?"

The woman on the stairs. "Son of a bitch." Yuri slammed his fist on the steering wheel. No wonder Jozwiak escaped so easily. She was good. Yuri had taken one look at the scared rabbit on the stairs and dismissed her. A decoy. Imagine that. "Where did the cab take them?"

"Hotel Harbizon. I go now."

To further placate Korioff, Yuri said, "Good. Bring the American spy to the hotel. Alive," he added with emphasis. He couldn't take the chance that Jozwiak no longer had the memory chip. In three days, he had time to hide it or pass it off.

"What about woman?" Korioff asked.

"She is nothing."

"Okay. I kill her."

* * *

Sam didn't expect to lean on Daria so much. She led him out of the hotel to a dull gray Buick parked at the curb. The perfect get-away car. Nondescript. Except for the specialty license plate with the colors and logo of the University of Iowa, the "I bleed Black and Gold" bumper sticker and the decal in the back window. "You're quite a fan."

Red tinged her cheeks. "Are we going to stand here and chit-chat?"

"Do you have a blanket in the trunk?"

"Are you cold?" Amazing how quickly she went from exasperation to solicitude.

"No, I don't want to ruin your seat if *my* seat starts bleeding again." Considering how rotten he felt, he was rather pleased at himself for coming up with another bad pun.

"That's very considerate of you." She sounded amazed.

Hey, he could be considerate when he wanted to be.

When she unlocked the trunk, he gaped. Besides a large rolling suitcase, the trunk was loaded with several shopping bags, two jugs of water and a picnic cooler. "Ever hear of traveling light?" he said.

"Do you know how expensive food is here?" she shot back. She pulled a black and gold stadium blanket out of the corner then slammed the trunk lid.

"Don't tell me. You brought sandwiches."

She spread the blanket across the gray bench seat. "I don't know why I even bother. I hate this car."

"Pardon?"

"Oh, never mind. Do you need help getting in?"

Despite her hovering, Sam managed to get into the car. Sliding on his left cheek was awkward because the blanket slid, too. Worse, the Tylenol hadn't kicked in yet.

When she put the key in the ignition, she glanced over at him. "Buckle your seatbelt."

He was probably going to bleed to death from a butt wound, of all things, and she worried about injuries from a car accident. He couldn't reach the seatbelt. He tried again. When he finally did, he couldn't fasten it, so it snapped back into place. Again he tried to reach it and broke into a sweat.

"Sorry. I didn't think. Let me help you." She leaned

across and pulled the belt. Her hair smelled of strawberries, and her breast brushed his arm. He flinched.

"Sorry," she repeated, quickly fastening his seatbelt. "You look terrible. We have to get you to that doctor quickly." She pulled away from the curb.

He might look terrible, but he felt worse. The little exertion getting down to the car had done him in. He'd been wounded before and never felt this weak, this useless. He always patched himself up and continued on.

He realized they were waiting at a stop sign. No traffic. "Are we going or what?"

"Directions would help."

"Take a right. Doc is in Brooklyn."

"He works in an all-night clinic?"

"No. Out of his home."

"Shouldn't you call the doctor first? I'm mean, it's after midnight."

Automatically, he patted his shirt pocket. Empty. He tried his jacket. The cell phone was light, but he should have noticed the weight. Or lack of. "Where's my phone?"

"I never saw a phone. Wait. In the lavatory. I think I saw one on the counter."

"I took it." He glanced over his shoulder then stretched his hand to reach the backseat. "Give me your purse. I can't get it."

"Oh, no. You are not dumping out my purse again. Especially not in the car, in the dark. It took me almost an hour to put everything back in place." She took a deep breath. "We need to get something straight. Trust. I said I didn't take your phone. I don't lie."

"Really? I've never known a saint before." He directed her to take another turn.

"I might not tell everything, but I won't flat-out lie. Can I expect the same from you, Sam Johnston?"

Every time she called him by that name, he inwardly cringed. He never told her that was his name, but he'd let her continue using it. She was safer that way. Just like he didn't tell her why Grashenko and partner were chasing him. Unlike her, he had no problem lying. He did whatever it took to accomplish his mission.

"All right," he said. "Trust. But, if you didn't see my cell after the lavatory, where is it?"

"I don't know. Oh, my," she exclaimed. "Is that the Brooklyn Bridge?"

She'd already expressed delight at seeing the Empire State Building—which, she'd informed him, she went to the top of yesterday—and the Chrysler Building with its unique roof line. He remembered his own awe seeing new sights. Another lifetime ago.

Lately, nothing seemed new. His mother, God rest her soul, thought he was lucky to travel so much in his *consulting* job. Travel was just a necessity. He didn't even *see* the wonders of Europe anymore. Paris, London, Moscow held no allure. They were cities, just like Detroit, Atlanta and LA.

He felt stale. Tired. Because of how he botched this mission, Sam worried he'd lost his edge. "Turn at the next light."

"The cab," she exclaimed. "You fell over in the seat. It could have fallen out of your pocket. I should have checked when we got out."

"Not your fault." He'd definitely lost his edge if he left the agency phone behind and, worse, not even known it.

"You can use mine," she said. "It's in the front pocket of my purse."

"And have you accuse me of messing it up again? I'll pass. Doc's accustomed to late night visitors. Or he used to be."

"Why did you say 'used to be'? Is he retired?"

"Yes." After the change in agency leadership a year ago, Doc left. Like several good agents. Friends who refused to work for a bean counter instead of one of their own. "You can slow down. Hang a left at the next street."

Daria drove into an older, established neighborhood. Red brick bungalows, some old two-stories. Most were modest and well-kept. She could have been in a residential neighborhood in Des Moines. She expected Brooklyn to look . . . different.

"Turn right at the next block." Two blocks later, he told

her to turn right again.

"But—"

"No questions."

Another three blocks and another right turn.

"Why are we circling?" she asked.

"Go around this block one more time. Slowly. This is no Indianapolis 500."

"Did you forget which house?"

"No." He'd made an effort to sound patient but didn't quite succeed. "Stop." He pointed to a small opening almost obscured by high hedges. "Turn off your lights and pull in there."

It was a narrow, two-rut path. The tall bushes scraped the car as she pulled in.

"Sorry about your paint job," he said. "Pull all the way in."

The streetlights weren't high enough to penetrate the hedges. Clouds obscured the moon. No headlights yet he wanted her to keep driving?

"I can't see ahead." She stopped and looked into the rearview mirror. She could barely see behind her. She thought the tail of her car was level with the beginning of the bushes.

"*I* can," he said. "Keep going."

She crept ahead until he said, "Angle to the right and pull up to the garage door."

Daria never even saw the garage until he mentioned it. She inched forward, squeezing the car against the hedge on the right. "You won't be able to open your door."

"Not a problem. We'll use yours." He reached over her head. "Kill the engine."

With the dashboard lights off, she could hear movement. Sam leaned against her. "What are you doing?" She edged closer to the door.

"Taking out the light bulb so when you open your door, it won't act like a beacon."

"Why?" She thought about his insistence that she circle the block, turn out the headlights and hide the car between two very tall hedges. "Do you think someone is watching the doctor's house? How would anyone know—"

"Doc used to work for the same people I do."

"And they are . . ."

"Now, Dahria," he exaggerated her name. "You know I can't tell you that. Quietly open your door. And no talking once we're outside."

Even angled to the right, she could only open her door a small space. She wondered if *she* would be able to squeeze through, let alone a big man like Sam. Holding her purse to the side, she made like a snake and slithered out of the car. It was so dark she could only hear him slide across the seat, along with a barely audible wince.

She reached in to help him, and they cracked heads.

"Damn it," he whispered. "I won't have to worry about Grashenko finishing me off. You'll kill me with all your damn hovering."

Stung, Daria pulled back. Stars still danced in front of her eyes. She forced herself not to retort. *Remember the wounded animals.* She sidestepped to the back of the car, giving him plenty of room to get out. With no hovering.

She heard the scrape of the door against the prickly hedge and smiled. With all the scratches, she could justify a new paint job. Anything was better than this ugly gray. A new car would be even better. A Camaro, for instance. Yes. A red Camaro.

A hand grasped hers, and she jumped. She couldn't see a thing in front of her—not even the body attached to the hand. She never heard the door latch after Sam got out. He pulled her toward the front of the car. The bushes snagged her hair, pulling it out of the French braid. She had to put her other arm up to shield her face from being scratched.

Daria could feel his irregular rise and fall as he limped around the side of the hulking garage. More hedges grew close to the structure. She hoped he could see as well as he claimed. People usually stored trash cans behind or beside garages.

When Sam stopped, she ran into him and realized he'd turned around to face her. He wrapped his arm around her back and drew her close. He bent his head and whispered, "When I turn around, tuck your hand in my belt. We're going through a narrow opening. I don't want to lose you."

His warm breath on her neck generated skittery feelings she had no business experiencing. Not now. Not here. Definitely not with this man.

She tucked her hand in his belt. Through the denim shirt, heat radiated from him. He could be running a fever. It was a good thing a doctor would check him over. After two steps, she was sure Sam made a mistake. There was no opening. She pressed her forehead against his back so she wouldn't get scratched. Twenty baby steps later, they came to a small backyard, next to a dark house.

From his vantage point in the shadow of a large evergreen, Yuri watched the two men walk away from the park bench in disgust.

"I can't believe that guy thought the phone fairy left him a present in a taxi cab," the younger one said softly.

"What a wasted trip." Teller's voice carried across the expanse of the park—something a good operative would know.

"Not my fault, boss. I told you where Jozwiak's *phone* was—not Joz. How was I to know he'd lost it?"

Yuri didn't recognize the younger man, but he'd heard about the new director of the clandestine agency. All he'd been able to learn was that Teller was a former accountant who advanced because he could balance budgets. Better this neophyte than an experienced agent directing operations. The advantage was on his side. He, too, was disgusted with the wasted trip. Unlike Teller, Yuri had a more philosophical approach. Sometimes, tips fizzled out.

His mobile vibrated against his hip. Probably Korioff with another dead-end lead.

Yuri made his way back to his car and was inside before he checked the display for the missed call. He was right. Korioff.

Yuri debated calling him back. Korioff hadn't proved himself very reliable so far. However, Yuri knew his boss wouldn't blame Junior. If this mission failed, Yuri would be lucky if he were only blamed. Korioff Senior didn't suffer fools, except for his son.

The injustice stuck in Yuri's craw.

Where the hell was Doc?

Sam rang the bell again. Through the solid oak back door, he heard the faint sound, so he knew the bell worked. Still no response.

"Guess he's not home," Daria whispered.

He checked the house on the left. Dark. Good. No witnesses. Wait. Did a curtain move? Sam froze. He searched the windows on the second floor. Nothing. He must have been mistaken. Because of the tall hedge, he couldn't see the house on the right.

"Not a problem," he whispered back. He took the tool—disguised as a frequent diner's card—out of his wallet—and slipped it between the door and the jamb. He gave the card a little wiggle and, voila', the door opened. He slipped inside, dragging Daria behind him. The hall was dark, like the rest of the house.

He told her to wait and limped to the bottom of the stairs. "Doc? You here?"

No response.

"I can't believe you broke into this house." Daria hadn't waited. She was at his elbow, hissing in his ear. "What if he wakes up and thinks we're burglars? He could shoot first and ask questions later."

"Nah, Doc's not here. Besides, he knows me," Sam said out loud. "And if I told him once, I told him a dozen times to install better security. C'mon." He headed back down the hall to a closed door on the left.

"Wait up. I can't see."

After grabbing her wrist, he pulled her along. At a heavy oak door, he paused, took out his tool again and slipped the lock. As soon as they went in, he shut the door and turned on the light.

She blinked several times. "It's an examining room."

"It's also an interior room. No windows." White stainless-steel cupboards lined the walls. A few were locked. To Sam, they presented as much a problem as the doors.

Daria looked around. "You're not going to steal drugs,

are you?"

"Borrow." He began opening cupboards. After collecting gauze and bandages, he put them on a stainless-steel tray stand that could be wheeled to the examining table. He found a suture kit and added that to his collection, along with a pair of latex gloves.

She stood against a small, old-fashioned sink that hung from the wall and folded her arms across her chest. Her hair straggled from the braid while fresh scratches decorated her hands and wrists, a couple along her neck.

"Sorry about the bushes," he said. "After you sew me up, you should put anti—"

"After I what?" She straightened away from the sink. "Oh, no. I am not sewing anything. I failed home ec."

"You did not." He poured normal saline into a steel bowl. "You are an excellent seamstress." He added hydrogen peroxide.

The bloom on her cheeks told him he'd caught her in a lie.

"So much for trust," he said. "And never telling a flat-out lie."

Her blush deepened. "What makes you think I can sew?"

"Your dress."

She took off her coat and hung it on a hook on the back of the door. "What's wrong with my dress?"

"Nothing. That's what's wrong. The plaids match at the seams."

"How do you know something like that?"

"My mother sewed."

He toed off his bloody shoe then staggered when he attempted the other.

"Let me help." When she stooped to help him, he grabbed her upper arms and pulled her up.

"Put gloves on first. Always protect yourself."

She gave him another of those teacher stares. "Are you diseased?"

"As a matter of fact, I'm not. I get tested often. I'm just telling you not to take chances."

"Really." She stepped back. "I've been taking chances since I crossed the Mississippi River last Friday."

This woman had a lot of spunk. As much as he hated involving anyone outside the agency, he was grateful Daria Mason had come into that restroom. And not some wimpy female who would've gone screaming down the stairs about a man in the ladies' room.

He let go of her arms. Despite being slender, she was no wimp. She had muscles.

"Balance yourself against the table." Daria snapped on the gloves. She wasn't convinced that she could do more than remove his shoe. Maybe his sock. The shoe was stained dark red, nearly brown. At least, she'd managed to stop the bleeding earlier. Just thinking about his ragged wounds turned her stomach. She gritted her teeth.

After unbuckling his belt, he unzipped his jeans. She gulped. "Uh, wait a minute."

"Judging by the bandage on my rear, you've seen all this before. It's not like I have anything different from other guys you've seen."

She wasn't going to tell him she'd never seen a totally naked man, in the flesh, so to speak. She had her share of curiosity. In high school, she'd looked at the *Playgirl* magazines her friend Heather snuck from her mother's stash. Then, there was Josh Lawrence, but she'd been too embarrassed to look.

Now, this stranger she'd known for less than twelve hours was going to strip naked from the waist down. And he wanted her to sew up his butt? He asked too much. She gritted her teeth again to halt the urge to puke.

"I didn't agree to this," she said. "I said I would drive you to your doctor friend."

He steadied himself by putting his hand on her shoulder. "You're going to have to help me. If I could see my a—butt, I'd sew it up myself."

She was surprised at his catch. He actually cleaned up his language for her. Oh, dear Lord, she would have to stick a needle into his flesh. Not just once, but over and over. She felt herself getting light-headed.

"Don't freak on me now, Daria." He clasped her suddenly icy fingers. "You've been a real trooper. I promise you can go your merry way back to the Corn Belt as soon as we finish. I can recuperate here. Doc won't mind. There's no telling where he went or when he'll be back. So, right now, I need you."

The look in his brown eyes was so convincing she knew he was right. She took several deep breaths. The room smelled of antiseptic, but it wasn't swimming anymore. His hands were warm, gently chafing hers. She swallowed hard. "Why don't you turn around and lean against the table? I'll, uh, pull down your jeans."

He leaned his forearms on the table. "Might just as well drag the briefs down, too. And, no nasty comments about a hairy butt."

He was trying to make her laugh, trying to put her at ease. As if.

Keeping him at arms' length, she managed to get his jeans and briefs off. She helped him lie on the table, face down, without looking at his, uh, *equipment*. Under other circumstances, she might have looked. Probably would have enjoyed looking. But, the prospect of sewing up his flesh, made her queasy. The lightheadedness returned.

"I can't do this." She staggered over to a straight-back chair in the corner.

"Put your head between your knees," he ordered from the table. "Take deep breaths. Not too many or you'll hyperventilate."

After several seconds with her face buried in her full skirt, Daria thought about Alexa Tremaine. Would her heroine faint at the sight of a wound? No. Would she wimp out when someone needed her? No. Would she upchuck all over a patient? No. Alexa would suck it up.

And so would Daria. She straightened her spine. *Suck it up, girl.* She walked to the table on shaky legs that grew stronger the closer she got to Sam. She took a deep breath and smacked his left buttock. "Okay, boy-o, let's get started."

Sam bucked. "Holy shit, what was that for?"

"Just getting warmed up. I'm not giving you Novocain because I'm not sticking any more needles in your butt than I have to. So, suck it up." Daria couldn't believe she said that. It did bolster her courage, though. Carefully, she tried to get her fingernail under the duct tape to remove the *bandage.*

"Oh, for God's sake. Just rip the damn thing off."

The too-big gloves made her clumsy. The doctor must have large hands. She finally got hold of a corner of duct tape and ripped.

He let loose with the mother of all swear words.

"You watch your mouth, Sam Johnston, or I'll use my Epilady on your chest."

A quiet clapping came from behind them. Sam reared up from the table and Daria nearly tripped over her feet as she backed up. A tall, older gentleman stood with his back to the door. He had entered and closed the door without either of them hearing.

CHAPTER EIGHT

"I sure hope you're the doctor," Daria said at the same time Sam called out, "Hey, Doc, where ya been?"

"If you must know, Samuel, I had a date. With a lovely woman. Not as lovely as the young lady playing doctor with you." The older man, with a hint of an accent, tsked. "At your age, too. I thought you had outgrown little games."

What was with all the Brits she was running into?

"A man's never too old to play that game." Sam leered back at her before resting his chin on his folded arms.

"He's been shot. And I d-don't know what I'm doing?" Daria's chin wobbled. Hot tears prickled behind her eyes.

"You took one in the arse, Samuel? How very undignified."

"And in the leg," Sam added. He looked over his shoulder at her. "Okay, kid, thanks for your help. You can go back to Kansas now."

She opened her mouth to correct him. He knew she was from Iowa, but those damn tears of relief suddenly started running down her cheeks.

"My dear." The doctor steered her toward the door. "I would be ever so grateful if you made coffee. The kitchen is through the pocket door across the hall. I turned the light on over the stove. That should be enough for you to see."

She swallowed past the tears, ashamed that she'd broken down. "Is making coffee like telling an expectant father to boil water?" She gave him a weak smile.

The man with pure white hair and a Van Dyke beard patted her shoulder. As she pulled the door closed behind her, he began chastising Sam for involving a civilian. She never thought of herself like that. Of course, she was. And they were part of a clandestine organization.

Through the pocket door to the kitchen, she saw a white coffee maker on the counter. Filters and coffee were in the cupboard next to a window with its shade drawn.

Sam mentioned someone named Grashenko after they collided heads. That sounded Eastern European. Russian? Was that the name of the man she met on the stairs? The one who sounded like a character from a British mystery on PBS.

Sam must be with the CIA. They were involved in the international stuff. He mentioned national security. Was he serious? When he asked for her help, she knew he was in trouble. Though she was ninety-nine percent sure he was a good guy, she thought he exaggerated the situation. National security, for heaven's sake. She helped him because he was injured.

She'd sipped half a cup of coffee by the time the doctor came in. "Is Sam going to be all right?" she asked.

He poured a cup of coffee before saying, "I prefer not to lose a patient."

"Bad for business." Pale and holding onto the doorframe for support, Sam limped into the kitchen. "Coffee smells good." His look was so pathetic, Daria poured for him.

"I told Samuel that as much as I enjoy his company, it is not safe for him to stay here."

She stopped the cup halfway to her mouth. "What do you mean *not safe*?"

"What Doc means—" Sam winked. "—is you're stuck with me a while longer."

"No." She thunked her cup down on the counter. "I've done my part for king and country . . . or president and country . . . or . . . whatever. You know what I mean. I got you here. That's it. I have to go back to my conference. I have an important meeting tomorrow. I can't miss it. Besides, I'm not cut out for this espionage stuff, if that's what it is. I'm a second-grade teacher from—"

The doctor yanked her to the floor. "Did you see that?" he whispered.

Sam pulled a gun out from behind his back. Where did he get a gun? He hadn't had one so far. She'd seen just about all of him, and he didn't have a place to hide a weapon. He pressed his back to the wall, the gun upraised and looked at the back door. "Shadows on the shade? Yeah." He, too, whispered.

Oh, dear God, Daria thought. What was happening?

Someone pounded on the back door. "Doctor Forester, police. Open up."

The doctor helped Daria off the floor. "I'll deal with this." He took off his shirt and tossed it under the sink. He wore a thin undershirt, the sleeveless kind. He had bony arms, little muscle, and white hair on his arms. He toed off his shoes. They and his socks followed the shirt under the sink. As he rumpled his hair, he said, "Samuel, you know where to go."

"Doctor Forester, police." More pounding.

"Coming," Doc said hoarsely.

Sam pulled Daria down the hall. Before they got to the bottom of the stairs, he yanked one of the posts. A panel silently slid open revealing a hidden place under the stairs.

"Inside," he whispered over the sound of more pounding and the doctor calling, "I'm coming. I'm coming."

Daria bent over and crab-walked into the hidey hole. Sam followed, though how, she didn't know. It was dark as pitch after he closed the panel. The space wasn't big enough for both of them. She banged her head on the underside of a step. She felt Sam sit on a built-in bench, then he pulled her down on his lap. She let out a tiny shriek.

"Be still," he whispered.

His whiskers scratched her neck almost as badly as the hedge. It was unnerving to be in absolute darkness, sitting on a man's lap. His hip. She was too heavy to be sitting on his lap when he could barely sit himself. She tried to get off.

He wrapped his arm around her waist and held her tight. "Don't wiggle."

"There must be a mistake, Officer." The doctor's voice was muffled by the paneling. "There hasn't been a break-in."

"Sir, your neighbor reported a burglar entering your house. Actually, she said two burglars. A man and a woman."

The doctor laughed. "Ah, Mrs. O'Reilly. I think if you check down at the station, you'll find she often sees burglars when, indeed, it is the homeowner returning."

"She said you live alone, Doctor. She said she saw a woman, too."

"I brought my date home with me, Officer. The young lady and I had plans for the rest of the evening, which you

71

interrupted. I can call her down here, if you wish."

So that's why the doctor practically undressed in the kitchen, Daria thought.

"Since Elvira O'Reilly is the worst gossip in the neighborhood," the doctor continued, "we tried to be quiet. Unfortunately, it didn't work. Believe me, Officer, I would know if my home was burglarized. I do thank you for your quick response."

"Yes, sir. Sorry to bother you."

Daria heard the back door close. She started to stand and rapped her head again on the step. "Wait," Sam whispered. "Doc will let us know when it's clear."

The panel slid open. Doc reached in for Daria's hand. "A little cozy in there," he said dryly. "Hope you weren't too cramped."

"Thanks, Doc." Sam exited the hidey-hole. He'd hidden in there before. Cozy was not the word he would use to describe the cramped space. Having Daria on his lap brought about a purely involuntary reaction. One that surprised him, considering his gunshot wounds. Whatever Doc shot into his butt numbed his backside but not the rest of him. There were some things a guy just couldn't help.

"You need to leave." In the dim light, Doc's face was drawn. He was deadly serious. "I have done my best to protect you, Samuel. I would do more if I could."

"I know." He clapped his friend on the shoulder. "Appreciate the warning."

Doc leaned in close. "Remember, don't trust anyone."

Daria gave the men a startled look. She must have heard. Sam cuffed her around the neck. "Present company excepted."

Doc went into the examining room, motioning them to follow. "I didn't block your car although I wasn't pleased that I had to park elsewhere."

"Sorry." Sam was glad to hear they'd have a clear shot leaving.

While Daria retrieved her coat, Doc loaded her purse with bandages, antibiotics and pain pills.

"You can just forget those," Sam said. "Tylenol's good enough."

"Aspirin for fever," Doc continued giving her instructions. "If the pain gets bad, one of these every four hours." He tapped a paper envelope.

"Excuse me. I'm the patient here," Sam said. "I said no pain killers."

Daria shot him a look before turning back to Doc. "Did you hear something? Like an annoying buzz? Some nonsense about—"

Sam froze. So did Doc. No annoying buzz. Someone was at the back door, jiggling the knob.

Daria held up her hand and whispered, "I am not going back in that hole."

"It might not be the good guys this time," Sam said. "We need to leave."

"Out the front," Doc whispered. "It's sheltered. No one can see you from the street. I let the bushes grow tall for just such a necessity. Be careful. You'll have to go over the porch rail. Stay close to the house until you get to the corner."

There was a pounding on Doc's door. He killed the light in the examining room. Sam took Daria's hand. It was cold, clammy. The way it had been after he told her she had to sew him up. Poor kid was scared.

"Hang in there with me, sweetheart." He squeezed her hand. After a moment, she squeezed back.

Sam checked the peephole in the front door. It was specially designed to give a wider than normal fisheye view of the outside. Clear.

They slipped out. Hopping over the porch rail proved more than Sam could handle. He fell to his knees.

"Have you seen Sam?" Teller asked the doctor who used to work for the agency. "I think he was shot."

"What?" the old man looked down at him. Teller hated that.

He narrowed his eyes. "He was supposed to meet me this afternoon. We've been searching for him, even monitoring the police band. You had some trouble here tonight. Was it Jozwiak?"

"It was my crazy neighbor. She thought she saw

burglars."

"If it was Sam, you would've called, right?" Teller shoved his hand through his hair. It felt thinner. Christ, on top of everything else, he was losing his hair.

"In case it slipped your attention, I retired," Doc said. "I'm not with the agency anymore."

"Yeah, well, Jozwiak would come to you if he was hurt, even if you are retired. You don't mind if I look around, do you?"

"As a matter of fact, I do. I would like to retire."

Teller harrumphed. "Sam's one of our people. He needs help."

The doc nodded. "Of course."

"Boss." Hardesty came running up behind him. "I talked to the neighbor who called the police."

"Good work. What did she tell you?"

Hardesty grimaced. "She will only talk to somebody in charge."

Daria knelt next to Sam. The doctor was right about the bushes. They were so dense they completely blocked the front entrance. The thick bushes and lack of a paved walkway discouraged anyone from using the front door.

When Sam went over the porch rail, she didn't expect him to fall. His body barely made a sound as it hit the ground. "Are you okay?" she whispered.

"Give me a minute."

She gave him ten seconds. They needed to leave. Whoever was at the back door might send someone to the front. A lookout, hearing Sam fall, would investigate.

"Put your hand on my shoulder to steady yourself," she whispered. Sound carried on the nighttime air. It wasn't going to be because of her that anyone heard them.

She helped him stand. All they had to do was get around the corner of the house and shoot across a small patch of grass without being seen. She hoped she could find the opening in the hedge. The sliver of moonlight was a blessing and a curse. When they raced across the yard, they would be visible.

Daria halted at the corner. Sam gave her shoulder a reassuring squeeze. Keeping as close to the house as possible, she angled her head around the corner.

A large man, with his jeans and shorts around his ankles, was preparing to squat.

"Here is my superior, ma'am," Hardesty said. "She wants to see ID, sir. The police have already been here."

"And they didn't believe me," the woman said shrilly. "I know what I saw and it wasn't the doctor and his *ladyfriend*. Unless the old goat is robbing the cradle."

He took out a flat folder and flipped it open. "I'm Detective Teller."

The old woman squinted. Her eyesight was probably so poor a Lone Ranger badge would fool her.

"Ma'am," Teller said in his take-charge voice. "What did you see?"

"It was quite dark and my precious Poo-Poo here woke me up."

The animal in her arms started yapping and clawing at the screen. Both men quickly stepped back before 'precious Poo-Poo' shot through the screen door. Hardesty stumbled off the small cement slab.

"Ma'am, restrain that animal," Teller snapped.

"Well, I never. Poo-Poo is just being protective."

"Yes, ma'am. Now, could you tell us what you saw? We're tracking—"

"Oh, my Lord. You're after a burglary ring, aren't you?"

Teller hid his smile. It wouldn't take much to lead her on.

"I saw them sneaking around the corner of the doctor's house. I know one was a woman because her skirt blew out from the breeze. It sure has gotten chilly this evening."

"Woman? What woman?" The call Hardesty picked up mentioned a burglar.

"How would I know that?" the old lady retorted.

Teller clenched his teeth. "Could you describe her?"

"I heard a car go around the block two, maybe three times." The old woman clearly ignored his question. She just plunged on. "I thought that was suspicious, so I got up and looked. I heard it turn in. I couldn't see, of course, because the doctor keeps those hedges on that side of his house so tall. And the ones in front, why they are a disgrace. I've called the city but—"

"Ma'am. About the burglars?"

"When they ran from the hedges to the house, they tried to keep to the shadows. The moon wasn't out like it is now and, as you can see, the light in the alley doesn't work."

Teller gritted his teeth. "Describe the woman."

"I was getting to that. You are just as impatient as the other officers who were here. Why aren't you wearing a uniform?"

"Detectives don't wear uniforms. About the burglars?"

"Yes, well. The woman was almost as tall as the limping man. She probably has dark hair. I know because blonde hair would stand out in the dark." She smiled triumphantly.

Tall. Dark hair. Not Quinero. "Very astute, ma'am."

The old lady preened.

"And you say the man was limping?" he asked.

"Yes. I don't understand how they expected to burgle a home if one was a cripple."

The bloody paper towels in the restroom. Jozwiak was hurt and Doc lied. "Shit."

"Really, young man. There is no need to use that kind of language."

"Ma'am—"

"That's the trouble with you young people. No language skills. No vocabulary."

"Ma'am—"

"And another thing. In my day, a gentleman would never—"

"Ma'am—"

"Don't interrupt. I taught school for forty-five years. You have no respect for—"

A commotion erupted from the opposite side of the house.

* * *

Daria didn't know who was more surprised. Herself or the man she'd caught with his britches down. She thought he was the man from the antique store. The one wearing a gray sweater.

"What's the hold up?" Sam whispered as he leaned around her.

The man straightened. Oh, brother, that was way more than she wanted to see of him. He started to reach for her. Without thinking, Daria straight-armed him in the chest.

She grabbed Sam's hand and ran. She didn't even wait to see Gray Sweater fall on his bare butt into the thorny shrubs. She didn't need to. As she and Sam raced for the hedge, Daria heard a crash followed by a stream of foreign words.

She ran flat out, and Sam kept up. She only found the opening because his hand on her back steered her in the right direction. He shoved her through the hedge at breakneck speed. Branches slapped her face, snarled her hair. Her purse banged against her hip. Sam pushed her to go faster.

They burst through the hedge. As they rounded the garage, she struggled to open the little pouch in which she kept her keys. By the time she got them out, Sam shoved past her. He pulled her between the hedge and the car, tugging on her wrist so hard she nearly dropped the keys. He yanked open the door and shoved her into the car.

"Give me the keys," he hissed.

Daria scrambled across the seat on her knees. Sam bumped her getting in and she dropped the keys. She bent over and flapped her hands around on the floor boards.

"Give me the goddamn keys, woman." He shoved the seat back to accomodate his long legs.

"I would if I could find them. You made me drop the keys on the floor." Her hand brushed against metal. "Here. Here they are. Hurry."

The car started with a roar. Before she could warn him they were too close to the hedges, he rammed the gearshift into reverse and floored it. Daria fell off the seat. She was wedged under the glove box, rump down, feet in the air, her skirt up to her waist.

She could see nothing except the tall hedges whizzing by, but she could hear. Dirt from the two-track spit out from under the spinning wheels. Stones hit the undercarriage while branches shrieked against the sides of the car. Sam didn't slow down for the street.

Oh, dear God. They could be hit by a passing car.

The Buick bounced over the curb and shot into the street. He slammed on the brakes, shoved the protesting gearshift into Drive and floored it again. Tires squealed, and Daria was thrown against the dash. It was a good thing she had a hard head.

She struggled to get her legs under her. When she finally did and tried to rise up, Sam put his hand on the top of her head and shoved her back down. "Stay put. If anyone comes after us, they won't care who they hit."

She could have figured that out by herself. "Do you see anyone?"

"Can't see a damn thing."

"Can't you find the lights? It's the switch on the—"

"And give away our position?" He barreled around a corner without hitting the brakes. The Buick's tires squealed in protest.

"Why aren't you braking?" she yelled. No lights. No brakes. Dear God, he was going to get them killed.

"Brake lights? I might just as well have a searchlight follow us."

She felt the car take two more corners. It was probably better that she couldn't see. She curled up into a ball and prayed for salvation from this mad man.

"What the hell was all that about?" Teller caught up with Hardesty who'd taken off across Doc's backyard. They stood at the corner of Doc's house.

"A flasher hanging onto his pants ran through that hedge." Hardesty pointed. "I heard a car take off. I think he's gone."

"Go through there and check."

"Uh, boss. I don't have a weapon. You told me this was just a surveillance op."

Teller hesitated. He had a weapon, but he wasn't fool enough to go charging through bushes. A guy could get killed that way. "A flasher?"

"Uh, huh. Foreign dude. I think he was speaking Russian. Not sure, mind you."

"And you think he had a car on the other side of the bushes?"

"Didn't you hear somebody lay a patch? So, yeah, I think he's gone."

Teller swore. "I'll bet Doc knows more than he's saying. If he doesn't give me some answers, you're going to shake it out of him." He headed back to the house.

"Me?" Hardesty squeaked.

The rookie was not showing the proper amount of gratitude for the opportunity to work in the field. And Teller wasn't happy. Hardesty's attitude needed an adjustment.

Without bothering to knock, Teller let himself in and went straight to Doc's kitchen. He smelled coffee and needed a slug of caffeine.

"So, Doc, who's helping Sam?" Teller took a gulp of coffee and shuddered at the bitter taste of the end of the pot. Three mugs were sitting on the counter with various amounts of coffee in each. Either Doc was a three-fisted drinker or, contrary to his claim, he'd had visitors.

Teller hit the light switch in the hall. "Doc?"

No answer. He pushed open a door on the right. He felt around on the wall and found the switch. An examining room. Bloody bandages filled the waste can. The paper sheet on the examining table was smeared with blood.

Teller walked back out into the hall. He stood at the bottom of the stairs and yelled, "Doc, get your ass down here. I have more questions."

Again, no answer.

"Hardesty, run up there and see what Doc is doing. Get him off the can, if you have to. I need answers." Teller carried his now empty cup back to the kitchen. Damn stuff tasted awful, but he could feel the caffeine kick in. He needed to keep the lid on this op. No sense letting his superiors know how badly—

"Boss?" Hardesty clumped down the stairs. "I think the doc flew the coop."

CHAPTER NINE

"You can get up off the floor now," Sam said. After his mad dash out of Doc's neighborhood, he drove at a sedate speed so as not to attract attention. He'd put about a dozen or so miles between them and the Russians.

He didn't understand why Grashenko didn't wait until Sam left Doc's to grab him. Yuri had more patience than to announce himself by jiggling door knobs. The Russian must have been monitoring police calls to have found them.

Sam never would have thought the last visitor was Yuri until they came across Junior Korioff in the bushes on the side of Doc's house. So, why did Yuri knock? The only logical explanation was that he didn't want the neighbor to call the cops again.

Daria uncurled herself, looking disheveled and scared out of her wits. It was a good thing she'd pulled down her skirts. Just a glimpse of yellow flowered underwear distracted him while making like Dale Earnhart, Junior on the streets of Brooklyn.

"You did good back there," he said. "Lucky for us Korioff was taking a dump in the bushes. He was probably supposed to watch the front of the house. I can't believe how you laid him out. Good work."

She stabbed at the seatbelt buckle three times before getting it to latch. She straightened the skirts of her coat and dress. "My hands are still shaking."

He put his hand on top of hers. "It's to be expected."

"We could have been killed," she said flatly.

"But, we weren't. Korioff never got close."

She shook off his hand and punched him in the shoulder. "Not the Hulk with his pants around his ankles. You! You were driving like a maniac." She hit him again.

While she continued her tirade—no more punches, thank God—he looked for a place to park. He found a fastfood restaurant that didn't open for breakfast. He parked

80

near the back and unbuckled his seatbelt. "Come here," he said gently.

She looked ready to take another swing at him.

"You wouldn't hit an injured man *again*, would you?" He let his mouth quirk up.

That was all it took to push her over the edge. She burst into tears.

Like most of the male species, Sam was uncomfortable with female tears. When he couldn't stand it any longer, he pulled her into his arms. Poor kid had been through a lot since she hooked up with him. He glanced at the dashboard clock. Her crying jag lasted a good three minutes.

"I was so scared," she mumbled against his jacket.

"Yeah. Me, too."

She lifted her head, swiping at the tears on her cheeks. "Really?"

He smoothed her hair away from her face. Her bangs flopped back. He touched the scratch below her left eye. "I'm sorry."

She leaned back to look at him. "It doesn't hurt."

Sam blew out a breath. "I didn't mean the scratch, though I am sorry about that, too. I meant this whole mess."

"Not your fault."

"Yes, it is. I involved you. I should have let you leave when you wanted to. In the restroom." He was having an attack of the guilts. He didn't think he had enough of a conscience left to feel guilty about anything.

He'd done too many things in the service of his country to have a conscience. Things no decent person like her would ever dream of. He'd probably broken every commandment in order to complete his missions. All in the name of patriotism. He'd do anything to get the job done. The country's loyal guard dog.

Protecting the U.S. from madmen was Sam's job, so innocents like the woman in his arms could rest, assured that the enemies of democracy were kept at bay.

"Those two guys would've caught you." She totally surprised him by laying her hand gently against his cheek. "I'm not sorry I stayed."

He cleared his throat. "Yeah, well, I am."

She leaned closer and lightly kissed his lips. "Don't be."

Her gentle touch. That sweet kiss. Something snapped inside him. He pulled her tight against his chest and kissed her mouth. Taking from her all the sweetness, the gentleness. He gave nothing in return. Ferocity roared through him. He devoured her.

Daria was shaken down to her toes. Once she worked her arms out from between them, she threw them around Sam's neck. Dear Lord, she'd never been kissed like this. His hunger was palpable. A corresponding hunger surged through her. She kissed him back with abandon. His whiskers scratched her lips, her cheeks. She didn't care. She couldn't get enough of him.

She went up on her knees, trying to get closer to him. He shoved her coat off her shoulders. Buttons popped as she ripped open his shirt. His white T-shirt was in the way. She yanked it out of his jeans. His hands slid up the backs of her thighs, under her skirt. Oh, God. She held him tighter, got her hands under his T-shirt. The muscles in his warm back tensed and flexed.

Suddenly, he pushed her away. She toppled back against the door. He gave her such a look of anguish she cried out. He turned away, wrapped his arms across the top on the steering wheel and rested his head on them. Great heaving breaths shook his body.

"Are you all right?" she asked.

Her breaths came nearly as rapidly as his. She struggled for composure. She didn't think she'd done anything wrong. Unless kissing him like she wanted him was wrong. Dear Lord, she wanted him.

"I'm sorry." His voice was muffled against the steering wheel. "That shouldn't have happened."

"All right," she said slowly.

When the silence stretched between them, she picked up her purse. The contents were strewn across the floor boards on her side and his. She picked up her brush. The visor had a lighted mirror. She attempted to put her hair in order. When she realized it was a useless cause, she flipped the visor back in place, not wanting to look at her swollen lips, the whisker burns on her cheeks—evidence of a kiss he regretted.

She pulled her braid over her shoulder and began unplaiting it. She would gather it into a pony tail and be done with it. At least, it would be off her face.

He didn't say anything more after his apology.

"I'm not sorry I kissed you," she said quietly but firmly. "Neither am I sorry that you returned the kiss. What do we do now?"

He lifted his head but didn't look at her. "Nothing. This goes no further. I lost control."

"What are you talking about?"

"For God's sake, woman. I had my hands in your pants. What the hell did you think was going to happen next?"

She wasn't stupid. She knew exactly what would have happened had he not called a halt. Another couple of minutes and she would have been flat on her back on the bench seat of the Buick begging Sam to have his wicked way with her. Daria never lost her head, never let things get out of control. Yet, tonight she did, and there he was taking all the responsibility.

She wasn't going to argue about who was to blame. "When I asked what we were going to do, I was talking about your flight from the bad guys."

"Hmph." Sam stared out the windshield, apparently transfixed by the dumpster behind the restaurant. Finally, he said, "May I use your phone?"

Daria found her old cell phone under her seat. When Jimmy gave her the new one, she didn't take time to leave her old one home. While he dialed, she picked up her lipstick and the bottle of Tylenol before they rolled under the accelerator. "Who are you calling?"

"A colleague."

Although Sam held the phone to his left ear, she could hear a woman answer. Daria didn't expect his colleague to be a woman although she shouldn't have been surprised. Women were capable of being spies.

"Hi, there." The woman's voice was bright and cheery, with a hint of sass. "You missed me. Try again later."

Sam clicked off the phone.

"Aren't you going to leave a message?" Daria asked.

"No. She's still out of the country."

"How do you know?"

"Her outgoing message would have been different if she was back." He sounded more than disappointed then dialed another number. It went straight to voice mail. "Damn." With that one word, he sounded defeated.

"Are you okay?" she asked.

His mouth twisted. "Yeah. Fine."

"That was like a code, right? Her message," she said, pleased with herself for figuring it out. "Okay, who else can you call? Oh, right. Doc said not to trust anyone."

"There is another."

A minute later, no one answered that call, not even a message. When he returned her phone, she took a good look at him. His eyes drooped.

"You should drive now."

He must be really exhausted if he was giving up the steering wheel. The men she knew wouldn't give up control unless they had to.

"Don't get out," she said. "I can run around the car faster than you can. Although the way you shoved me through those bushes, I thought you were going to run me over if I didn't move fast enough."

He stopped her from opening the door. "You're a good woman, Daria Mason."

"Yes, well . . ." She cleared her throat. Although that was just about the sweetest thing anyone had ever said to her, she would rather he said she was sexy, hot, gorgeous, anything but *good*.

"You don't deserve to be saddled with a broken-down wreck like me."

He sure didn't act like a broken-down wreck when he was kissing her. She would do well to forget her lapse in judgment.

She jumped out of the car, ran around and opened the driver's door. Sam was slowly sliding over to the seat she vacated. In the rush of flight, she hadn't thought about him driving with wounds in his right leg and hip. Accelerating and braking must have put a strain on his injuries.

"Thank you for getting us out of there," she said. "I'm sorry I yelled at you . . . and I'm sorry I hit you."

When he stabbed at the seatbelt latch several times, she shoved his hands aside and did it for him. "Any idea what we should do now?"

He was silent for a moment. "I can't force you to take me any farther."

"You didn't force me."

"Back at Doc's you said you weren't cut out for this. I don't blame you." He took a deep breath and exhaled slowly. "Drop me off at the airport. I'll go on from there."

"Are you nuts? Those guys will have the airports staked out. Oh, don't give me that look. I read mysteries, write them, too. *I'd* have the bad guys stake out the airports. Train and bus stations, too, if there were enough henchmen." She thought for a moment. "Rental cars are out because you need a credit card for them. If these guys are smart, they'll watch credit card transactions. So, I'm not taking you to an airport."

She didn't mention that he'd probably keel over from exhaustion or his wounds after she dropped him. "What other options do you have?"

He gave her a weak smile. "I could take your car and drop *you* at the airport."

"Oh, no. I'm not flying. There's nothing but air between those glorified aluminum cans and the ground. Uh, uh." She vigorously shook her head, causing her ponytail to swish against her shoulders. Flying scared her more than bad guys. "Besides, you would hate this car. I hate this car."

He took a strand of her hair and let it sift through his fingers. "Don't knock it. It got us this far."

She exhaled noisily. "Where do you need to go?"

"Forget it. I was joking about taking your car. At Doc's, you said you have to go back to your conference."

"Yes. Yes, I do."

"Drive back to your hotel." He gave her directions then leaned his head against the passenger window.

She started back to her hotel. From there, she knew how to get to the one where her friends were staying. She saw the lights of the Brooklyn Bridge. All she had to do was cross over and be back in Manhattan.

"Sam? What street did you say to take after the bridge?"

He didn't respond.

"Sam?"

Nothing.

She pulled over to a curb then shook his shoulder. "Sam?"

He groaned. "Huh?"

There was no way he could make it on his own. Those guys would catch him for sure. She took a deep breath. If she didn't go back to the conference, she would miss the appointment with the editor. But if she did, what would happen to Sam?

Daria couldn't leave him behind. She would never forgive herself if the bad guys caught him because she wasn't brave enough to help.

She shook his shoulder again. "Sam? Where do you want to go?"

"Shi—" He shifted in the seat. As he leaned toward her, his head landed on her shoulder. "Chicago."

CHAPTER TEN

Yuri found Korioff sitting on the sidewalk holding the back of his bleeding head. At first when Korioff didn't answer his mobile, Yuri thought he might be in a tight situation and couldn't risk it. When he still didn't answer, Yuri thought it might be payback from when *he* didn't answer Korioff's call.

Yuri had been watching the traffic going in and out of the back of the doctor's house for nearly an hour. He hadn't made it there before the police after the call about a burglar. He'd had to pick up Korioff. Yuri had forgotten about that Brooklyn doctor, or he would have staked out this house earlier instead of chasing down stolen mobile phones.

As soon as Korioff told him about the burglary, Yuri knew it was Jozwiak. Yuri was patient and waited until the police left. Teller and his young helper nearly caught Yuri when they showed up.

"What happened?" he asked when he came up to Korioff on the sidewalk.

"Johnston." Korioff moaned. "The woman."

Yuri helped the heir apparent to a powerful crime syndicate into the car. When Korioff touched the back of his head and moaned again, Yuri retrieved a chemical ice pack from the First Aid kit under the seat. Those Americans invented the most useful items. Give the bag a twist and a shake, and it became cold without refrigeration. Amazing.

He handed the bag to Korioff and told him to lean back in the seat. Yuri had to make another stop. Korioff seemed too dazed to ask questions.

Waiting for Teller and his partner to leave the doctor's house had given Yuri time to come up with a plan. He would pay a visit to a nearby precinct. A policeman there still owed him a favor from the old days.

* * *

Daria headed away from New York City. It was the right thing to do. In the morning, rather later in the morning, she would call the conference and cancel the appointment. She would take Sam to Chicago. It was on her way home, after all.

The meeting with the editor wasn't the only thing she would miss. The Women's Rights Hall of Fame and the Rock & Roll Museum would have to wait for another trip. And, by golly, she was going to take another trip, even if she had to go by herself. No more sitting around home. She was going to see more of the U.S. Maybe even more of the world.

Of course, she'd probably have to fly if she wanted to see any more of the world.

Sam stretched his legs and groaned. "Where are we?"

"On the way to Chicago," she said. "How do you feel?"

"Like I was run over by a truck." He scrubbed his hand down his face. "Thought you were going back to your conference."

"Changed my mind."

"Why are we going to Chicago?"

She shot him a look. "That's where you said to go."

"I did? Hmm. Okay, that will work." He yawned. "Five o'clock? Feels later."

"It's six a.m. here. I live in Iowa, remember? Central Time. I didn't want to reset the clock twice, so I just left it. You should try to sleep."

Sam shifted against the back of the seat, trying for a new position that didn't cramp his good leg or pain his bad one. He'd been stupid to kiss her. What the hell had he been thinking? She showed a little gratitude and he mauled her.

"I'm sorry, Daria."

"Quit beating yourself up," she said.

"What?"

"You couldn't have done things any different. In the restroom, you couldn't let me go in case I ran into Grashenko. You were protecting me."

Sam didn't have the heart to disillusion her. It wasn't her he'd been protecting but himself.

"You need some rest," she said. "Besides, you have enough on your mind about keeping whatever you have away from Grashenko and the Incredibly Clumsy Hulk."

"You've made some interesting deductions." God, she had no idea how close she was to the truth.

"That's what comes of being inquisitive by nature."

"Is that another word for nosy?" He kept his tone as neutral as hers.

"I prefer inquisitive." She sounded very pleased with herself. And not the least bit afraid of him.

She reached over and squeezed his hand. "Everything will be all right."

Such an optimistic thing. He hoped to God she was right. "I was apologizing for attacking you in the parking lot. After we left Doc's."

"Attacking me?" she said.

"When I, uh, kissed you."

"Oh, that attack." She laughed. "You have got to stop trying to take all the responsibility. I started it."

"What are you talking about?"

"That kiss was consensual. So would whatever came next. I wanted you." She shrugged. She kept her head turned just enough away that he couldn't see if she was blushing. "Call it an after effect of danger. A rush of relief that we made it. A momentary lapse when both our defenses were down. You wanted me, I wanted you. No biggie. Build a bridge and get over it."

In the early morning light, Sam could swear he saw red along her jaw.

"It's a good thing you want to go to Chicago. That's on my way home."

Had he really told her Chicago? Odd. He hadn't wanted to go home since his mother passed. Was his subconscious telling him what to do? "We'll be taking a slight detour. Instead of Chicago, I need to go to Michigan."

"What's in Michigan?"

"Someone I trust."

"Hardesty, what did you find out?" Teller demanded into the phone.

Since he couldn't get out of his standing Wednesday morning meeting without lengthy explanations, he'd left

Hardesty in New York and flown back to DC.

Teller couldn't let *The Powers That Be* know an agent disappeared. They would think he didn't have control of his agency. He couldn't give them an opportunity to second guess his management decisions. He wasn't Saint MacDonald. When were the *overseers* going to remember they didn't want John MacDonald anymore?

Teller needed to keep a tight lid on this op. He couldn't give them reason to regret appointing him Director. Not now, anyway.

Hardesty's voice came through the cell phone crystal clear. "You know how I traced Jozwiak's cell phone—the one he lost—back to the cab where he lost it?" Hardesty was still in Teller's apartment playing with the agency's super-sophisticated laptop. For what that thing cost, it should be made of gold.

"Yeah, yeah," Teller said.

"I talked to the driver who picked up two people near the old Guttschenheimer Department Store. A tall woman with long, dark hair and a man who was drunk. Now, the way I figure it, we already know Joz was wounded so that might look like intoxication."

Jesus, the guy liked to talk. "Skip the dissertation, Hardesty. Get to the point."

"They were dropped off at the Harbizon Hotel," Hardesty proclaimed in triumph.

"And . . ." It was like pulling teeth to get the information he needed.

"I've accessed the hotel's guest list. And I'm looking for a woman who is alone."

"Good job. If that doesn't pan out, start talking to the housekeeping staff, doormen, parking valets. See if anyone remembers that woman."

"Uh, boss? A *friend* of yours came by. She, uh, had a key."

Sweat broke out on Teller's forehead. Christ. Now, Hardesty knew one of his secrets.

* * *

Daria was running on empty.

How she wished she could stretch out on the seat, like Sam, and sleep. Ever since he nearly strangled himself on the seatbelt, he lay across the seat with his head on her leg.

He moaned and rubbed his face on her skirt. He'd nuzzled her thigh before, which she'd found strangely erotic. Okay, maybe not strange—just erotic. New and erotic. Like when his hand was under her skirt earlier.

She still couldn't believe how wild she'd become when he kissed her. A man's kiss never made her wild. If Sam had gotten his hands inside her underpants—which he hadn't— she would have helped him rip them off. She would have had wild monkey sex with a man she'd known less than a day. Just thinking about what might have been made her feel quivery, jittery. Hot.

Quit thinking about that kiss, she admonished herself for perhaps the tenth time. At least, it kept her from nodding off at the wheel.

Her arms ached, she was butt-sore, and her eyes felt gritty. A stop at McDonald's two hours ago recharged her batteries. Sam was awake but didn't want anything to eat. She managed to get the antibiotic into him. Because of his previous moaning and restlessness, she'd given him a pain pill, too. He didn't seem to notice, but he rested quietly ever since.

Now, Daria was fading fast. The Seneca Falls city limits sign came as welcome relief. She didn't think she could drive any farther.

She nosed the car into a parking space away from the office of the Green Acres Motel. She didn't want the clerk or anyone else to see Sam. Willing her nerves to stop jumping around, Daria walked into the motel office. It was the first time she'd ever registered for a room by herself. Although Daria went in with her, Ginnie had taken care of registering on their trip east. She traveled often with her husband and kids, while Daria had only traveled on school trips or with her brothers.

The clerk looked about twenty with a rangy body and lank over-long hair. When he stood, he hastily dropped the magazine he'd been reading. It flopped open on the chair.

Oh, my goodness, how did that girl walk upright?

"Can I help you?" He looked like he wanted to help Daria right out of her clothes. First, the guy in the bookstore. Now, this one? How did she find these guys?

"I'd like a room, please."

"A single?" he asked with a hopeful grin.

"A double. My husband's asleep in the car."

The clerk's mouth turned down for a moment. Then, he gave her a conspiratorial wink. Like he didn't believe her. He handed her a registration form to fill out. She carefully wrote 'Mr. & Mrs. Sam Smith'—just in case she slipped and called him by his first name. It asked for the make, model and license number of her car. Holy cow. She didn't realize she had to give out that much information. She switched the numbers and reversed the letters. Close enough that, if the clerk checked, he'd think she just made a mistake.

The clerk glanced at her registration form and then at her hands. No ring. She should have thought of that. She shoved her left hand into the pocket of her dress. He gave her a knowing look when she handed over cash. She couldn't very well use a credit card in the name of Daria J. Mason when she'd registered as Mrs. Sam Smith.

The clerk handed her a key. "It's the last unit on the left. Real private like, for you and your . . . husband."

She gave him a quizzical look and left. Sam was still asleep on the front seat. While she was inside, he'd sprawled more onto her side of the bench seat. She nudged him over, so she could slide under the steering wheel. After driving down to the end unit, she parked in front. Meanwhile, the clerk came out and leaned against the fake portico.

When she opened the door to the room, she discovered the source of the motel's name. 'Green Acres' summoned up the image of new vegetation, maybe a meadow. Not the case here. The color of the room resembled old swamp scum.

She started to go back for Sam when it hit her. She spun around and looked. One bed. A king but still one bed. She should go back and ask for a room with two beds. No, she quickly decided. She wasn't going to give the clerk another opportunity to leer.

She had a more pressing problem. Getting Sam out of

the car into the room without the nosy clerk observing.

As she walked outside, a car pulled off the road and up to the office. The clerk looked Daria's way, shrugged and went in to take care of the customers who'd gotten out of their car. The older man and woman did the arthritic shuffle for a few steps as they worked out the kinks from sitting too long. Both went inside.

Daria let out a sigh of relief. If she hurried, neither the clerk nor the customers would see Sam.

"Sam, wake up." She shook his shoulder.

He didn't. She shook him again.

She had to hurry before more customers arrived or the ones registering came out. She swung Sam's legs out of the car and then draped his arms over her shoulders. "C'mon, Sam, help me," she whispered.

His only response was a muffled grunt because he'd buried his face in the crook of her neck. The intimacy of the man's lips against the side of her throat reminded her of their sizzling kiss. None of that now, she told herself. He regretted the kiss. She'd told him to get over it. Good advice. Maybe she should take it.

Daria grabbed the back of Sam's belt to lever him out of the car. And nearly fell over from his weight. His arms tightened around her. She could do this. She just needed to steady herself. She shifted until she had them both balanced.

She nudged the car door closed with her knee, shifted again and started the mile-long walk to the room. Six steps at most, but they seemed like a mile. Sam's feet dragged against the pavement and one foot caught on the cement curb. She thought she'd lost him on that one. Finally, they staggered into the room. She used her foot to close the door then edged Sam closer to the bed.

"Okay, Sam, a little more. Another step and you can lie down."

"Grashenko, I hired you to teach my son the business."

Yuri wiped his palm down the crisp fabric of his blue jeans. So, the little shit called his papa. Yuri should have guessed.

He willed his hand holding the mobile phone to stop trembling. Even across two continents and an ocean, the man's voice made Yuri cringe. He never broke into a sweat outwitting the CIA, MI-6 or the Israeli Mossad. Yet, Yuri felt his insides liquefy and feared he would soil himself.

"I am teaching Ivan the business." He cleared his throat. "He is learning surveillance."

"With a concussion?" the senior Korioff shouted.

The thickening in Yuri's throat would not clear. He dared not clear it again. "The hospital examined him. He did not have a concussion." Yuri wasn't altogether certain young Ivan wasn't faking the injury, except for the small cut on the back of his head.

"Double vision is a sign of a concussion," Korioff exclaimed.

"He did not inform me that he was having difficulty seeing. It is necessary—"

"What is necessary—" The man's soft voice was more menacing than his bellow. "—is that you retrieve what was stolen."

Certain that Korioff had not finished, Yuri shifted in the chair of the tacky motel room. After the hospital visit, he had to stop and get some rest. He'd lost Jozwiak but not for long. Yuri had no doubt he would pick up the trail. Young Korioff needed to rest, too, after the trauma to his head.

In the old days, Yuri's accommodations had been first class—compliments of a government department with unlimited resources. Spying upon the Capitalists was a proud profession worthy of the expenditures. His new employer had the resources but chose not to spend them on his employee's comfort.

Yuri couldn't complain about his salary. He just did not expect that his job expenses would be microscopically examined. If he wanted better accommodations, he had been told after his first job, he could pay the difference out of his *generous* salary.

Yuri had other plans for his salary.

When the silence stretched, he shifted again. This time the chair creaked, giving away his agitation. Sweat broke out on his upper lip.

"You are an intelligent man, Yuri Grashenko." The satisfaction in the man's voice proclaimed that he correctly interpreted the sound. He *knew* he'd unnerved Yuri. "I was certain you understood that your mission is two-fold. Retrieving what was stolen is imperative. I hold you responsible for not protecting it."

Yuri knew better than to protest. The unfairness stuck in his craw. He'd warned Korioff about the lax security, about not leaving passwords where they could be found. As usual, Korioff did as he pleased and ignored the warnings.

A little longer, Yuri reminded himself. He could tolerate this pig a little longer. This job and one more should do it. Then, like a gunman of the American West, Yuri would hang up his gun and start a new life.

"The second part of your mission is to train my son. If he is ever injured again and you do not call me immediately, I will be most upset."

CHAPTER ELEVEN

Sam tried to roll out of bed then promptly wished he hadn't. The entire percussion section of the University of Iowa's marching band was holding practice in his head. He must have gone on some drinking binge, considering the hang-over.

His eyelashes hurt. And his teeth were numb. Even his butt hurt. He hoped he enjoyed the alcohol because he wasn't enjoying much of anything now. His mouth tasted like dirty gym shoes. Really dirty gym shoes.

"Sam, are you okay?"

Oh, God. He'd been so drunk he picked up a woman.

Sam never had indiscriminate sex. Too dangerous. Besides AIDS and other STDs, the risk of going to bed with a Mata Hari kept Sam from indulging in one-night stands. He was no James Bond.

The woman snapped on a light which drove red-hot pokers into his closed eyes.

"Shut off the goddamn light," he growled.

She did. At least, she obeyed—whoever she was. Damn, he wished he could remember whether he'd had a good time or not. At least, he was still alive. She hadn't slit his throat while he was sleeping.

"I'm sorry, Sam. Are you okay? You've been sleeping so long I've been worried. The doctor said you needed sleep, but you're scaring me."

Doctor? Good Lord, he was groggy. Sam slit one eye open. The room swam for several seconds. The only illumination came from a sliver between the curtains and the nearly-closed bathroom door. At least, he guessed it was a bathroom. He was in a hotel room. Okay, he remembered waking up here before.

No, not here. He shook his head. Big mistake. His stomach revolted. When he tried to sit up, a knife ripped from his right hip down his leg.

"Sam, be careful. You'll pull out the stitches." That woman again.

Stitches?

Everything came flooding back. Running from Grashenko, the bullets, the woman in the restroom. Daria. The grade school teacher from Iowa who wasn't cut out for espionage. Daria, who kissed like a wild angel. Daria, who hadn't deserted him.

He buried his head between his knees. He didn't want her to see how pathetically grateful he was. He also needed to wait for the nausea to pass.

A few seconds later, he felt something cool on the back of his neck. A wet cloth.

"Would you like help getting to the bathroom?" she asked.

He lifted his head five millimeters—all that the percussion section would allow. She knelt in front of him, a shadowy figure full of motherly concern. A memory of fierce arousal, soft skin and delicious womanly scents flickered through his consciousness. Not sensations associated with *Mother*.

"Come on, Sam, let me help you up. You can lean on me."

His stomach was holding its own, but his bladder clamored for relief. "I can manage. Just don't get between me and the door, okay?"

She scrambled out of his way. "I'll stay close in case you need me."

She let him take two steps before coming to his rescue. Good thing. His right leg had the structural stability of Jell-o. She draped his arm around her shoulder and wrapped her arm around his waist, which plastered her breast against his side. Pain should have ruled out sexual arousal. Wrong.

Once they got to the door of the bathroom, he grabbed the frame for support. He hated depending on her. Hated depending on anyone. He shrugged off her arm. A rejected puppy look crossed her face before she stiffened her shoulders.

"Maybe I should come in with you in case you are too weak to, uh—"

"I can take it from here, Ms. Nightingale." He squinted against the four-hundred-watt bulb above the sink.

"Just call out if you need me." She backed away as he closed the door.

Daria waited outside the bathroom, praying that Sam wouldn't fall. She'd never get him up off the floor. She couldn't believe how long and hard he'd slept. Despite her fatigue, she only dozed in the chair. His occasional moans always brought her fully alert.

He must be exhausted from those two Russians chasing him. He'd slept hard in her room at the Harbizon, but their race across Doc's side yard and through the hedges, let alone driving as fast and as far as he did, must have been more than his body could handle.

She turned on the lamp next to the bed. By now, his eyes would be used to the light especially after the weak bulb in the bathroom. She straightened the curtain where the two sides failed to meet. Then, she picked up the blanket which had fallen off the bed. What was taking him so long?

She knocked on the door. "Are you all right in there? Do you need any help?"

The toilet flushed, and water ran before the door opened. Sam leaned against the doorjamb. "Do you always fuss this much?"

"Only when someone's been shot and then is unconsciousness for hours."

He held onto the jamb and from there to the upholstered chair. By the time he eased himself into the chair, his face was pasty and sweaty.

"You need your pills." She took two envelopes out of her purse.

"Keep those damn things away from me."

"What? The doctor said you need antibiotics to prevent infection and the other is for the pain. I'll need to examine your wounds in a bit."

"I can examine my own wounds. Don't need you hovering over me like I'm an invalid. Give me those envelopes. Did Doc mark which was which?"

Ignoring his surly tone, she held onto the pills and read out loud the information the doctor had scrawled on the outside of each envelope.

"Throw those goddamn pain pills down the toilet." His vehemence surprised her.

"You'll need them tonight when the pain gets bad."

"No way. Throw 'em out."

"Are you playing Macho Man?" She lowered the timbre of her voice. "Real Men tough it out. Real Men don't take pain pills."

"Cute. My chauffeur is a comedienne." He shifted in the chair to find a comfortable position. She could have told him there wasn't one. "I'm not a glutton for punishment. I can't tolerate certain drugs. They put me out faster than alcohol—and are twice as dangerous."

"What?" An awful feeling dropped into her stomach.

"Drugs won't kill me," he said. "They make me vulnerable and *that* will kill me."

"Oh, God. I didn't know." She swallowed. "I gave you two of the pain pills, one around nine this morning and the other around two."

"What! You gave me pain pills after I specifically said I didn't want them?"

She gulped. His anger frightened her, yet she had to tell him the truth. "You were hurting. I-I thought . . . I'm sorry. I didn't realize."

His anger vanished. "That explains a lot." He gave her a long look. "You didn't have to tell me. I wouldn't have known. Just chalked it up to no sleep for almost a week."

She felt even more guilty. He hadn't slept for a week? How could he abuse his body so much? She was wiped out from missing one night's sleep.

She hadn't planned on telling him about the pain pills she'd given him at lunch. But, she remembered something they'd discussed before. "Trust," she said. "If we don't have trust between us, we're going to have real problems."

"As opposed to the *unreal* problems we already have? Like two Russians who want me dead? Seems pretty real to me."

She ignored that. "You need the antibiotic to combat infection. Your body's run down. It won't be able to fight off an infection without help."

"You're right," he conceded. "Let me hold off for a bit. My stomach's still doing the back flip."

He refused lunch when she stopped earlier. She picked up her purse. "You need food. I'll go out and get dinner. I was waiting until you woke up."

He nodded. "Where are we?"

"Seneca Falls. In the Finger Lakes."

"You only got this far? I told you I needed to get to Michigan. What time did you stop, for God's sake?"

Well, that capped it. Here she was doing him a favor by getting him out of New York City and away from the bad guys and he was complaining she stopped too early.

"Listen, Mister Sleeping Beauty. This is the route I planned to take home. I stayed off the turnpike because of the security cameras and those electronic signs they use for warnings and Amber Alerts. I thought it wouldn't be as easy to spot us on secondary roads—if they learned about my car. I stopped because I've been awake, unlike some people, for two days straight, and I nearly fell asleep at the wheel. So, put that in your pipe and smoke it, buster." *Whoa.* That sounded almost as tough as Alexa.

"Okay, okay, don't get your knickers in a twist. I shouldn't have yelled at you."

"No, you shouldn't have."

He scrubbed his hand down his face. "I need to get to . . . my friend's as soon as possible."

"You should call to make sure this friend is home. I'd rather you didn't break into any more houses while I'm around."

"My friend doesn't have a phone."

"Get out. Everybody has a phone. Half my second graders have cell phones."

"He doesn't."

"Will his place be safe?"

"Oh, yeah."

"All right then." She stood. "What do you want for dinner?"

"Doesn't matter."

She walked to the door. When she looked back, he'd put his elbow on the desk and was resting his forehead in his palm. "You won't go anywhere, will you, Sam Johnston?" She stared at him until he looked up.

"Not likely, the way I feel."

"Good. Wouldn't want those bad guys to find you passed out in the parking lot."

When the door closed behind her, Sam wondered if he even had the strength to make it as far as the door, let alone out to the parking lot. Just taking a leak was a monumental effort. Must have been those damn pain pills. They always made him weak.

He didn't think he'd lost that much blood. On the floor at the foot of the bed lay the shoe that gave testimony to how much blood he'd lost. Nearly soaked through. He gave a snort of disbelief. She'd put a plastic bag under the shoe. What? She was afraid it would stain the carpet? Nothing much could damage this one.

But, if someone did notice a new stain, it might raise questions. She was clever. He had to give her that. Staying off the turnpike was a good idea, too, even though it meant they would travel slower. It was unlikely, though, that Grashenko would figure out in which direction they were headed. He would watch planes and trains to DC. He'd never guess they were going to Michigan.

Very few people knew about Mac's boat on Lake Michigan. The Orion Agency had been John MacDonald's life. At age sixty-five and still going strong, he'd been forced out. A discard in a disposable society. When he retired, Mac shook off the dust of Washington and disappeared.

On a rare vacation last fall, Sam had visited his mentor and former boss. They fished, walked the beach and talked. Sam had been surprised at Mac's insistence that he turn off and lock his cell phone in the trunk of his car. Not only did Mac not have a phone, he refused to allow one aboard his boat.

Sam's head was still muzzy and he felt like he'd been run over by a truck. If it wouldn't hurt so much, he'd get out of this lumpy chair and flop on the bed.

* * *

"Hey, boss, I got lucky," Hardesty announced over the phone with pride.

Teller suppressed a sigh. He hoped this news turned out to be luckier than the last dead end. They didn't have a clue where or how Joziak disappeared. The man was a goddamn gopher.

"I talked to the housekeeping staff at the Harbizon. There's some kind of writers' conference going on, and they're real busy."

Teller didn't have time for this. "Get your gear and get back here."

"But, boss." Hardesty practically whined. Teller hated whiners. "I talked to the parking valet."

"I don't care if you talked to the chef. Get to the point. I have other problems here besides an agent who doesn't know enough to come in out of the cold."

"I think it's 'come in *from* the cold' which is a leftover from the—"

"Are you lecturing me, rookie?" Teller couldn't believe Hardesty's nerve. "Tell me you found the woman with the braid."

Hardesty cleared his throat. "Uh, right. Sorry, boss. The woman." His voice brightened. "I told the parking valet I was her brother and was worried about her."

"Get to the damn point or get off the phone."

"You aren't going to believe this. Someone else was looking for her."

"And I care about this why?"

"It was a Russian."

Teller's heart stuttered. Hardesty found out about Grashenko and that meant Grashenko knew about the woman. Damn. The man was two steps ahead of him. "Old guy?"

"No. Late twenties but definitely a Russian accent. But that isn't—"

Not Grashenko. "Rookie, get to the point."

"She's a grade school teacher."

"What!"

"Yeah. She's a teacher. I couldn't believe it, either. From Iowa."

"Iowa? A teacher from Iowa is helping Jozwiak? Does she have a name?"

"Of course. Daria Mason. But, wait. There's more. She and Joz went to the same college. University of Iowa."

Teller snapped his fingers. "It's a cover."

"Huh?"

"Grade school teacher, my ass. That's a cover. Find out who she really works for. In fact, get your ass back here. You'll need the agency resources to dig into deep cover."

"But, boss, she's lived in Prairieville, Iowa her entire life. You won't believe who her brothers are. They're—"

"You don't get it, rookie. She's a mole."

"Where the hell have you been?" Sam demanded when Daria opened the door. "What did you do—drive back to the City for dinner?" He'd fallen asleep again in the chair. When he woke up and realized she hadn't returned, he'd started to worry. He'd gotten her into this mess. She was his responsibility.

Plainly ignoring him, Daria tossed two Walmart bags on the bed before setting a third bag on the minuscule desk. Shopping? He'd been worried, and she went shopping?

"What's all that?" He pointed to the rumpled bed where bags were spilling their contents. Jeans, packages of underwear, shirts, shoes. All men's, he noted with chagrin.

She opened the bag on the desk and took out two small white cartons. "I found a Chinese restaurant. I thought egg drop soup and rice would be light enough for your flip-flopping stomach."

He shifted in the uncomfortable chair and then scrubbed a hand down his face. Old Foot-in-Mouth strikes again. "Thanks," he said grudgingly.

After handing him the carton of soup and a spoon, she gave him a pinched-mouth look then headed out the door. He recognized that look. His mother could turn him to stone with that one.

Daria returned with more bags which she set on the bed. No flinging this time. Something clanked and clinked. Bottles? Cans? She started to go back outside.

"For God's sake, get back in here." he called after her. "Where's your dinner?"

She ignored him. Well, nuts.

He heard the trunk lid shut, and then she edged in sideways carrying the cooler. He started to get up to help her. The pain from his leg nearly knocked him over. He sucked air through his teeth. *Damn it to hell.* He fell back into the chair.

"Stop this in-and-out business," he said. "What do you think this is? A family vacation? We're on the run, for God's sake."

With another plastic bag dangling from her fingers and still wrestling the cooler, she stopped to give him a baleful look. "Really? Anyone observing my behavior would think this *was* a family vacation—not a get-away."

She was right, damn it. He unhooked the bag from her fingers. A square white box. Her dinner. He pointed to the straight-back chair tucked under the desk. "Sit. Eat."

She glanced at his unopened food cartons. "You didn't have to wait for me."

He gave her a crooked smile. "My momma would've whupped me good if I didn't wait for a lady first. C'mon, Daria, you can get the rest later."

"That's all there is." She set the cooler on the floor under the window. "You know what I think, Sam Johnston? I think your bad mood is the pain talking." Finally, she pulled out the desk chair and sat. "You should take one of the pain pills."

He paused while opening the carton of soup. "And have a repeat of today? I can't stay awake. Consequently, I can't protect you from the people after me."

She opened the white dinner box. General Tsao's Chicken. One of Sam's favorite dishes. His mouth started salivating over the scent of the spicy dish.

"What makes you think you have to protect me?" she asked. "I've proven I can take care of myself . . . and you. Haven't I?"

"Yes, well . . ." He ate the soup while glancing longingly at her dinner.

"What?" she asked.

"That isn't General's Chicken, is it?"

"Yes." She forked a piece of breaded chicken and let the sauce drip off before taking a bite.

"You aren't going to eat *all* of that, are you?"

"There's not that much. Ah, now I get the picture," she said with a knowing smile. "I've seen better pleading looks from my second graders."

He tossed the empty soup container into the wastebasket next to the desk. "The soup wasn't very filling."

She pushed the other carton toward him. "You forgot the rice."

He stared at her box. "I'm a growing boy. I need more than soup and rice."

"But you said—" She started to laugh. "I take it you're feeling better? Your stomach has settled down?"

He nodded just as eagerly as a second grader. God, he was pathetic. She nudged her box toward him.

"You're a sweetie." He scooped a spoonful of chicken and sauce into his mouth. Hurriedly followed by another. He couldn't remember when he'd eaten last. Yesterday morning? The night before that? What day was it, anyway? Wednesday?

When he returned for a third spoonful, she rapped his knuckles with her plastic fork. "Take it easy. That stuff is pretty hot. Your stomach will be doing backflips again."

"You just don't want to share."

She smiled. "That pout is worthy of an eight-year-old."

"Meanie."

"I thought I was your sweetie." As if realizing what she just said, she busied herself cutting a large piece of chicken into a more manageable size.

Don't go there, Ace. Get this conversation back on track. "That was before you decided to hog all the good food."

She didn't look at him. Instead, she pulled the box toward her. "No more."

"Sharing your dinner made us look like a family, you know," he mocked.

She jumped up. "I'll get us something to drink." She opened the second batch of bags she'd brought in and rummaged around until she held up a container of juice. "It's not cold." After setting the bottle of juice on the desk, she grabbed the plastic bucket. "I'll go and get some ice."

When she tried to scoot past him, he snagged her wrist. "Sit." He didn't let go. If he did, she'd probably fly out of the room. She was that jumpy.

She tried to pull away. "That's okay. I'll just—"

He easily removed the bucket from her fingers. "If you leave now, you won't get any more of the chicken."

"You would eat my—" She stopped. She must have seen his lips twitch even though he gave a half-hearted attempt to keep from laughing at her outrage over his threat to steal her meal. "Sam Johnston, you are a pain in the tush."

Once again, a twinge of conscience shot through him as she called him by his other name, but he did nothing to correct her. "I'm the one with a pain in the tush."

He stroked the tender skin on the inside of her wrist. Her eyes darkened. In that brief moment, longing sweet and desperate shot through him. Not the fierce need he felt when he kissed her. That had been the rush of the chase. An adrenaline high.

When her eyes darkened to a midnight blue and the same sweet longing filled them, he promptly released her hand. *Not good.* He'd bet dollars to donuts she didn't have indiscriminate sex, either. He knew her type. She believed in commitment, happy ever after. He was a rolling stone.

"Eat your dinner," he growled.

Sam's slow, gentle rub on the inside of her wrist sent Daria's pulse racing, her breath catching in her throat. Don't stop, she wanted to say. But, of course, she didn't. She stood there, waiting. Waiting for that smoldering look he'd given her before, wanting him to take her hand again.

"Daria?" His thicker-than-caramel voice sent another shiver through her, this one deep into her belly.

For a second, his brown eyes flared, like a lick of flame from a banked fire. Then, his eyes flattened. She continued to stand, transfixed by the echo of the sensations.

"Daria, finish your dinner."

She blinked. Why was she standing there with her mouth open? All he'd done was grab her wrist. So he didn't want ice. *She* needed ice. A whole bucket of it.

"I want something to drink." Her voice was husky. She

would die if he knew she nearly melted on the floor from his touch. She was still embarrassed by her abandon when she kissed him. She couldn't bear a repeat of his self-disgust.

She cleared her throat. "I hope I'm not coming down with a cold."

The corner of his mouth curved up.

"I'll just get a cup." *That's right, babble away.* She opened one of the bags on the bed, grateful to turn her back on him. Yet, he still unnerved her. As if he knew what he'd done by stroking her wrist.

He didn't say anything when she poured juice into two cups. Nor did he say anything when she set one closer to him. Well, she wasn't going to look into those smoldering eyes again. She ate two bites of her chicken before she realized how quiet he'd gotten. He hadn't taken a drink, either.

"If you don't like white grape, I bought—"

His head bobbed once then stayed on his chest. The man dropped off to sleep faster than anyone she knew.

After finishing her dinner, she began cleaning up. She pulled out the duffel bag she bought for Sam and quickly dispensed with the sealed pouches containing the underwear. Folding a man's underwear seemed more intimate than bandaging his butt.

She hadn't had to guess at sizes since his jeans sported his waist and inseam on the leather patch above the back pocket—thirty-four, thirty-four. She'd noticed the tag in his jacket when she hung it in the closet. An XLT. Easy enough to find shirts and a windbreaker. Long enough jeans had been more difficult. Although she didn't find the same brand of athletic shoes he wore, at least the store carried size thirteens.

And, she'd found an ATM. She'd needed to use her credit card at Walmart. If anyone found out who she was and tracked her to Seneca Falls, using the ATM wouldn't make any difference. By using cash from now on, she wouldn't make tracking any easier.

She laid out a change of clothes for him and packed the rest in the duffel. The toiletries she put in the bathroom. All the 'housekeeping' chores done, she opened her own tote bag. Now that she knew Sam wasn't going anywhere without her, she could take a few minutes for herself. She hadn't realized how stiff her shoulders had become. Napping in that poor excuse for an upholstered chair, along with the driving, didn't help.

What she needed was a soak in the tub. She collected her nightshirt and toiletry bag and headed for the bathroom. As she passed Sam, she realized how uncomfortable he looked sprawled and slipping sideways in that awful chair. He should be in bed.

After putting her things in the bathroom, she came out and straightened the covers. Then, she tried to get Sam up. The man was practically dead weight.

"C'mon, Sam, help me out here." She tried the trick she'd used to get him out of the car—putting his arms over her shoulders and hoisting him by holding onto the back of his belt. "Sam, could you wake up a bit?"

He was out cold. Okay, she could do this. She planted her feet, pulled . . . and catapulted Sam right out of the chair and onto the bed. That was the good part. The bad part was she didn't get out of the way in time. She was sandwiched between the man and the mattress.

"Roll over, Sam." She pushed on his shoulder with the hand that wasn't pinned between them.

Nothing.

She tried again. And, again, he didn't move, except to start nuzzling her neck. His whiskers itched and scraped, sending skittering sensations along her skin. She tried to twist away.

"Cut that out. Just roll over, and I'll get out of your way." She bucked and pushed. And didn't move him an inch.

Instead, he burrowed his face deeper into her neck. "You smell good."

She managed to free her arm. This time using both hands, she pushed on his shoulders. He groaned. Guilt shot through her. She must have hurt him, but he did roll over.

And dragged her with him. She tried to slither away, but he clutched her closer. "Don't go, Sally," he muttered. "Need you."

"Sally?" she exclaimed.

He held the back of her neck and opened his eyes. He

blinked twice before closing them. "Not Sally. D-Da— Not Sally." He brought her head closer, until their lips were merely a breath apart. "Daria."

His lips closed over hers. Sweet, so sweet. Very unlike their kiss this morning. Soon, not only sweet but spicy. Like the General's Chicken. A delayed reaction. The initial sweetness fooled her. Hot, spicy. Needy. He needed her. A crazy demanding hunger. A need that called to a corresponding need inside her.

Following hard on the fire of need, common sense slapped her in the face. She didn't know this man. She didn't believe in casual sex. No one-night stands for her no matter how intense the need was. Not that she'd ever had intense need while kissing any guy back home. Besides, he was kissing her, but he was thinking about another woman.

The reality of their situation penetrated her brain. The man was injured. As soon as they got to Michigan, she'd never see him again. He was also snoring in her ear. By falling asleep, he'd made the choice between physical need and common sense for her.

Daria disentangled her legs from his, his arms from hers, and got up. The poor man lay sprawled crosswise on the bed. His legs dangled off the edge. She lifted them, taking care not to bump the injured one.

With a lot of straining and lifting, she got him situated properly on the bed. He didn't look comfortable wearing street clothes. Maybe she should unbuckle his belt and unsnap his jeans. He'd be more comfortable not wearing the jeans at all. She stared down at his zipper. The bulge beneath it gave her pause.

Daria swallowed. How was she going to get his jeans off without touching him?

Carefully, very carefully.

She could pretend he was one of the kids. *Right, Daria, that's no eight-year-old's body.*

She could pretend he was her brother. *Yeah, sure.* Those weren't sisterly feelings racing through her.

Just get it over with.

She started to unzip the jeans and stopped. How was she supposed to get it past that bulge? Maybe if she slid her hand

between the zipper and—
    "Find what you're looking for?"

CHAPTER TWELVE

Daria shrieked, whipped her hand out of his pants and stumbled backward. She tripped on the cooler and sat down hard on top of it.

Sam propped his elbow on the bed and half-sat up. "If you wanted to go at it, you should've waited until I was fully awake."

Daria's mouth worked, but nothing came out. Speechless. She, who could quell a classroom of twenty-five with a single word, couldn't speak if her life depended on it.

"What's the matter, darlin'? Cat got your tongue?" He gave her a knowing smirk—right before a knock sounded on the door.

Sam bolted upright, wincing sharply. "Where's my cig?" he whispered.

"What?" She stumbled off her perch on the cooler. "You want a cigarette? Now?"

"My weapon. The one Doc gave me. Where is it?" He levered himself off the bed. When they first arrived and she'd gotten him into bed, she removed his holster and gun to make him more comfortable. She'd wrapped it in his jacket and put it on the shelf in the closet. Now, she brought him the bundle.

The knock sounded again. "Are you all right in there?"

"The clerk," she whispered. "Get under the covers and turn away from the door."

"I am not hiding under the covers. I'll deal with him."

"We don't want him to see your face."

Sam pulled the Sig out of the holster. She was right. If the clerk saw his face, he might remember if someone tracked them there. Grashenko wasn't stupid. It was only a matter of time before he picked up their trail.

Sam went into the bathroom and turned on the shower. He stayed behind the door, leaving it open a crack. There was a click of the latch and the rasp of the chain. Good girl. She'd kept the safety chain on. It was a slight deterrent. If someone really wanted in, one swift kick would rip the chain out of the woodwork.

"Is there a problem?" she said in that school-teachery tone she often used on Sam.

"I, like, came down to see if you, like, needed anything. I heard you yell."

"That's so thoughtful of you to be concerned." Her voice had taken on a syrupy sweetness. "I tripped over the cooler."

"Well, I, uh, was like making sure you're okay. Do you like need anything?"

"Everything is fine," she said. "Please remove your foot so I can close the door."

The bastard. "Hey, honey," Sam called out. "Is someone at the door?"

"It's the clerk," she called back.

Sam turned off the shower. "Problems?"

"Got it covered," she said.

"Y-You really, like, have a guy with you." The bastard sounded amazed.

"I *told* you my husband was sleeping in the car," she replied. "We tried driving straight through from Des Moines to Boston, but we didn't make it."

Sam admired her quick thinking.

"Well, like if you need anything . . ." The clerk was still tripping over his tongue.

"Just a good night's sleep. Thank you for your concern." She dismissed the jerk.

When Sam heard the door close, he came out. She was leaning back against the outside door, her eyes shut.

"Good job," he said as he worked his way over to the bed. *This damn weakness.*

Her eyes flashed open. She fisted her hands on her hips. "That little twerp."

Sam chuckled. "You handled him just fine."

"He thought I was alone." She was shaking. "What if I *had* been alone?"

"You would've handled the situation just fine," he said. "You probably would have straight-armed him the way you did Korioff."

Her chest rose and fell in agitation as she moved away from the door. "If this was part of a motel chain, I'd report him to their general headquarters." Her shakiness had given way to anger.

"Hey, take it easy." He kept his voice low and tugged her hand until she sat next to him on the bed. "You did good. Very clever telling him we're going to Boston."

She gave him a brief smile, but the anger wasn't gone from her eyes. She turned sideways toward him, curling her knee on the bed. She pushed her hair out of her eyes. Her braid was nearly undone. "I wanted to punch that smile off his face."

He tucked the errant strand of hair behind her ear. "He won't bother us again. You probably froze his libido with that dismissal."

"You think?" A small grin curved her lips.

He liked kissing those lips. Soft, luscious. Pliant, willing, eager. Her taste. He remembered her taste, sweet, tentative, wild.

No, he was mixing up their kisses. He'd woken up with her sprawled across the top of him and her lips inches from his. He was only human, as she found out when she began unzipping his jeans.

Sam reminded himself he had a mission to complete. He didn't have time for this kind of distraction.

Wham. Wham. Wham.

Startled, Daria woke up with a splash. Water sloshed over the side of the tub.

"You fall asleep in there?" Sam was hitting the bathroom door with his palm.

"I'm fine. Don't you dare come in here." The water was tepid. She examined her pruney fingers. How long had she been in the tub?

"Wouldn't think of it, sweetheart. Just didn't want you to drown. Dead bodies mean too many questions. Might give away my location."

"I'll be out shortly." She hurried through her washing

and got out of the tub. A wet rope hit her in the back. Oh, darn. She hadn't pinned up her hair. She might as well wash it even if it would take forever to dry before going to bed.

That was the trouble with long hair. One of these days, she was going to get the courage to whack it off. Lil, at the Curl Up & Dye, had been on her case for years to change her hair style.

She shampooed her hair, thinking about what Sam said about giving away his location. She'd gotten him away from the bad guys, but what if they did find him? She wasn't that naïve to think they wouldn't kill him . . . or her.

He did make two calls. But, why didn't Sam phone someone else? Did anyone besides the doctor realize he was in trouble? She stilled, toothbrush in her mouth. Minty foam dribbled down her chin. What did that doctor say? *Don't trust anyone.* Maybe it wasn't safe for Sam to 'phone home.'

Speaking of phoning home, the boys were probably having fits that she hadn't called tonight. She rinsed, spat and wiped her mouth. She slipped her watch back on and realized she'd been in the bathroom for almost two hours. It was after eleven already. Since it was an hour earlier in Iowa, she still had time to call.

As soon as she opened the door, Sam hit her with "About time." He levered himself off the bed.

She scooted past him. "Sorry." Moments later she heard the shower running.

While Sam was in the bathroom, she retrieved the new cell phone from her purse. She did not want to make this call. When the shower went off, Daria figured she'd better make this quick. If she was in luck, she'd get anyone but Jimmy. She turned on the phone and the 'missed call' message lit up. She ignored it and clicked the automatic dial-up.

"This better be you, Dar. It's about time you called."

"Hello, Billy, how are you? I'm fine," she said sweetly.

"Knock it off." That didn't sound like easy-going Billy. "Jim called your hotel and they said you left *last* night."

He'd checked up on her? "Actually, we left early this morning. We wanted to get an early start. You wouldn't believe how bad the traffic is in New York City."

Sam opened the bathroom door. She held her hand up to

indicate she'd only be a few minutes. His brow furrowed. She gulped when she saw what he was wearing. Rather, what he was not wearing. He had his jeans and shirt in his hand. She hastily glanced away from the sight of his bare chest and his long, hair-roughened legs. In between, he was wearing a new pair of plain white briefs. Whoa. The briefs left little to the imagination. And she had quite an imagination.

". . . home, Daria?"

She stopped ogling the near-naked man and tried to concentrate on what her brother was saying. "Billy," she said patiently, "I told you we were going to do some sightseeing on the way home. Now, how are you and the other boys getting along with Mrs. Howard? Is she fixing things you like to eat?"

"Yeah, she made lasagna for dinner tonight. Not as good as yours, though." Was her brother pouting?

"That's not a nice thing to say about her cooking. I'll make a nice dinner when I get home. I'm sorry to call so late. We went to a movie and just got back." She glanced at Sam with a shrug. So much for not telling flat-out lies. She regretted looking at him again. *Lordy, he should put some clothes on.* "Now, don't go giving Mrs. Howard any grief. I don't want her mad at me for leaving you boys."

"Jesus, Dar, you make us sound like we're kids."

"Did you remember to put the trash out? Tomorrow's pick up. Now, tell the rest of the boys good-night for me. I'll call tomorrow. Love ya." She ended the call before one of the others wanted to know where she was. Something Billy didn't think to ask.

"Who was that?" Sam leaned against the doorjamb to the bathroom. Though he'd assumed a casual pose, his voice contained an edge.

"One of the boys. I was checking up on them." She turned off the phone and put it in her purse.

"The boys?"

"My brothers," she said with a wave of her hand. She did *not* want to discuss her over-protective brothers.

"You live with your brothers?"

"Actually, they live with me."

After college when Daria made noises about getting her

own apartment, the boys put the house in her name. She supposed they meant well. Lately, she suspected they did it to keep her from going out on her own.

"What about your parents?"

"They died years ago. That's why the boys live with me. If I don't call each night, they worry." She unwrapped the towel from around her head and started rubbing her hair to hasten its drying. That way she wouldn't look at Sam's near-naked body. He hadn't put his shirt back on. He stood there watching while she dried her hair. Stood there in white cotton briefs and nothing else.

Sam pried himself away from the frame. Coming out of the bathroom and finding her on the phone nearly put him into cardiac arrest. He first thought she was turning him in. But her expression and later explanation quickly dispelled that fear. She didn't look so much guilty as embarrassed.

So, she checked on her brothers every night. No big deal. The little guys must be worried that their sister was out having fun by herself. Some things started to make sense, like why she was still single at twenty-nine. Being responsible for little kids would put a real crimp in a girl's love life. Not too many men wanted to get involved with a woman who came with so much baggage.

"Hang on. That wasn't the phone I used to call Sally."

She blew out a breath. "I accidentally gave you my old one. I got a new one before I left."

"And they didn't transfer everything to your new one?"

"I don't know." An odd look came into her eyes.

"What?"

She shook her head. "Not important."

Sam eased into bed and pulled up the sheet. He wasn't feeling so hot. Every time he got up and moved around, he felt weak. Oh, hell. The medicine. As much as he hated to do it, he threw back the sheet and swung his legs over the edge. "Where did you put those antibiotics?"

"Don't get up." She went over to her purse which she'd tucked in the far corner of the room between the bed and the window—something Ginnie told her to do. "I'll get the pills."

"Just the antibiotic, remember?"

"Of course, I remember. I saw what those pain pills did

to you. Do you think I want to have to deal with an unconscious man again?"

"Yeah. I might wake up and find your hand inside my pants again."

"You wish." She handed him the antibiotic.

"Florence Nightingale to the rescue." He hated this damn weakness, hated depending on Daria.

"Which wound is giving you trouble?" Daria's question broke into his thoughts.

"Both." He took the pill and washed it down with juice.

"Better take some Tylenol." She handed him the bottle. "Then, roll on your stomach so I can check your wounds."

"You just want another look at my butt."

"Of course." The pink in her cheeks belied her bold words.

"No thanks, Florence. I checked in the bathroom and my wounds are fine."

"Darn." She snapped her fingers.

"I can't believe that idiot Korioff actually hit me. And in the butt, for God's sake."

"Speaking of being shot, would you put that away?" She motioned toward the weapon he'd placed on the nightstand.

He set it on the floor just under the bed. Not as easy to reach, but she looked upset about seeing it.

"Why do you call your gun after cigarettes?" she asked.

"I don't."

"Yes, you called it a cig."

"It's a Sig Sauer 40."

"Six hour?" she exclaimed. "It's only good for six hours? What does the forty stand for? Forty shots?"

He gave her a look of disbelief before spelling out the name. "The forty is the caliber. Why all the questions?"

She lifted her chin. "I'm doing research. For my book."

"If you're going to write about weapons, you need to research them better."

"Thank you," she said with fake sweetness. "I'll be sure to contact you when I have more questions." She pointed to the granola bar on the desk. "Eat or your stomach will give you problems."

"Quit hovering. I'm not a goddamn invalid." He

unwrapped the bar and took a bite. He couldn't remember the last time he'd had one. Eighth grade? Granola bars reminded him of junior high cafeteria and girls with budding breasts.

He glanced at Daria who was rubbing her hair with the towel. With her reaching up like that, the over-size shirt brushed the tops of thighs. Long legs were almost as good as budding breasts. Only Daria's weren't budding. They were lusciously ripe. And she wasn't wearing a bra. Fascinating.

She bent over, rubbing the long thick strands which shone darkly from dampness. He could see the edge of her underpants curving over her bottom. White cotton underpants with tiny pink flowers. Sweet Jesus, he was only human.

He cleared his throat. "I shouldn't have snapped at you."

She straightened to shake her hair away from her face. Thank God, she sat down so he wouldn't have to look at her thighs and pink flowered panties and imagine . . .

With her head tilted back, the long tresses hung down her back nearly to her waist. Sam hadn't realized how much he liked long hair. He wanted to bury his face in it. Have it swish across his chest as she made love to him.

He groaned. The room had gotten hotter, smaller, and his briefs a lot tighter.

"You're in pain," she said quietly.

"Don't be so goddamn understanding," he barked, pissed at the lust roaring through him. "And don't be a goddamn doormat."

She stiffened, her hair forgotten as it draped over her shoulders in damp ripples. "I would appreciate it if you would refrain from using that kind of language."

With that prissy remark, she picked up a wide-tooth comb and began to comb out her long, dark hair. She was ignoring him. It wasn't pain that made him irritable. A small motel room, one bed, a beautiful woman. Hell, she didn't deserve his anger because he was horny as hell.

"Okay," he said reluctantly. "I can be a real pain in the a—butt sometimes."

She arched an eyebrow. "Sometimes?"

* * *

Daria straightened her legs, shifted onto her other hip and curled up again. She pulled the blanket over her shoulder. Yet another red numeral of the clock on the nightstand morphed inexorably into the next. Twelve forty-eight.

Something Sam said earlier had been niggling around in her brain. Something that didn't occur to her before. When Jimmy had the new phone activated, he didn't transfer her number which would have disabled her old phone. He must have gotten a new number. Oh, boy. Now, she was going to have double the expense on her bill. She'd have to take care of that when she got home.

He really should have discussed that with her. Typical Jimmy. Always taking charge and doing what he wanted to do. She shifted in the chair. Well, she was going to have words with him when she got home.

"For God's sake," Sam growled from across the darkened room. "Would you quit trying to find a comfortable spot in that chair? There isn't one."

He was right about that. She'd been trying to sleep for the past half hour. "I'm okay." She thought he'd gone to sleep.

"You aren't going to get any rest if you stay there."

He was right about that, too. She had a full day of driving ahead of her. With any luck, they could be through Ohio by tomorrow night. Maybe even as far as Detroit. If that was where they were going.

"And neither will I," he added, as he turned on the light next to the bed..

Didn't that put things into perspective. She thought he was concerned about her.

He patted the space next to him. "There's plenty of room and the way I feel I can guarantee your virtue is safe. Even if you crawled in here buck naked."

Heat rushed through her at that image. How did he know she was thinking about getting into that big bed and lying next to him? Not naked, of course. She looked longingly at the empty half of the bed. More than half. She wouldn't take up much space.

He pointed to the wide expanse of bed next to him. "Just get your ass over here so I can get some sleep."

"Okay, but you don't have to be so crude." Carefully, she lifted the heavy bedspread. She would lie on top of the sheet with the spread covering her. That way, she'd be separated from Sam. She lay flat, her hands clasped on her chest.

"Christ, you look like a sacrificial virgin."

She dropped her hands to her sides. "Actually, I was thinking along the lines of a funeral pyre."

He chuckled as he turned out the light. "Glad to see you haven't entirely lost your sense of humor." He patted her leg just above her knee. "Get some sleep."

Relax, she told herself. She was lying in bed with a man. She tried deep breathing exercises. A man who was wearing only tighty whiteys. A skittery feeling raced along the nerve endings of her skin. She pressed her hands to her lower abdomen, to quell the fluttering.

"Daria?"

Oh, God, he was still awake.

"Listen, kid. Even if I wanted to, I couldn't, uh, perform. So, settle down, close your eyes and think of something else besides the fact that we're sleeping together."

CHAPTER THIRTEEN

Daria woke with a start. Sam's arm was around her waist and he'd pulled her back snug up against his chest. He nuzzled the side of her neck. The heat of his breath warmed her ear sending tiny electrical sparks along the nerve endings. His beard rasped against her skin, more erotic than irritating. When she tried to move away, he tightened his grasp.

"Don' go." His lips grazed her earlobe.

Sam's hand splayed across her abdomen. Through the nightshirt, his fingers burned into her flesh. Her brain was muzzy from sleep but not so muzzy that she didn't know what he was doing. He ran his big palm across her hip and then down her thigh. Those skittery feelings accelerated. If she didn't move, maybe he'd think she was still asleep. As long as he kept his hand on the outside of her nightshirt.

How the heck had his hand gotten *under* her nightshirt? And under the waistband of her underpants? She bolted out of bed.

"Huh?" Sam blinked several times. "'Smatter?"

Daria pasted a bright smile on her face. "Time to get going."

Sam groaned and flopped against the pillow. "Going? Oh, right."

She grabbed her toiletry bag and the clothes she'd laid out the night before and beat it into the bathroom. "I'll only be a minute."

She quickly took care of her needs and dressed. Again, she put on a bright smile before opening the bathroom door. She needn't have bothered with the smile. He'd fallen back to sleep. Now what?

After giving Sleeping Sam another look, she decided to pack up the car. By the time she finished, he would need his antibiotic again and some Tylenol. They had to leave before

121

the rest of the motel guests came out to their cars.

"Sam? Time to get up," she said in her best cheerful voice.

Nothing.

Holding the cup of juice and the pills in one hand, she gently shook his shoulder. "Sam, get up. We're burning daylight here."

With a groan, Sam worked his way up the headboard. Obediently, he took the pills.

"Here are some clean clothes. Let's get you into the bathroom and—"

"I can take it from here." He took the clothes and shrugged off her offer of help.

"Are you sure—"

The closed door in her face was his answer.

While he was in the bathroom, Daria made a sweep of the room to see if she'd forgotten anything. Then, she sat at the desk and spread out the map she'd brought in from the car along with the driving directions she'd gotten off the Internet at home.

She turned on the television, hoping for a weather report. The sky was overcast and she hoped it wasn't going to rain. Ordinarily, she liked rainy days on vacation because she could curl up with a book. Rain while driving made her nervous.

The local news was wrapping up at the bottom of the hour. ". . . late breaking news. Police are looking for a man who carjacked an Ohio tourist last night in downtown Manhattan."

A picture of a younger, clean-shaven Sam appeared on the screen.

The quick rap on his door brought Teller's attention from the agent's report he was supposed to be reading. That was Ryerson's job. The AD would pick today of all days to go AWOL.

"Director?" his assistant Gloria stuck her head around the privacy wall that faced the outer door, a security measure Teller rather liked. Nobody could see what he was doing or if he was in, even though getting past Gloria was a feat in itself. She guarded him better than a dragon.

"I asked not to be disturbed today," Teller said.

"But it's—"

"Hey, boss, I'm ba-ack." Sally Quinero scooted around the wall and strode into the room. The little redhead wearing a black shirt and cargo pants, as usual, and with little regard to propriety acted as if she owned the place.

"You're supposed to be in Nicaragua." Seeing his assistant still hovering in the doorway, he added, "You may go, Gloria."

He went back to reading—or not reading the boring report—and let Quinero stand there cooling her heels. He did not like anyone barging in on him. That's why he employed an assistant, a gatekeeper. Quinero needed to watch herself.

Though he didn't invite her to sit, she did anyway. Leaning back in the chair in a nonchalant pose, she propped her ankle over her knee. Damn confident, he thought. She was a tough, little broad. A damn good agent who thought Saint MacDonald walked on water.

Finally, he looked up and folded his hands on the leather blotter. "It's good you're back early. We have a problem." He took a long breath, playing for suspense. "An agent's gone off the reservation."

"What?" She dropped her foot to the floor.

Ah hah, he thought trying to disguise his satisfaction. He'd caught her totally by surprise. *Good.* She needed a comeuppance.

She gripped the arms of the chair and leaned forward. "Who?"

"Sam Jozwiak."

Daria's heart skipped then charged full-speed ahead as she watched the television in wide-eyed, open-mouthed astonishment.

"The man, believed to be Sam Johnston of Arlington, Virginia, is a white male, thirty-two years old. He is six feet, two inches tall, weighs one hundred ninety pounds and has dark hair and eyes. He may have been wounded in an earlier shootout with police. The unknown tourist was driving a dark blue Toyota Camry with Ohio plates. She is white, in her late twenties, approximately five-ten and one hundred fifty pounds. She has dark brown hair worn in a long, single braid. If anyone has information or sees the vehicle, contact the Tipster Hotline at . . ." A telephone number appeared on the screen.

"Sounds like us," Sam drawled from the doorway.

"This is awful," she cried. "We have to get out of here before anyone sees us."

"Wrong car."

"Not the wrong people." She pointed. "Your socks and shoes are on the bed."

He limped over to the bed and sat down. He gave her a sharp look. "These aren't my shoes."

"Remember? I bought them yesterday. One of your old ones was a mess." Her stomach churned just thinking about the blood-soaked shoe.

"Where are my old shoes?" he demanded.

"I wrapped them in a plastic bag and put them in the trunk. I'm going to toss them out at the first rest stop we come to today."

"No." Again, his voice was sharp. "Keep them in the trunk. I don't want anyone finding them."

She nodded. "Those bad guys could figure out where we've been and then maybe where we're going."

"You catch on quick." He looked around. "Where's the rest of the stuff that was here last night?"

"I already packed the car. We need to leave." She grabbed his bag then opened the door and looked out. "Okay, the coast is clear."

She wrapped her arm around his waist to steady him. They made it out to the car before anyone else came out. As soon as she got him inside, she grabbed a floppy hat from the back window ledge. She tried tucking her braid under it but then the hat looked like it was perched on top.

"What are you doing?" Sam asked after she'd fiddled several times with the hat. The best she could do was jam it down on her head.

"On the news announcement, they mentioned my hair."

"Don't worry about it. It's me they want."

Daria headed out onto the main road through town. Maybe she could just get a glimpse of the museum. She never thought she'd get so close and not be able to even see the building commemorating women's struggle for equal rights.

Sam lowered the visor against the morning sun. "You're going the wrong way."

"I told that nosy clerk we were going to Boston. This will fake him out. Besides, I want to see something."

"Hell. You're doing the thinking for both of us. I'm still groggy from yesterday. Between Doc's shot and those damn pain pills you gave me, it's a wonder I can think at all."

Daria experienced a twinge of guilt. She'd only done what she thought was right. "Oh, my. There it is." She pulled over to the curb.

"What?"

She pointed to the sign in front of the red brick building. "The Women's Rights National Historic Park." She leaned toward Sam so she could look out his window. She gave a longing sigh.

"You want to go in there?" he said. "We need to get to Michigan."

She pulled away from the curb. "I know. Besides, it's too early."

She took a circuitous route, so as not to pass the motel as they headed west.

"What was the big attraction back there?" he asked.

"The park commemorates the struggle for equal rights. Elizabeth Cady Stanton organized the First Women's Rights Convention there in 1848. Can you believe that? A hundred and seventy years ago. The women—and some men—signed a Declaration of Sentiments using words just like Jefferson did in the Declaration of Independence when he listed the grievances against the king. Only these were grievances against men."

"Men?"

She shot him an indignant look. "Yes, against men who kept women under their thumbs. And this was back when women not only couldn't vote but had absolutely no rights at all."

"Aw, geez," he groaned. "Nobody in their right mind would ever accuse you of knuckling under to a man."

"What?"

"If you lived back then, you probably would've marched with Stanton."

Not me, Daria thought. She was such a wimp she couldn't stand up to her brothers. Except for this trip and she hadn't exactly stood up to them. More like she ignored their objections and went anyway. She shrugged. "Sorry, I got carried away. You can take the teacher out of the classroom, but you can't keep her from lecturing."

"Must come with the territory. My mom was like that, too. While all my friends went to Disney World, Mom would take my sister and me on 'encyclopedia' vacations." He gave her a rueful grin.

"Your mother? What about your dad? Or wasn't he in the picture?"

Sam snorted. "He was there. The old man's idea of vacation was sitting out in the backyard in his skivvies, reading the sports section and pissing off the neighbors."

Daria laughed. "My dad liked to sit outside in his boxers, too. Only our nearest neighbor was a half mile away."

"Tell me more about that museum back there. You seemed to know a lot about it."

"I did research on the Internet before we left—on it and all the other places Ginnie and I planned to visit. But this is really special. I admire women who stand up for what they believe. Sure wish I had their courage."

"Getting me away from Grashenko took a lot of guts." His praise warmed her.

"I was scared to death."

"Acting in the face of fear is what courage is all about." He yawned widely. "Damn, I just got up, and I feel like I could go right back to sleep."

"Not yet. I want to swing through McDonald's and get us some breakfast. I haven't had my coffee yet."

She began to unplait her hair. Maybe she could wrap it into a knot.

"What are you doing?"

"I don't want the cashier at McDonald's to notice my

126

hair."

"Why?"

"Didn't you hear that news flash? They mentioned my braid."

"Your hair is distinctive," he said. "It was the first thing I noticed about you."

"Really?" She combed her fingers through the sections of hair to blend them.

"Oh, yeah. I wondered if it was long enough for you to sit on. By the way, you're going to get in an accident if you don't keep both hands on the wheel. Pull over." He pointed to an empty parking lot in front of a school. The low, rambling, tan brick building looked a lot like the one in which she taught. Again, she realized that even though she was hundreds of miles from home, things still looked familiar.

When she stopped the car, he pulled the scarf he'd worn as a disguise out of the pocket of her coat. He folded the scarf into a triangle and tied it under her hair, instead of under her chin. "There. Now, don't worry about your hair."

At the drive-through, she gave her order then pulled around to the first window to pay. One more person would see her and Sam together. At least, the police were looking for a different car from a different state.

While they were at the first window, Sam bent his head and opened the glove box as if searching for something inside.

"Here's your change. Drive up to the next— Omigod, your hair's beautiful," the teen-age cashier gushed.

CHAPTER FOURTEEN

Daria gave the cashier a weak smile and drove to the next window. Once she had their food, her first instinct was to floor the accelerator for a fast get-away. She quelled that notion. Nobody expected an ugly pedestrian car like the Gray Goose to peel off.

"I hate this car," she muttered as she drove away at a sedate speed.

"What?"

"Oh, never mind. I swear, when I get home I'm dumping this Grandpa-mobile for a red Camaro. Unwrap my sandwich please."

As he pulled the wrapper off her sausage-and-egg biscuit, he said, "Cops love to pull over muscle cars. Especially red muscle cars."

"Darn it, you sound like—" She broke off. She was not going to think about the boys. "Oh, never mind. I told you people would notice my hair."

Sam handed her the sandwich before unwrapping his own. "If they're busy noticing your hair, they aren't paying attention to me."

He was probably right. Maybe he was right about her obsessing over her hair, too, but she didn't want to be the reason Sam was caught.

"A red Camaro, huh?"

She smiled. "Oh, yeah. I am definitely getting a Camaro . . . someday." She remembered a movie in which Tom Cruise said "someday" was code for never. Nope. Not never. She *was* getting a new car. And she wouldn't let her brother talk her out of it.

The road stretched out, curving slightly, over gently rolling countryside. Farmland, not so different from home.

"How did the police get all that information about us?" she asked before taking a last sip of her now-cold coffee.

Sam shifted to give his good leg a respite. His right hip still hurt but not as bad as yesterday. "Grashenko has contacts here. Obviously, he knows a woman is helping me. You said you met him on the stairs, so he knows what you look like." Sam didn't like that one bit. Grashenko knew entirely too much.

"You know this man well?"

Sam laughed, ruefully. "We go back a long way. He's tried to put me out of action a few times."

"Sam!"

"I never thought he'd actually do it. I used to think he went through the motions. Like his heart wasn't in it."

"My God, Sam. You talk about him wanting to kill you as if it were nothing. As if you and he are playing a game."

That's exactly how it had been in the past, he thought. A game. One side won and then the other. Not this time, though. Too much was at stake. Sam wadded up his new jacket to use as a pillow against the window.

After several minutes, she said, "I do *not* weigh a hundred and fifty pounds."

He chuckled. "I wondered when that would hit you. It's your coat and the dress."

Like yesterday, she was wearing another loose dress, green plaid with a lime green shirt underneath only now she had on a light-weight jacket instead of the long coat.

"Are you going to tell me who you really are?" she asked.

"Who do you think I am?"

"Oh, no, none of that stuff." When he didn't respond, she blew out an exasperated breath. "All right, I'll tell you who, or what, I think you are. You're probably CIA. I don't think you're FBI because they deal with national stuff and the CIA is international."

"Hmm."

"You're not going to tell me, are you?" When he didn't say anything, she continued, "I'll bet you're part of a covert op. Or maybe a black op group."

Alarm bells went off in Sam's head. Very slowly, he said, "How do you know about black ops?"

She shot him a look. "I'm a mystery writer. I read mystery, suspense, espionage. I go to movies. You can't tell me they make up names like black ops out of thin air. I'm right, aren't I? You're from some agency that *doesn't exist*."

She had no idea how close she was. How she'd nearly sent him into cardiac arrest when she joked about telling her friends she'd rescued a spy from the Russians. Now, she was talking about black ops and agencies that didn't exist.

Of course, the Orion Agency existed. It's just that nobody had heard of it. As it should be. She was wrong about black ops. The Orion Agency was strictly intelligence gathering. No going in and blowing up things. Just get in and get out with intel that would protect America. Not that he could tell her any of that. "You have a good imagination, Daria Mason. That must come in handy for a writer."

"Okay, I get the message. This is hush-hush stuff." After a moment, she said, "So, you think that Grashenko character fed false information to the police?"

"Probably. There's something I can't figure out. With all the correct info they had on us, why were they so far off on the car?"

Daria shot him a triumphant look. "I took care of that. I bribed the parking attendant to steer wrong anyone asking about me. Actually, I was thinking about you."

"Me?"

"You scared me. I didn't want you to know who I was or come looking for me."

"Wise decision. What made you change your mind and come back for me? And don't give me that business about signs."

"It's going to sound silly," she said.

"Even if it is, I promise not to laugh."

"Okay, you know how you always went through doors first?"

"I'm the professional. I had the weapon. Even if it was a dinky, little box knife."

"The terrorists on 9-11 used box knives. They're not so dinky."

"You're right. I had a weapon, so I went first."

"I know," she said. "And that made sense. But when we got to the first floor and I said I should go first, you let me. You trusted my instincts."

"That's what made you change your mind?"

"That and the fact that you have a cute tush."

"You think my tush is cute?"

"I can't believe I said that." Her cheeks were glowing pink.

"Just how long did you look at my *tush* while I was out cold?" He was enjoying her discomfort.

"Long enough." She cleared her throat. "Now, you face looks pretty scruffy. And your hair is longer. Do you think that's enough of a disguise?"

"Good enough. The picture in that news bulletin is an old driver's license photo." One the agency used for fake ID, like the one he carried.

She tapped her fingers on the steering wheel. "I'm not so sure. They could use CGI to add a beard, mustache and various disguises. Or even to add years."

His internal antennae started vibrating. She knew about 'black ops' and agencies that 'didn't exist.' Now, she was talking about CGI—computer-generated imaging. "How do you know so much?"

"My—" She broke off. "I know someone in law enforcement. I always ask him technical questions, so my details are accurate."

That made sense. She said she was a writer and read espionage books. His suspicions died down. A bit.

"By the way, I want to ask you some questions. Research for my book. How many women work for your agency? How old do you have to be when you enlist? Is that the right word? Enlist? Oh, and what does a spy carry with him when he goes on a mission?"

"Good grief. How the hell would I know?"

"Oh, give it up, Sam. I know you're a spy. I'm not stupid."

That was for sure. In fact, she was too smart for her own good. "Daria, I can't answer your questions."

"Oh, of course. A code of silence, right?"

"Where are you coming up with this stuff? I work for a *research* agency. We do research on topics of interest to certain people."

"Uh, huh." She smiled. "Like who?"

"People high up in the government." He held up his hand. "I can't name names. Surely, you understand that."

"Right. And don't call me Shirley." She gave him a cheeky grin.

"Fell into that one, didn't I?"

"All right then, how did you end up stealing something from . . . Grashenko, is it?"

"No, I stole something from his boss. I found out something else by accident and stole that, too. Listen, kid, enough interrogation. I'm getting tired. Think I'll take a nap." Sam tried to lean against the window without putting his weight on his hip. Maybe she would take the hint and stop asking so damn many questions and jumping to conclusions.

Well, darn, Daria thought. He'd evaded her questions . . . with all the skill of a professional spy. At first, she thought he was just faking fatigue. It wasn't even nine in the morning. Then, she glanced over and saw the even rise and fall of his chest. He wasn't cataloging the scenery. He'd gone back to sleep.

She started thinking more about whatever he stole. If that Grashenko and his hulky partner were trying to retrieve it that meant *it* was something tangible. So where was it? All he had with him when she got him away from Grashenko were the clothes on his back. It followed that whatever he stole had to be small. She'd worn his jacket, picked his pants up off the floor in the doctor's exam room. She hadn't checked his shirt pocket. But if his phone could fall out, he wouldn't have kept the stolen item in his pocket.

Maybe it was surgically implanted in his hip—like in that adventure/spy movie where the guy lost his memory. She thought again. Sam said he'd been on the run for four days before she met him. He wouldn't have had time for surgery. Besides, she'd seen his hip. No fresh incisions. Just the ragged trench from a bullet.

Maybe he left it at Doc's. If he'd left the object behind, it made sense that he would try to lead the bad guys away from his hiding place.

As she drove, Daria thought about the news bulletin. If the police were involved, would they give Sam a chance to explain who he really was? If Grashenko could get the police to put out an APB, he could convince them to turn Sam over to him.

The more she thought about the broadcast, the more she worried about her hair. She'd been proud of its length and glossy shine. Other than trims, she hadn't changed her hair style since her parents died.

Mom's nightly ritual had been to brush Daria's hair. A hundred strokes. It was a private time for them. Just her and Mom. Dad often tweaked her braid and made her promise never to cut her hair. And she hadn't.

Lately, she'd begun wondering why she didn't change. All her girlfriends had gone through numerous hairstyle changes. Not Daria. Of course, most of her friends were mothers now and wore short, easy to care for styles.

She wasn't a girl of thirteen anymore. Keeping her hair the same because of a long-ago promise to her father was silly. He wouldn't have expected her to stay the same. For the past three months, she'd wondered how her hair would look if she tried something different. She even started looking at hairstyle magazines when she went in for a trim. She'd thought, looked, wondered, but never had the courage to follow through.

Teller sat back and watched the emotions cross Sally Quinero's face. Her redheaded temper was legend around the agency. In typical Quinero fashion, she leapt to her feet and slammed her palms on his polished desktop. Damn. He hated finger and palm prints on the elegant rosewood finish.

"Listen up, you weenie. Sam is no more a traitor than I am."

"Interesting way of putting it," he mused, ignoring her pejorative.

"You dumb shit. Sam's the best agent we have. They should've given him the Director's job—not some goddamn bean counter."

He sucked air. If he didn't need her to find Jozwiak, he'd fire her ass for insubordination.

"Now, Quinero. Derogatory names are uncalled for. Frankly, I can't believe what I've recently learned about

Jozwiak." He let that sink in, for a moment. "Sam hasn't checked in. Early Saturday morning, he reported finding highly sensitive information, and Yuri Grashenko was on his tail. He was scheduled on a flight out of Paris Tuesday morning—Monday night, our time—to New York. We have no trace of him after that."

Quinero sank into the visitor's chair. Apparently, she could rein in her temper enough to gather info, which made her one of his best agents. Even if she had a mouth like a sailor. "He's being chased by the Russian Mafia? Maybe he didn't lose Grashenko."

He'd thought that, too. "Why doesn't he call for extraction?"

"Maybe he can't." She got up and paced Teller's spacious office. "Maybe he lost his phone. Or, it was stolen."

"Ever hear of pay phones, Quinero? They still exist. *Or—*" He drew the word out. "—he could buy a damn burn phone from any drugstore. Listen up. We have to find Joz before he does something stupid."

She stopped and whirled around. "What do you mean by something stupid?"

"He could sell the intel to the highest bidder."

Outside Buffalo, Daria saw what she was looking for. She pulled into the Walmart parking lot. Quickly, she switched off the engine. If she didn't do this now, she wouldn't have the courage to do it later—when she gave her idea more thought. "I'll be right back," she said as she bolted out of the car. "Don't go anywhere, okay?"

Not waiting for Sam to answer, she raced into the store, quickly found everything she needed and, five minutes later, she was back in the car.

"Going to tell me what that was all about?" Sam drawled as they drove off.

"Not right now." Oh, no. She wasn't giving him an opportunity to nix this idea.

Two miles later, she saw the perfect motel. Just like Green Acres, it had been around since the 1950's and suited her needs. Unlike the chain motels, it wouldn't be hooked into a central computer system.

"It's too early to stop for the day. I told you I have to get to Michigan."

"Not stopping for the day. I've got to do something. I, uh, I need a nap. Yeah, I'm really tired, Sam, and I need to rest. So do you."

The clerk—an older man this time—gave her a smirk when she said she just wanted the room for a few hours. "Ain't no price reduction no matter how long you use the room, missy."

"That's all right." She paid him in cash and signed the registration card 'Mr. & Mrs. Thomas Matthew.' Her brother would laugh if he knew she'd used his first and middle names. Only time 'Mr. & Mrs.' would ever appear in front of his name.

She handed the card to the clerk. "I want a room in the back . . . where it's quiet."

The old geezer smirked again as he handed her the key. "Ri-ight. You just drive around. Nobody'll see your car from the road."

What was it with motel clerks? They had secret smiles as if they knew something she didn't. After she parked the car, Sam didn't need her help getting out.

"Hey, kid, are you feeling all right?"

Now that was a switch, Sam asking if *she* was okay.

"Yes, no." She leaned into the back seat and grabbed the smallest package from the store. "I don't know. It's just . . . I have to do something." Then, she remembered she'd said she was tired. "I want to go to bed."

He gave her an odd look. "All right."

She stopped him when he started toward the trunk. "I've got everything I need. We aren't going to be here that long."

As soon as she locked the motel room door, she turned around. Sam was standing right there. He put his hands on the door caging her against it. "I know last night I said I couldn't get it up but—" He smiled. "—I think I could manage a mid-day quickie."

* * *

135

Teller called the rookie into his office for an update. Hardesty kept harping on the woman with Jozwiak. Teller no more believed she was a schoolteacher from Iowa than he believed the Washington Nationals would win the pennant.

"Quinero's our best shot at finding Jozwiak," Teller said.

Disappointment crossed Hardesty's face. Teller would love to get into a poker game with him. His face was a billboard.

"Sure, boss, I understand. She has more experience. I'll turn over everything I've got to Ms. Quinero."

Teller held up a hand. "Whoa, not so fast. I want you to work a different angle. We'll use this as a test of your ability to be a field agent. An agent often works alone, has to depend only on himself."

"Excuse me, sir. I mean no disrespect, but didn't Mr. MacDonald have the agents work in teams? Wouldn't that be more efficient?"

For a year, the old-timers had thrown Saint MacDonald in Teller's face. The man was a goddamn legend. That's what came of being in a job too long. Like Hoover at the FBI. Men like that thought they were god, and everyone treated him as such.

"What does this say?" Teller pointed to the nameplate on his desk.

"Bart Teller, Director," Hardesty read.

Teller knew he got the point when a red flush crept up his neck. "Let's get something straight, rookie. I'm in charge. If MacDonald's methods worked, he'd still be sitting in this chair."

"Yes, sir. Sorry, sir."

"Okay." Teller shot his cuffs, enjoying the play of light on his gold cufflinks with a diamond in one corner of each. "As I said, Quinero is our best bet. She and Jozwiak are lovers so—"

Hardesty held up a tentative finger. "Excuse me, sir. They used to be lovers. When I did a deep background check on him, I found out their affair—which wasn't very long-lived—ended six years ago. Most people think—"

Teller blew out a breath. "You are more long-winded than a politician. Listen up. Quinero will find him. I want you to follow her."

"Sir?"

"I've got her writing up a report on her trip to Nicaragua. That'll keep her busy for at least a couple of hours. While she's here, you do the works. Bug her condo. Tap her land line. Use her cell phone to track her."

Hardesty's eyes bugged out of his head. "Sir? She's one of us."

Teller leveled a hard look. "The security of our homeland is at stake." He leaned forward conspiratorially. "I'm trusting you to keep what I tell you in the strictest of confidence. It's possible Joz is a rogue agent. Quinero may be helping him."

"What!" Daria dodged under Sam's arm and went to stand in the middle of the room. "What are you talking about?"

"Oh, sweetheart, I knew you were horny last night, so if you want to do it now . . ."

"A quickie? Are you talking about sex? Are you nuts?" She dropped the bag on the bed. "Oh, my goodness. That's what that old man at the front desk must have thought." She sank onto the bed and buried her burning face in her hands.

Sam limped over to sit next to her. "Nothing to be ashamed of, sweetheart. Everyone has urges. Thanks for getting the condoms at Walmart. I don't have any on me."

She bolted upright. "Condoms?" she shrieked. He thought she bought condoms?

"I mean, it's not like you have a lot of opportunities with those brothers of yours and all," he continued.

"The boys? Oh, no." She buried her face in her hands again. How was she going to explain to them about the police looking for her? Better yet, how was she going to face them after she—

"I'll do my best to make it good for you." Sam patted her back. "But you know I'm not exactly running on all thrusters here."

"Thrusters?" She jumped up. "Thrusters?"

Red crept up his neck. "Okay, poor choice of words."

What crazy thoughts had gone through his head while she was registering for the room? She fisted her hands on her hips. "Look, Sam Johnston, in case you forgot, not only are some demented Russians hunting for you, so are the police. We do *not* have time for a quickie."

"Then, why did you stop in the middle of the day at the No-Tell Motel?"

"That is not the name of this place. What kind of a name is that?"

Sam groaned. "Just tell me what's going on, okay? I'm too tired to think anymore." He slowly stretched out his leg.

"Personal stuff." She didn't want to tell him what she planned to do. If he was anything like her brothers—and she suspected he had some of their less desirable traits—he was going to pitch a fit.

"Sam, I'll need to be in the bathroom for a while so if you want to use it first . . ."

Something flickered in his eyes. "Sorry for the misunderstanding. I get it now. You don't have to be embarrassed. Give me a minute and the bathroom's all yours."

When the door to his office slammed against the wall, Teller nearly dropped his cell phone. Quinero rounded the security wall. "What the f—"

An ex-Marine security guard and Gloria barreled the same wall before Quinero got to Teller's desk. She sat in the visitor chair just as nonchalantly as before.

The guard had his weapon drawn. He motioned to Sally. "Assume the position."

"She threatened me, sir," Gloria the Gatekeeper babbled at the same time. "I wouldn't let her in, and she pulled a gun on me. She was going to shoot me if I didn't let her—"

While Teller gaped, Quinero smiled. "My report is finished."

God, she was a bitch. Arrogant, reckless and, he hated to admit, a damn good agent. "Out," he said to his admin.

"Everything's under control," he said to the guard. Then, he turned to Quinero. "Next time just wait until I'm available."

"Guess you're available now, huh?" She smiled again.

The guard shook his head at her. "One of these days, Quin . . ."

"I need info on Sam," she said as soon as the door closed behind the guard and Gloria. "The rendezvous he missed, his contact, the nature of the intel he brought back."

Teller narrowed his eyes. "Why would you need to know that?"

"It will give me a starting point, a strategy."

"I already told you. He brought intel out of Russia, missed a rendezvous and hasn't contacted anyone. Or has he?" Teller arched his eyebrow and let that sink in.

Her mouth gaped. "You think he contacted *me*?"

He folded his hands and waited.

"Hell, no." Quinero's eyes flashed in anger. "Wouldn't I report that?"

"I don't know. Would you? You two are pretty tight. Maybe you're covering for him."

She jumped out of the chair, just like before. Only instead of just leaning on his desk, she reached across and grabbed a handful of his shirt and tie. "Listen up, you goddamn son-of-a-bitch. Sam is the most loyal agent we have. The most trustworthy. And don't you ever question my loyalty again."

For such a small woman, her grip was so strong black started edging in from his peripheral vision. He was going to die. Right there in his office. All the security in the world wasn't going to help him if they were down the hall.

Just when he thought she was going to choke the life out of him, she released her grip, took a deep breath and blew it out. He struggled to suck in air then covered up his fright by straightening his Hermes tie and his Armani shirt. He doubted the wrinkles would come out. If he didn't need her . . .

While she strode to the door then to the window overlooking a courtyard and back to the visitor chair, he held onto his own temper. He had a lot of experience doing so. Every time his wife went off about the time he spent on the job. Or his latest purchase. Well, damn it, she expected him to dress for success then begrudged him the money to do so. Hell, she was loaded yet nickel-and-dimed him to death. He was going to fix her, by God. Just not yet.

"Why did Sam go to New York?" Quinero's question brought him back to his more immediate problem.

"Because I said so." His harsh tone made her sit up.

"All right then. I need to go to New York. I've done as much here as I can."

He had a good idea she would delve into the case without him asking. Typical Quinero. He was right. Her relationship with Joz made her eager to prove he wasn't a rogue. She would find him.

"Have Gloria book you on—"

Quin laughed. "Gloria doesn't like me much. She'll book me on a flight to hell, with stopovers in Hades and Gehenna."

"Do you blame her? What is wrong with you? Pulling a gun on my assistant?"

"I'll take the agency jet."

"No."

"It will be quicker," she continued.

"No."

"I'll be more flexible following Sam's trail."

"I said no."

"C'mon, Bartley. Give me the keys."

Teller's face flushed. He hated his first name. He was sure she used it on purpose. "Do you realize how much it costs to fuel that plane?"

"You're worried about money when Sam's out there in danger?"

"Why do you think I was hired?" He gave her a smug smile. "To get this agency's budget under control."

"You'll probably ration bullets next," she muttered.

"Good idea, Quin. Remind me at the next staff meeting."

She rolled her eyes. "Please. Let me have the jet."

He couldn't believe she was pleading. He rather liked that.

"Either fly commercial or take the bus."

She twisted her mouth, apparently accepting defeat. "Who else is working on finding Sam? We should coordinate, compare notes."

"It's just you, Quinero."

She gaped at him. "That's stupid. It makes no sense to—"

"When they approve *your* appointment as Director, you can make the decisions." *That'll be a cold day in hell.* "We need to keep a tight lid on this. Sam's been a good operative. We don't want to tarnish his rep if it's not warranted."

"I told you Sam is not a rogue. He would never—"

"Yeah, yeah. You would say that. So, listen up. We need to find him pronto. The fewer people who know about this debacle the better." When she got up to leave, he said sharply, "Sit down."

She shot him a startled look. Good. The agents needed to know who was in charge. She sat.

"The next time you pull a stupid stunt like you did with Gloria, I will assign you to watch paint peel in Hamtramck." He let that sink in before adding, "If you ever attack me again, I'll ship you down to Gitmo."

Sam jerked awake, his heart racing. He was still shaking from the dream. He'd been running down a long, narrow alley toward a far opening. As hard and as fast as he ran, the opening never got closer. But those chasing him did. He heard their pounding steps—like jackals after wounded prey. He knew they would catch him this time.

The question was who were *they*? It didn't feel like the Russians. Then, who?

He couldn't ever remember falling asleep so much. He'd stopped a bullet before and never felt this wiped out. Of course, he'd been a lot younger then. Running through Europe on sheer adrenaline for four days prior to nearly getting caught back home didn't help. Add in jetlag and something had to give. He was enough of a realist to know sleep was his body's way of mending itself.

The room was silent. Had Daria left? He wouldn't blame her if she did. If the police caught her with him and she denied she was kidnapped, they'd think it was Stockholm

Syndrome.

The bathroom door was open. He rolled over to check the rest of the room and—

"Jesus H. Christ!" He bolted upright, ignoring the stab of pain in his hip. "Who the hell are you?"

"Tipster Hotline."

"Well, like, there's a reward or something, isn't there, for like information about that guy you're looking for? The one wanted for carjacking."

"Yes. Did you see him?"

"Not exactly. See, yesterday, this like bodacious babe walks into my motel, ya know? I mean, like it's not *my* motel. I just like work there. But, anyways, this babe wants to rent a room and I mean she's like really a hot babe. Smokin', ya know, man?"

"Your point?"

"I figure she's just one of those cautious women traveling alone so she says her husband's out in the car." Snicker. "So, like I go on down to her room later on, like when I figure she's like getting ready for bed, ya know?"

"You have not explained why you are calling."

The caller plunged on. "So, I knock on her door and when she answers this like dude calls out from the bathroom and I'm like, holy shit, she really does have a husband and then I see on TV about a carjacking and the woman is real tall and has a long braid."

"Yes?"

"The babe who was here last night was tall and had a long braid."

Yuri Grashenko smiled.

CHAPTER FIFTEEN

The slinky blonde with wild curly hair rose from the chair in the corner and walked toward him. She wore skin-tight jeans and an equally tight red shirt. "Sam?"

He was hallucinating. The woman sounded like Daria. A tiny angel charm nestled in the hollow of her throat above the low-cut shirt. An angel just like Daria's, but—

"Sam, I'm glad you're awake. We can leave now."

"Oh, shit. Where's your hair?"

She self-consciously touched the froth of blonde curls that brushed her shoulders. "No time to talk. We have to get on the road again. I needed—"

"I thought you needed the bathroom because you were constipated not because you wanted to turn yourself into a—a floozy."

"Constipated? You thought—" Her cheeks matched the color of the ultra-snug top and the slash of lipstick across her mouth. What happened to her fresh-scrubbed look? Good Lord, her eyelashes were all gunked up.

Sam swung his legs off the bed. He planted his elbows on his knees and buried his face in his hands. "Your beautiful hair," he moaned.

Gone. She'd cut it off. Instead of long and wavy from the braid, her hair was sticking out like she'd stuck her finger in a light socket. And it was the brassiest color he'd seen since his sister and her girlfriends experimented on each other in ninth grade. She'd even replaced her gold studs with large silver hoops that dangled from her ears.

"This is a good disguise, Sam. Come on, admit it." She walked toward him, unsteady on her feet.

He looked down and saw why. Instead of cute penny loafers, she was wearing black boots with three-inch heels. He looked up those mile-long legs. "Your jeans are too damn tight. That penny in your pocket was minted in Denver in

143

1994."

She tried to wriggle her hand into the pocket before she gave him a suspicious look. "I don't have a penny in my pocket."

"Well, if you did, I could read it."

She blew out a breath. "You sound just like Jimmy. What a wet blanket."

"Who's Jimmy?"

She fluttered her hand. "Never mind."

He reluctantly got to his feet. He couldn't believe he'd slept through her going out to the car for the clothes she must have bought at Walmart. "Well, nobody would ever say you weigh a hundred and fifty if they saw you in that outfit."

"Really?" She gave him a quick, uncertain smile. "Well, uh, we should leave."

"Give me a minute." He limped into the bathroom, bemoaning the loss of the sweet innocent girl he'd shanghaied into getting him away from Grashenko. Not bothering to close the door, he splashed cold water on his face and blotted it with the only towel available. The water helped. He hung the towel over the bar.

A glance in the mirror showed a haggard face. He looked like shit. Felt like it, too. He scrubbed a hand across the heavy growth on this face. As a disguise, this worked. Even though he didn't want to admit it, so did hers.

What the hell was she thinking to ruin her beautiful hair like that?

"Boss, you gotta listen to this."

Teller looked up from Quinero's report on her recruiting efforts in Nicaragua. Damn stuff was boring as hell so he welcomed Hardesty's interruption. Still, he had to make sure the rookie understood how things worked.

He held up his finger for Hardesty to wait, skimmed a couple of paragraphs then looked up. "What do you have?"

The rookie set a recording device on Teller's desk.

"Careful. Do not scratch the finish." He'd paid handsomely—rather, the agency paid handsomely—for the highly-polished rosewood desk. Last year when he first walked into his new office, he'd taken one look at MacDonald's battered monstrosity and ordered it hauled away. A director wouldn't be taken seriously unless he looked the part. And Teller always made sure he looked the part— what he wore, what he drove and especially his office furniture.

Hardesty gave him a quick look of chagrin before carefully moving the device to the leather desk pad.

"I assume since you barged in here while Gloria was at lunch that this is important." Teller raised his eyebrow.

"Very. Just listen." He started the recording.

"How the hell did you get in?" That sounded like Sally Quinero.

"Wouldn't be much of a spook if I couldn't do a little B & E."

"Is that Ryerson?" Teller asked.

Hardesty nodded. "The AD doesn't sound very sick, does he?"

"How've you been, sweetheart?"

"Don't you sweetheart me." It sounded like she stomped across the floor. Hardesty's bugs were more sensitive than Teller thought.

"I couldn't reach you this morning. They told me you were sick. I was worried about you, old man."

"I tried to catch you when got back from Nicaragua. You'd better check your cell phone. I called, but you were unavailable."

"Yeah, well that's the message I got when I tried calling you." There was a pause. *"Shit. My goddamn cell is dead. That never fucking happens."*

"Tsk, tsk," Ryerson chided. *"You still haven't cleaned up your language."*

"Fuck my language, old man. What's this bullshit about Sam and why didn't you answer your cell? After your lecture, you'd damn well better not have a dead battery, too."

"Not dead. I got rid of it in case it was bugged."

"What? Your phone is being monitored?"

"It's a possibility."

"Who knows your number . . ." Her voice trailed off. *"Besides the agency."*

"Always knew you were a smart girl. Be careful."

Crap, Teller thought. She might figure out her cell was bugged. He glared at Hardesty who shrugged.

"You haven't answered my question about Sam."

"I don't know." Ryerson sounded dejected. Or tired. Yeah, probably tired. The man was pushing Medicare age. He should have retired with MacDonald. Damn Powers That Be kept him to ease the transition, so they said. Teller figured they kept him on as a safeguard in case he—Teller—screwed up. Damn politicians.

"What do you mean you don't know? You're the assistant director."

"I didn't realize Teller had taken over Sam's op until two days ago."

"Hang on. Teller ran the op? No wonder it got fu—screwed up."

Hardesty cringed. "Sorry, boss."

After Quinero's crack, Teller wondered how she'd like a post in Nuevo Laredo. He heard the drug cartels just loved female Federales.

"I knew they were going to phase me out but not like this." Ryerson.

"Is that what you think is happening? That this is an elaborate scheme to get you to retire? Is Sam just a pawn in some weird power play? Teller ordered me to find him."

"Why do you think he had your place bugged?"

"Pause it." Teller glared at the rookie. "How the hell did Ryerson know? Did he catch you?"

"No, sir. I got in and out clean."

"Hmph. Ryerson's playing with us. He knows her place is bugged. Shit."

"Then, why would they keep talking?"

"They want me to know. They're taunting me. Damn agents." Teller blew out a breath. So much for that strategy. "Play the rest."

"Just a little bit left."

"Teller is using me to find Sam to arrest him." The incredulity in Quinero's voice sounded as fake as the conversation that preceded it.

"I think she's onto you, boss."

Teller rolled his eyes. "Ya think?"

"Sorry, boss. I have another idea."

"It sure as hell better work out better than bugging her phone."

Hardesty had the good sense not to point out that bugging Quinero's home and phone wasn't his idea.

"I'm listening," Teller said. "Make it good."

"I do not look like a floozy."

"She speaks." Sam had been getting the silent treatment for the past thirty miles.

When she walked into the restroom of the old Guttschenheimer Department Store, she made him remember why he'd gotten into this business. She looked honest, decent, unspoiled. A prime example of what he worked to safeguard, to keep untouched by the ugliness of the world. He hated her new look. Sexy as hell. But then, he'd been turned on by her former appearance. Hell, no matter what she wore, she turned him on.

"I wanted to look like Sandy in *Grease*," she said softly.

He remembered that movie. "Goody-Two-Shoes and the Greaser. You used to look like her. Not anymore."

Daria shook her head and the blonde curls bounced. So, did the earrings. "No. At the end. Where she turns herself into what she thinks he wants."

"Dumb idea."

"I agree," she said. "Sandy should have been true to herself."

"Not her. You. Cutting and bleaching your hair was a really dumb idea."

"Ouch."

"You didn't think *I* wanted you to look like that, did you?"

She blew out an exasperated sigh. "Of course not. I wanted to look different."

"You look different, all right. Your own mother wouldn't recognize you." At her sudden silence, Sam grimaced. "Sorry. I forgot your mother is, uh, gone."

"You can say *dead*. My mother has been dead for a long time."

Sam winced but plunged on. "You looked fine before. Fresh, wholesome."

"Right. Every girl wants to hear she's wholesome," she spit out the word. "I'd rather look sexy."

She was sexy last night. And totally unaware of how she affected him. Especially, when she bent over to dry her hair, and he got a good look at her pink-flowered panties. Lying next to her in a too-small king bed had been agony. And not because of being shot, twice. He'd wanted Daria. Because of the way she looked and acted—unconsciously innocent, no, guileless—she brought out his protective instincts. And something else.

The smokin' hot babe sitting next to him brought out lust instead of protectiveness. If they shared a bed tonight, it wouldn't only be for sleeping.

"What are your students going to think when you waltz into the classroom looking like . . . like this?"

"I did it to protect you," she said indignantly.

"Oh, no. You're not laying this on me."

She continued as if he hadn't spoken. "I don't expect your gratitude."

"You aren't going to get it."

"I think this is a great disguise. Nobody will recognize me. You said so yourself."

She was right. As disguises went, it was a good one. Nobody would connect the new Daria Mason with the woman described in the news bulletin.

"Why the hell didn't you just buy a wig?" he asked.

"I figured no half measures," she said. "Since I was going to change, I decided to go all the way."

"You didn't have to make the change so . . . permanent."

"Yes, I did. I'm not going back to being Goody-Two-Shoes. Do you know what it's like living in a town where everyone knows everything about you, including the color of your underwear?"

"White cotton. Tiny pink flowers."

"What!" She swerved and nearly ran them off the road.

What in heaven's name made him blurt that out? He'd be damned if he dug himself into a deeper hole. "I, uh, I'm guessing that's what you wear."

She shot him a suspicious glance.

They drove for several minutes before she said, "You're right. I didn't change just because of you, to protect you. Although that was the impetus," she hastened to add. "I, uh, I did it for me."

"Why?"

"I am so tired of everybody assuming I'm a *good* girl."

"What's wrong with being a good girl? Most guys like good girls. They lust after bad girls but marry the good ones. Just like girls do with guys. They want to walk on the wild side before settling down with a *nice* guy."

"Maybe *I* want to be lusted after." She lifted her chin.

"If you only knew . . ." he said under his breath.

"Pardon?"

"We could have come up with a disguise without cutting your hair." He groaned. "Your beautiful hair."

"Oh, give it a rest. My hair's gone and that's that."

Sam bolted upright. "Your braid. What did you do with it? And the hair coloring paraphernalia?" Evidence that they'd been in that crummy motel. Evidence the maid might report, if she heard the news.

"In the wastebasket . . . at the motel." She gave him a startled look. "Not my braid but the coloring stuff. I—I should have bundled it up and brought it with us, shouldn't I?"

What wastebasket? He should have seen it. He sank back against the seat. "Too late for shoulda/woulda's. It's done. We can't go back for it."

"Why not? We haven't come that far. I could just tell the old man I left something in the room and—"

"And he's supposed to recognize you . . . how?"

Her shoulders slumped. "You're right. Maybe the maid won't think anything of it."

"If the news is kept local—in New York. *If* the city police don't bring in the state police. *If* they haven't already brought

149

in the FBI because they think I kidnapped you. *If* it isn't a slow day news-wise and it doesn't hit the national networks. *If* the maid is too tired and doesn't listen to or watch the news."

"Oh, my. I'm sorry, Sam. I am so sorry." She sounded like she was ready to cry.

"Forget it." In the series of screw-ups dominating this mission, his negligence in not checking the bathroom was probably the least of his worries. "What did you mean *not* your braid? You didn't leave that behind?"

"No. I'm donating it to an organization that makes wigs for people who've lost their hair due to chemo treatments."

He started wondering if cutting her hair was really a spur of the moment decision. Who would think of saving their shorn hair for such a noble cause? Unless that person had been thinking about it ahead of time.

They'd just passed the sign for the city limits of Erie, Pennsylvania when he felt the car slow. "I told you we can't go back to that motel."

"I know." She pulled into a Burger King. "I need lunch. It's after two, and I'm starving. Do you think it's safe for you to go into the restaurant? Or do you want me to bring the food out?"

Sam realized he was hungry, too, but he wasn't going inside a restaurant. "Let's put some more miles between us and that news bulletin." He pulled out his wallet while telling her what he wanted to eat.

"We can settle up later," she said.

He stopped her from opening her door. "You've been paying for everything—food, gas, motels. Even my clothes. I should have given you money before." He handed her some bills.

"Holy cow! This is three hundred dollars." She tried to hand it back. "I don't—"

Sam closed her fingers around the bills. "Just say thanks and go get our food. It's going to take me a while to work the kinks out so I can walk to the restroom."

He watched her saunter across the parking lot toward the door. The jeans clung tight to her rounded butt. Oh, mama.

In those boots, she had a different walk. A sexy walk. Others thought so, too. One guy almost ran into a car. Another tripped over the curb trying to get to the door to open it for her. She gave them that sweet smile of hers—so at odds with her new get-up. And that smile only encouraged them. One guy was chatting with her.

Sam clenched his fists. Damn. He should have gone in with her. She was an innocent who was suddenly a lust-inspiring sex object. She needed protection.

Right. A lot of protection he would be. He could barely walk.

"You are actually getting on the turnpike?" Sam asked as Daria sailed down the entrance ramp. She accelerated to match the speed of traffic. He was glad to see she wasn't timid about merging. It drove him crazy when people slowed down at the bottom of the ramp. Then, he noticed her knuckles on the steering wheel. Paper white.

"We have to use the expressway to get through Cleveland quickly. Surface streets will be too slow. Would you check the map?" She didn't take her eyes off the road or her hands off the wheel. She jerked her head toward the map on the seat between them. "Tell me how to get to US-6."

Sam checked. "I-90 splits. Follow US-2 and that will get us to 6. Or you could just stay on 90."

Traffic was heavy. She cautiously maneuvered the Buick into the middle lane and there she stayed. She had lanes on either side of her for vehicles that wanted to pass and away from the traffic getting on and off. Very sensible. Someone taught her well. But, Sam didn't think she had much experience driving in rush hour traffic. If she thought this was bad, he couldn't wait to see her tackle Chicago traffic.

But, of course, he wouldn't. She was leaving him in Michigan and heading through the Windy City all by herself.

Her caution made him edgy. She obediently drove the speed limit even though the traffic was going five to ten miles an hour faster. Cars switched lanes around her and frequently cut her off. He decided that watching road signs was better than digging his fingers into the armrest.

151

As they passed one particular sign, he heard a deep sigh and glanced over. Her shoulders were slumped.

"What was that for?" he asked. Among other downtown attractions, the blue sign had listed the Rock & Roll Hall of Fame. He recalled hearing that deep sigh before—in front of the Women's Rights National Historic Park. "Get in the right lane," he ordered.

She promptly obeyed and earned a horn blast for her maneuver. "Why? Did you see something? Is someone following us?"

"Get off at the exit."

She did.

"Now, turn right and follow the signs."

They were stopped at a traffic light. She looked around. "Signs to what?"

"Where you wanted to go. The Rock & Roll Hall of Fame."

She slapped him. "You idiot! You nearly gave me heart failure."

He couldn't believe she actually took her hand off the steering wheel to slap him. He rubbed his shoulder. "The light's green. You can go. Now, be a good girl and turn before those people behind you get really pissed."

She turned. On a long exhale, she said, "Sam, we don't have time. That was very thoughtful but—"

"Just cruise past. At least, you'll be able to say you *saw* it."

When they got there, she pulled in front and looked longingly at the glass and steel building. Then, she swallowed and drove away. "Another time. There will be another time. I'll make sure of it." She sounded as if she were trying to convince herself.

"Sure you will. You can be one determined lady when you want to do something. What else is on your list of things to see on your way home?"

"The Gateway Arch in St. Louis," she said reluctantly.

"St. Louis isn't that far from Iowa," Sam said. "Why haven't you ever been there?"

"One of my brothers has a thing about heights. He'd never admit to being scared, mind you." She chuckled. "So, we never went."

"What about Chicago? Were you going to go to the top of the Sears Tower?"

She gave him a cheeky grin. "Been there, done that. Senior class trip. Only it's called the Willis Tower now."

CHAPTER SIXTEEN

"You have a knack." Sam surveyed the motel room.

Daria set her tote and his bag on the low dresser that doubled as a TV stand. "How so?" Without waiting for his response, she headed for the bathroom.

He hated that she had to bring his duffel in from the car. She'd parked in front of the door so he didn't have too far to walk. He could manage not to limp for three or four steps but not if he carried anything.

"This is the second ugliest room I've ever seen," he said to the closed bathroom door. The winner of the Ugly Room Prize was the one they'd stayed in last night. Even the No-Tell Motel in Buffalo had better décor.

When she came out, she shot him an accusing look. "Why didn't you tell me my hair looks like the Wrath of God?" She unzipped one of the pockets of her giant purse, pulled out a brush and went back into the bathroom. She didn't close the door this time.

"And have you accuse me of spoiling your disguise?" he called after her.

When she came out again, her hair was even worse. "It looks like a Brillo pad," she moaned. "Maybe I shouldn't have used that instant curl product."

He tried to hide his smile. "It's not so bad," he lied. "Besides, doesn't that stuff wash out?"

"I hope so." She walked across the room to the window. "This place is okay."

Beige walls, brown carpet. The bedspreads and matching drapes were brown, orange and yellow. "The Wayback Machine threw us into the 1970's," Sam drawled.

Daria opened the window then adjusted the drapes. A fresh breeze dispelled the faint mustiness of a little-used room. "Wayback Machine? Don't tell me. You're a Rocky and Bullwinkle fan." She licked her index finger and made a short downward stroke in the air. "That's another one."

"Another one what?" Sam had parked himself in the lone chair when she went into the bathroom. Now, he stretched out his right leg. Still sore but not as bad as the day before. "Was that some kind of scorekeeping?"

"Yes. I'm counting the ways you and my brothers are alike. I can't believe you like that old cartoon show. It is so corny. Next, you'll say you like the Three Stooges." She sat on the edge of the double bed nearest the window and began taking off her boots. "Ah, relief." She wiggled her toes before peeling off her thin socks.

"And what's wrong with the Three Stooges?"

"It's gotta be a guy thing. You and my brothers." She made another mark in the air, accompanied by a snort of disgust.

"Moose and Squirrel are classic television. So are the Stooges."

"Whatever. Listen, I don't care what this place looks like. It's clean." She yawned a great, jaw-cracking yawn. "The lady at the check-in desk said her parents opened the motel in 1954. She and her husband are retired and run it now. I would have gotten the entire history of the place if I hadn't said we were exhausted from driving from Sioux City. By the way, we're headed for Boston. Again."

"Good job." Sam leaned forward, his hands dangling between his knees. "How do you do it?"

"What?"

"How do you get people to talk to you so easily?" he asked. "Like the valet at the hotel in New York who faked out Grashenko. The one you said was studying . . ."

"Journalism. He's from Minnesota. His mother didn't want him to—"

"See? That's what I mean. Just like the couple who own this flea trap. People tell you their life stories."

"It's a gift," she said dryly.

"You'd make a good spy." He instantly regretted saying that. Words didn't just pop out of his mouth. He was never careless, and he never used the word *spy*.

She appeared startled. "What do you mean?"

"Are you staking out that bed?"

"Yes. The other one is closer to the bathroom, so you won't have to walk so far."

"That's considerate."

"Right. I'm a real considerate girl. Quit changing the subject. I want to know why you said I'd make a good spy. You can't just toss that into a conversation then drop it."

She would make a good agent. She had all the right instincts. She lulled people with her open, honest look. If she had a conniving bone in her body, it was well hidden.

"People talk to you," he said. "You smile at them, and they just spill their guts."

"That's a charming image." She flopped backward on the bed. "I'm so glad I'm not driving another mile."

He glanced at the bed closest to the bathroom then at hers. "I take it we're not sharing a bed tonight?"

"You wish."

"Hey, is that any way to talk to a wounded man? How about a little TLC?"

"You've had your TLC. I think my thigh is numb from your head resting on it while you were sleeping."

Sam waggled his eyebrows. "What makes you think I was sleeping?"

That stopped her for a moment. "You drooled on my new jeans."

"*If* I drooled, it was because of those jeans. Any guy would drool."

"Don't go there, Johnston." Daria threw her arm across her eyes. "Good grief, I can see the lane marker behind my eyes."

"You done good, kid. I didn't expect you to keep driving after dinner. Where are we? Toledo?"

"Almost. I got a second wind, but it ran out right after Sandusky. Like you in Brooklyn. I still can't believe how you drove away from that doctor's house. You'd better let me check your leg and, uh, hip. To make sure the stitches are all right."

"No stitches. Doc used Super Glue."

"What?" She lifted her arm to peer under it at him.

"They've got this glue-like substance that's better than stitches to hold skin together. Doesn't leave a scar from the stitches."

"I can see how scars would worry you." Her droll sense of humor always snuck up on him. "Especially on your behind."

"Don't be a smart ass—aleck. Doc glued me together."

"Amazing." She yawned. "I can't believe how tired I am."

Even in the dim light, he could see shadows under her eyes. And that made him feel like shit. He thought about putting her on a plane in Detroit tomorrow and borrowing her car to drive to Mac's boat. Reluctantly, he discarded that idea. It would take him twice as long to get there, if he made it at all. His butt and leg were still sore. But, that wasn't the only reason. He kept dozing off. The sound of wheels on pavement had such a lulling effect he didn't trust himself not to fall asleep at the wheel.

She had to be exhausted from all the driving she'd done that day. He made a rough estimate of over four hundred miles, which wasn't that far except for a novice driving solo. He could feel her tension halfway across the room. He limped over and sat on the edge of her bed. "Scoot over."

She dropped her arm. "We are not sleeping in the same bed."

"You have a suspicious mind, Daria Mason. I was planning on giving you one of my famous backrubs."

She eyed him. "Famous?"

"World class." When he put his hand on her shoulder, she jumped. "Easy. Your muscles are tight. Now, roll over. I promise I have no impure thoughts in my head."

"Impure thoughts?" She chuckled. "Were we in the same religion class?"

"Sister Horseface. I mean, Hortense. Fourth grade preparation for confession class where we learned about *sin*." He waggled his eyebrows. "We learned so many new ways to be bad that year. Horseface took the boys while Sister Immaculata took the girls. They got the better deal."

Daria rolled over on her stomach. "No, we didn't. We learned about occasion of sin and how not to be one."

He had her scoot higher on the bed and then toward the middle until she was where he wanted her. Not exactly where he wanted her but since he couldn't have her naked and holding her arms out to him, he got her situated for a massage.

"Oh, yeah." He began to rub her shoulders. "You girls are such temptors. Boys have no chance *not* to sin around you."

"That's right. Blame it all on us." Her voice was muffled against the pillow. "Take no responsibility for your own actions."

"Would you settle down? You're spoiling all my hard work by tensing up like that. Relax and let my magic fingers do their work." He worked on a particularly tight spot on the side of her neck. She had three light freckles below her neck, about where a tank top would expose her skin to the sun.

"I hate to complain," she said. "But that hurt."

"No pain, no gain." He eased up and moved to a different spot. He could always come back to that knot later. Her skin was soft, smooth. He had to be careful to keep his touch impersonal. "Put your arms down next to your sides. I don't want you to get any funny ideas about what I'm going to do next."

"Sounds ominous. What are you going to do next?" Was she laughing at him?

"I'm just going to move your shirt. It's in my way."

He slid the scoop neck of her stretchy shirt down her arms. And saw that her bra matched her shirt. Fire engine red. It was a wonder his fingers weren't singed.

"And why would I get *funny* ideas? I believe you also moved my bra strap."

"Mmm. So I have. Must have been in the way."

He worked his hands down her back, paying attention to the tight muscles under her shoulder blades. Even though he'd slid the straps of her bra down her arms, the rest of the bra was in his way.

On second thought, she needed to trust him more, so he went back to that knot along her neck. Gently, firmly, he worked until the tension was gone.

Her back invited kisses. Butterfly kisses along each vertebra. All the way down to her waist then beneath her jeans. And there would go all her trust. He unhooked her bra.

When she stiffened, he said softly, "It was in my way."

"Gee, how did I know you were going to say that?"

"Is that cynicism I hear? What happened to the sweet, innocent Iowa farmgirl I coerced into helping me escape the Russian Mafia?" Sam alternated using his fingertips and the heel of his hand in the massage.

"She took a hike. What are you doing?" Her voice held a tinge of panic as he slipped her left arm out of the sleeve.

"Making you more comfortable." Before she could protest, he added, "You looked like you were in a straightjacket. Now, relax." He leaned across her and pulled the sleeve off her other arm.

He could see the half-moons of the sides of her flattened breasts. Perfection. Just like her back. A small mole decorated the side of her left breast. If he kissed it, she would probably deck him and storm out to the car, leaving him to fend for himself when Grashenko showed up.

That wasn't the only reason. Despite her new appearance—blonde hair, sexy shirt and jeans—she was the same Daria Mason from Small Town America inside. The teacher, the writer, the Good Samaritan, the girl who took care of her little brothers. The good girl a man took home to meet Mama. Not the kind of girl to have a one-night stand with a washed-up spy.

He slowed the circles he was making down her spine. Her breathing deepened, became rhythmic. When he lifted his hand, she moaned in protest. So, he went back to torturing himself. He smoothed her back in long strokes, more caressing than therapeutic. Sweat broke out on his forehead. Dangerous territory. He sat back. Look, but no more touching, he told himself.

She didn't protest this time. She didn't even move.

"Daria?" he whispered. "I'm done."

Still she didn't move. She was asleep.

He was done, all right. Done for. He bent and pressed his lips to one of the sweet freckles. No more. Just . . .

He kissed the spot below her ear. That was more than he should have. Desire surged through him with intensity so strong it was all he could do not to roll her over and push her shirt down to her waist. He would kiss that sweet mole and then—

Sam Jozwiak was going straight to hell.

* * *

Daria was having a wonderful dream. Sam was kneeling over her and kissing the side of her neck. So sweet, so tender. His mouth had more magic than his fingers. His tongue caressed her ear. She groaned at the sweet ecstasy.

He kissed the first bump of her spine. His tongue worked its magic on the space between the vertebrae. He did the same for each bump and space. She wanted to feel his magic hands and lips on her breasts. She tried to roll over. Her legs twitched but didn't move. She tried to tell him what she wanted. No words, only a small sound, came out.

"Daria?"

How could his voice sound so far away when his lips were hovering over her back?

"Daria, why don't you get ready for bed?"

She opened one eye. Sam was sitting at a small table, the road atlas open in front of him. He was across the room. Not sitting on the bed next to her. He wasn't kissing her neck and back. She closed her eyes in mortification. She'd been having an erotic dream, starring Sam Johnston.

She must have fallen asleep while he was rubbing her back. She rolled over and realized he'd slipped her arms into the sleeves and pulled her shirt back into place. But, something felt . . . different. He'd he taken off her bra. And she slept through it.

She glanced around the room. A small bundle of red lay on the nightstand between the two beds. Weren't they two of a kind? Both sleeping while the other removed clothing. She wished she had the nerve to ask why he didn't wait until she was awake. The way he did when she tried to take off his jeans yesterday.

She found it amazing how much she trusted a man she barely knew. Had she only met him on Tuesday? So much had been jammed into two days. It was Thursday, wasn't it? She glanced at the clock. Eleven fifty-six. Almost Friday. Depending on where in Michigan Sam's friend lived, they should be able to reach him the next afternoon. And then, this Grand Adventure would be over.

Daria sat up. She could tell from the shape of the map that Sam had the atlas open to Michigan. "Is your friend in the Lower or Upper Peninsula?"

Sam looked up. "Why?"

"I hadn't planned out that leg of the trip. I should do it tonight, so I have the route planted in my brain. Don't look at me like that. I'm a visual person. After I study a map, it will be imprinted, and I'll *see* it behind my eyes." She always hated trying to explain that. It sounded weird.

"You don't need to know. I'm working out the route."

He still didn't trust her. That stung. What happened to their earlier camaraderie?

"I want an idea of how long it'll take to get there. I need to know whether I'll have enough time to keep driving after I drop you off, or if I have to get a room for the night."

"Guess that depends on how tired you are."

"You're a lot of help."

He didn't trust her, and that was that. She stood and stretched her arms over her head and arched her back. Sam was staring at her. Not at her eyes but lower. The edge of her shirt tickled her midriff.

Sam sucked air. He shouldn't look at that narrow strip of exposed skin between her shirt and unsnapped jeans. But, damn, he was only human. He figured he'd earned enough credit to look by only unsnapping the jeans while she slept and not putting his hand down inside them—the way she had in his.

He was disappointed when she dropped her arms. Then, he was promptly rewarded when she tucked the shirt into her jeans. The stretchy fabric clung to her unbound breasts. Sliding her bra out from under her when it bunched up had been difficult. Not sliding his hands in the bra's place was torture. Oh, the credit he was racking up with his self-restraint. Penance for his impure thoughts.

A cold shower helped, too.

Now, her shirt molded full breasts. A guy would have to be a eunuch not to stare at her beaded nipples.

"Thank you for the backrub, Sam, and for waking me up." She mustn't have noticed the drool sliding down into his beard.

He scrubbed his hand down his face. Dry. Damn, he was sure he'd been drooling.

Sitting back in the chair, he stretched out his legs. With a little maneuvering to take pressure off his hip, he propped his right leg on the bed. "You were moaning. I thought you were having a nightmare. Besides, I figured you'd get a better sleep if you got out of those clothes."

That really helped, Ace. Nothing like telling her he wanted her naked.

She gave him an odd look. Was she reading his mind? Nah, she took what he said at face value. That he'd meant she would rest better wearing that sleepshirt thing not street clothes. The sleepshirt that reached mid-thigh. With flowered panties underneath. Or, maybe no panties at all.

While he was ogling and speculating, she'd opened her tote and pulled out her sleepwear. She tried to hide a tight roll of flowered cotton under her sleepshirt. Blue flowered cotton.

She stared pointedly at his leg blocking her way. "Kindly move your leg."

"You can cross over. Your legs are long enough." Oh, yeah. Her legs looked a mile long in those tight jeans.

When she started to tap her bare foot, he said, "Only funning ya, darling."

She waited two seconds then swung her leg over. At the same time, he took his leg off the bed. Their legs tangled. Her arms flailed as she tried to maintain her balance. She dropped the sleepshirt, and the panty roll went flying. He caught her around the waist before she fell. When she landed in his lap, he let out a whoosh.

"Oh, my goodness, did I hurt you?" She tried to get up, but that only made things worse. She'd pressed on his bad leg.

"Give me a minute." He held her still. "I think you broke something."

"I'm so sorry. Let me up so I can check. Maybe you're bleeding."

"No. Don't move."

"I hurt you. Oh, Sam, I'm so sorry." Again, she tried to get up, pressing near a more vital spot. "I didn't mean—"

"No problem," he said in a falsetto. "I'll live."

She tried to twist around. "Let me up. I'm hurting you."

"I'm okay." He snugged her against him. Very okay. Her on his lap, his arm around her waist, just under her breasts. Oh, yeah. He liked this position.

She went still. "This is not a good idea."

He could feel her heart beating under his hand. It wouldn't take much to slide his hand upward. She must have realized that, too, because her heart started beating faster. Her breaths became shallow. Tension radiated from her. But, she didn't leap out of his lap.

Sam rested his chin on her shoulder. Not a good idea. In fact, it was a very bad idea to hold her. To want her.

He pressed his lips quickly in the hollow of her shoulder and released her. "You can get up now. You weigh a ton." He lightly swatted her hip.

Daria scrambled off his lap. She bent over to pick up her panties that had rolled toward the bed. When she stood, she caught the expression in Sam's eyes.

"You were looking at my tush," she accused him.

He pointed to his chest. "Moi? Why would I look at your tush? Mine's cuter."

CHAPTER SEVENTEEN

Daria rolled over for the fifth time. The nap following the backrub kept her awake. That and thinking about the erotic dream. She felt strange. Edgy. The warm shower hadn't helped—either her nerves or her hair. Contrary to the package, the instant curl did not wash out.

"Can't sleep?" Sam's soft voice in the darkness startled her. She didn't know he was awake. Unlike her tossing and turning, he'd been still, his breathing even.

"I'm sorry. I didn't mean to wake you," she said.

"I haven't gone to sleep yet. Too many naps in the car."

"I can't claim that excuse."

"Good thing. At least, not while you're driving." He chuckled softly. "I'm the one who needs to apologize. I should have let you sleep earlier."

Daria could hardly tell him she, too, wished he'd let her sleep instead of interrupting her dream. "No problem."

The silence stretched between them. Awkward, unsettling. This was worse than when she shared a bed with him. Last night, he was exhausted and in pain. He'd even reassured her he couldn't *perform*—not that she totally believed him. She hadn't worried since he'd immediately started to snore.

Tonight, his exhaustion seemed nearly gone. The antibiotics were healing his injuries. A palpable difference filled the atmosphere of the room.

"Why haven't you married?" Sam's question came out of nowhere, startling her more than realizing he was awake and listening to her restlessness.

She'd asked herself that question at each of her friends' weddings. She stalled. "Why do you ask?"

"Curious. You're the kind of woman who gets married to her high school sweetheart, has kids, does the church-school-scouts volunteer thing."

In her teens, that was exactly the life she envisioned for herself. Like her mother. But, it was rather tough to do considering she had no high school sweetheart, thanks to her brothers. They had taken their over-protectiveness to extremes and intimidated any guy brave enough to ask her out. And it didn't end with her high school graduation. Never mind that the government considered her an adult at eighteen. Her brothers didn't. They scared off nearly every eligible bachelor within fifty miles of Prairieville. Too bad they hadn't scared off Josh Lawrence.

Nobody was good enough for their sister. It had gotten so bad she started meeting dates at restaurants rather than have them pick her up at home. But, that made her feel like she was sneaking around. And it didn't work. Somehow, the boys would find out and, oh so casually, just happened to have dinner at the same restaurant where they managed to sit at a nearby table. She was rarely asked out for a second date. Finally, she just gave up. She saw her life stretching out before her, an old maid living with four old bachelors.

Then, two years ago she began writing. As her character, Alexa Tremaine, evolved, Daria found her secret dreams coming to life through Alexa's acts of daring heroism. Alexa was strong. She took responsibility for her actions. She never blamed others. More importantly, she went after what she wanted. That's when Daria realized she'd *allowed* her brothers to chase off potential suitors. She hadn't cared enough about any of the men she dated to insist the boys leave him alone.

What if she really wanted a man? What if she found the love of her life? Would she cave and lose him? Or would she stand up to her brothers?

"Oh, my God." Daria bolted out of bed. "I didn't call home."

She tripped over her boots, yelped at bruising her big toe and stumbled around the corner of the bed before Sam switched on the light.

"Jesus. You act like you're a kid who didn't make it home before curfew. It's almost one o'clock. Your brothers are sleeping, which is what you and I should be doing."

"Billy's a night owl. He'll be up. Besides, it's not even midnight there." Daria rifled through her purse. "Where is my phone? You didn't use my phone while I was sleeping, did you?"

"Try the pocket with the snap." Sam propped himself up on the pillows. "Where you always put it."

That's where it was. She hated that he was right. She switched the phone on and found five messages. All from home. Something horrible must have happened, Daria thought as she speed-dialed her home number.

"Mason," the brother closest in age to her answered.

"Andy, what's going on? Is everything all right?" She should have played the messages. Then, she would've had a clue what was wrong.

"Oh, DJ. Are you ever in for it."

"What? Me?" Daria heard the faint sound of arguing. Andy had probably covered the phone. She had a bad feeling about this.

". . . give her a break, Jim." That was Tommy. "Maybe there's a good explanation."

"Daria Jean Mason, where the hell are you?"

Oh, boy. "Hi, Jimmy. What's wrong?"

"Your turning off your phone is what's wrong. What if this had been a real emergency? Keep your—"

"What do you mean what if this had been a real emergency? You mean it isn't?"

"I ran into Doug Campbell tonight."

She felt as guilty as a kid with her hand in the cookie jar. "Really? How's he doing?"

"Funny thing." Jimmy didn't sound like he thought it was funny. "Doug told me Ginnie is in Florida."

"What?" She snapped her fingernail against the tiny mouthpiece. "You're breaking up, Jimmy. What did you say?"

Sam raised his eyebrow. She turned her back on him. Bad enough she had to deal with her brother. She didn't need Sam questioning her, too.

"You have the best cell phone on the market," Jimmy was saying. "I made sure of it before I let you go off on this wild goose chase."

"*Let me?*" she said softly. "Did I hear you correctly? You

let me go on my trip?"

Her brother was treading on thin ice and didn't even know it.

"There is nothing wrong with your phone, Daria. Keep the damn thing turned on at all times. I want to know where you are. Why the hell didn't you tell us you were alone?"

Darn that Jimmy. He took interrogation to new heights. Of course, that was part of his job, but he didn't need to use the bright lights and rubber hose on her. She rummaged through the snacks she'd brought in from the car. The bag of chips would work. She held out the phone and crunched the chips.

"Jimmy?" she said hoarsely into the outstretched phone and crunched again. "Jimmy? I can't hear you." Crunch, crunch.

"Daria? What the hell is going on?" His voice came through loud and clear.

Crunch, crunch. "Sorry . . . must have . . . bad connection." Crunch, crunch. "I'll call tomorrow. Bye." She ended the call.

"I take it your brother was giving you a hard time?" Sam said.

When her phone rang, she promptly switched it off. "That darn Jimmy. He thinks because he's the oldest, he can tell me what to do."

"Maybe he misses you," Sam ventured.

"Yeah, like a migraine." She threw her phone into her purse. "I don't want to talk about the boys. If it weren't for them, I'd be married by now."

Sam watched her stalk over to the bed and plop. She sat cross-legged After seeing where he was looking, she pulled the sheet up over her lap. *Damn.* He only caught a glimpse of those blue flowered panties. Carefully, he rolled on his right side.

She looked almost mutinous leaning back against the headboard, her arms folded. The nightshirt pulled across her chest, emphasizing the swell of rounded breasts. And if he continued to stare, she was liable to take whatever caused her anger out on him.

"Well, I guess that answers my earlier question," he said. "The one that took you so long to answer I thought you'd fallen asleep. Why you haven't married."

She reached over and turned out the light between them. "That isn't true." In the dark, her voice softened. "What I said about my brothers. It's not entirely their fault."

"Care to explain?"

"My parents died when I was thirteen. My oldest brother suddenly became responsible for all of us."

"You're not the oldest?" All along that's what he thought. The way she talked about her brothers, calling them *boys*. He assumed they were middle or high schoolers.

"Goodness, no." She chuckled. "I'm the youngest. The *baby* and the only girl. The way they act, especially Jimmy—he's the oldest—you'd think I was still thirteen. They've taken *responsibility*—" She made it sound like a dirty word. "—to new heights. Which was okay when I was thirteen and through high school, I guess. Taking care of me, protecting me was their Number One objective, especially Jimmy. The others go along with whatever he says."

Sam thought protecting her wasn't such a bad thing. "So, they've scared off all the guys in Iowa." Not a bad thing, at all. He could like those guys.

"Again, that's not entirely true," she said, resignation in her voice. "I let them. That's what I was figuring out earlier, after you asked me why I wasn't married. I never cared enough to fight for what I wanted. Then again, if a man is so easily intimidated by the boys, he isn't the right man for me. And the reason I haven't married is because I haven't found the right man. But, I'm going to find him. He's out there. Somewhere."

"Tell me about your Mr. Right." Damn, that came out wrong. It sounded like he was mocking her. *Maybe because, Ace, you don't want her to find Mr. Right.*

"He'll be kind, sensitive."

"Wimp," Sam scoffed.

"No, he'll be strong enough in his masculinity to be sensitive to me, to my needs."

"Did you get that out of a magazine?"

"Tall," she went on, plainly ignoring him. "He has to be taller than I am. I hate dancing all hunched over."

"Tell me about it." Sam had the same problem. "I suppose he'll have to be handsome, too."

"Of course." Was she smirking? He wished he could see her face. But, he had a feeling if he turned on the light, she would clam up.

"And they call men superficial," he said.

"And rich." Was that laughter in her voice? Was she mocking him?

He couldn't believe she said that. "How rich?"

"Oh, he has to be worth at least five million." She was lying. She had to be lying.

"That lets me out. I'm short a couple of mil." Like three or four. He never thought about it much, but he guessed he was worth about a mil or two if he counted the value of his condo and his stock portfolio . . . and only if the market didn't take another dive.

"Right. As if you were ever in the running, Johnston."

"Ouch. DQ'd before the race begins."

"Okay," she challenged. "What about my other criteria?"

"We-ell," he drawled. "I am taller. And handsome, too."

She made a derisive sound. "Your ego is showing."

"You're the one who told your friends—the ones you stood up Tuesday night—that you'd met Mr. Tall, Dark and Handsome."

"And somehow you thought I meant you?"

"Ouch, again."

"What about kind and sensitive?" she taunted.

"Kind and Sensitive are my middle names. Quit making those noises or I'm going to think you don't like me. I rubbed your shoulders, didn't I? Wasn't that being kind? Wasn't I sensitive to your needs? See? I meet your requirements— except the rich part."

"There is another qualification. A real deal buster. Mr. Right won't let my brothers chase him off."

"Piece of cake."

She snorted. "Tell me that after you meet them. As if that's ever going to happen. You and I are parting company tomorrow."

"That's right." He had a mission to finish. He didn't have time to indulge in fantasies about Daria Mason.

"All silliness aside, Sam, if—no, when—I find Mr. Right, I'll recognize him. It won't matter if he's classically handsome or not. And I was teasing about him being rich."

"Really?" He could tease, too. "Were you yanking my chain?"

"You didn't think that I really meant—" She broke off when Sam chuckled. "Oh, you. You knew all along I was joking."

"Gotcha. So, what's going to happen when you find Mr. Right?"

"For starters, I won't let my brothers chase him away. I will fight tooth and nail to keep him."

"I believe you would." Sam meant that. He wondered what kind of man would inspire such fierceness.

"And I'm going to find him soon. I have six months."

What? Was she sick? Dear God, she wasn't dying, was she? Slowly, because he wasn't sure he wanted to hear that she had a terminal illness, he asked, "Why six months?"

"I'm going to find Mr. Right and marry him before I turn thirty. On October third."

Okay, she wasn't dying. Relief washed over him. What was the matter with him that his imagination had gone into high gear? A lot of women heard their biological clocks ticking. Hers was sounding the alarm.

She was going to find some yoyo who met all her criteria and marry him in six months. Sam felt a spasm of pain ripple through his chest. Pain that had nothing to do with his gunshot wounds. Daria and some Mr. Right getting married.

Wait a minute. Why should he care who she married? He wasn't going to see her after she dropped him at Mac's boat.

"Oh," Daria said brightly. "I should have mentioned. He has to want children. Lots of children."

An image of Daria swollen with child flashed through Sam's mind. Another man's child. Jealousy streaked through him. He had no business thinking like that. This game was getting out of hand. Yet, he persisted.

"How do you define *lots*?" he asked.

"I used to want six."

"Six?" Sam choked out.

"Uh huh. I come from a large family and even though my brothers can be real pains in the tush, I wouldn't trade my life with them for being an only child." In the dark, she heaved a sigh. "I don't think about six any more. I won't have enough time. Even if they come close together, there isn't enough time to have six before I'm thirty-five."

"So, you have two goals and a timetable. Be married by thirty and have as many children as you can by thirty-five?"

"Yes. It's important to have goals. I didn't used to. I sorta . . . drifted, satisfied with the status quo. Not anymore. I'm glad we talked, Sam. When I get home, I'm going to stop letting life happen to me. I'm going to make life happen. Things are going to change. *I'm* going to change." The determination in her voice reminded Sam of an eight-year-old punctuating her decision with a foot stomp.

"You've gotten a headstart on changing today with your hair and those clothes. You'd better be careful. You're liable to attract Mr. Wrong."

There she went making derisive noises again.

"I'm serious, Daria. Stay away from bars and dance clubs. A girl like you can get into all kinds of trouble in those places."

"What do you mean a girl like me?"

"Trusting. Inexperienced. Naïve."

"Gee, thanks. Why not throw in gullible and stupid?"

"You are not gullible." He recalled her reaction to Grashenko. She saw through his impersonation of a police detective. Sam went on, "And I'd never call anyone stupid."

Okay, maybe Teller who didn't have a clue about field work.

Sam continued, "Don't get all riled up or you'll never get to sleep. We have a long drive ahead of us tomorrow. Today," he corrected since the clock was edging toward two in the morning.

"What about you, Sam? Ever been married?"

Oh, no. He wasn't going there. "Daria, be a good girl. Roll over and go to sleep."

"Why?" she persisted. "Turnabout's fair play. I bared my secrets to you. Your turn. Why haven't you married?"

"We're leaving at six, you know. That's in four hours."

"I'm going to lie awake and wonder. And then what shape will I be in to drive?"

"You're just going to hammer away at me, aren't you?"

"Uh huh. It's part of my new persona. I won't take no for an answer."

"God, you've turned into a monster."

"Of course. And it will be all your fault if I'm too tired to drive in the morning."

"Playing on my guilty conscience isn't going to work. I don't have a conscience—guilty or not."

Sam's conscience quit working during his second mission. When he killed the woman. It didn't matter that she was in the process of betraying the team. That she would have killed them all. He knew he had no conscience because he felt nothing when he looked down at her dead body. She was the first and, even though he wasn't a *terminator*, she wasn't the last.

"You have a conscience, Sam," Daria intruded into his thoughts. "You might think you don't, but I know it's there."

"What are you?" he growled. "Some kind of cockeyed optimist? I've killed people, Daria. I steal, lie, cheat—kill," he repeated, just in case she missed it the first time. "It's my job. It's who I am."

He couldn't believe what he'd blurted out.

In the dark, he heard a rustle of bedclothes, the creak of bedsprings. Then, he felt the dip of the mattress and Daria's weight pressing against his hip. Her soft hand touched his chest. She patted upward until she cupped the side of his scruffy face.

"Sam, you are not the job. You do what you have to do, to protect us. To survive."

She was wandering too far into forbidden territory. Too far. "You're pushing your luck, kid. Don't you know better than to come to a man's bed in the middle of the night?"

She didn't leave.

"If you have no conscience—no sense of right or wrong—you wouldn't issue warnings." She leaned forward and kissed his forehead, her lips cool on his super-heated skin. Then, she patted his cheek. "Get some sleep. We have a busy day tomorrow."

With that, she climbed back into her own bed, leaving Sam to wonder why he hadn't grabbed her and tumbled her into his.

CHAPTER EIGHTEEN

Sam had wanted to get an early start, ahead of rush hour traffic. That was shot when he woke at eight. Since Daria was still out cold, he let her sleep while he took a quick shower, careful not to let his Super-Glued wounds get too wet.

After his shower, he checked in the mirror. The area around his butt wound was red. Could be from the shower. He touched it. Warm. Tender. Not good. The antibiotics should have kicked in by now. If it wasn't better after he got to Mac's, he'd get it checked out.

When he put on clean underwear, he gave Daria silent thanks for her thoughtfulness. She was a good woman, a nurturer who was caught up in a dangerous game. Not just between him and Yuri Grashenko, but between the United States and those who wanted to bring about its destruction. A destruction far worse than destroying buildings and killing the people inside.

Overt attacks were not effective, and America's enemies were not slow learners. Far more insidious was an attack from within. When those entrusted with government secrets conspired with the enemy, disaster loomed.

It wasn't going to happen. Not on Sam's watch.

"Yuri, you are such a naughty boy. Tsk, tsk, tsk."

Yuri Grashenko let out a hearty laugh, the first since the debacles started back in Smolensk. "Ah, the redoubtable Ms. Sally Quinero."

"Redoubtable? Cain't say Ah ever heerd of that word afore," she said in a mockingly slow drawl. Her exaggerated dialect belied her cunning intelligence. "Does that there word mean y'all think Ah'm smart?"

Yuri lost his smile. "Do not insult my intelligence, my dear. I wondered when you would enter the fray."

"Fray? You ain't seen nothing yet, buster." She chuckled. "So, how ya doing, Yuri? Long time, no see."

"I have had better weeks."

"I'll bet you have. With your talents, you shouldn't be working for that idiot Korioff. Why don't you come on over to the good side?"

And run the rest of his life? Always looking over his shoulder for another of Korioff's minions? No, thank you.

"Okay, don't answer now," she said. "Think about it, Yuri. Just think about it. I have another question. How did you con the media into giving out your cell phone number for the tipster hotline?"

Yuri gave the Brooklyn policeman a momentary thought. Collection of that debt had been particularly enjoyable. "Trade secret."

The beep of Call Waiting sounded in Yuri's ear. Ordinarily, he found it quite annoying that any conversation could be so rudely interrupted. Sally Quinero was a worse annoyance. He wouldn't put it past her to be tracing his call and he certainly did not want her to discover where he was.

"I have another call, my dear. Ta-ta."

Daria white-knuckled through construction on I-75 in Toledo. "You should have woken me up sooner," she said to Sam. "I hate rushing around. I didn't have time to do something with this." She flipped the ends of her hair.

She'd thought it looked terrible last night. That was nothing compared to her shock this morning when she looked in the mirror. She should have taken time after her shower last night to dry her hair. Now, she had the worst case of bedhead she'd ever seen.

"Gee," Sam drawled. "Have you mentioned that before?"

Daria didn't dignify him with a response. She may have mentioned it one or two times. Okay, maybe three or four. She saw signs for Detroit and groaned. "Please tell me we're not going to Detroit. I hate big cities. If I never drive in a big city again, I'll be perfectly happy."

"You'll never be perfectly happy. Nobody is. We just take our snippets of happiness when we get them." He directed her onto US-23 toward Ann Arbor.

"That's cynical. Don't you think people deserve happiness?"

"Some."

"Do you?"

"No." He turned to look out the passenger window, effectively cutting off their discussion. Daria thought that was the saddest thing she'd ever heard.

She stopped at a Welcome Center and got a Michigan road map. She needed to imbed the map firmly in her brain before driving any further. If Sam hadn't let her sleep so late, she would have checked her road atlas. This map was even better.

He still wouldn't tell her where they were going, despite her inquiries. She memorized the expressways while trying to figure out their destination. She hated not knowing. I-75 went through Detroit and up the middle of the state, across the Mackinac Bridge, on up to Sault Ste. Marie. She'd heard that *Yoopers*, people who lived in Michigan's Upper Peninsula, were a hardy lot. Since Sam's friend eschewed modern necessities like a telephone, it was quite possible he lived up there.

Sam finally told her his friend lived on a boat. Daria didn't think he meant the boat was on a small lake. Michigan was nearly surrounded by the Great Lakes. She guessed Sam's friend was in the same business as Sam before he retired. Her next conclusion was that he would moor his boat where he could make a quick getaway in the event someone from his past attempted to settle a score. It made sense to her that he would want to be on a very large lake. They were going the wrong way for Lakes Ontario and Erie. Which left Superior, Huron and Michigan.

Too many choices.

And then she didn't have time to worry about where they were going. They weren't going anywhere. Traffic had come to a complete halt.

Construction.

* * *

"Boss?" Hardesty caught Teller coming out of the men's room. The newbie's timing stunk. "Got news for you."

Teller glanced around. The hall was empty, but anyone could come by. He motioned for Hardesty to follow him into his office. The eager beaver practically danced on his toes unable to contain his enthusiasm. Teller had to remind him to close the door.

He sat at his desk, a reminder to the rookie that *he* was in charge. "All right, what's so damn important you had to follow me into the restroom?"

"Well, technically, sir, I didn't follow you into the restroom, I met you out—"

"Get to the damn point."

"You know how you had me monitor Ms. Quinero's phones?"

"She called Joz. Halleluiah. Where is he?"

"Uh, boss." The kid shifted his feet. "Uh, no. Uh, that is, she, uh. This is kind of bad. I mean—"

"Who. Did. She. Call."

"Yuri Grashenko."

"Holy shit."

Hardesty nodded. "I know this is bad. Him being Russian Mafia and all. And with Agent Jozwiak and Grashenko . . ." The rookie cleared his throat. "Sir, you may be right. I didn't want to think that Joz would—"

"You *think* I might be right? You just *think*?"

Hardesty held up his hand. "You're right. Agent Jozwiak has gone over to the enemy. And Agent Quinero is helping him. They are both traitors."

Sam was champing at the bit for Daria to drive faster. Traffic was limited to one lane in each direction with concrete K-rails dividing northbound cars from those going south. The speed limit was forty-five, but they weren't even going that fast.

Where the southbound lanes had been, mechanical hammers broke up the pavement. Their thuds gave him a headache even across the median. Enormous trucks hauled away the pieces of concrete and other, equally enormous trucks hauled in sand. Each time a flagman—usually a woman—halted traffic to let the outgoing trucks into the lane, Sam's blood pressure rose.

"Are you sure it's okay to drive on the expressways?" Daria said. "I keep looking for toll booths and cameras."

"Michigan doesn't have toll roads. In fact, they use the terms freeway and expressway interchangeably."

"How do you know about freeways? Are you from Michigan?"

"Nope. Chicago. Right after college, I worked in Detroit."

"Great. I can ask you questions about both cities. I am learning so much on this trip," she enthused. "Great research for my book."

They were stopped again. "Tell me about this book of yours," he said. Might as well kill time. They weren't going anywhere. "How far along are you?"

"Actually, my first book is finished. It features a female detective. Sort of Nancy Drew on steroids." She giggled. "Alexa Tremaine is the protagonist. She's a real kick-a—uh, she's a kick-butt kind of woman."

Sam stretched his legs under the dash and folded his arms. They would be on this stretch of US-23 for a long while. Listening to Daria helped pass the time. He'd caught up on his rest thanks to her driving. At night, he'd slept surprisingly sound with Daria next to him. That was a switch. A civilian guarding him.

"Do you identify with this Alexa?" Sam asked.

"Maybe." When she giggled again, she reminded Sam of the fresh-face farmgirl he met three days ago. Not the smokin' hot babe in tight jeans sitting next to him.

She wore another snug shirt, an electric blue tank top. When they left the motel, she wore a windbreaker. At the Welcome Center, they discovered the day was warming quickly, and she shed the jacket. Her bare arms were slender, nicely shaped and winter white with faint tan lines from the previous summer.

"You did knock Korioff on his butt," he reminded her. She had more strength than she gave herself credit for.

"That was a fluke. I caught him with his britches down. I simply reacted. Still I wish I were more like Alexa. She is awesome, if I do say so myself. You know," Daria said in a soft conspiratorial tone, "this is the first adventure I've ever had."

"Some adventure. Being chased by the Russian Mafia. You are aware that this is not a game." Without realizing it, his voice turned sharp. "Those were real bullets that tore up my leg and ass. Do you get that, Daria Mason? This isn't some goddamn adventure." *Where the hell did that come from?*

She sucked in a breath. "Perhaps we should find another topic."

Old Foot-in-Mouth strikes again. "Aw shit." He scrubbed his hand down his face. "My remark was uncalled for. Forget it."

"Was that supposed to be an apology? 'Forget it'? I'm tired of being on the receiving end of your pain and frustration. Just once would you say you're sorry?"

"I'm sorry."

"Oh, yeah. That was real sincere. Just like my kids. Just like my brothers. You guys think apologizing is a sign of weakness. A strong man who is in the wrong, who hurts someone's feelings, apologizes and means it." She was on a roll, blaming him for the sins of the male species.

"Lecture over?" he asked, after reining in the sarcasm.

She blew out a breath and turned up the radio volume. She'd been listening to an oldies station. The Ventures "Wipe Out" blasted through the speakers. Appropriate. He'd not only wiped out. He'd crashed and burned.

He reached over and lowered the volume. "I'm sorry. I acted like an ass."

"Yes, you did. But I would prefer you refrain from using vulgar words."

"Up ahead you're going to need to get in the left lane," Sam said.

They didn't reach Ann Arbor until noon. The construction ended just north of there. Now they were

179

making good time. "Watch for the sign for I-96 toward Lansing."

"Lansing? That's the capital of Michigan," Daria exclaimed.

"Why am I not surprised you know that?"

"Go ahead and scoff," she said. "My fourth grade teacher made the class memorize the state capitals. Uh oh."

Sam groaned. The exit to westbound I-96 was closed for bridge repairs. They joined the long line of traffic snaking through the town of Brighton.

"Yuri, I do not understand why we are flying to this . . ." Korioff looked at his ticket as he paced in a circle around Yuri in the Buffalo airport. " . . . Grand Rapids. It is in Michigan. The woman lives in Ohio."

"And do you know where in Ohio she lives?" Not that Yuri needed to know. Samuel Jozwiak was not going home with the woman. Who, by the way, did not live in Ohio. A fact Yuri chose not to share with his inept partner. Korioff had vengeance on his mind ever since the woman or Jozwiak— Korioff's story frequently changed—gave him that knot on the back of his head. Yuri had to keep reminding Korioff that Sam *Johnston* was their target.

It was a shame that the old motel clerk waited until that morning to call the Tipster Hotline. From him and the young clerk in Seneca Falls, Yuri learned the correct license plate, color, make and model of the woman's car. He even had her real name and home address. More information he chose not to share with Korioff whom Yuri made wait in the rental car while he interviewed the clerks on the pretense that his formidable size might deter the men from talking. Korioff bought it.

"Why are we not going to Virginia?" Korioff asked that question a minimum of ten times since they left New York City. "Johnston live in Virginia."

Yuri's prey was heading west. Seneca Falls, Buffalo. Not south to Virginia. Samuel Jozwiak was not turning over what he stole to the Director of Orion Agency.

Samuel was too loyal, too patriotic to just run and hide

until Yuri's boss called off the search, which he wouldn't do. Gregor Korioff never gave up. Copying financial records was bad enough. Destroying the originals was a death sentence.

Jozwiak knew exactly how volatile the other information he had was. How essential it was to ensure that what he risked his life for was utilized to prevent a catastrophe.

Something Yuri had to prevent.

The Internet was Yuri's friend. There were no secrets from those with the skill to uncover them. Like himself, he thought with no modesty whatsoever.

John MacDonald had mentored Jozwiak, grooming Samuel to take his place before his unexpected forced retirement. The old man was still a viable player in the espionage game. Still a threat.

So, Yuri kept tabs on the former Director of the Orion Agency, the same way he monitored Jozwiak. MacDonald—McIntyre as he called himself now—was the quintessential spy. He buried his true identity and whereabouts under layers of false names and bogus corporations. Child's play for a man with Yuri's technological skills.

MacDonald lived on a boat registered in Holland, Michigan, a short drive from Grand Rapids. Sam was planning to deliver the information he'd stolen to his old mentor.

And Yuri would stop him.

CHAPTER NINETEEN

"I can't believe all this construction," Daria exclaimed. They'd driven around Lansing, and she'd been disappointed not to see the Capitol Building. Now the highway was down to one lane while crews repaired the other. From the looks of the pavement, it was a good thing. You could lose a VW Beetle in some of those pot-holes.

"'Tis the season," Sam replied. Though he didn't wiggle or squirm in his seat, Daria felt the tension radiating from him. When she occasionally glanced over, she saw him clench and unclench his hand on his thigh.

They'd picked up lunch as they drove through Brighton. She was getting royally sick of fastfood and longed for a nice sit-down meal. She was glad some fastfood places offered salads so she could avoid fatty foods. Sam didn't seem to have the same concerns. Eating a salad was not conducive to driving, which either meant longer delays while she scarfed down her lunch or Sam drove.

After driving about five miles of stop-and-go, he pulled off at an exit and they switched drivers. The white lines around his mouth meant his leg and hip hurt. He took some of her Tylenol, but she didn't think it helped.

"Tell me more about your book," Sam said.

"Why?"

"Anything to pass the time."

"You could tell me about your adventures," she said. "I'll bet you could fill several hours about your missions."

"Too boring. I'd really like to hear about your story."

Since he sounded sincere—not mocking as before—she talked about her favorite subject. "My idea is for a series of mysteries starring Alexa Tremaine. Series books are very popular right now."

Daria loved talking about Alexa, who had become such a real *person* to her. "Well, mystery series aren't anything new.

I mean, look at Nancy Drew. She's been around for over eighty years. And then there's Agatha Christie's Miss Marple, Raymond Chandler's Philip Marlowe and Janet Evanovich's Stephanie Plum."

"I get the picture."

She checked if he was being sarcastic. When she saw he wasn't, she said, "I was going to set Alexa's adventures in Chicago. She is definitely not a small-town girl. Besides, nothing ever happens in small towns so there would not be a story." She ought to know. "Now, I'm thinking about setting the second one in New York City. It was so exciting to be there, to walk the streets, to see the people. I gathered so much detail. Did you know the Manhattan subways stink? I don't think there are any restrooms and people just . . . well, you know. Anyway, I think I'll set each book in a different city. With your help, I could learn enough to set the third one in Detroit. Oh, sh— Sugar Jets. We could've driven through Detroit."

"Oh, my goodness," he mimicked. "Were you about to swear?"

She could feel the heat in her cheeks. "I have enough self-restraint to avoid using vulgar words."

"God, you sound so prim and proper and look at you. Wild, bleach-blonde hair. Those tight jeans and tighter shirt."

"Would you please get off that topic?"

"Holy cow." He used another of her expressions. "I can see the lace of your bra."

"You cannot." She shifted to turn away from him. Apparently, not soon enough.

"I can see your nipples. Did I just turn you on?"

She nearly ran off the road. Only the rumble strip along the edge of the expressway brought her back into her own lane.

"I-I'm cold," she lied and punched the Heat button and slid the temp lever to H.

Sam shoved the lever back to C and hit Vent. Moderate—not cold—air wafted from the vents, just like before. "I thought you said honesty is important. Honesty and trust. It's okay to get turned on. Shows you're human. Christ, I've been horny since you walked into that restroom. It took you a while to catch up."

Oh, my word. What did he just say?

"You can't do anything about how your body reacts," he went on, unaware that she was dying of embarrassment. "We're two humans in close confines and under dangerous circumstances. I'm attracted to you, and you're attracted to me. Not unusual. What counts is what we do about our mutual attraction. Which is absolutely nothing. Like you said the other night. We build a bridge and get over it."

If Daria could crawl under the dashboard and still keep the car on the road, she would've done so. She grew so warm at his frank talk about physical attraction that she thought she was having hot flashes. Could a woman go into menopause at twenty-nine? Heat spread from between her legs. She wanted to squirm.

She cranked down her window hoping the fresh air would cool her. Making her lie about being cold more obvious. Goosebumps broke out on her bare arms. Furtively, she glanced at Sam. He was staring at her chest. If he made one comment about her nipples standing at attention, she was dumping him along the side of I-96. He could jolly well walk to his friend's boat. The only good thing was that they'd gotten through the construction zone and were going faster now.

Hoping to calm down and get control of herself, Daria took several deep breaths. She only succeeded in bringing her body's reaction into prominence.

She groped for an innocuous topic of conversation. *Groped*? What a word choice. She was a writer with a better command of language than that. He'd thought she was groping him in the Green Acres Motel when all she was trying to do was unzip his pants. Oh, dear Lord, that sounded even worse.

"I don't know what you're thinking about," Sam said. "But it might be a good idea to slow down. The speed limit in Michigan is seventy."

She glanced at the speedometer. Seventy-eight and climbing. She backed off the accelerator. What she wouldn't give for a cold shower.

* * *

"When is your book coming out?" Sam asked. They were almost to Mac's. Sam could hardly sit still.

What should have taken less than four hours had stretched to seven thanks to the Michigan Department of Transportation's efforts to improve the highways and an accident east of Grand Rapids. Using the map she'd insisted on picking up at the Welcome Center, he discovered a short-cut. A highway, built after he left Michigan, cut across the south end of Grand Rapids. That would shave at least thirty minutes off the trip. Maybe even more.

Daria's shoulders slumped. "That's a problem. I've been querying editors, and I keep getting these darn 'dear author' rejection letters."

"What's wrong with the book?"

She shot him a lethal look. "There is nothing *wrong* with my story."

There went the peace. He held up his hand. "I'll rephrase that. Why hasn't anyone recognized your brilliant writing?"

"Sam Johnston, you are so full of it." She gave him a crooked smile while he felt that recurring sense of guilt when she called him by his alias. He was about to correct her when she said, "I figured out—with help from the other writers— that my query letters aren't very good."

The opportunity to tell her his real name blew past . . . and he let it go. "So this conference you went to really helped."

"Oh, yes. I learned so much, met some really nice writers, people who take me seriously. Not like my brothers who think it's just 'Daria's little hobby'." She snorted. Then, she sighed. Her shoulders slumped.

"What's wrong?"

"I had a chance to pitch my story to an editor. Oh, well. Water under the bridge."

"You blew your chance?"

"Sort of." She took a deep breath and sighed. "I rescued a spy instead."

"I lost you."

"I had an appointment Wednesday morning." She

shrugged.

"That's why you wanted to go back to your conference." Now, he felt like a heel. He'd dragged her into his problem and made her miss an opportunity.

He shifted. God, he was butt-sore. Shot in one cheek and the other numb from sitting so long. Now that he wasn't sleeping so much, he was antsy doing nothing. Soon, he reminded himself. Soon, he would reach Mac and complete his mission. Meanwhile, he sat next to a woman who made him hornier than he'd been for months. How long had it been since he'd gotten laid?

He shifted again, this time to relieve the fullness in his jeans. "Tell me about your story, and I'll tell you if it's any good."

"That is so like a man."

"Now what?"

"You'll *tell* me if it's any good? You arrogant so-and-so."

"Arrogant? Me?" He was just trying to help.

She shot him one of those 'teacher' looks. "Why don't you tell *me* a story? How about a story that ends in the women's restroom in an old New York department store? I think I deserve to hear how that one began—since I know how it ended."

"Are you sure it has ended?" Even he wasn't sure how it was going to end.

"You know what I mean. I want to hear why those Russian guys are chasing you. What do you have that they want?"

"Good question." As if he'd tell her.

"I thought so," she said with a smug grin. "Was it something you found in Paris?"

"What makes you think I was in Paris?" he asked sharply.

"The airline ticket in your wallet. Why, is that a secret?"

He forgot she'd rifled his wallet and, honest woman that she was, hadn't helped herself to his cash. He toned down his suspicions. "You're very observant."

Daria smiled, obviously pleased by his compliment. That should distract her from realizing he'd evaded her original question.

"Does Grashenko have a grudge against you?"

The distraction hadn't lasted. "You are persistent." In fact, he could swear steam was coming out of her ears. "Yuri and I have gone up against each other a few times, but it's always been professional. Never personal."

"Shooting at you is darn personal. It's a good thing he didn't do more damage."

"If Yuri Grashenko was aiming, I'd be dead."

"Dear God, Sam. How can you talk so glibly about that?"

"It's part of the job. You get in and get out. Hopefully, in one piece. The most important thing is completing the mission. In this case, the mission isn't complete."

"What a quaint town. Look at the tulips," Daria exclaimed.

The streets of Holland were lined with rows of tulips. Hundreds, no thousands had been planted along the curbs.

"Not good that they're blooming this early," Sam said.

Daria was fascinated by the colors. Red, yellow, white and a purple so deep it appeared black. "Why not? They are gorgeous."

"Because the Tulip Festival isn't for another two weeks. The visitors won't get to see this treat." He snorted. "They'll have to call it the Stem Fest, like they did one year when all that was left of the tulips were the stems."

"Tulip Festival? Is that where people wear wooden shoes and dance in the street?"

"After they wash it first." Sam laughed at her expression. "You've heard of the Scrubbing Dutch? They do it big here. Especially for the tourists."

"One of my high school friends went to Hope College. She told me about the festival. Mostly, she groused because the students had one day at the end of the semester to vacate because the school rented the dorm rooms to visitors."

Sam directed her past Windmill Island with its reconstructed authentic Dutch windmill and fields of tulips.

"Oh, I definitely want to come back here for the festival," she said.

"When you do, be sure to go a little north to the Dandelion Festival."

She shot him a suspicious look. "There's no such thing."

"Sure there is. They don't have a Grand Marshall, but they get somebody to sit on a manure spreader and lead the parade."

"You are making that up."

"Once," he went on, ignoring her disbelief. "I saw a poster advertising the festival. A wooden shoe filled with dandelions was crushing a tulip."

"That's sick."

"But, memorable." Interspersed in their conversation, he'd been giving her directions. "Pull into that marina," he said. "That's Lake Macatawa. It leads out into Lake Michigan."

Friday afternoon and it looked like many people had gotten a head start on the weekend. The parking lot was nearly filled while boat slips were conspicuously empty. The lake shimmered in the sunlight. White sails and sleek boats of all sizes were either stationary on the lake or headed out to Lake Michigan.

"Listen," Sam said as she pulled into a parking spot. "Drop me off and get going. You can probably make it into Indiana before stopping for the night."

She turned off the ignition. "No." She wasn't leaving him until she knew he was safe with his friend.

"You've done enough. Go home, meet Mr. Right and have a bunch of kids."

She got out of the car. "Which way to your friend's boat?"

Sam didn't argue. Good thing.

The weather was glorious. On the way through town, they passed a bank where a sign indicated the temperature was seventy-eight degrees.

"What a gorgeous day," she enthused. "Perfect beach day."

They walked along the main dock from which several shorter docks jutted out into the lake. Her heels clattered on the wood slats competing with the squawk of seagulls.

"You won't want to go swimming yet," he warned. "If this was a hard winter, there might still be ice floes in Lake Michigan."

She stopped. "You're joking."

"Nope. I'm surprised so many boats are in the water this early in the season. The ice fisherman probably brought in their shanties last weekend."

"Now I know you're joking."

"Okay. Two weekends ago."

She felt a forced jocularity in Sam. Tension radiated from him. Why wasn't he jubilant? They'd made it.

"Where is your friend's boat?" she asked.

"Over two more docks. At the end." His steps quickened. He still limped, though not as badly as before. She hastened to keep up.

They rounded the last pier. "Which boat is his?"

Some slips were empty. Paraphernalia left behind indicated they were recently occupied. There were cabin cruisers and cigar boats. A very large boat blocked the view of the far left of the dock. Good grief, that had to be a yacht.

When the end of the dock came into view, Sam stopped. Still gawking at the *ocean liner*, Daria ran into him. His shoulders sagged. Deep disappointment etched his face. The last slip was empty.

"Shit."

Though his voice was soft, Daria was startled by his vehemence. For once, she didn't chide him for his vulgarity.

"Are you sure this is the right place?" she asked, hoping he'd merely gone down the wrong pier. Or had the wrong marina. But, knowing Sam as well as she could know anyone in only four days, she was sure he hadn't made a mistake.

His friend was gone.

CHAPTER TWENTY

"This is the right place, goddamn it," Sam spat out. "Mac's boat isn't here."

Daria tried to inject some hope. "Maybe he just went out for a couple of hours."

"Ever the optimist. Don't you get tired of playing Merry Sunshine?"

Daria stumbled backward as if from a body blow. Even though she was tempted to push him into the lake, she hid her hurt, unwilling to add to his troubles.

"Hey," a husky voice called out from the yacht. "You folks looking for Johnny?"

Daria looked up at the luxury boat expecting to see a man. A woman in white shorts, an orange shirt and deck shoes leaned over the rail above them. A cigarette dangled from her fingers. She was in her sixties and sported a deep tan acquired from long hours on the water with no sunscreen. If the cigarettes didn't kill her, the sun would.

"Johnny?" Sam asked.

"Yeah. You're looking for Johnny McIntyre, aren't you?"

Sam hesitated. "Yes, that's right. I'm just surprised he let you call him Johnny."

"Oh, honey. He doesn't *let* me. I call people what I damn well please." The woman laughed and coughed. "Name's Marge, folks. Wanna come aboard for a drink?"

"No."

"No thanks," Daria called out, hoping the woman didn't take offense at Sam's abrupt answer. "It's a little early."

"What?" The woman struck a pose. "The sun's gotta be over the yardarm or some other damn fool nonsense? Honey, it's five o'clock somewhere. Nothing ever stopped me from having a drink with friends. Any friend of Johnny's is a friend of mine, I always say. Isn't that just like him? I keep telling him to get a cell phone, but you know him."

Sam's mouth twisted. "Yeah, I know him. When did he leave?"

"Let's see now." Marge shoved her sunglasses into her hair and looked at her watch. "Around one, one-thirty."

Daria could almost hear the Sam's thoughts. They'd missed his friend by three hours. If not for all the traffic delays, they could have been there before Mac left.

"Johnny never would've left if he knew he had company coming."

"Did he say how long he'd be gone?" Sam asked. "Where he was heading?"

"Didn't say how long. He did say maybe Traverse City or even up as far as Mackinaw City."

"Shit," Sam whispered.

"Too bad Johnny missed all of you. He'll be real disappointed."

"Yes," Daria responded while Sam smoldered under the only dark cloud within a hundred miles. "We're real disappointed, too."

"Hey, honey. I didn't mean just you and Mr. Gorgeous. Johnny will be real disappointed he missed his friends from England."

"English friends?" Sam demanded.

Daria stomped on his foot before he went into interrogation mode. "Really? I wonder if they're the people you met when you were here last fall, Sam?"

"Naw. Never saw them before. You—" Marge pointed at Sam with her cigarette. "You, I remember, even though you need a shave. Tell him not to kiss you, honey, until he gets rid of that beard. You'll get whisker burns. Johnny doesn't get many visitors, so I remember them all. There's the little woman with red hair that never came out of a bottle and a tall, skinny old dude. Old Skin and Bones comes at least once a month. The redhead not so often. Don't know about during the winter. I head for South Beach."

Sam put his arm around Daria's shoulder and leaned close. "We gotta go."

She waved up at the gossipy woman. "Nice talking to you, Marge. Tell Johnny we're sorry we missed him."

191

"Did you come far? You could wait here for him. I got plenty of room."

Daria resisted Sam's efforts to urge her back to the car. She just couldn't walk away while Marge was talking. The woman must be lonely, desperate for company.

"Thanks, but I guess we'll catch him the next time we're in town."

Sam rushed her down the dock. She leaned in and said, "Aren't you glad now that I insisted on coming with you? Otherwise, you'd—"

"No, I'm not." Sam glared. "Those *English* friends are Grashenko and Korioff."

Yuri Grashenko waited inside the convenience store for Korioff. The man used the toilet more than an old lady. Yuri pretended to examine feathered lures. He was amazed at the gay colors and the variety of shapes. In the village from which he'd come, if a man wanted to fish, he dug up worms. Which were also for sale, a sign proclaimed, at an outrageous price.

Yuri disliked waiting in the shop crowded with children whining to parents to buy them candy or souvenirs. But, he did not want to stand outside where Jozwiak might see him. Yuri wondered what kept him. Too bad John MacDonald had taken advantage of the weather and gone fishing.

Korioff came out, adjusting his trousers. The man was such a pig. Through the large window overlooking the marina, Yuri caught movement out on the dock. A blonde, with long legs that Yuri wasn't too old to appreciate, was walking away from the dock where MacDonald's boat should have been. She was animatedly talking to her companion. A man with a dark beard. A man who was limping.

Jozwiak.

The blonde. Yuri didn't recognized her, even though he'd interviewed the old man at the motel in Buffalo who was only too happy to tell 'British Intelligence' all about the woman with the long braid, an empty box of Miss Clairol and stained towels left behind a shower curtain in the tub.

"Hurry," Yuri called to Korioff who stopped to buy a candy bar.

"But, I—"

Yuri threw a dollar bill on the counter and yanked Korioff behind him. Even though the man was six inches taller and seventy pounds heavier, he followed.

They came out of the shop thirty feet behind Jozwiak. If the motel clerk in Buffalo hadn't bitched about what his customers left behind, Yuri never would have looked twice at the blonde. Who did she work for? She was like a chameleon and too damn clever.

"Why are we hurrying, Yuri?" Korioff said around a mouthful of chocolate.

Yuri elbowed him to be quiet and pointed. Up ahead, Jozwiak glanced over his shoulder. Recognition flared in his eyes. He grabbed the woman's hand and ran. And like Lot's wife—Yuri knew the Bible even though it had been banned in his homeland for most of his life—she looked back.

"Her." Korioff took off at a dead run.

Yuri had hoped to attract as little attention as possible. His plan had been to seize Jozwiak in the parking lot. Once again, Korioff disrupted the plan.

Jozwiak put on a burst of speed, but suddenly the woman stopped and spun around. Her sudden move threw her pursuer off balance before Korioff could grab her. With a twist of her body, she sent him flying off the dock. Korioff hit the water with a splash and a hail of Russian curses.

So much for not attracting attention.

Sam grabbed Daria's car keys. Once again, he shoved her across the driver's seat and climbed in behind her. She didn't fall off the seat this time. She even managed to buckle her seatbelt while he slammed the car into reverse, then forward. Daria just knew she was going to get whiplash.

He avoided hitting a pedestrian who was more interested in the contents of her purse than looking both ways as she crossed the parking lot. Daria just clung to the dash. Her heart was still racing from her 'close encounter' with Korioff. Twice now she'd surprised him more than he surprised her.

And that was a real stretch since she'd been really surprised to hear that big lummox pounding after her.

A bigger concern was Korioff's partner.

"Is he still following?" She twisted to look out the back window. "Grashenko. He was running after us. I don't see any cars tearing out of the parking lot like you did."

"He couldn't very well let his boss' son drown." Sam drove at a controlled speed. Over the posted limit but not enough to attract attention. "Korioff can't swim."

"How do you know he can't swim?" She smacked her forehead with the heel of her hand. "Du-uh. You speak Russian."

"Nice move back there."

"Thanks." She kept eyeing the sideview mirror. Sam made several turns. No new cars behind them.

"Where did you learn how to bodycheck?" he asked.

"Basketball with four brothers. We play a lopsided three-on-three. They never give any quarter. Only time they ever treat me like an equal. There are times when I almost wish they'd go back into *Protect Daria* mode. Then I could score more points."

Sam scoffed. "I don't believe that. You wouldn't want to win that way."

"How do you know?"

"I know you better than you think. You don't want special treatment. You're competitive. And you think fast on your feet. Good strategy to take the offensive."

"Oh." She sat back in surprise at his insight.

"Not too smart, though," he went on. "What if Korioff had been quicker? He could have backhanded you right into the water."

She wasn't too pleased with his post-mortem. Why did he have to give her a compliment and then spoil it with what could have happened? "I didn't think about that. I just didn't want to be grabbed from behind."

"We got lucky. Promise me you won't try anything like that again. I nearly had heart failure when you stopped."

"No promises. That was an act-first, think-later situation. Are you going to promise me you'll be careful?" When he didn't answer, she said, "I thought not. So, who are those other people who visit your friend? Skin-and-bones and the little redhead?"

Sam laughed. "Old Skin and Bones has to be the Assistant Director. The redhead has to be Sally."

So, Sally—whose name Sam uttered while kissing Daria—was small and a redhead. Great. Why should she care? She didn't. Not really. "Okay. So, what are we going to do next?"

"What?" He wound his way through Holland.

"Obviously, you can't give whatever you stole to your friend with the boat. So, what do we do now? Isn't there anyone else you trust who will help you?"

"Yeah."

"And does this person have a phone? Or is he another Luddite?"

"She," he corrected. "Yes, she has a phone."

"Then, why haven't you called her? You could have made a connection with her sooner and avoided this unnecessary detour."

"I tried. Remember? She's out of the country. I didn't think you wanted to drive to Managua."

"Nicaragua?" That took the wind out of her sails. She felt foolish for going off on him for not contacting this woman.

He sounded dejected. He must be very disappointed that his friend, Johnny McIntyre, wasn't where Sam thought he would be. The tension in his shoulders from their flight was gone. Now, they slumped.

"Is it possible she's back now?"

He seemed lost in his thoughts. "Possible."

Did she have to tell him everything? "Well, call her again, damn it."

"You swore."

"Yes, I did. You would make a saint swear."

"I'll need to use your phone. The one I used before."

"W-We sh-should c-call my f-father for help," Korioff said through chattering teeth.

After Yuri pulled his partner from the cold waters of Lake Macatawa, he'd wrapped Korioff in the blanket a helpful boater offered. Yuri was disgusted with Korioff, disgusted with himself. He had Jozwiak within his grasp only to lose him once again. If Korioff wasn't so miserably wet and cold, Yuri would have blasted him with recriminations.

But since he was in charge, the blame rested solely on Yuri's shoulders.

He'd gotten Korioff into the car. Even the heater on full didn't help. Korioff had to change out of his wet clothes and take a hot shower. There had been nothing left to do but to find a motel while Jozwiak's trail grew cold.

"No," Yuri said with exaggerated patience. "We will not call your father."

He never asked for help. That would be a sign that he couldn't handle the situation. A sign that he was no longer competent. In this business, a man was only as good as his last assignment. If he failed or needed to bring in reinforcements, there were others eagerly waiting to take his place. And in this business, there was no cushy retirement plan. No retirement plan at all, except for a bullet between the eyes from someone younger, faster, and smarter.

"Your father wants as few as possible to know his security was breached. He has entrusted this mission to . . . you." Yuri wasn't above pandering to Korioff's ego.

Predictably, the young man puffed up with pride. "He did? Yes. Yes, he did."

"How proud he will be when your father discovers *you* captured Johnston," Yuri went on.

"Yes." Korioff threw off the blanket. "He will be very proud."

Yuri remembered the last time Korioff was injured. "However, if your father knew about your fall into the lake, he will surely want to bring you home." He gauged the insecurity in Korioff's eyes. "He will think you are not ready for such responsibility yet."

"I am ready. We will find Johnston—and that woman." Korioff's eyes turned steely. "Her I will kill with my bare hands."

Yuri turned away so young Korioff would not see the relief in his eyes.

* * *

Sam opened the old flip phone and turned it on. The thing took forever to connect. He had two bars. Better than nothing. He started to input Sally's number when he saw an odd symbol at the corner of the miniscule screen. It took him a moment to recall what the symbol meant. He hadn't seen it in so long. All the phones he used were newer, more sophisticated.

"You have a missed call," he told Daria.

"Go ahead and look. Hit the middle button for Menu and—"

"Got it." He got something else. Eight missed calls all from the same number. Sally's. Damn. Why hadn't he remembered to check? He hit redial.

She answered on the first ring. "Yes."

"Hey, kid."

"Hey, you."

He sensed a world of meaning in her response. Worry, tenderness, relief.

"Where are you?" he asked.

"On the road. You?"

"On the road."

"We've got a big problem."

Sam snorted. "Yeah, I know."

"No, you don't. All hell's broken loose here. Boss thinks you've gone rogue."

His heart squeezed. He couldn't have heard right. "Run that by me again."

"You haven't checked in. You didn't turn over a *package*."

"I ran into an old *friend*. I couldn't hang around and wait for the boss."

"I heard. No wonder everything was fucked up."

"Past history."

"I talked to a friend. He said you were hurt. Bad?" She must have talked to Doc.

"Bad enough."

"Are you all right?" she said softly.

"Been better."

197

"You have a bigger problem. Boss thinks you've gone over to the Dark Side."

He still couldn't believe it. "That's what I thought you meant the first time. What do you think?"

"Damn it. You know me better than that. What do you need?"

He thought for a moment. "A ride."

"You got it. When? Where?"

"Sleepytime Motel. It's on I-80, near 294."

"You're joking."

The motel was nondescript, just like the others they'd stopped at. Besides, it would be along I-80 so Daria could jump back on to get home. "Know where it is?"

"I'll find it."

"Boss?"

Hardesty's phone call interrupted Teller's wife's weekly harangue. According to her, he never used to get calls in the middle of the night; he never used to leave her bed; he used to tell her where he went; he never lied to her before. Now, he was home in the middle of the afternoon, and he was still getting calls. The litany of his sins went on and on.

Teller held up his hand to silence his wife, but she kept yammering away at him until he went into the bathroom and locked the door. Christ. What kind of a deal was this? Hiding out in the john so he could take a goddamn phone call.

A little longer, he thought. He only had to put up with her a little longer. The way she was going on, he might reconsider his plan.

"What?" he said to Hardesty.

"You were right, boss. Joz contacted her."

"He did?" Teller didn't believe he actually would. "See. That's twice now she used the phone you bugged . . . like I told you." He reminded the rookie in case he forgot who was in charge.

"Actually, sir, she isn't using any phone we know about."

"Then, how . . ."

"When I searched her apartment, I found a call on her answering machine. It was a hang-up, but the call took place early Wednesday morning. I thought it might be Jozwiak so I checked out the number on her Caller ID. It's the schoolteacher's cell phone."

Hardesty's attitude bordered on 'I told you so.' Teller was going to have to talk to him about that. Just not now. "Did you find out where Joz is?"

"Not exactly. The conversation was too short, but I know where he will be. Quinero's meeting him at a hotel outside Chicago, almost to Joliet."

"I knew she'd come through." After a moment of silence, Teller amended, "I knew *you* would come through. Get the jet ready."

"Done. I'm on my way to pick you up."

Teller pulled down his fist. "Yes." He would've done a happy dance, but the half bath was too small.

"What did she say that upset you?" Daria asked.

"What?" Sam looked at the dashboard clock. Twenty minutes had passed since he returned her phone and they switched drivers.

Twenty minutes of digesting what Sally had said. Twenty minutes of disbelief followed by anger. And betrayal.

"Whatever she said upset you."

"It's nothing." Nothing he wanted to talk about.

"I'll beat her up for you," Daria offered. Her words brought the first hint of a smile. God, she was beautiful. Ready to do battle for him.

"I believe you would."

"I mean it, Sam. I'll claw her eyes out for upsetting you. You've had a bad enough day, week. Why did you call her anyway?"

"Take it easy. I'm not upset at Sally. She, uh, gave me some . . . unwanted news. So, don't kill the messenger." He gave her a weak smile. "You would like her. Under other circumstances, you two would be friends."

"Somehow I doubt that."

"I'm serious. Sal is a good friend. She's a lot like you. Fiercely protective. Loyal."

"So, that was Sally. I thought as much. You love her," Daria said with resignation.

"What makes you think I love her? I mean, I do but how . . ."

"Your voice when you talked to her and talk about her. When you were out of it from the pain pill I gave you by mistake, you thought I was her. You kissed me, tried to make love to me—only you called her name."

"Wish I'd been awake for that." He hoped his teasing would ease the sinking sensation he felt since Sally dropped her bomb. His own agency thought he was a traitor.

"You and Sally are lovers."

"Used to be lovers. The operative word there is 'used' to be. We were. We aren't anymore. I haven't been in a relationship for a long time. I couldn't want you as much as I do if I was in a relationship with another woman. I don't betray—"

Sam was going to say he didn't betray people or his country. But, he didn't want Daria to know what his agency believed him capable of. He couldn't bear to see the doubt in her eyes. The uncertainty would be there. Oh, she'd protest that she believed him. But, what did she really know about him? She'd known him for three whole days. Half the time he was being a smartass and the other half sleeping.

She didn't even know his real name.

"Jozwiak," he said.

"I beg your pardon?"

"My name isn't Johnston."

"But your passport, driver's license—"

"Fake. My real name is Samuel Joseph Jozwiak. The rest of the information is fake, too. My birthday was last week. April third. I'm thirty-four." The date, year and place of his birth had been altered to prevent anyone who had the time and patience to search from figuring out his real identity. "The 'home' address on the license is headquarters. I went to the University of Iowa on a basketball scholarship. I grew up in a mixed ethnic neighborhood in Chicago. Poles, mostly. Some Russians, Ukrainians, Slavs. Because I speak or understand five eastern European languages, I was recruited by—I can't tell you the name of the agency. I'm asking you to trust me that it's part of the U.S. government."

"You don't have to tell me all this."

"Yes, I do."

CHAPTER TWENTY-ONE

"I thought Michigan construction was bad," Daria said. They had come to a complete stop in northwest Indiana.

She'd seen the large orange signs preparing travelers for delays. She didn't expect this. Bumper-to-bumper, crawling, stopping, creeping ahead, now a dead stop. An SUV's chrome grill filled her entire back window. Too many vehicles, too close. Her hands were sweating, despite the goosebumps on her arms from Sam's open window. Exhaust fumes and grit from the construction filled the car along with the cold air.

"Sweetheart, welcome to Chicago."

"Are you ever going to tell me what that woman said?"

Sam was quiet for so long she thought he'd fallen asleep. "It seems the director of the agency I work for thinks I'm pulling an Aldrich Ames."

"Who? You mean the CIA agent who sold out his colleagues to the KGB?"

"Yeah." Sam laughed mirthlessly. "Because I didn't meet him in New York City, he thinks I'm holding an auction for Korioff's files. God knows, his rivals would want them."

"Back up. I thought your boss was the one who didn't show up for your meeting."

"Yeah, well, I haven't contacted him."

"But your doctor friend said not to trust anyone."

"Yeah. That's a problem."

Sam was worse than a caged animal. He paced the motel room in suburban Chicago while Daria tried to stay out of his way. Although he told her to drop him off, she was too tired to drive any farther. Since she paid for the room, with his money again, she told him she might as well get a good night's sleep and leave in the morning.

In truth, with all his missed connections, she was afraid to leave him behind. What if this Sally person didn't show up?

Daria was exhausted from driving since nine that morning. Twelve hours later, all she wanted was time to unwind. She thought about what she bought at the drugstore, hoping to take her mind off what was about to happen.

Sam was leaving.

And she would never see him again.

During Sally's last phone call, she'd said she would pick up Sam close to midnight. There was plenty of time. If Daria had the nerve. But how to go about it . . .

"Your phone is on, isn't it?" He strode to the dresser/television stand combo where she'd set her purse.

Maybe if she came up behind him and circled his waist. Or—"

"What's this?" Sam held up a small spiral-bound notebook.

"Put that down." She bolted out of the chair as if poked in the butt by a cushion spring. "Don't you dare open that."

"Never could resist a dare." Sam gave her a devilish grin. Before she even took two steps, he started to read aloud. "Eyes: Hershey's semi-sweet chocolate. Hair: 'mahogany.' Crossed out. 'Dark walnut.'"

She raced across the room. She needed to retrieve the log of her most personal thoughts and observations before he read any further.

"Voice: velvet and steel. Crossed out. Too cliché. Kraft—" He broke off as she reached him then held the book in the air and continued reading. "—caramels. Definitely food-oriented. Are you describing someone?"

"Give me that." She tried to reach but his height and longer arms prevented it.

He laughed. "This is better than finding my sister's diary. What is this?" Using his thumb to hold the pages open, he held the book higher. "Tight butt."

Daria grabbed his arm and tried to pull it down. "You are acting so juvenile." She discovered he was stronger than she thought.

He laughed again. A small part of her brain—the part not furious at him or embarrassed that he was reading her private thoughts—registered that he wasn't pacing, that he was thoroughly enjoying himself. At her expense, of course. For a few minutes, he forgot to worry about his mission.

A magnanimous person would rejoice. Daria wasn't feeling very magnanimous. She wrapped both hands around his elbow to bring the book in reach. Nothing. She put her weight into it. He didn't budge. She was nearly swinging from his arm when she felt it move.

Her jubilation was short-lived. He merely switched the book to his other hand.

"Buns of steel. Smooth. Sexy. Whoa. Daria, I'm surprised. You like butts. Whose—" His eyes widened. "Torn flesh. Rivulets of blood. Nausea."

Daria couldn't stand it anymore. He couldn't read the rest. The part about his kisses. She climbed onto the wooden desk chair. "You have no right to snoop. Give me my book." She lunged for the journal.

At the same time, he sidestepped. The chair tipped. Daria lost her balance.

Sam didn't expect Daria to tackle him. He dropped the notebook to catch her before she hurt herself. Her full weight caught him in the chest. He lost his balance. He twisted to cushion her as they fell to the floor.

Daria sprawled on top of him. "Look what you did."

"Me? I wasn't the one playing Peter Pan off the chair."

When she tried to scramble off him, Sam tightened his arms. Didn't he owe himself this moment? The feel of her long legs entwined with his, her lush body full length against his. He would hold her just a moment longer, torturing himself with what might have been had they met under different circumstances. When he wasn't running for his life.

"Sam, you can let go," she said softly.

He'd worked so hard to restrain himself while they lived in each other's pockets. While they spent hours cooped up in a car. While she slept beside him.

"Sam?" She sounded a little breathless. Her pupils were wide, rimmed by a slim halo of blue.

He tucked a straggling curl behind her ear. "In a minute," he whispered. He drew two fingers along her jaw. Her skin was soft, the way a girl's should be. But he'd seen that jaw tighten and become stubborn. Last night, she talked about how she let her brothers walk all over her. She made promises about standing up for herself. Didn't she realize she already had that strength?

He traced her cheekbones, her dark eyebrows so at odds with her new hair color, her nose with its slight upturn. And then her lips. Full, sensual.

She parted her lips and touched his finger with her tongue.

Sam's restraint crumbled. He cupped the back of her neck and brought her closer. "You've been a temptation from the get-go."

He kissed her. And, glory halleluiah, she kissed him back. All fire and urgency. She kissed him with a hunger that took his breath away. Sweet Jesus, she was wild. And hot. She made him hot.

"Touch me," she demanded before sucking on his earlobe.

Sam covered her breast with his hand. Through her shirt and bra, he felt it swell. He rubbed her nipple, and she writhed on top of him. Her moans drove him crazy.

"I want you," he said, his voice husky.

"I want you, too." She sounded just as husky.

"You have on too many clothes." He slid his hands under her shirt. He had to touch her, had to feel—

As she shifted, her knee banged against his right hip. A spasm of pain shot through him. He couldn't control the groan.

"Oh, Sam. I'm sorry." Daria rolled off on his left side. "I forgot about your wound. Are you hurting?" She knelt next to him, anxiety in her voice and expression.

"Yes," he said through clenched teeth. He lay on the motel room floor, practically in fetal position.

"I am so sorry. I should have been more careful. I forgot all about your gunshot wounds. I'm—"

"If you say you're sorry again, I will slap you," he said.

"You won't," she said with conviction. "I know you better than that. You don't hit women. You protect them. Now, hold still." She reached around his waist and tried to unbuckle his belt.

He slapped her hand away. "What the hell do you think you're doing?"

"I need to check your wounds."

"No, you don't. I'm fine." Hell if he was fine. Jesus, his hip hurt like a son of a bitch.

"Sam Johns—Jozwiak, either drop your drawers or I'll do it for you." She said it with such ferocity he figured he'd better obey, or she'd do more damage to his wounds trying to take off his clothes.

"Bathroom." He crawled to the fallen chair and used it to lever himself up. She was right there helping him. Good little Nursey followed him into the bathroom. "Do you think I could have some privacy?"

"No. I think something's wrong."

"Hell, yeah, there's something wrong. You almost killed me."

"I did not." She sounded so indignant he almost laughed. "Do not give me any more grief. Bend over."

"Didn't know you were into kinky sex. You should've told me."

When she went into second-grade teacher mode—pursed lips, narrowed eyes, tapping foot—he complied. Leaning over the vanity while the woman he lusted after pulled down his briefs about as humiliating as it gets. For the past four days, she'd seen him helpless, vulnerable, unmanly. A first for him and he didn't like it.

"Oh, Lord. Sam, your hip is red and swollen. I don't think your antibiotic is working." Then, she did the "mom" thing and put the inside of her wrist against his forehead. "You're quite warm. You probably have a fever."

"Ya think maybe I'm hot because I wanted to have sex with you? Jesus Christ, unprotected sex. I'm not a kid. I don't carry condoms in my wallet in case I get lucky on a mission."

"Not unprotected." She pointed to the bag from the drugstore sitting on the counter. She'd stopped for what she called *unmentionables* before they got to the motel. What she withdrew from the bag sure as hell weren't tampons.

She held up an economy-size box of Trojans. "I told you I like to be prepared. In case *I* got lucky." She smirked.

Sam groaned. God, his butt was on fire. What had he been thinking holding her, touching her? He hadn't been thinking. He'd let longing and lust take over his brain. What the hell was he blaming himself for? Apparently, she'd had seduction on her mind when she ran into the drugstore earlier.

She edged around him in the miniscule bathroom and turned on the faucet. "You need a hot compress." She was muttering under her breath as she wrung out a washcloth and applied it to his butt. Words like "stubborn, typical male, obdurate." He thought she said "hardheaded" a couple of times, too. She certainly had an extensive vocabulary where men were concerned. Only by force of will did he keep from yelping over how hot the cloth was. How did she squeeze out the excess water without burning her hands?

He glanced up and saw worry in her eyes and tightness around her mouth. "Take it easy, okay?"

"You should have told me your hip wasn't healing right. Don't you know two signs of infection are redness and heat?"

He let her vent. No excuses. Yes, he knew the signs. His training went beyond basic first aid. An agent had to take care of himself in the field. Foolishly, he thought the antibiotics Doc gave him just needed time to work. His hip had been red and tender this morning, but he thought he'd get to Mac's and then get his wounds checked out. He hadn't planned on another full day on the road.

As with this entire mission, nothing went according to plan.

Daria was wringing out the washcloth again. He took it from her. "You don't need to burn your hands taking care of me."

"It's nothing." She was lying. Ms. Prim and Proper was lying. Her hands resembled lobsters.

He held her reddened hands. "I never wanted you to get hurt on my account. I'm not worth it."

God, that sounded pathetic. He meant to sound—what? Selfless, altruistic. Nope. He just sounded pathetic.

She turned her hands around and held his. "I wanted to, uh, make love with you." She wouldn't look him in the eye.

With his knuckle, he lifted her chin. "I don't do one-night stands. And I don't think you do, either."

She gave him a tentative smile and shook her head. "I just . . . I just wanted to know what it felt like."

Sam had a bad feeling. "What what felt like?"

"A, uh, an orgasm."

He groaned. "Please don't tell me you're a virgin."

She turned away and ran the hot water again. "Not technically." She soaked the washcloth.

"What do you mean 'not technically'? Either you are or you aren't."

She quit wringing the washcloth. "Are you asking about my sexual history?"

"Yes, damn it." God, he'd nearly—he'd wanted to make lo—have sex with a virgin.

"I suppose that is the proper thing to do these days. A person can't be too careful."

"You said you're technically not a virgin. Did you have an . . . accident?"

Her mouth twisted. "I guess you could call Josh Lawrence an accident. He got the condom on, did the deed and came within twenty seconds."

"The son of a bitch."

"Gee, that was so much fun. Your turn."

"One? You had one lousy lover?"

"He was no lover, but he sure was lousy. Your turn," she repeated.

"Hold on. When did this happen?"

"Oh, ages ago. In college. Back to you. How many women have you had?"

"That sounds so crass. I don't *have* women. I make love with them. And I hold out a hell of a lot longer than twenty seconds."

"I'll bet you're wonderful, too." She leaned over and kissed his temple. "Do you feel well enough to continue where we left off?"

"Stop that." He wanted to make love with sweet, sexy Daria. But, he couldn't. He couldn't make—have sex with practically a virgin. As he said, he never had one-night stands. Once his ride got here, he was never going to see her again.

He wasn't a hit-and-run man. He would hate himself in the morning.

Making love with Daria and then leaving would be cruel. As cruel for her as it was for him. She would haunt his dreams. As it was, she made him long for what she represented. Home, hearth, all that was good and normal. He hadn't lived a normal life for over twelve years.

Daria Mason scared him more than Yuri Grashenko. He'd let his guard down with her. She made him think of what might have been.

He'd nearly had sex with a woman he forced into driving him halfway across the country. That bordered on coercion. No, it was coercion. He was going straight to hell. He was a bastard. A real bastard.

The muffled ring of a cell phone came from the other room.

Daria so didn't want to explain her extremely limited sexual history. She ran out to grab the phone from her purse. At least answering the phone gave her an excuse to leave the small confines of the bathroom she'd shared with Sam.

She'd wanted so badly to make love with him. Something to remember from her brief time with him. Not that she'd ever forget Sam John—Sam Jozwiak.

She wanted to give him a memory to carry away with him. The memory of the woman who loved him.

Dear Lord, when had that happened? She'd fallen in love with Sam.

The phone rang again. Daria clicked it on. "Is this my idiot brother? The one who thinks I'm incapable of traveling alone? You'd better not be checking up on me again."

A woman cleared her throat. "Actually, this is the idiot who needs to talk to the man you're traveling alone with."

Daria looked at the phone. She'd answered her old one and hadn't even noticed. Force of habit. She shook her head and held it out to Sam who'd followed her out of the bathroom. She'd only beat him to her purse because he had to pull up his pants. "Your ride's here," she said, hating the unseen woman who sounded sexy and pretty.

Sam took the phone, listened for three seconds, then hung up and shoved the phone into his pocket. "We gotta go." He grabbed his jacket and his weapon out of the closet. He threw her windbreaker at her.

She batted it aside. "In case you forgot, I'm staying. *You're* leaving with Sally Whatshername."

He limped into the bathroom and gathered her toiletries and the medical supplies she hadn't had a chance to use on him. He threw everything into her bag. Every other step brought a spasm of pain.

"Daria," he said sharply. "Grab your things. Somebody's following Sally."

CHAPTER TWENTY-TWO

Daria felt like a deadbeat, sneaking out of the motel. She'd paid cash, used Alexa Tremaine's name when she checked in so there was no way Grashenko could track them to the room. But, Sam wasn't waiting around to find out, and he was dragging her with him.

Using the peephole, he checked the hall then carefully opened the door and checked again. He barely waited when she went back for the little spiral notebook under the desk. That notebook was to blame for her lack of judgment. She wasn't leaving her journal for anyone else to read.

When they first arrived at the hotel, Sam instructed her to back into a parking slot at the opposite end of the unit. Since Sally was going to pick him up, it hadn't been important. Now, Daria worried that it was too far for him to walk.

He made her wait between the double entry doors while he checked the brightly-lit parking lot. "Okay." He motioned for her to come. "Don't open the trunk. Just throw everything in the backseat and hit the road."

She did and didn't even wait for Sam to buckle up before she put the car in gear and took off. He grabbed her purse from the back seat and pulled out her new phone. Then, he pulled her old one out of his pocket.

"What are you—"

"Just drive," Sam said.

A flash of headlights yanked her attention from Sam back to the road. A Cadillac barreled in off the street. She swerved to avoid a collision. In that split second, she saw surprise on the man's face. It probably mirrored hers.

Sam bounced against the door. "What the hell was that? I told you to drive carefully. Holy shit." He ducked as Daria pulled out onto the street.

"What are you doing with my phones?" she asked.

"Never mind." He stayed scrunched down.

"What?" She looked wildly around at the cars passing them on the service drive that led from the main road to the motel. "Did you see Grashenko?"

"That was my boss."

"What?"

"The black Caddie trying to avoid hitting the motel sign."

"You mean your boss who thinks you're a traitor?" she exclaimed. "Let me find a place to turn around, and we'll go back. I'll give that guy a piece of my mind."

"And have him arrest me as a traitor? I don't think so. We'll connect with Sally. Her, I trust."

Daria remembered Doc's warning. *Don't trust anyone.*

Sam had her old flip phone open in one hand. He was texting in the new one.

"What are you doing?"

"Contacting Sal from your new phone. If someone followed her, her phone was compromised. So was yours, the other one. SOP when followed means changing phones."

"SOP?" Before he could answer, she said, "Oh, standard operating procedure. Gotcha. So, if my old phone was compromised why do you have it out?"

"Sally got a new phone. I'm texting that number from your new one and then we need another phone. Find that drugstore we stopped at before."

"Another one? How many phones do we need?"

"Enough that they can't be traced."

Her new phone rang. Sam answered, "Okay, Sal. What's the plan?"

There was silence for so long Daria glanced over at Sam. In the light of passing cars, she could see his face. It had turned a strange color. Must be an effect of the headlights and the green display from the dash.

"Wrong number?" she asked.

He handed the phone to her. "Not exactly." He cleared his throat. "It's for you."

"Hello?"

"What the hell are you doing in Chicago?" It was Jimmy.

"How do you know I'm in Chicago?"

"GPS in your phone."

"You are tracking my phone?" She couldn't believe it. "How dare you?"

In the background, she heard the other boys.

"I can see why you've never been asked to be a hostage negotiator," Andy said while Billy said, "I told you to let Tom call."

"Who was that man?" Jimmy demanded. "Are you all right? What the . . ."

She held the phone away from her ear while Jimmy continued his interrogation from over three hundred miles away. She smiled at Sam. "You're right. It's for me." She didn't bother to cover the phone.

"Who is Sal?" Jimmy shouted. "Does he have an accomplice? Just tell me you're all right. Give me your safe word."

"An accomplice? What are you talking about? Why are you calling?" Daria fired back. He wasn't the only interrogator. "And what do you mean by tracking this phone. Why are you checking up on me?"

"Checking up? You didn't call tonight. I thought you were all alone since Ginnie is in *Florida*. A man answers your phone, and all you can do is complain about me calling?"

"It's nearly midnight," she managed to cut in. "Maybe I'm in bed."

"If a man answers your phone, you sure as hell better not be in bed."

"She's in bed with a man?" Daria heard Billy yell.

"And why not?" Daria glanced over at Sam and winked. "I'm a healthy woman with a healthy woman's sexual appetite."

She heard a choking sound, followed by silence. She wondered if Jimmy swallowed his tongue. Unfortunately, the silence didn't last.

"Listen, you numb-nuts," Jim barked without covering the phone. "Our sister is with a man. What the hell is she doing?"

"Gee, I don't know, Jim," Andy said. "What *would* a man and a woman be doing at midnight?"

Bill guffawed while Tom cleared his throat. Typical of her middle brother.

"Daria Jean is not a woman," Jim declared. "She's our baby sister."

That was the problem. They still thought of her as their little sister. Enough of that. "Gotta go." She ended the call. The phone rang again and she tossed it to Sam. "Turn it off."

"I think you'd better tell me who that guy was," Sam said.

"Why? Jealous?"

"Are you trying to make *him* jealous?"

"Of course not." Daria felt the heat of his glare. "Sally calls you."

"That's different. I told you Sally and I aren't lovers. Now, are you going to tell me who that guy was? I thought you said you hadn't had a lover since Speedy Gonzales. Josh Whatshisname."

"He's not my lover, that's for sure. By the way, what did he say to you?"

"You mean after demanding who the hell I was? He said if I hurt you, he'd follow me to the ends of the earth, rip the skin off my balls, chop them into little pieces and shove them up my ass."

"I want to hear about your sexual history," Daria said as she cruised down a side street. "I told you mine. You were saved by the phone."

"Not now." Sam's head hurt. "I have to think about what we're going to do next." Concentrating on a plan seemed more than he could manage. From the way his body felt, he knew he had a fever. "Where's that drugstore—God, I can't believe you waltzed in and bought condoms."

"I didn't waltz in. I was so embarrassed my face had to be bright red. Thank goodness, some teenager wasn't behind the register."

Sam propped his elbow next to the window and rested his head. "Gotta hand it to you. You're a surprise a minute. Just when I think I have you figured out, you do something totally out of character."

"Maybe you don't know me as well as you think." She pulled up in front of the twenty-four-hour drugstore. She turned off the car and twisted in the seat to face him. "Okay, why do we need another phone?"

"We need one that can't be traced."

"What? Do you think someone is listening in on our calls?"

"Someone is following Sally. Could be Grashenko. He has the smarts and the equipment to listen in on cell calls. He could track cell phones with GPS."

"My new one has GPS." She hit the steering wheel with her palm. "That rotten Jimmy has been tracking my phone."

"Shit."

"My sentiments exactly. Do you think Grashenko found out who I am and is tracking my phone, too?"

"Could be. Maybe somebody else. I don't like it that Teller just happened to show up at the motel where we were staying. Sally wouldn't tell him. She hates his guts." Sam felt the same way.

"I'd better get that phone. Do you need anything else?" she asked.

He was so tired, he could hardly think. "Get two phones plus long-distance phone cards." He managed to find his wallet and pull out three bills. "Then, I'll call Sally and find out what Plan B is."

CHAPTER TWENTY-THREE

Sam woke up disoriented. He was sweating, yet cold despite the blanket wrapped around his shoulders. His head was on Daria's breast and his arms resting around her waist under her jacket. The steering wheel was inches from his nose. She had her back to the door and sound asleep.

Sam levered himself away from her, half-afraid he'd drooled on her electric blue shirt. The car was tucked between two semis. Over the rumble of diesels, he heard faint traffic sounds. Through the rear window, he could see dawn begin to color the sky.

Where? Why had she stopped?

Okay, Ace, think. The last thing he remembered after she came out of the drugstore with the new cell phones and a bottle of aspirin—she claimed he had a fever—was trying to call Sally. And getting no answer.

Daria stirred. She opened one eye, blinked and smiled. "You're awake."

"Yeah. Where are we?"

"Almost to the Mississippi. Last service plaza before Moline." She yawned and tried to stretch, but the steering wheel was in her way. "I'm sorry. I just couldn't—"

"What the hell are we doing here? Sally's in Chicago. Shit."

She bristled. "Don't you swear at me. I nearly ran off the road because I fell asleep. If it hadn't been for rumble strips, we would've flipped or hit a bunch of trees."

Sam scrubbed his hand down his bristly jaw. "I'm—"

"Listen, Buster, until two this morning, I did everything you asked. I drove you to a doctor, but he wouldn't let you stay. I drove you to your friend's boat in Michigan, only he and the boat were gone. I even drove through Chicago on a Friday night during rush hour. Why? So you could meet up with another friend who didn't come. Your plans suck. You fell asleep. So, I took charge. I decided to go home. Don't forget. You're just a stray I picked up in New York City."

"Wha—"

"Just like Rover. And Archy and Mahitabel and Ling-Ling and—"

"You're making up those names."

"I am not. Rover is a mutt who was dumped at the end of my drive. Archy and Mahitabel are kittens someone threw in a sack and pitched into the ditch. Ling-Ling was a finch who broke his wing falling out of the nest in the tree next to the kitchen window."

"You name all the wounded strays?"

"Then, I patch them up and shove them out the door." When she didn't look at him, he knew she was lying. He'd lay odds that the dog and cats were still in their happy home.

"When we get home, I'm dumping you. I'll turn you over to my brothers. I'm through with trying to help you only to have you go off on me."

"What about Sally?"

"I got hold of her on the burn phone when I stopped at the rest area. You know, that's a good idea using different phones. I'm going to use that in my book. Anyway, I told her my plan."

"And she agreed?"

"It's better than anything you two have come up with." Her mutinous look softened. "Sam, my brothers will help."

"Why do you think they'll help me?" How had he lost control of the situation?

"Because I'll tell them they have to." She smiled. "They won't let me down. They might be pains in the tush, but they're trustworthy. Now, I'm going to use the restroom and then we're getting back on the road. We still have a ways to go."

Bart Teller woke up with a mother of a headache plus a crick in his neck and back pain that only his chiropractor could relieve.

He'd only meant to rest his eyes for a few minutes. It was almost eight. The sun was up and the service plaza nearly empty. When he stopped east of the Mississippi to use the restroom around three, the parking lot was crowded with semis, RVs and a few cars.

Last night, he had been so close to his goal. What spooked Jozwiak into running? Thanks to Hardesty, Teller had the right place—the Sleepytime Motel. Thanks to a desk clerk only too willing to help the *police*, Teller even had the room number. When no one answered his knock, the clerk opened the door. Gone.

Not only that, but Hardesty was gone. When Teller returned to the jet, he found Hardesty's resignation. Stupid shit. How the hell was he supposed to get to Iowa?

Teller was now convinced Hardesty was right about the importance of the woman. She was returning home and taking Jozwiak with her. With Hardesty gone, who was going to fly the plane?

When did his life turned to shit?

Teller swore at the roadhog who cut him off. Then, he realized he hadn't been paying attention to the speed limit. He pushed the pedal to the floor and the Caddie responded like a dream. He always drove Cadillacs. It was all about appearances, according to his wife, the rich bitch. Act successful, and you'll be successful. Well, just a while longer and he wouldn't have to listen to her anymore. He almost had enough socked away. He chuckled as he thought about how easy it had been.

Damn. That truck just cut him off.

He floored it, passed the truck then flipped the driver the bird. *How do you like that, sucker?* Nobody cut off Bart Teller and got away with it.

This debacle should have been over days ago. If he'd gotten the evidence in New York. If his goddamn plane hadn't been delayed. If Grashenko hadn't shown up and sent Joz on the run. If that Mason bitch hadn't helped him, Joz would have called the agency.

The fact that he was driving across the goddamn country trying to find his operative made Teller furious. Get to Podunkville, Iowa. Get Jozwiak. Get the—

The siren and flashing lights in his rearview mirror made him glance at his speedometer. Eighty-five. Well, shit.

* * *

"Talk to me," Daria demanded. "Despite my nap, I'm having a hard time keeping my eyes open."

In the sideview mirror, Sam could see the sun behind them. He knew he should offer to drive, but he didn't have the strength. He'd thought he was getting better, that the gunshot wounds were healing. An illusion that was coming back to bite him.

"Sure. What do you want to talk about?"

"Your sexual history. Which you keep avoiding. No excuses."

"Thought you wanted to stay awake. My *exploits* will put you to sleep faster than a knock-out drug."

"You're stalling."

He swiped his hand down his face. "I can't believe you're asking about this. Nothing is going to happen between us. Once I connect with Sally, I'm gone."

"I know. But, I told you about Josh Lawrence."

"I'm a little sick about hearing his name."

"Sam, I'm waiting . . ."

He blew out a breath. "I'm a healthy male. I've always been careful. I've been in a couple of relationships. They didn't last because of my job. I'm not in one now. Haven't been for quite a while."

"Is that why you've never married? Because of your job?"

"Yeah. Funny how that works. A wife actually expects her husband to come home on a regular basis. And when he's called out in the middle of the night, a wife expects to know where he's going."

"Agents don't get married?"

"Some do. Most get divorced. I'm not putting a woman through that. I don't want my wife to doubt that I'm faithful. Or to doubt herself."

"She wouldn't if she loved you. She would trust."

"Trust has to be built. When a man is evasive about where he goes at a moment's notice, trust erodes. And what about kids? You think bad guys postpone their nefarious deeds for dance recitals and Little League games? How the hell would I tell my daughter I can't come to her T-ball game or my son that Daddy has to miss the Pinewood Derby? I sure as hell am not telling my children that saving the world is more important than they are."

Daria sat in stunned silence. He'd obviously thought long and hard about having a family. He wanted one. She could hear it in his voice, in the way he said 'my daughter' and 'my son.' But, Sam must have weighed his choices and sacrificed family for duty.

"Daria," Sam said urgently. He pointed to the dashboard.

A red light flared from the instrument panel. *Temp.* She quickly looked at the temperature gauge. The needle, which usually hovered near the mid-mark between C and H, had shot to the H. Carefully, she slowed down then edged to the side of the tollway. When the car stopped, white smoke billowed out from under the hood.

"Oh, my God, the engine's on fire!" She quickly shut if off before the car blew up taking them with it.

"No," Sam said quietly. "If there was fire, the smoke would be black. That's steam. You've lost a radiator hose."

Why couldn't the car break down closer to an exit? They'd passed Iowa City and were almost home.

She reached for the door handle, but he said, "Wait. We can't do anything yet. Pop the hood and let the steam dissipate."

When she pulled the hood release, more steam spewed out. Radiator? After he'd thoroughly checked over the car before her trip, Tommy was going to have a hissy fit.

"We can't just sit here." She drummed her fingers on the steering wheel.

Sam covered her fingers with his big hand. Warmth and reassurance flowed from him. "Be calm. Wait."

He was right about the steam. The early morning breeze quickly blew it away. Suddenly, she remembered something she'd read.

"Hold on," she said brightly. "I know just the thing to fix this."

She checked for approaching traffic. This time he didn't stop her. Instead, he met her at the back of the car where, by the time he hobbled around, she'd opened the trunk. "The steam is coming from the other end," he said.

"I know." She rummaged in her tote bag. Triumphantly, she held up the roll of duct tape. "I told you it has many uses."

He acknowledged that with a rueful smile and grabbed a rag tucked into the front of the trunk near the latch. "Didn't I see jugs of water in here?"

She pushed aside her coat in its long garment bag. It was covering up the jugs of water that had been shoved to the very back of the trunk. She leaned in as far as she could, stretched and pulled them out.

When she turned around, Sam had a strange look on his face.

"Are you okay?"

He looked away. "Uh, yeah."

"Were you staring at my butt?" she demanded.

He cleared his throat. "Flashlight."

"Yes, Doctor." She slapped a Mag-light into his open hand. "But, I don't see why we need a flashlight. The sun is up."

"Bring the water."

"Yes, sir."

Daria followed as Sam limped to the front of the car. When he propped up the hood, she could see steam still spitting from a hose.

"Stay back," he warned. "I don't want you to get burned. At least, it's a hose on top. I wasn't relishing crawling under the car." He held onto the frame.

"You should get back in the car," she said. "I can take it from here."

"I'll do it. Just hold the flashlight so I can see what the hell I'm doing."

Now, she understood why he wanted the flashlight. The upraised hood blocked the sun. "I am capable of dealing with this, you know." She shone the big flashlight on the engine. "It's a good thing I'm prepared."

Sam used the rag to wipe off the hose. He rolled the silver-gray tape around it. "Good thing you had the water, too." Sam poured water into the radiator until he was satisfied. "The tape won't hold for long. You said we're not far from your exit?"

She nodded.

"Okay, let's get out of here before some Good Samaritan stops to help us. With our luck, it'll be Grashenko and Company."

Getting the lay of the land, Yuri Grashenko slowly drove through the sleepy town of Prairieville. The main street was three blocks long. Two streets crossed it with a courthouse in the middle. It didn't take long for those locals who were up and about early on a Saturday morning to stop and gawk at the stranger in their midst. He should have remembered how provincial, how insular these places were. He came from just such a village. He could not wait until he returned to the City.

He would, just as soon as he retrieved what Jozwiak had taken. Then, Yuri would climb back into his rented Towncar and make his superior very happy.

Of course, he would have to pick up Korioff in Chicago where he'd left him searching motels for his elusive prey. Yuri lost Jozwiak too many times because of that damn fool to bring him along for the finale. He wasn't going to lose Jozwiak this time.

Korioff was so angry at the woman he'd lost sight of the goal. Nothing Yuri said had any effect. Korioff was bent on revenge. The only reason he agreed to search for Jozwiak was to find the woman.

Yuri knew he was taking a chance coming to this village. He'd missed Jozwiak at the Sleepytime Motel and barely escaped detection by Teller. When Jozwiak didn't get rid of the Mason woman, Yuri knew she was the key to getting what he wanted. He'd already driven past her home. Isolated. The nearest neighbor approximately a kilometer away. However, at the present time, three vehicles were parked in the large garage. Trusting, these Americans who did not close doors. Through the open windows of the house, he saw men moving around. He would have to wait until they left.

He noticed a restaurant into which the early risers were entering. The Wheel Inn, which sat across the street from the courthouse, reminded him of KGB training films made in the

1950's about Middle America. And television episodes he and other prospective agents watched that would prepare them to infiltrate the decadent capitalist society. However, "The Andy Griffin Show" and "Father Knows Best" did not prepare him for New York City or Los Angeles.

Yuri hoped for a properly brewed cup of coffee. Not the sludge he'd gotten three hours ago at a service plaza along the Illinois Tollway. He'd actually given thought to sleeping in the car, like others in the last plaza before Iowa. Instead, he'd pushed on hoping to get to the Mason farm before his quarry. A lot of good it did, though.

He chose a booth next to the broad front window where he could watch the main street. The lone waitress assured him she'd be right back to take his order then complained to the people in the next booth about another waitress who hadn't shown up for work.

The coffee—when it finally came—was hot and delicious. The aromas emanating from the kitchen made his mouth water. He had just decided to order breakfast when he noticed three cars cruising up the street. He recognized them from the Mason woman's farm.

Hurriedly leaving money on the table for his coffee, Yuri rushed out to his car. He needed to be in place before Jozwiak and the woman got to the farm. He whipped the Towncar away from the curb only to be stopped by a sudden jolt and a screech of metal on metal. Followed by another screech—of the human variety.

"My car. You ruined my car."

Yuri climbed over the floor console to use the passenger door. He walked around to inspect the damage. Through the open window of an older vehicle, an elderly woman grieved over her car. He'd embedded the left front headlight of the Towncar into the side post of the woman's door. Until she backed up, he was unable to go anywhere.

Yuri did not have time to waste over a silly traffic accident. He quickly walked around to the driver's side of the other car. "Madam, if you will please reverse your vehicle, you will no longer impede traffic."

"Oh my goodness." She immediately changed from grief-stricken to fawning. "You're English, aren't you?"

Yuri gave her his best British nod—royalty to peasant. "You have a good ear for accents, Madam. Might I impose upon you to reverse your vehicle?"

Her companion leaned across to look at him. "Oh, no, you don't, sonny."

He was perhaps ten years younger and she called him *sonny*? This woman was even shaking her finger at him. "You don't move the cars until the police come. That's what my husband, the late Mr. Carmody, always said."

People came out of the restaurant to gawk at the spectacle. Two old men left their wooden chairs in front of the hardware store and ambled across the street. One held a cell phone up to his ear.

"Lloyd's calling Sheriff Jim," the other old man announced.

"Sheriff's coming," the man with the cell phone said. "Wasn't your fault, Gladys. Don and I saw the whole thing."

"Gladys, don't say a word," her companion said. "Mr. Carmody always said never admit anything. Can you move your head? Maybe you have whiplash."

"Harriet, this nice gentleman is from England." The driver got out of her car.

Yuri looked over at the Lincoln, the color of silver smoke. The rental company would not be pleased.

The passenger didn't stop talking as she scooted across the seat to get out. "That *nice gentleman* just cut out in front of you. You should look where you're going, sonny."

"Here comes Sheriff Jim," the old man named Lloyd said.

A tall man in a brown uniform hurried down the broad courthouse steps and crossed the street. He surveyed the knot of people around the cars. "Well, well, well. What have we here? Miz Arbuckle, Miz Carmody." He nodded to the women.

Yuri groaned. Of course, in a village this small the police would know the citizens. He was the outsider. He would be at fault, even if he wasn't. He would have preferred not to encounter the authorities.

"James Allen." Mrs. Carmody bustled up to the sheriff. "Arrest that man."

Adrenaline shot through Yuri's system. Arrest? That old woman could not possibly know who he was and why he was there.

"Miz Carmody, we do not arrest people for fender-benders. All right," the sheriff said to those gathered in the street. "You lookee-loos go on about your business."

Some went back into the restaurant. Most stayed on the sidewalk. Yuri remembered his own village. This was probably the most excitement they'd had all week.

"But he's a furriner," the Carmody woman insisted. "He'll probably skip town leaving Gladys to foot the bill, and it was all his fault."

Relieved that he'd misinterpreted the woman's demand for his arrest, Yuri decided it was time to take control of this situation. He walked up to the officer, stretching out his hand. He held the forged documents in his other. "Good morning, sir. Archibald Rutledge. As you see, we had a small altercation. I have my international driver's license, the rental agreement on my vehicle and proof of insurance. If you could expedite the paperwork, I shall be on my way out of your fair city."

"Hold on there, sonny," the Carmody woman said. "None of that fancy talk. We're just plain folks here. James Allen, don't you let him get away." She peered at his chest. "Where is your name tag? How are furriners supposed to know you're our sheriff?"

The sheriff didn't need a name tag. His uniform and the weapon holstered at his side were enough identification for Yuri.

The sheriff patted his chest. "Guess I got dressed in a hurry, Miz Carmody. Sure glad you're here to keep me on the straight-and-narrow." He gave her a rueful look. "Miz Arbuckle, you want to move your car over to the curb so you aren't blocking traffic?"

"I knew it, Harriet. I knew I should have moved my car."

"We'll go over to the courthouse and fill out the paperwork. Miz Arbuckle, bring your license, registration and proof of insurance."

The driver gave him a sheepish look. "I-I forgot my purse. I was in such a hurry to pick up Harriet that I . . .

forgot."

"James Allen, you've known Gladys since she was your kindergarten teacher. You don't need to see her license."

"It's the law, Miz Carmody."

"You weren't so anxious about following the law in fifth grade when you—"

"Miz Arbuckle, you bring in your license and registration today or I'll have to issue you a ticket," the sheriff said, before turning to Yuri. "Come with me, sir. If everything is in order, you can pay your fine and be on your way."

Of course, everything was in order. Yuri only engaged the best forgers.

"A fine?" the Carmody woman exclaimed. Neither she nor the driver had gotten into the car, let alone moved it out of the street. "You're only giving him a fine? Look what he did to Gladys's car!"

"Miz Carmody," the sheriff said patiently. "Let the insurance companies duke it out. We only put murderers, thieves and spies in jail these days."

For a full second, Yuri's heart stopped. *Spies. A hidden message?* No, it was a joke. The sheriff was looking entirely too pleased with himself.

"Gladys, are you going to let—"

The driver cut off her companion. "Harriet, I know you mean well, but that's enough about my car."

"But—"

"I do not want to hear another word about the accident."

"But—"

"I mean it. Not another word. Now, I have to go home and get my purse and come back to town so I don't get a ticket, too. Are you coming?"

"He didn't mean you had to get them now. We'll just get something to eat and—"

"No. I am going home now."

While the two women argued and finally drove away, Yuri followed the sheriff to the last place he wanted to be. On his perusal of the village, he'd noticed a small sign on one side of the courthouse. County Jail.

CHAPTER TWENTY-FOUR

Ka-pow!

Sam flattened himself across the seat. When he heard the unmistakable thump-da-thump of a flat tire, he felt absolutely foolish. What was the matter with him? He knew the difference between a blow-out and a gunshot. He straightened and gave Daria a weak smile. "Sorry."

"What did you think?" She wrestled the car onto the narrow shoulder of the two-lane road. Only moments before, they'd left the toll road. "Oh, my goodness, you thought someone was shooting at us."

Instead of answering, Sam got out of the car. He limped around to the driver's side. With resignation, he inspected the tire. "It's flat."

"Only on one side." She grinned. Then, she sobered. "I can't believe this. We're almost home."

"Since you're always so prepared, I assume you have a can of instant tire inflator?"

"I sure do. Stay here, and I'll get it." She ran back to the trunk. When she returned, she'd left the trunk lid up as a warning to anyone passing by. "I'll do it. My brother showed me how."

She was so determined to prove she could handle road emergencies, Sam let her. She followed the directions. The tire inflated . . . and then quickly went down again. "It didn't work," she groaned.

Sam bent over to look, ignoring the pain in his calf and rear. "What in the world did you run over? You have a hole as big as the Grand Canyon. I'll have to change the tire." He limped back to the trunk and groaned. He'd have to take out everything—luggage, cooler, shopping bags—to get to the spare.

At the sound of a car coming from town, Daria exclaimed, "Wait. We'll catch a ride home and one of the

227

boys will take care of the car." She stepped into the middle of the road and waved her hands.

As much as he hated to leave the job for someone else—especially Daria's brothers—Sam pushed his male ego aside and decided to follow her suggestion. Just getting out of the car had been more exertion than he expected. He was sweating and feeling queasy. And he didn't relish the thought of squatting to change a tire. The skin around both wounds felt like plastic wrap stretched beyond its limit.

Daria ran up to the driver's side of a blue-green Chevy Impala, circa 1971. It was built like a tank with a mile-long hood. The elderly driver was so short it was a wonder she could see over the steering wheel.

"Hi, Mrs. Arbuckle. Could you give us a lift?" A moment later, Daria ran back to her car, leaned in the driver's side and came out with her purse. "C'mon, Sam. We've got a ride."

He grabbed his bag and shut the trunk. When he hobbled over to the Impala, Daria threw a smug smile at him. "See, I told you someone would give us a lift." She opened the back door and slid across the seat so he didn't have to walk around the car. "Mrs. Arbuckle, Mrs. Carmody, this is my friend Sam."

"Darla Jean, what have you done to your hair?" the passenger exclaimed.

Daria shrugged at Sam and whispered, "She has never gotten my name right. Not even when she was my fifth-grade teacher."

The elderly woman didn't wait for Daria's answer. "You will never guess what happened this morning—"

"Harriet," the driver said sharply. She struggled with the steering to make a three-point turn, narrowly missing Daria's car.

"I know, I know."

In the silence that ensued, Daria gave Sam a bewildered look and shrugged. "Mrs. Carmody, how's your daughter? Has she had her baby yet?"

As they drove down country lanes, past fields of new growth, Mrs. Carmody went on at length about the birth of her grandbaby four days ago, and Sam learned more than he wanted to know about the delivery. But, that wasn't the worst.

"Hemorrhoids," Mrs. C. announced in a voice of doom. Then, the driver began extolling the benefits of different brands of fiber supplements, stool softeners, and laxatives. Sam leaned his head against his seat and wished he was back in Toledo or even the Green Acres Motel in Seneca Falls. Anywhere but in a car with two old ladies who were putting the local pharmacist's kids through college.

The driver turned onto a washboard-rough country lane. Mason Road.

"You have your own road? Aren't you special?" Sam said to Daria.

"My great-great-grandparents homesteaded here before there were roads. Oh, Mrs. Arbuckle, you don't have to pull up into the drive. Just drop us off here. Thanks."

When Daria tried to open her door, Mrs. Arbuckle said there was a problem and to get out the driver's side.

"That's what I tried to tell you," Mrs. Carmody began. "We—"

"Harriett," the driver said sharply.

Harriett clamped her mouth shut so hard her teeth clashed. Daria just gave Sam a confused look and shrugged. She had to wait for him to get out first. They were on a gravel driveway next to a white three-story farmhouse with dark green trim and a wide front porch. A large garage and barn stood back from the house.

The Impala backed out of the driveway and headed in the direction from which they'd come. Sam noticed the surprise on Daria's face. "I guess she does have a problem with that door," he said.

"I'll bet Mr. Arbuckle is turning over in his grave," Daria said as she walked toward the back of the house. "He never had a scratch on that car. She only got to drive it after he passed away."

There were no cars in the drive or in the open garage. "I take it you don't worry about burglars? Or maybe you think the no-goodniks won't find your place?"

"Sam, nothing ever happens here. The most crime we had last year was when somebody painted the water tower red and gold with 'Go Cyclones' on it."

"Whoa." He managed a weak smile. "Pretty dangerous in Hawkeye territory."

She sighed. "My brothers aren't here. I can't believe they left so early on a Saturday morning."

"I thought you said they didn't expect you back until tomorrow."

A little reddish-brown mutt raced out of the garage and danced around her. She bent down for kisses. "Oh, Rover. I missed you."

The dog ran up to Sam, sniffed his legs then sat, tail wagging, tongue lolling. Sam bent over, ignoring the screaming pain in his hip, and scratched behind the dog's ears.

"You have a friend for life." Daria smiled. "Sam, this is Rover. Rover, shake hands." And, by golly, the little dog held up a paw, which Sam obediently shook.

"Now, you've seen his entire repertoire of tricks."

"Rover? One of your wounded strays? One you shoved out the door?"

She ducked her head but not before he saw her blush at the lie. She led him to the house while the little dog danced around her legs.

The low porch in front of the back door had a broad overhang. The porch appeared to be the drop-off point for assorted tools and muddy boots. The size of the boots gave Sam pause. They were very large boots.

When Daria opened the back door without a key, Sam said, "Isn't this carrying trust a little far? Or does that man-eater keep them at bay?"

"Sam, you are so silly. Rover wouldn't hurt anyone. Just set your bag down anywhere. Oh, my goodness. Mrs. Howard—our part-time housekeeper—left a streusel swirl coffee cake, and the boys didn't touch it. They saved it for me." She smiled. "They know how much I like her coffee cake."

She just kept talking and Sam didn't need to say a word. "It feels so good to be home. Now, if you need to use the bathroom, just go through the laundry room." She pointed to a door at one end of the kitchen. "I'll use the one upstairs."

Without waiting for his response, she hurried through a

broad doorway then ran lightly up an oak staircase to the right. Since she'd strutted and stomped in those boots before, he expected to hear her clomp on the stairs.

A creature of habit, he checked out the surroundings. At the end of the kitchen was the lavatory/laundry room Daria mentioned. A wood screen covered with calico fabric was supposed to separate the laundry area from the toilet and sink. The screen had been pushed to the side and a pile of men's clothing lay on the floor in front of a heavy-duty washer.

The kitchen had a closed door across from the back door. He checked. Basement. Daria's little dog ran to the back door and barked twice. Sam let him out. The way the dog took off, Sam guessed he'd seen a rabbit.

The broad doorway to the right of the basement door, through which Daria had gone, led into a living room. He was grateful the house was empty. How the hell was he going to introduce himself to Daria's brothers? If they were half as protective as she said, he'd have a lot of explaining to do.

Again, Sam surveyed his surroundings. The oak staircase with its white balustrade formed a natural boundary between the casual living room and a formal dining room. Together, both rooms spanned the front of the house. At one end of the living room was a fieldstone fireplace. But, the focal point was a large, flat-screen television hanging above it. The fireplace was surrounded by well-used, substantial furniture. He was about to check the mantle full of photographs when Daria came down the stairs, again very lightly despite her boots.

She was yanking a brush through her hair. "My hair looks absolutely awful."

Sam gave her a wary look. No matter what he said, she'd make sure he regretted it. "Nice place." He nodded to the living room. "Comfortable."

She smiled. "It's home." She set the brush the stairs. "I don't know about you, but I'm starved. I'll make coffee, and we can have a piece of coffee cake. How does that sound?" She headed through the archway into the kitchen.

"That sounds very good. I, too, could use some nourishment." Yuri Grashenko stood in the middle of Daria's kitchen, the PPK in his hand.

CHAPTER TWENTY-FIVE

Yuri Grashenko backed Daria and Sam into the living room. For the first time since she realized the man she rescued from the ladies' restroom had a gun, she wished he was carrying it now. Out of deference to her, Sam had stowed it in his bag when they were in the car. She remembered how quickly he'd grabbed the bag out of her trunk before they hitched a ride. His bag was sitting on a chair at the kitchen table. Darn.

Grashenko motioned toward the stairs. From his vantage point, he would be able to watch the back door as well as the front and driveway side of the house. Nobody could sneak up on him from those directions.

"Well, shoot." She glanced at the gun in his hand. "Not literally, please."

The man chuckled. "She has an unusual sense of humor," he said to Sam who hadn't said a word. "Don't you think so, Samuel?"

Daria felt Sam's tension. If he was worried, she should be, too. But, after her dealings with this man's partner, she couldn't summon the necessary fear. His country gentleman attire—tweed jacket, wool flannel trousers—made him appear almost trustworthy. If it wasn't for the gun in his hand.

"Hold on. Where's Rover?" Daria demanded. "What did you do with my dog?"

"Calm yourself, my dear. I shoot people, not innocent animals. He is tied up behind your barn enjoying a box of dog treats."

That didn't pacify Daria, not one bit. Rover was never tied up.

"Yuri, this is between you and me," Sam said. "One professional to another. Let her go."

"As one professional to another, you know I can't do that. Please sit." Using the gun he motioned toward the

233

stairs.

Stay strong, Daria reminded herself. "Where's your sidekick, the Incredibly Inept Hulk?" She gave Grashenko a smug smile. "Still all wet?"

"That was most unkind of you. He has vowed revenge."

Hah. She taught second graders. She could give him lessons in intimidation. "I am so scared. Did you finally ditch him? Smart move." She thought about that for a moment. Not so smart for her and Sam, since the Hulk had been the reason they escaped Grashenko's traps.

"Sit on the stairs," he repeated. The motion with his pistol was more menacing.

Since the bones in her knees suddenly liquefied, Daria sat on the fourth step. Sam sat beside her and reached for her hand. His reassuring squeeze said they would get out of this alive. She wasn't as convinced. What would her heroine, Alexa Tremaine, do? Would she let this guy intimidate her? Of course not.

"What kind of gun is that?" Daria asked.

"What?" Grashenko exclaimed.

"Daria." Sam groaned. "This is not the time to do research for your book."

"It doesn't look like your gun," she said to Sam.

"You are unbelievable." Yuri leveled the weapon at her. "Do you not realize I could end your life with this?"

All she had to do was convince him she wasn't scared until she came up with a plan.

"Yeah, sure." She fluttered her hand, as if totally unimpressed, while her heart marched double-time. "I still want to know what kind of gun that is."

He blew out an exasperated breath. "It is a Walther PPK."

"Cool. Just like James Bond. But, it's smaller than Sam's gun."

He looked up at the ceiling.

"Are you praying?" she asked. "Or examining the water spot on the ceiling from when the tub overflowed?"

"Daria." Sam gave her hand a warning squeeze.

"I am not a religious man," Yuri said. "Even though religion is now tolerated in my homeland. But, *you* would drive a saint mad."

She sighed. "That's what Sam says."

"You are a smart man, Samuel. How did you ever get mixed up with her? Such curiosity. Research, indeed." Grashenko turned his hard eyes on her. "This weapon is just as deadly as Samuel's."

She felt all the blood drain from her head. She couldn't pass out. Sam needed her help. The clanging had just started when he shoved her head between her knees.

"What are you doing?" Yuri demanded.

"She's going to faint," Sam said.

Daria looked up through the cloud of brassy blonde hair. Sam kept his hand on the back of her neck. She'd really thrown Yuri with that trick. The clanging got softer, but her heart still raced so fast she thought it would pound out of her chest. This was not at all how she imagined Alexa Tremaine would feel facing a weapon. Daria wiped her hands down the sides of her jeans. While her palms were dripping, her mouth was so dry she could barely swallow.

The farm was isolated. It never bothered her before that the nearest neighbor was half a mile down the road. Nobody would hear a gunshot. Sam was right. This wasn't a game. Her Grand Adventure had turned deadly serious.

How did she forget that Grashenko was a professional assassin?

It was time to start acting like she was scared. *That* wouldn't take any acting skills at all. Slowly, she straightened. "I-I'm sorry. Sometimes my mouth starts running before my brain is engaged." She gave him a tremulous smile. "I-I won't give you any trouble."

"Of course, you won't."

This time, Sam squeezed her hand so hard he nearly cut off her circulation. "Daria, shut up and let me handle this."

Startled by Sam's reprimand, she shrank back against the step. Something poked her in the back. The bristles of her hairbrush.

"Wise move, Samuel. It is time. Hand over that which you stole from my employer."

"You're too smart to work for Korioff," Sam said. "He's mixed up with some very nasty people who would sooner behead you than look at you. When your usefulness is over, they'll do just that."

Daria was surprised that Grashenko listened.

"Your talents are wasted working for Korioff," Sam went on.

Grashenko smiled. "Are you offering me a deal?"

"Turn away from the Dark Side, Yuri," Daria said, figuring out where Sam was going. "Sam will help you, won't you, Sam?"

Slowly, Grashenko shook his head. "Nice try. Ms. Quinero also tried to *reform* me. It was a waste of time. And time is running out. Your right shoe, Samuel."

"What?" Daria exclaimed. Why did he want Sam's shoe?

"My what?" Sam asked at the same time.

"Did you not think about surveillance cameras?"

Sam tensed, but showed no change in expression. "Yuri, surely you don't think I kept the memory chip. It isn't here. I will take you to it."

Suddenly, Daria got it. Sam had hidden the memory chip in his right shoe. But, Yuri didn't know those weren't the shoes Sam wore when he was caught on 'Candid Camera.' She'd bought those shoes in Seneca Falls.

Sam put his hand on the step to lever himself up. A sheen of perspiration covered his forehead. His eyes were dull. The man looked sick.

Daria didn't think it was fear. He must have faced down men with weapons before. It had to be his wounds. She knew they weren't healing properly. If he was running a fever, he wouldn't be thinking right. Still, he was trying to lead Grashenko away from here, away from her.

"Do not insult my intelligence." Grashenko's voice was hard, his eyes as menacing as Daria remembered from their first encounter on the stairs of the old department store. "You would not leave anything that valuable behind."

"I've led you on a merry chase away from it, haven't I?"

Grashenko looked momentarily perplexed, as if that possibility—one Daria thought of and dismissed—hadn't occurred to him. Slowly, he shook his head. "I do not believe you. You have tried so hard to contact Sally Quinero. Give me your shoe."

"What?" Daria exclaimed. "You know about Sally?"

"That horse's ass Teller wasn't the only one monitoring your calls. How do you think I was able to follow you? Too bad you haven't been able to make contact."

Sam's boss was monitoring the phone calls? And he didn't try to help Sam?

Hold on. Grashenko didn't know Sally was on her way here? The drugstore cell phone and long-distance cards really couldn't be traced. All they needed to do was hang on until Sally got there. But, what if she was too late? What if she couldn't find them?

"Your little red-headed friend is not coming, Samuel. Now, give me your goddamn shoe." Yuri was starting to lose it.

Daria jumped to her feet. "If all he wants is your shoe, Sam, just give it to him."

"Don't you get it," he said. "Once I hand it over, he will kill me and then he'll do you."

"No, he won't. He promised to let us go."

"Stay out of this, Daria. I'm handling it."

"Well, you're not doing a very good job." As her voice rose in anger, she flung the hairbrush at Grashenko.

Instinctively, he flinched at the flying object. In that moment of inattention, Sam launched himself into Grashenko. His weapon skid across the carpet and under the couch. Daria dove for it. On her knees, she felt around under the couch until her fingers encountered metal. "I got it," she called out in triumph.

"Daria," Sam yelled. "Behind you."

CHAPTER TWENTY-SIX

Sam knew his warning came two seconds too late. He was going to lose Daria and there was nothing he could do.

"I fix you, bitch," Ivan Korioff bellowed as he grabbed Daria from behind and lifted her in a bear hug. She dropped the weapon.

Sam was still rolling around on the floor with Grashenko who, despite his age, was surprisingly strong. Sam couldn't let go of Yuri to help Daria.

"Not you!" she yelled. "Where did you come from?"

Yuri squirmed, clawing at the carpet, trying to reach his weapon. Sam hung on. Even if he reached Yuri's weapon, Sam couldn't shoot Korioff. The man held Daria in front of him like a human shield. Sam was an excellent marksman, but the chance of hitting a wiggling Daria made his blood freeze. He'd promised to protect her, and he failed. Despair's dark cloud enveloped his soul.

"You think you leave me in Chicago, Yuri." Korioff shifted his grip, probably to avoid those lethal heels on her boots. "I smarter. I follow you. I much smarter. I put tracker on your car."

Daria continued to struggle. She was squirming as much as Grashenko. Korioff held her off the ground. She scissored her legs, trying to get away. Just as Grashenko was about to reach his weapon, she managed to kick it away. The gun slid under a swivel rocker that was so much smaller than the other furniture Sam knew it had to be Daria's.

He finally got Yuri in a hammerlock and then subdued him by pressing on the carotid. Grashenko slumped unconscious.

Sam wasn't sure what happened next. As he scrambled to his feet, Daria brought Korioff to his knees, doubled over and gasping for breath. Once again, she got on her knees and came up with a gun. She stood with her feet apart, the

Walther PPK clutched in both hands. Nancy Drew on steroids had nothing on Daria Mason.

"Whew. 'That PMS is a bitch.'" Daria wiped her brow. "'Go ahead, punk'," she said to the moaning Korioff. "'Make my day.'"

"Daria, when you're finished quoting movie lines," Sam drawled. "Give me the weapon and find something to tie them up with."

"I know just the thing." After handing Sam the weapon, she raced out to the kitchen. Moments later, she returned, holding up a gray roll.

Sam groaned. Duct tape.

"A hundred and one uses," she declared.

He held Korioff's arms behind his back while Daria wound the tape around his wrists. The man was still pale and, considering the curses in Russian, had to be in extreme pain. If Korioff hadn't tried to hurt Daria, Sam might have felt sorry for him. He used a strip of duct tape over Junior's mouth in case he started cursing in English.

"Was that your Jackie Chan impression?" he asked as they bound the still unconscious Yuri.

"Nope. 'Miss Congeniality'—SING—solar plexus, instep, nose, groin. Nice Vulcan neck pinch on Grashenko."

"I thought so."

She stood and dusted her hands. "I don't know about you, but now I'm famished. That coffee cake in the kitchen is calling my name. Taking down Russian Mafia hitmen really worked up my appetite."

He walked toward her. "So, I wasn't doing a good job handling the situation." Sam crowded her into the corner next to the stairs.

"Uh, Sam. What are you doing?"

He caged her with his body. "Do you realize how dangerous our situation was? Do you realize the chance you took when you threw that brush? Don't you have any sense? He could have shot it, and hit you."

"He didn't," she protested. "I was distracting him for you. And it worked."

"It might not have." He yanked her against his chest and held onto her. "I thought I was scared when Yuri threatened you. But, I have never been so scared as I was when I looked up and saw Korioff about to grab you."

Her mouth quirked in an uncertain smile. "I nearly wet my pants when he did."

"Oh, God, babe. Don't ever do anything that foolish again." Holding her was all that mattered. He buried his face in the sweet curve of her neck.

She clung to him, more frightened than she let on. When he kissed her, her hunger took his breath away. His own hunger, deep, desperate, nearly overpowered his fear.

He had no doubt Korioff would have beaten her senseless. The man was that out of control. Daria could have been killed. Because of Sam. Had he not involved her, danger would never have come into this house. He brought danger into her home.

He held onto her tightly, more to reassure himself she was safe.

The sound of a faint frustrated bark pulled Daria out of Sam's arms. "Rover," she cried and ran through the kitchen.

"I'll, uh, just keep an eye on these two," Sam said.

Daria spun around at the screen door. "What are we going to do with them?"

"Sally and I will take them back to DC. We'll get info out of them and then make sure they're put away for a long time."

"You're sure Sally is coming? I thought she'd be here by now."

"She'll come. If it will make you feel safer, call the local police and—"

"Prairieville eliminated its police force in a budget cutback. The sheriff serves us."

"Okay, call the sheriff."

An odd look crossed her face. "That might not be a good idea."

"You have a problem with the sheriff?"

"You could say that. I have to get Rover." She took off across the backyard.

Sam cast a glance at the two in the living room. Korioff shot him a lethal look, but he wasn't going anywhere. Grashenko was still in dreamland. Sam stepped out onto the porch in time to see the little brown dog race around the corner of the barn with Daria following. Rover ran past Sam and lunged at the back door. Then, he stopped, perked his ears and ran toward the driveway.

At the sound of gravel crunching, Daria gave Sam a helpless shrug. "The jungle drums have been active."

A gold Lexus braked to a stop in front of the garage and the tall, dark-haired driver stepped out. The man in gray pin-stripe trousers, tie and dress shirt was as polished and elegant as the car.

"Andy," Daria cried and flew into his arms.

A streak of jealousy stabbed Sam. Jealousy? Was this the guy on the phone?

The man she called Andy held her at arm's length. "My God, DJ, what have you done to your hair?"

Wrong voice. Sam silently breathed a small sigh of relief. After the wrestling bout with Grashenko, Sam wasn't up to another match.

Andy zeroed in on Sam. "Who's that?"

"My friend," Daria said. "Come and meet Sam."

The man strode to the porch. "Drew Mason. You are . . ." He didn't offer his hand.

"Oh, Andy, quit that lawyer intimidation stuff."

Lawyer?

"DJ, cut the crap. Is this the guy from last night?"

Daria gave Sam an exasperated shrug. "When he isn't pretending to be Big Brother, he's usually a lot of fun."

Brother? Then, the man's name registered. Drew Mason. The headache throbbing behind his eyes and Daria calling him Andy had momentarily confused Sam.

Daria's brother was a lawyer. And not a happy one, according to the steely glare he aimed in Sam's direction. A burgundy Buick came up the drive at a more sedate pace, but there was nothing sedate about the speed with which the driver got out.

"Tommy!" Daria hugged the man dressed in black with a reverse collar.

If this was a brother, Sam was going straight to hell for lusting after his sister.

"What happened to your beautiful hair, honey?" The

priest was as tall as the lawyer. Both topped Sam by at least two inches.

"That's what I'd like to know," Sam muttered.

"Is that a hickey on your neck?" The priest then looked at Sam the way God must have looked at the serpent in the Garden of Eden.

A black 4x4 complete with bug lights roared up the drive. Sam was still stunned by the fact that one of her brothers was a lawyer and the other a priest when a mountain of a man jumped down from the truck. He made the other two look like shrimps. If this was another brother, Sam was turning in his secret decoder ring.

Daria whirled out of the priest's arms and into the newcomer's. "Billy."

Late morning sun sliced through the big oaks shading the backyard. Sunlight glinted off Daria's swinging earrings and made her hair look twice as brassy.

The sumo wrestler picked her up and swung her around. "Holy shit, Dar, what did you do to your hair?"

She gave him a smacking kiss on the cheek. "You can put me down now, Billy."

"About time you got here," the lawyer said. "Meet our sister's new *friend*."

Before Sam could say 'Oh, shit', Sumo Brother dropped Daria and stomped up to the porch. He literally picked Sam up by the front of his shirt and lifted him high enough so that Sam's feet dangled. *Oh, God.* His life was over.

"You the guy who was with her last night?"

"She's got a hickey," the lawyer said. Three pairs of glacial blue eyes turned on Sam. He was a bug impaled against the post.

"A what?" Sumo Brother's roar sent the throbbing in Sam's head into high gear.

"Billy, put him down," Daria ordered in her school teacher voice. "Sam, don't you pay any attention to these numbskulls. Put my friend down, William Robert. Right this very minute."

Apparently, Sumo Brother knew she meant business. He unhanded Sam, none too gently. Sam staggered for a moment before grabbing the porch post for support. The

Russian assassins hadn't scared him as much as Daria's three brothers. Sam shot her a look. "You do realize that you give an entirely different image of your brothers."

"What?"

"You call them *boys*." As Sam spoke, the three stared at him. "You call them by childish nicknames. I had the impression they were . . . smaller."

"He's right about the names, DJ," Drew, the lawyer, said. "You make us sound like little kids."

Daria looked puzzled. "Hmph. I never thought about that."

"How'd you guys find out she was home?" Sumo Brother asked.

"Jim called me, and I called Tom," Drew said.

"Jim called you? I found out from Mrs. Carmody. She and Mrs. Arbuckle caught me at the Wheel having breakfast."

"Well, Mr. Mayor, somebody has to be the last to know," Drew smirked.

Mayor? Sumo Brother was the mayor?

Daria's brothers were a lawyer, the mayor, and a priest. It couldn't get any worse.

"I thought Jim was going to call him," the priest said. "By the way, where is he?"

"Look, guys." Sam held onto the porch post. His leg ached, his butt hurt, he had the mother of all headaches, and he wasn't sure he could take all this talking. "I'll wait inside with the prisoners while you and your sister—"

"What prisoners?" the lawyer said.

A white sedan emblazoned with 'Prairie County Sheriff' across the side pulled up behind the three vehicles. As the man dressed in brown got out, Daria strode up to him. She shook her finger under his nose. "James Allen Mason, if you even try to intimidate Sam, I'll—"

The sheriff was lean and mean and, from the way Daria spoke to him, another brother. The three others stepped away from Sam.

"Are you Jozwiak?" It was the voice from the phone. The one who threatened to discontinue Sam's family line.

He was toast.

CHAPTER TWENTY-SEVEN

That was it. Sam was too stupid to live. He'd shanghaied a woman with four super-size brothers. A lawyer, the mayor, a priest and the sheriff.

Sam hadn't been this close to such big men since basketball at the University of Iowa. At six-two, Sam didn't have to look up at too many men except on the court. These guys made him feel like the playground weenie about to be pounded into dust. Sam figured his odds of getting out alive would be greatly increased by keeping his mouth shut.

"You put my sister in danger." The sheriff rested his palm on the butt of his revolver.

"Leave Sam alone," Daria ordered.

"Not now, Daria," the sheriff said impatiently. "This is between him and me."

"Oh, no you don't. James Allen Mason, you leave Sam alone." She pulled on his arm. When he easily walked away from her—toward Sam—Daria jumped on her brother's back. She wrapped her legs around his waist and had him in a stranglehold with one arm around his throat while pulling his hair.

"Oh, God, Daria," Sam groaned. "What are you doing?"

"Hey, Jimbo." That was the priest. "Need any help?" Sumo and Lawyer Brother were laughing too hard to talk.

The sheriff swung around. "Would you three get your thumbs out of your butts and get this leech off my back?"

Since none of them moved, Sam grabbed Daria around the waist and swung her off her brother's back. "Now, I understand why you have a problem with the sheriff." He set her on her feet. "When you said your brothers were trustworthy, you weren't kidding."

"Don't start on me, Sam. I didn't rescue you from the Russian Mafia just to have my brothers gang up on you."

"Russian Mafia?" the priest said.

A quiet clapping came from behind Sam.

"That's right, girl. Don't put up with shit from men." Sally and the new hire—Haggerty? Hardesty?—came around the sheriff's car. "Looks like you've got your very own bodyguard, Sam."

"It's about time you got here," Sam said. "What took you so long?"

That had to be Sally, Daria thought. She was everything Daria wasn't. Petite, slim, with gorgeous red hair that 'didn't come out of a bottle', which was how Marge at the Holland marina had described one of Mac's frequent visitors.

For such a short woman, Sally had a long stride. She came up to Sam, grabbed him around the neck and pulled him down for a kiss. On the mouth. Daria saw red—and it wasn't just the woman's hair.

"Glad to see you survived," Sally said. "I thought I was bringing backup, but I see you have plenty. So, what's the plan when Grashenko arrives?"

"We've already taken care of him," Daria said proudly. "He and his buddy are in the living room."

Daria's brothers looked at her like she was speaking in tongues. Why didn't they give her credit for anything? She ignored them—and Sam—and led Sally into the house. Grashenko and Korioff were lying spoon-fashion on the floor. A piece of duct tape lay nearby and Korioff's head appeared to be very close to Grashenko's rear end.

"Oh, Yuri." Sally chortled. "I never knew . . ."

Both men started then scuttled away from each other. Grashenko turned a dull red, while Korioff's face flamed. Apparently, he was trying to use his teeth to remove the tape around Grashenko's wrists.

"Good job, Sam," Sally said. "You got them both."

"Excuse me," Daria said. "I helped."

Her brothers laughed. They'd followed and had crowded into the living room.

"She did more than help," Sam said. "In fact, she's taken down Korioff three times." That earned a baleful look from

Korioff.

"Daria?" Billy exclaimed.

"Shut the front door." Sally walked up to Daria and gave her a high five. "Way to go, girl."

"Daria?" Jimmy snorted.

Daria wanted to deck him the way she had Korioff. Her brothers would believe her then. But, on the hopes of having nieces and nephews someday, she restrained herself.

Sally turned to Jimmy. "Okay, Wyatt, can I borrow some cuffs?"

"Wyatt?" Daria asked.

"Wyatt?" The rest of the boys hooted. Sam, who looked paler than Daria had seen him that day, leaned against the side of the stairs.

"As in Wyatt Earp?" Tommy said. Tom, Daria mentally corrected. She was going to have to work hard not to call them by the names she'd called them all her life.

Now it was Jimmy's turn to be embarrassed. Daria couldn't remember the last time anyone got the best of him. It served him right for being so overbearing. Jimmy—Jim shot them all looks that promised retribution before handing Sally a pair of handcuffs. "Bill, get me an extra set of cuffs out of the car."

Before Bill could leave, an imperious voice came from the kitchen.

"Excuse me. Let me through. I'm in charge."

"Well, if it isn't Teller the Turd," Sally drawled. "Let our boss through, boys."

Andy, Tommy, Billy—nuts to remembering what to call them—and the young man who came with Sally crowded Sam against the stairs, effectively blocking him from sight. With Tom, Jim and Sally on the other side, they formed a gauntlet. Teller was oblivious. He strutted between them just like a bantam rooster who thought he was king of the barnyard.

"Good job, Quinero, Hardesty," Teller said. "You can help me load these two into the chopper, and I'll take them back to DC. Did you find Jozwiak?"

"Jozwiak? Who Jozwiak?" Korioff asked.

"Chopper? What chopper?" Tom asked.

"Hold it." Daria marched up to Sam's boss. "Are you the

man who thought Sam was a renegade?" She poked him in the middle of his three-piece suit that looked like an Armani she'd seen in New York. "The one who thought he was a traitor?" Another poke. "Why didn't *you* show up at the rendezvous?" Poke. "Why did you leave Sam all alone to fend off—" Poke. "—Tweedledum—" Poke. "—and Tweedledee?" She jerked her head toward Grashenko and Korioff. "Why didn't *you* take care of your agent, you dumb shit?"

"Daria!" Jimmy exclaimed.

"You've got his number," Sally muttered.

"Oh, Daria." Tom just shook his head.

Sam limped around her brothers to stand next to Daria. He leaned in and whispered, "Do we really need an audience while you flog the head of my agency?"

Daria looked around the crowded living room and began issuing orders. "Andy, I mean, Drew, return to your office. Tommy, er, Father Tom, back to the rectory. And, Bill, if you didn't finish your breakfast, go back to the Wheel."

When she directed her attention to the silent young man clutching a laptop, he visibly paled. He jerked his thumb over his shoulder. "I'll just wait in the kitchen."

"And, you—" She pointed to Sam. "—sit down before you fall down."

Grateful to be off his leg, Sam sunk into a big recliner. Daria could give a general lessons. And her three brothers hopped to. First, they groused like kids about being left out, but they left.

The sheriff said, "What about me, your highness? Going to order me back to the courthouse?"

"You may stay," she said in an imperious tone. "I might need you."

To Sam's surprise, the man didn't argue. And Daria thought those men ruled her life? She had them marching to her tune, and she didn't even know it.

Meanwhile, Teller looked conspicuously at his watch, though he still gave Daria a hesitant look. After the dressing down she gave him, he *should* be hesitant around her.

Sally just smirked. Since Daria hadn't ordered her out, she stayed, too. If Sam was feeling better, he might have wanted to see those two square off. On second thought, he didn't think Sally stood a chance when Daria went into teacher mode and treated everyone like her second-graders.

"Now," Daria said. "What's the plan?"

"Joz comes with me," came a voice from the doorway.

Daria spun around to look at the latest newcomer.

"Ryerson, I outrank you," Teller huffed. "Jozwiak comes with me."

Daria sat on the arm of Sam's chair and leaned close. "How does it feel to be a bone between two dogs. Who's the new guy?"

"Assistant Director Ryerson."

"He's the guy who visits Johnny, right?" she whispered. "The one Marge called Old Skin and Bones?"

Sam nodded.

"By whose authority, do you tell me what to do?" Teller demanded.

"By mine." Mac stood in the doorway to the kitchen. "Sheriff, I have a Federal warrant for this man's arrest." He pointed to Teller. "Take him into custody."

Teller sputtered. Daria gasped. Sally smiled.

And Sam thought his head was going to explode.

"The reason we were late, hot shot," Sally said to him, "is that Mac wanted me to bring the sheriff."

"I am so confused," Daria muttered. "This is worse than Who's on First."

"So, your people finally wised up," Grashenko said to Teller.

"You knew about Teller?" Sally asked.

"What about him?" Daria sounded as confused as Sam felt. His head hurt even worse trying to figure out what was going on.

"I'm going to need another set of cuffs," Jim said. Amid the chaos of everyone talking, Hardesty offered to get them.

"Jozwiak, what are you doing sitting on your ass?" Mac said with his usual finesse before nodding to Daria. "My apologies, Ms. Mason. On behalf of a grateful nation, thank you for keeping this poor excuse of an agent out of harm's way."

"Daria?" Jim asked.

Sam levered himself out of the recliner. "If it weren't for

your sister, I'd be dead and information vital to our nation's security would be in their hands." He nodded to Grashenko and Korioff.

"Daria?" Jim said again.

An hour later, Daria still didn't have the answers she needed. Nor was she allowed time with Sam. Jim and a deputy guarded the two Russians and Teller locked in patrol cars, waiting for federal officers summoned by Mac before his surprise arrival. Sally, Mac and Ryerson—Old Skin and Bones—kept Sam at the dining room table bombarding him with questions. Since they kept their voices low, Daria didn't know what transpired.

The boys—Daria mentally kicked herself for calling them that, but old habits die hard—never did leave. They stayed in the kitchen with Hardesty, the young man with the laptop while she hovered in the archway hoping to hear what Sam was saying.

When those at her dining room table rose, Daria thought for sure she'd get a chance to talk to Sam. Mac brushed past her and strode through the kitchen. He pointed to Hardesty. "We're leaving."

Daria found the short, wiry man too brusque, too impatient to take Sam away from her. She knew he had to leave, but she wanted more time with him. Needed more time. She followed the men out to the backyard.

"Hold up," she said with more boldness than she felt. "I want answers. I want to know why you people didn't help Sam. I want to know what's going on with Teller. I want to know—"

"Sorry, Ms. Mason." Mac didn't sound sorry. "National Security."

"You are playing that card? After all I did to save your agent, you are pulling that crap on me?"

"Daria." That was typical Tommy, scolding.

"Saddle up, boys and girls," Ryerson said. He jerked his head toward the stealth helicopter next to the barn toward which Mac was walking.

Sam came up beside her. "Not yet. She's right. She deserves some answers."

Over his shoulder, Mac shot him a glare. "What did we just talk about?"

"Joz, say your good-byes and get aboard," Ryerson said. "We're burning daylight."

While he and Mac headed across the yard, Sally said something to Jim before joining them.

When Sam took Daria's hand, she knew this was it. He was going to leave with them. She didn't want her brothers and his colleagues to hear what she had to say so she urged him away from them.

He protested. "I have to go."

She just ignored him. "I figured as much. You be sure to get medical treatment." She placed the inside of her wrist against his forehead. "You definitely have a fever."

"Joz," Ryerson demanded. "Get over here."

"Yeah. In a minute," Sam called back before turning to Daria. "Thanks for . . . what you did, Daria."

"For saving you?"

"Yeah." He kissed her forehead. "Have a good life."

Daria stopped him. *Please let me get through this without breaking down*, she prayed. "Will you keep in touch? I'll have more questions to ask you . . . about . . . well, about research for my book. If it sells—"

His mouth quirked. "*When* it sells," he corrected.

"When it sells, I'll dedicate it to you. The spy who—" She almost made a joke of it. A James Bond movie title.

"Daria, don't . . ."

"To the spy who taught me I'm stronger than I think."

He pulled her close. His lips brushed her temple. "Thank you for keeping me safe. Forget Alexa Tremaine. *You* are the real kick-ass heroine."

"Sam—"

He set her away from him and gave her a cocky grin. "Listen, kid, this was fun while it lasted. Be a good girl and get on with your life here in the cornfields."

She stood there frozen until she realized what he meant. That was a brushoff if she ever heard one. Damn him.

Sam wasn't sure how he managed to walk away from

Daria. He reached for the grip to pull himself into the helo when she yanked him back by his collar. She grabbed his arm and turned him around. And he let her.

"Not so fast, Sam. You owe me this." She wrapped her arms around his neck and kissed him. It was a poignantly sweet kiss. A knife sliced through his heart. His last kiss.

"Do not leave. Stay." Her blue eyes were bright with unshed tears.

He hated that he was the cause of the tears. "I can't. I have to go."

"Come back soon, then." Her plea tore through him.

"You know I won't. Find Mr. Right and have those six babies." He let the corner of his mouth quirk.

She grabbed the front of his shirt. "I found him, and he's too stupid to know it."

"Daria . . ."

"Jozwiak," Ryerson hollered again from inside the helo over the roar of the engine. "Get your ass in here."

"You just wait a minute," Daria shouted back. She gripped Sam's shirt harder, standing on her toes so she was right in his face. Her look hardened, tears gone. "Listen to me, Sam Jozwiak, and listen good. I am the best thing that ever happened to you. You're in for a long, lonely life without me so you'd damn well better come back."

Tom held Daria while she cried. She'd waited until the helicopter was a speck in the bright April sky. She didn't want Sam's last view of her to be that of a weak, blubbering fool.

"What are we going to do with you, Daria Jean," Tommy said softly.

Her brother, who'd postponed going into the seminary until after she graduated from high school, had come home last year to take over the reins of the parish when their pastor retired. Although he had a perfectly good rectory in which to live, he'd chosen the family homestead in which to hang his biretta, the black three-cornered ceremonial hat with a tassel on top she bought for his ordination.

Father Tom—it felt weird to hear people call him that—used the office in the rectory but had turned the building's use over to the youth minister and the church council. Tom came home to dinner and slept in the same room he had as a child.

As did the other three. When their parents were killed in a car crash three days after Daria's thirteenth birthday, Jim and Bill had closed up the apartment they'd shared in town and come home. Tom was supposed to start seminary that fall. Drew was a junior in high school.

The older boys postponed their lives so that she could have as normal a home life as possible. She'd always idolized them. Later, she realized how much they'd given up for her. And she appreciated the sacrifices they'd made. Really she did.

Tom held her at arm's length. "I have a question for you."

"Ask away."

"What exactly were the sleeping arrangements on your trip from New York?"

Heat rushed into her face. "Is this confession time, *Father* Tom?"

"I trust you, Daria. You're an attractive woman. But, that man didn't kiss you as if you were a mere acquaintance."

Daria allowed a slow grin to curve her lips. "Definitely not a mere acquaintance."

"Seriously, honey, do we need to worry about anything?"

"That is none of your business."

"Hey, you guys, come inside," Bill called. "Senator Canfield has been arrested. CNN is replaying a press conference he gave."

Daria watched the television in horror as a wan Howard Canfield, his wife at his side, faced reporters outside his Washington townhouse.

"This morning," the senator from Iowa said without preamble, "I notified the President that I've withdrawn my name from consideration as Director of Homeland Security."

There was an audible gasp from reporters.

"When one is young," the senator went on, "one often does foolish things. One of those foolish things recently returned to haunt me. They say there's no fool like an old fool. Instead of telling my wife I cheated on her when I was twenty-two and she was a new mother, I hid the truth. Recently, I allowed someone to use knowledge of my indiscretion to . . . control me."

Daria felt sick to her stomach. She'd believed in the senator, had even worked on his campaign, and felt terribly betrayed.

Canfield took a deep breath. "Among other things, I revealed information regarding security precautions for the President of the United States to terrorists. Even though those precautions were outdated, I knew it was wrong. After I informed the President, I called the Secret Service and the FBI. I offer no excuses. Only my apologies to the fine people of Iowa who trusted me to represent them for the past fifteen years, and I apologize to the people of the United States."

"Always the politician," Daria said in disgust.

"Sh-h," Drew whispered.

Canfield went on. "I have tendered my resignation to the Senate and will accept the punishment I deserve."

While reporters went on and on about the senator, several things hit Daria. Terrorists. Controlling him. The timing.

My God. Was this the intel Sam found?

"You still haven't told me about Teller," Sam said to Sally. "Why was he arrested?"

Mac wouldn't tell him anything back at Daria's. There, at her dining room table, the info went one way—to them. Every time he asked questions, they asked a different one. The noise inside the helo from Prairieville to Midway Airport in Chicago hurt too much to even try to talk. The Lear that Ryerson procured for Sally was now airborne, and she'd engaged the auto-pilot before coming back to talk to him.

She chortled. "Embezzling."

"You're joking." He knew Teller had expensive tastes but figured that came from having a rich wife.

"The Whiz Kid discovered it," Sally said. "He was like a

bird dog on a scent."

Hardesty apple cheeks glowed red. "Actually, sir, I stumbled over it by mistake."

Sam chuckled. "That's how I found out about Canfield."

Sally gave him a questioning look. "What's this about Canfield? You mean the senator? The one who was supposed to be the next Director of Homeland Security?"

"What do you mean 'supposed to be'?" Sam asked.

"He was arrested," Sally said. "Hardesty and I heard it on the radio. He's been feeding classified information to terrorists."

Hardesty gaped. "Was that the intel you brought back from Russia?"

Sam lifted the corner of his mouth. "Along with Korioff's financial records."

"You stole his financial records?" Sally chortled. "No wonder he sent Grashenko after you."

"Especially after Sam loaded a worm into Korioff's computer that corrupted all his files." Mac gave them all a sly look.

"You knew?" Sam said.

Mac smiled enigmatically. "Who do you think told the FBI?"

Trying to process all this new information increased Sam's headache. "You knew about Canfield. You knew about the intel I brought from Russia. Why did you let me bumble around like a goddamn idiot? With a civilian?"

"Couldn't play my hand too soon. You did all right."

"By the way, someone else is after you besides Grashenko," Sally said. "I was followed in Chicago."

Ryerson shrugged. "Good help is hard to find."

"You?" Sally stared in astonishment. "You had me followed?"

"Ryerson contacted me after he talked to you in your apartment," Mac said. "You were our best shot at finding Joz."

"It sure would've helped if you two had trusted us," Sally retorted. "We were working blind."

Sam remembered what Daria said about trust. About how a wife needed to trust her husband. And it made him think about how much he trusted her to get him to Doc's, to drive him to Michigan and then to Chicago. All along she trusted that he was one of the good guys.

She trusted him, and he'd walked away from her without a backward glance.

CHAPTER TWENTY-EIGHT

"Jozwiak, your head has been up your ass ever since you got back from Iowa."

For the past year, Sam had actually missed Mac's bull-of-the-woods style of management. Not lately, though. Mac had ridden him about what he referred to as Sam's Major Screw Up. Of course, Mac conveniently forgot that Sam was responsible for corrupting Korioff's financial records and discovering the connection with Canfield. Mac's major complaint was Sam's not contacting him first. That and trusting Teller.

Maybe Sam should be grateful Mac laid off for the first week while he fought off a major infection. He hated to admit Daria was right. By the time Sally dragged him to an emergency room, he had a raging fever. The docs pumped him full of super-antibiotics. Sam slept for four days and finally recovered. When he wasn't sleeping, he worked hard at putting Daria Mason out of his mind. A futile effort.

Instead of going back out into the field, Sam had to endure extensive debriefing with Mac—now acting director— Ryerson, Sally, and Patrick Hardesty.

For a kid who'd learned how to shave last week, Hardesty had shown himself to be very resourceful. He broke through password-protected files on the memory chip and discovered more than even Sam thought he'd stolen. He wanted the kid on his team from now on. If he ever got a team again.

After the debrief, Sam was swamped with report writing. Not just about the mission, but analyzing all the data Hardesty uncovered. When Sam finished those reports, Mac made him go through all the reports out of Eastern Europe and write reports of those analyses. Sam hated writing reports. For crissake, he was a field agent, not a writer. Like Daria.

He kept thinking about her. He'd write a couple of paragraphs and remember her straight-arming Korioff and knocking him on his bare ass at Doc's or into the lake in Holland. Then, Sam would snap out of his reverie and discover an hour had gone by.

"This is a piss-poor excuse for a report, Jozwiak." Mac threw the papers at him. "And pay attention, goddamn it, when I'm chewing your ass."

"Yes, sir."

"I've cut you some slack since you were injured."

Sam made a concerted effort not to snort. "Begging your pardon, sir, I haven't asked for special treatment. I have asked to be sent back out into the field."

"And get somebody killed because you're thinking about that Amazon in Iowa?"

"With all due respect, sir, Daria is not an Amazon."

"Sorry." Mac didn't sound sorry. "That's what Sal calls her."

"Anyone over five-five is an Amazon to her."

Sally was another person who rode Sam's butt. She kept asking him if he talked to or emailed Daria. After the tenth time, he finally shut her up by asking if she wanted to know about Daria or her brother Jim. For the first time, as far as Sam could remember, Sally Quinero blushed.

"Neither here nor there," Mac continued. "You aren't any good to me in the field. You are undermining morale around here with your short temper and your failure to respond to requests by the staff."

"What requests?" Sam may have been distracted, but he never ignored staff requests.

Mac waved that aside. "I've got a whole lot of patching up to do around here to repair the damage Teller did to my agency. I don't have time to babysit a field agent."

"Sir, I don't—"

"Either get your act together, Jozwiak, or I'll have to replace you. I can't use an agent whose mind isn't on his job."

For four weeks, Daria watched her email and checked the answering machine at home. Sam was going to call. She was sure of it. Worse, she didn't even have a phone number to call him. Which was pretty dumb on her part. She'd slipped one of the business cards she'd made for her conference into his shirt pocket. Not that he couldn't find out her number. He was in intelligence. However, the rat hadn't given her anything in return.

Her brothers told her she was foolish to think he was coming back. She finally shut them up with an Alexa Tremaine stare.

But, she didn't just sit by the phone each night waiting for Sam to call. She started making the changes to her bedroom that she'd promised herself before she left for New York. Stripping wallpaper and preparing old walls for paint was more work than Daria anticipated, but it occupied her evenings and weekends and kept her from thinking. Each night, she fell into bed exhausted. And lonely. She thought about him anyway.

Finishing last week filled her with pride. The walls were a rich burgundy. She couldn't believe how many coats it took to cover the primer. The addition of ecru draperies and cream sheers plus a cream quilt with burgundy and hunter green accents brought about the effect she wanted. Classy yet livable. All she needed was a certain tall, dark and handsome spy in her new queen-size bed.

Although her brothers praised her work—when they weren't offering to help—she wanted someone else to see what she'd accomplished.

Sam.

She was sure he would come to his senses and figure out they belonged together. It had been five long weeks and not one word. Her curse backfired. The curse about the long, lonely life. That appeared to be her fate. What did she know about curses anyway?

Last night, she finally gave up waiting for him to call or come to her. She was just going to have to go to DC and rescue him again. This time from himself. What good was having a fantastic bedroom if the man of her dreams wasn't there to share it with her?

First, she was going to have to eat some crow and ask for help. That night, she fixed her brothers' favorite dinner. With gusto, they polished off the sweet succulent ham cured by their neighbor, Daria's special macaroni and cheese plus apple cobbler for dessert. When they sat back replete, she propped her forearms on the table and interlaced her fingers.

"I need a favor," she said with more apprehension than she'd felt that long-ago Friday morning before leaving on her adventure.

"Sure, whatcha need, Dar?" Bill was the first to respond.

Tom nodded, but Drew, the typical lawyer who wanted all the facts before committing himself, hesitated.

"What exactly do you want, Daria Jean?" Jim said evenly.

"Sam Jozwiak's home address and phone number." She stared straight at the one who could get it for her.

The proverbial pin drop could have been heard in the silence that ensued. She waited. And waited.

Chairs creaked. Shoes shuffled. Throats were cleared.

Tom was the one who spoke first. "Now, Daria, honey . . ."

"That is not the answer I want." She didn't take her eyes off Jim. "Get me his number. I know it's unlisted, buried under all kinds of safeguards. But you can do it."

Jim gave her a leveling look. "Are you pregnant?"

"No!" That was the last thing she expected him to say. Then, she recalled Tom's mini-inquisition when she broke down after Sam left.

"Why keep banging your head against the wall?" Drew asked. "He hasn't called. He isn't coming back."

"He will." She was surprised at how cool and confident she sounded. Sam would come, but he needed a kick in the pants first.

"It's a secret agency. Nobody knows—"

She cut Jim off. "Sally gave you her card. I saw her hand it to you."

The tips of Jim's ears turned red.

"I want that number," Daria persisted. "I'll call her and get Sam's address."

"I threw the card away. You saw how she kissed Jozwiak. I hate to break this to you, Daria, but—"

"Don't," Drew said sharply.

Tom and Bill gave Jim warning looks.

"Okay, what's going on?" she asked.

"They're trying to protect you from the truth," Jim said.

"I don't need or want protection. Tell me."

"All right." Jim planted his tightly clenched fists on the table. "You want the truth, here it is. Jozwiak and the Quinero woman are lovers."

"Old news," Daria shot back. "They used to be lovers."

Jim snorted. The others gave her pitying looks. She remembered the kiss Sally had laid on Sam and, for a moment, her resolve faltered. No. He told her they weren't lovers anymore. She believed him. She had to.

"Jozwiak used you to escape," Jim went on ruthlessly. "He did what he had to do. You were transportation. That's all. Don't make three days into a relationship."

"It was five days." She stood. "I'm going to him. School is out next Friday. My flight leaves at six."

She wasn't sure which scared her more—flying or seeing Sam. And she would see him. Nothing was going to stop her.

Sam came to a decision. His life wasn't worth shit. Alternately, Sally and Mac told him he was all kinds of a fool. Although Sam paid attention, wrote reports, analyzed information coming out of Russia, Mac still would not send him out on assignment. Never mind Sam had wanted out of the field. That was long ago. Now, he wanted, needed activity to forget.

"You're not ready," the old man said.

"Bullshit."

"You're a menace to yourself and others. Make a decision, Sam. This is your last warning. Either start acting like an agent or rethink your career options. Until then, I don't want to see your ugly mug in here."

It took Sam three days to figure out he'd royally screwed up. He had no job and no woman. He thought he couldn't have both. Now, he had neither. It was his own fault. Sam thought about Daria's parting words, about the long, lonely life ahead of him. Oh, yeah. He really wanted that. But, what was he willing to do about it?

He'd given up the woman he loved for his job, and he had no job. What was the sense in that? The job wasn't going to keep him warm at night, sure as hell wasn't going to give him kids. He never realized how much he wanted children until she talked about wanting them. He didn't want just any children. Sam wanted to father Daria's children.

He could make it work. Field work was too dangerous so he'd give it up. He could parlay his skills into another line of work. Daria was more important than any job. He just hoped his "cockeyed optimist" would forgive his stupidity.

The kicker was if she would take him back. She'd told him she loved him. And what did he do? He walked away. Told her to find somebody else. She'd be a fool to risk letting him stomp on her heart again. What if she wrote him off because he never called? What if—

No more thinking, or second guessing. He had to take the risk.

Mac hadn't come into the office yet when Sam placed his resignation on his desk. He wasn't afraid Mac would bellow and tell him how the agency couldn't do without him. Sam couldn't bear to have Mac quietly shake Sam's hand and wish him well in his new profession.

Thursday was the last day of school for the kids, and they were antsy. Daria led her class out to the playground. A good walk around the schoolyard would settle them down. At least, the rambunctious children kept her mind so occupied she didn't think about Sam and her impending flight to DC. Correction—she didn't think about him much.

She chose Tony Avotino to lead the parade around the playground. Tony with dark hair, big brown eyes and the smartest mouth no eight-year-old should ever have. Something in his cocky walk reminded her of Sam. Or reminded her of the son she and Sam might have.

For a moment, her optimism waned. He could refuse to see her. Sam could reject her and mean it.

She swallowed and blinked rapidly. Couldn't have the second-grade teacher dissolving into tears on the playground. No red eyes, either. News like that would spread faster than liquid fertilizer on fields. And burn just as badly.

"Hey, Miz Mason, look at that red Camaro," Tony called out. "That's a boss car."

Daria shaded her eyes with her hand and watched a car turn into the parking lot. "Sure is, Tony. Real boss."

She wasn't going to stand around and drool over that Camaro the way she did at Lucky's five years ago. If she wanted a *boss* car, she'd go out and get one. In fact, when she got to Washington, that's exactly what she was going to do—trade in the Gray Goose for a red Camaro. "Okay, kids, let's continue our walk. Tony, lead on."

"I wanna go look at that boss car." Her leader headed over to the fence. The rest of the class followed. Soon all twenty-four noses were pressed through the links of the fence, ogling the shiny red Camaro.

The driver didn't get out. The reflection of the sun on the windshield kept the interior hidden.

"All right, kids." She clapped her hands. "Time to go in."

Nobody moved. Except the driver of the Camaro, who finally got out and stood beside the car. The man with dark hair and sunglasses wore a white shirt, a tie and a suit. The tie was loosened, and the collar of the shirt unbuttoned. The cuffs of his sleeves had been turned back twice, and he'd slung the suit jacket over his shoulder. Her heart twisted at the sight.

She knew that cocky stance. That set of broad shoulders. The dark brown hair that the wind tousled over his forehead. The man who wouldn't stay out of her thoughts, her dreams.

The kids crowded at the fence, silently staring at him. Except Tony who called out, "Hey, mister. That your boss car?"

Sam walked to the fence. She couldn't believe he'd finally come. When she'd given up hope. When she'd finally decided to take matters into her own hands and go to him. He was here.

"You like that car?" he asked Tony.

The little boy shouted an enthusiastic "Yes." So did several others.

Daria knew what her class was thinking. They were no dummies. If they talked to this man, their teacher wouldn't make them go inside and finish the math problems on the board. Their teacher was no dummy, either.

"I'm gonna have a car like that someday," Tony boasted.

Yeah, me too, Daria said silently. *Me, too.*

"The car isn't mine," Sam said. "It belongs to your teacher."

The entire class turned as one to stare at her, who stared at him. Her jaw dropped, as he probably expected.

"That your car, Miz Mason? Really?"

Her 'boss' factor just soared.

Sam came closer until just the chain link fence separated them. "How do I get on your side?"

"There is no gate. You have to go in through the school." She pointed toward the school entrance, about fifty feet away. Maybe that would discourage him. The last thing she wanted was Sam Jozwiak on her side of the fence. "Why don't you wait at the farm? I'll be there after school."

"Nuts to that." He set his jacket on the fence and vaulted over.

Well, shoot.

"You're gonna get in trouble, mister," one of the kids exclaimed.

"Nobody's allowed to jump the fence," said another.

Sam walked up to Daria. He removed his sunglasses and handed them to Tony. "Hang onto them, kid. Your teacher won't let me get into trouble."

"Don't count on it," she snapped, refusing to look into those warm, brown eyes.

"I'm counting on a lot of things." His caramel-coated voice reached deep inside her, thrilled her, discombobulated her.

She backed up. "We, uh, need to get back to the classroom. We—We were out for a l-little walk and—and it's time to go in."

"Am I making you nervous?"

She snapped her mouth shut. *Stop stuttering. Where's your backbone?* "Of course, I'm not nervous. Kids," she called, using the voice that never failed to bring order. "Line up."

They didn't. Ginnie's daughter tugged on Daria's slacks.

"Is he your boyfriend?"

Daria's cheeks flamed. "Of course not, Laura. Time to go in, kids."

"Teacher's got a boyfriend." The chant began. "Teacher's got a boyfriend."

"Now, look what you've done." She glared at Sam.

"Oh, well. In for a penny, in for a pound." He wrapped his arm around her waist, dipped her over his arm and kissed her. On the mouth. With tongue. The rat.

Oh God. How much she'd missed this. Her memory had been a pale imitation.

The girls squealed, the boys hooted, and several "yucks" were thrown in.

When he finally finished and brought her upright again, he gave the class a look worthy of a twenty-year teacher. He held up his hand and the little rascals instantly quieted. He slung his arm around her shoulder. "I'm not Miss Mason's boyfriend."

That announcement set off a few groans. Daria's heart sank.

"I'm going to be her husband." Cheers met that one.

She couldn't speak. Stunned didn't come close to how she was feeling.

He held up his hand. "But I have a problem, kids. Think you could help me out?"

They tried to outdo each other shouting "yes."

"Miss Mason hasn't agreed to marry me yet. What do you think? Should she marry me?"

Twenty-four voices rang out.

"Sounds like it's unanimous." His mouth quirked into a grin that she would have given anything to see for the past five weeks—ever since he left Iowa.

"A little overconfident there, Sam Jozwiak. The way I see it is you have a bigger problem. You haven't asked me yet." She clapped twice. "Line up, class. Now." Several groans. "I mean *right . . . now.*" She turned to Sam. "You got them all riled—" She broke off. "What are you doing?"

He was kneeling on one knee. When he tried to take her hand, she jerked it away. "Would you get up? You look ridiculous."

He managed to snag her hand. This time no amount of pulling would get him to release it. "Miss Daria Jean Mason," he said loud enough for those standing at the open windows of the classrooms that faced the playground to hear. "Will you marry me?"

"Mister, you got it wrong. You gotta say mushy stuff before you ask her to marry you." Tony Avotino, matchmaker, put his hands over his heart dramatically. "Like 'I looove you'."

Again, the girls squealed, and the boys hooted.

"Thanks for the advice." Sam winked at Tony who was wearing his sunglasses. "Miss Daria Jean Mason, I love you. Now will you marry me?"

"Miss Mason, what is going on out here?"

Daria scrunched her eyes shut. Mr. Leonard, no-nonsense principal and Danny DeVito look-alike, was heading her way.

"There are reports of a man out here. Where is he? Does he have a visitor's pass?" Leonard scurried up. The kids surrounding Sam must have shielded him from the principal. "Good heavens, man, what are you doing?" he said to Sam still on his knee.

"He wants to marry Miz Mason," Tony announced. "And he isn't done yet 'cause she hasn't answered."

"Harrumph. Well, get on with it. You are disrupting half the school." Leonard gave her a stern look before walking toward the windows, not only filled with students but teachers, too. "You people need to get back to work."

"Sam Jozwiak," she muttered, "this will be all over town before dinner."

"What's it going to be, Daria? Yes or no. Tell me no, and you'll break my heart."

"Like you broke mine?" she snapped. "Oh, get up. This is so embarrassing."

"How about if I take you to the Rock & Roll Hall of Fame and the Women's Rights Museum on our honeymoon?"

"Sa-am."

"Okay, the Gateway Arch in St. Louis and the Statue of Liberty, too."

"Would you stop this?"

Some of the kids wandered over to the monkey bars. Others to the swings. Tony and a few others stayed.

"All right. I'm playing hardball now. I have a box of blue cover Nancy Drew mysteries in the trunk."

Her eyes widened. "Blue cover? A whole box?"

"Yep." He grinned. "And that's my final offer."

"Miz Mason," Tony said in an exasperated voice. "Are you going to say yes or not?"

"Yeah," Sam said. "Say yes. Please."

She pretended to think about it. "Will you get up?"

"Not until you say yes."

A slow grin started in her heart and spread to her lips. "I'll need to look at the books first."

Sam followed Daria home. No cars were in the drive. Thank God, her brothers weren't home yet. He needed time with her first. Time to plead his case. Time to convince her he was her Mr. Right.

He hurried to open her door, but she beat him to it and jumped out of the car. Damn, she looked good. He'd thought that when he saw her on the playground and was even more convinced now. Classy. No schoolteacher in penny loafers and granny dresses. Not a smokin' hot babe in skin-tight jeans and shocking red or electric blue Tees, either. Today, her long legs were encased in beige pleated slacks. She wore a skinny, gold belt and a silk blouse in sage and cream. Yep, classy. Real classy.

He wrapped his arms around her. "Oh, babe, I've wanted to do this for weeks."

"What stopped you?" She pulled away.

"I was an idiot."

Folding her arms across her chest, she looked every bit the stern schoolteacher. "No argument there."

Damn. She wasn't going to make this easy for him. Not that he expected her to. He deserved everything she threw at him.

"I had some problems to work out."

"Do you think you can come here and bribe me into forgiving you with a new car? I'm not that cheap."

266

If he'd only heard her, he would have thought she was still angry at him. Good thing he was looking into her beautiful blue eyes and saw the twinkle there. His mouth quirked up. "There is that box of Nancy Drew books."

She dropped her arms and started to laugh. "I don't know, Sam. I still think I should look at those books before I decide."

"Oh, babe. Nobody would ever accuse you of being cheap. Unless they saw you in your blonde disguise." He crushed her to him and buried his face in her hair, which smelled of wildflowers. "I like your hair." It was a soft, light brown with gold highlights, stylishly cut to frame her face.

"Lil, at the Curl Up & Dye, repaired the damage." She leaned back. In a surprise move, she clasped his face between her strong, capable hands. Her long fingers brushed his temples. "You like pretty good without that scruffy beard."

"Yeah, well, you didn't exactly see me at my best." He gave her a wry smile. .

"Is that really what we want to talk about? My hair? Your beard?"

"No." He'd better get through this without breaking down and acting like more of an ass than he was. Erasing his smile, he pinched the bridge of his nose. "I don't want that lonely life you cursed me with."

"I don't want it, either, Sam. What changed? What made you come back?"

"You. I came back because I knew that I could no more live the rest of my life without you than I could live without air."

"Oh, Sam."

"You were so determined to get me away from the bad guys." He laughed. "You truly believed you could do it, too. When you found me, I was worn out. An old man at thirty-four. Cynicism colored everything I did. Then, you waltzed into my life, bravely facing down a pervert in the restroom."

She looked at him in surprise. "How did you know that's what I thought?"

"For God's sake, girl, I saw it in your eyes." He laughed. "I couldn't believe it when you ordered me to zip up and get out. God, you had guts. And I saw something else in you when you talked about the children you taught and about your writing. I saw something of my idealistic self in you. The way I was when I first went into the business."

"Maybe I wasn't such an idealist, just naïve and stupid."

"A little naïve. But never stupid." He kissed her temple then dropped his arms. This time, he backed away from her and leaned against the Camaro. "I quit the agency."

"Oh, Sam, no."

"Yes. I won't be an absentee husband and father. And I won't make you a young widow, either. Live is too short. I love you, Daria. I am so sorry for not contacting you, for not returning sooner. You *are* the best thing that's ever come into my life. I want you to stay in my life from now on."

When Daria threw her arms around his neck and began to kiss him, Sam knew he'd gone to heaven. He'd offered his heart to her, knowing full well she might reject it. Wonder of wonders. She still wanted him.

"Always knew you had some smarts, Jozwiak," she said between kisses.

The sound of automobiles penetrated his bliss. He looked up to find a caravan coming up the drive. Four vehicles came to an abrupt stop behind the Camaro. Oh, Lordy, the posse was here, ready to rescue their baby sister.

Jim slammed the door of the sheriff's car and strode toward them. "Hold it right there, Jozwiak. The four of us want to talk to you." The others were right behind him, fists clenched, menace in their eyes. Even Tom the priest.

Daria—his brave Daria—threw herself in front of him, arms wide protecting him just like she'd done five weeks ago at almost the same spot. "Oh, no you don't. You guys are not going to screw this up for me."

That actually stopped them in their tracks. They stared at Daria as if not recognizing her.

Taking her shoulders, Sam set her behind him. "Honey, I can take care of myself. You don't have to rescue me from your brothers."

She ducked under his arm to stand beside him, her arm around his waist. She looked up at him with a cocky smile then turned to her brothers. "This is the man I'm going to marry. You will not interfere. And just so there's no misunderstanding, he's sleeping in my room tonight and every night."

"Hey, no problem, Dar." Bill slapped Sam so hard on the back he stumbled.

"Right, DJ." Drew stepped forward and shook his hand. Sam didn't realize lawyers used the 'who can squeeze harder' intimidation tactic and did his best not to wince. "Hurt her, Jozwiak, and you die."

"Dre-ew!" Daria rounded on her brother.

Tom came forward next. "Welcome to the family." He shook hands in a civilized manner and, with a completely civilized smile, said, "Ditto what Drew said."

Daria rolled her eyes. Then, she stared at the lone man standing to the side. "Threaten him, Jim, and you'll answer to me."

"Wouldn't think of it, Daria Jean. You're a full-grown woman—"

"About time you recognized that," she said.

"—who has the right to screw up her life any way she wants."

"Jim!"

"You want him, Dar, go for it." Bill stepped close to Jim and shot him a warning look. "It might take some of us longer than others to agree."

"Good." She smiled. "I'm glad that's settled. Let's go inside."

"Are you going to let me say anything?" Sam said.

"Why?" she asked.

"Because it's one of your requirements." Sam looked from her to the four men who stood in a semicircle around him, caging him in. "You love your sister and have protected her." He squared his shoulders. "It's my turn."

"You've done a piss-poor job, so far," Jim said.

"The Russian Mafia came after her," Drew added.

"Hang on," Daria protested. "That wasn't Sam's fault."

"Yes, it was," he said. "I'll do better. I promise. Now, I won't ask your permission. I don't need your approval. Daria has made her choice. For her sake and because it's important to her, I will ask for your blessing."

There was a long pause before Jim stepped forward, his

hand extended to Sam.

"Hey," Bill said. "We've got even sides now for three-on-three basketball. Heard you played, Jozwiak."

"A little," Sam said.

"I remember you from Iowa," Drew said. "All American three years."

"How about a game before dinner?" Bill asked more excited than a kid.

"Only if I get Daria on my side," Sam said.

"And where else would I be?" she asked.

CHAPTER TWENTY-NINE

After the rousing game of basketball on the cement apron in front of the garage, Daria had bruises on her arms and ribs and scrapes on her knees. The boys played rough, gave no quarter as usual. But then, neither did she or Sam.

Tom and Bill told her to take Sam out to the front porch while they made dinner. She could barely move and feared if she sat too long she wouldn't be able to get up. Besides, with the windows open, the boys would hear everything she and Sam said.

"Let's take a walk." With Rover dashing ahead of them, she led Sam out to the stand of trees that separated the fields from the backyard. When they were sufficiently away from her brothers' prying eyes and keen ears, she turned to Sam who promptly took her into his arms. His kiss told her how much he missed her. She hoped hers told him the same.

But when she started to pull his shirt out of his slacks, he stilled her hands. "As much as I want you, I am not making love to you on the damn grass in full sight of your brothers."

Though disappointed, she laughed. "After that speech in the driveway, you're afraid of them?"

"No. Afraid if I get down on the ground, I won't be able to get up. God, I hurt."

"Where?" She gave him a coy smile. "I'll kiss it and make it better."

"And you know where that will lead. Is all that yours?" He waved toward the fields where the corn was nearly knee-high already.

"The land is. We lease it to our neighbor. Since you don't want to make out, tell me what happened after you left here. Why was your boss arrested?"

"Do we have to talk about that thieving bastard?" He leaned against a tall oak that held the swing her dad had hung on one of its branches when the boys were young.

"Thieving?" She settled onto the swing's board seat. With her toes, she set the swing moving.

"He was embezzling from the agency."

"Embezzling? Holy shit."

"Shit? Did you just say shit?" His incredulous expression was just as mocking as his tone. "Ms. Prim and Proper used a vulgarity?"

She jumped off the swing and stalked up to him. She grabbed the front of his dress shirt, which he'd taken off during the basketball game, and pulled him close enough so she was in his face. "You don't think I can utter vulgarities? How's this? I want to fuck your brains out."

A red flush shot from his neck up into his face. Good. She'd shaken him up. With a smug smile, she sauntered back to the swing and sat down. "Cat got your tongue?"

He cleared his throat. "About Teller?"

"Do I give a shit about that bastard?" She set the swing moving.

Again, he cleared his throat. "You've changed."

"Damn straight, I have. Have you?"

He came over and stood in front of her, stopping the swing with his hands on the ropes. "You know the answer to that. Are you going to forgive me?"

"I'm not a priest. If you want forgiveness, talk to Tom."

"It's your forgiveness I need."

She leaned back, wrapping her legs around his. "If I didn't forgive you, I would never have agreed to marry you. And I certainly wouldn't want to make love with you."

He disentangled himself from her. "Glad we got that straight. And I'm still not making out with you out here."

"Oh, be that way." She heaved a sigh. "Go on with your story about Teller."

"Thanks to his wife, he has very expensive tastes."

"I know. The Armani suit, gold cufflinks, the Rolex."

Sam gave her a crooked smile. "You noticed that, did you?"

"I thought it odd since he's—I mean, since he *was* a government employee."

"Just like you did with Grashenko, you noticed his clothes. Always knew you'd make a good spy." He winked.

"Teller grew accustomed to the finer things, but his wife controlled the purse strings. She kept him on a short leash. He must have thought he'd died and gone to heaven when he saw the agency budget. He saw all the money past administrations had thrown our way with little or no outside accounting. He didn't realize Ryerson tracks all expenditures."

"Ryerson? Old Skin and Bones?"

"Right. Teller knew he scrutinized the agents' expense reports but didn't realize Ryerson had the authority to track the Director's. Mac set it up that way, as a protection for the agency and himself. Ryerson was a watchdog. About three months ago, Teller put Ryerson on a special project, busy work to keep him from watching finances and figuring out Teller was siphoning funds and sending them to an off-shore account."

"That creep," she exclaimed.

"He started out with padding expense reports. He also charged the rent on his apartment in New York City to the agency."

"He has an apartment in New York?"

"His mistress lives there. She arrived when Hardesty was still there and that started him thinking. When Teller ordered him to illegally bug Sally's and my homes, Hardesty's conscience finally kicked in. The rookie did a little detective work and discovered Teller was embezzling and told Sally about it. Turns out Mac already knew, thanks to Ryerson."

"Good."

"It gets better." Sam came behind her and began to push the swing. "Canfield was blackmailing Teller."

She gripped the rope, worn from so many hands. "What?"

"Your former senator sat on the committee that oversees the intelligence agencies and was instrumental in getting Teller appointed Director. So, when Korioff started blackmailing Canfield, the senator leaned on Teller. Who better to send in an agent to retrieve the evidence Korioff had?"

She twisted around to look at him. "Teller set you up?"

"Yeah, and I didn't realize it. I'd heard a rumor about

Korioff laundering money for an extremist group. Ordinarily, I would have gone to Ryerson, but he was gone on a special project. I thought Teller's meeting me in the agency gym was a coincidence. He asked me if anything was going on, and I told him about the rumor. He said to check it out. If I could get to Korioff's office, I was supposed to insert a code that would let us access his computer from Virginia. Afterward, I realized that too was Teller's idea. He planned to examine the files himself and delete Canfield's evidence. He was subtle, feeding me just enough to lead me down the primrose path. Shit. I felt so stupid when Mac and Ryerson laid it all out for me."

"Sam, you trusted your boss. It's not your fault."

He snorted.

"If you put in the code and Teller accessed Korioff's files, why was Grashenko chasing you? Why did he want your shoe?"

"There was a major problem. Korioff's computer wasn't wired to the Internet. Not wireless, either. Not even a modem. I had to download his files into a memory chip, which I hid in the heel of my shoe. That put a major glitch in Teller's plans. I not only had seen the information on Canfield, but I had physical proof. With Canfield's appointment a little over a week away, I had to let Teller know right away. And he called Canfield."

"What? He knew the senator was revealing security details and warned him?"

"He planned to blackmail him, but Canfield turned the tables. The senator already had his own investigator trolling for something he could use to ensure Teller's cooperation if he ever needed a favor. Canfield told Teller if he didn't help, he would inform Teller's wife about his mistress. She would divorce him in a New York minute. And he wasn't ready yet to flee the country with the money he'd embezzled since he didn't have enough. Greed did him in."

"Holy cow! Blackmailers being blackmailed." Daria shook her head. "How did Korioff Senior find out so quickly and send Grashenko after you?"

"Surveillance cameras. Yuri saw me in Korioff's office. When he turned on Korioff's computer to see what I'd done, all of the financial files *disappeared*."

"That certainly endeared you to Korioff."

"That extremist group I mentioned would, literally, have Korioff's head for not protecting their dealings. We didn't just get financial records, we discovered their agents, suppliers, contacts. Korioff even had a file on their long-range plans."

"He'll be in deep trouble if they find out, right?"

"You got it." Sam's eyes hardened. "Every time I called Teller for extraction, Grashenko found me."

Daria nodded. "Let me get this straight. Teller called Canfield who called Korioff who told Grashenko where you were?"

"Until I stopped calling Teller, thanks to Doc. He, Ryerson, and Mac have always been tight. Ever since he left the agency, Mac's had his ear to the ground. I still don't know how he found out what was going on, but he told Doc to give me the message about not trusting anyone. Mac was working on a plan but needed time to put it into play."

"Now, wait a minute. If Mac doesn't have a phone, how did he learn all this?"

"I don't know. Sometimes, I think he and Ryerson have mental telepathy."

"So, what happened to Teller after he was arrested?" she asked. "There hasn't been anything on the news reports."

"The wheels of justice grind very slowly," he said in disgust. "It's been kept quiet. The public doesn't want to know you can't trust our own intelligence gathering agencies."

"Excuse me? I'm the public. I would want to know."

"Do you feel safer knowing?"

"I feel safer knowing that a traitor is in custody. What about Grashenko and the Clumsy Hulk?"

"They claimed diplomatic immunity and were let go."

"What?"

"Interestingly enough, they had documents proving they were diplomatic envoys. Probably forged but since State couldn't prove otherwise, the Dynamic Duo were shipped back to Russia and have become *personae non gratae* in the U.S."

"Good. I appreciate your telling me what happened. I understand it's all confidential."

"After all you did to keep the evidence safe, you had a right to know."

CHAPTER THIRTY

After dinner, the boys did something so unexpected Daria nearly fell off the kitchen chair. They left. Not just the kitchen. They got in their cars and drove off.

"Well, that sucks," she said as she started clearing the table. "They left us with the dishes."

Sam put his arms around her waist and drew her back against him. "Honey, they're gone for the night."

"What?" She twisted around to face him.

"Your brother, the priest, told the others they needed to give us space. I think they're all going to sleep at the rectory."

"That was very considerate of them."

He took the dishes out of her hands and set them back on the table. "And we're not wasting time down here. Now, where's your bedroom?"

She looked at the table. No leftovers. Nothing to put in the fridge. With a grin, she took his hand and pulled him toward the stairs. "I need a shower first." She sniffed. "And so do you."

"We could shower together. Save time." The hopefulness in his voice made her laugh.

"I'm not sure I'm ready for that." On the third step, she looked over her shoulder and caught Sam's disappointed look. "Yet."

His expression brightened. As she led him into her bedroom, she was so glad she'd made all the changes. When she turned to see if he liked it, she caught him staring at her luggage.

"Are you going somewhere?" Though his tone was light, she could see the uncertainty in his eyes.

"As a matter of fact, I have a flight out of Des Moines tomorrow."

"You? Fly? Didn't you say something about glorified tin

cans?"

She shrugged. "It's for a good reason."

"Vacation?"

"Sort of." She clasped his face and tried to smooth the worry lines. "It's a good thing you came today. We would've resembled an O Henry tale. You know, the one where the husband sells his pocket watch for hair combs."

"And she sold her hair to buy a watch fob. 'Gift of the Magi.' I don't get the connection."

"My flight was to DC."

"You were coming to see me?"

She smiled. "While you were talking to my brothers, I cancelled my flight. Now, take your shower. You can use the bathroom off Jim's room."

When she returned from her shower, Sam was already in her new bed leaning against the headboard, waiting for her, the covers pooled at his waist. At the sight of his naked chest, she hoped he was just as naked underneath the covers. She crawled in next to him and wrapped her arm across his chest, loving how solid he felt.

"You held your own, tonight."

"So did you." She groaned. "I won't be able to move in the morning."

"This isn't exactly how I envisioned our first night together. Both of us with aching muscles." He kissed her temple. "Did I tell you that every night after I left here I fantasized about taking off your nightshirt and those flowered panties?"

Like the ones she wore to get from the bathroom across the hall to her bedroom. Even if her brothers were gone, walking around naked was beyond her capabilities. She might have changed some in her attitude toward life but not that much.

"I have a beautiful nightgown that I bought just for you. I wanted to wear it on our first night together."

"No matter. You wouldn't be wearing it for long." He leaned forward and slipped his hands under her nightshirt. "Here's my fantasy come to life."

* * *

Daria lay curled in Sam's arms. Exactly the right place to be. He had come back. He wanted to marry her. She mulled that over.

The only problem she could see was that he'd given up a life he once loved. For her. That wasn't a good way to start a marriage. He was making a huge sacrifice. She remembered their long conversations in the car. How he talked about the reason he'd gone to work for the Orion Agency. How he wanted to make a difference in the world. How he tried to make America safe for the next generation.

"Something's burning," Sam said casually.

Daria jerked upright, sniffing. "I don't smell anything. The smoke detec—"

Sam tugged her down. "You're thinking too hard. Must be all those wheels and gears smoking."

She batted his shoulder. "I was thinking about your job."

"Forget about the job. I have a lot of vacation due and a good nest egg. Hell, I never had time for a vacation or a chance to use even half my salary. I'll find—"

His cell phone started vibrating on the table next to the bed. He picked it up, looked at the display and pressed a button to silence the phone. "Now, where were we?" He started to kiss the side of her neck.

"That isn't where we—"

The phone began vibrating again.

"Answer it, Sam," she said.

Reluctantly, he clicked it on. "Joz—"

The voice on the other end cut him off. It was so loud, she could hear every word.

"What are you thinking, boy? I am not accepting your resignation."

"I believe there are laws against forced servitude," Sam drawled.

"Is that Mac?" she asked.

"Don't act like a bigger ass than you are. I suppose you're in Iowa."

"Yes, sir."

"Have you eaten crow and kissed ass?"

Sam gave Daria a lewd grin. "I've certainly kissed ass."

She hit him with her pillow.

Mac loudly cleared his throat. *"I hope you got down on your knees and groveled."*

"Yes, sir. I've been on my knees. Groveling was involved."

Daria felt herself blush all over. Oh, the things he'd done on his knees.

"Good. Now get your sorry ass back here and take over."

"I beg your pardon?"

"For chrissake, Jozwiak, I need you to run this agency."

"Me? What about Ryerson?"

"Hell, he's retiring next month. Sally will make a good replacement for him. But somebody needs to run the agency. After the debacle with Teller, The Powers That Be gave me free rein to choose the new director. You might be a horse's ass in your private life, but you're a first-rate leader."

"Well, sir, I—"

Daria could see Sam was going to refuse. She grabbed the phone. "He'll think about your offer, sir," she told Mac.

"Tell him to think quick. I'm no spring chicken, you know. I could keel over from a heart attack and then where would the agency be? Ask him if he wants them to appoint another Teller?"

"Yes, sir. I'll give him your message. Have a good evening." She ended the call.

"Why did you tell him I needed to think about it? I'm not going back."

"Sure you are." She crawled on top of him. "I saw your eyes when he offered you the job. You want it."

She bent and kissed his chest, just below his left nipple. His heart thudded loudly. She slid lower, kissing and licking her way down to his navel. She swirled her tongue inside the indentation, knowing how much he liked that.

He hauled her up. "Think you can use sex to make me change my mind?"

"Will it work?" She wiggled until she felt him harden against her. "Think about it later. Something more important has come up."

She straddled him. She liked this position. It gave her a sense of control and she knew how much he liked watching her.

Later, she snuggled against him. "It will work, Sam. We'll make it work. Your country needs you."

"Your job? You love teaching. Those kids love you."

"I can teach anywhere. Take the job, Sam. It's what you want. It's what you're meant to do."

"How come you know me so well?"

"I love you, Sam. It's that simple."

"I love you, too, babe."

She put her arms around his neck and tugged him close. "Just think of the adventures we'll have."

Turn the page for a quick look at

The Case of the Bygone Brother: An Alex O'Hara Novel

by Diane Burton

An Excerpt from *The Case of The Bygone Brother:*
An Alex O'Hara Novel

She had trouble written all over her.

Like a scene out of *The Maltese Falcon*, a beautiful woman begs the P.I. for help. Shades of Sam Spade, with a slight difference. The elegantly-dressed woman pounding on my plate glass window was more than twenty years older than me and, even though my name is Alex O'Hara, I'm not male. But I am a PI —O'Hara & Palzetti, Confidential Investigations since 1965. Not that I've been around since 1965.

As soon as I unlocked the outer door, the woman burst through, a few maple leaves stuck to her Manolo's. Frankly, I was surprised she wore only a sweater. She must have been freezing out there. In spite of the fact that it was mid-October, the temp had dipped that afternoon to the low forties. We might even get frost.

"Ms. O'Hara, thank God you're still here. I was so afraid—" She broke off on a sob. Taking a small, white, lace-edged handkerchief out of her Louis Vitton purse, she dabbed at her eyes.

Now I'm not one to belittle a person's worries. However, I thought she switched a little too quickly from imperious knocking to damsel in distress.

Damsel? Not quite. I pegged her around fifty-five, give or take a few years, and well-preserved. Even in her Manolo's, she only came up to my chin. Next to her I felt like a hulking giant. Since I'm five-ten in my socks, I look down on most women. Despite her elaborate up-do, from my angle I could see her roots. A visit to her hairdresser might be in order. But I digress.

"What can I do for you?" I tried not to sneeze from her overpowering perfume. An oriental scent. Shalimar or Opium. I never knew which was which. I tried them on at the perfume counter at Macy's. That's the closest I'd ever get to wearing expensive perfumes.

"I need your help." Her breathy voice reminded me of Marilyn. As in Monroe, not Manson. "My brother is missing. I must find him."

About the Author

Diane Burton combines her love of mystery, adventure, science fiction and romance into writing romantic fiction. Besides the science fiction romance *Switched* and *Outer Rim* series, she writes romantic suspense and cozy mysteries (The Alex O'Hara Novels). She is also a contributor to the anthology *How I Met My Husband*. Diane and her husband live in Michigan. They have two children and five grandchildren.

For more info and excerpts from her books, visit Diane's website: http://www.dianeburton.com

Connect with Diane Burton online

Blog: dianeburton.blogspot.com/
Facebook: Diane Burton Author
Twitter: @dmburton72
Pinterest: dmburton72
Goodreads: Diane Burton Author

If you would like to know when a new book is released, sign up for Diane's newsletter. http://eepurl.com/bdHtYf

Thank you for reading **One Red Shoe**. I hope you enjoyed my story. It would be great if you let others know. Authors love reviews. If you have time, please consider leaving a review at Amazon and/or Goodreads — even just a line or two about what you thought of the book would be so appreciated.